When their cig... ... y and seltzer
had bee... ...sed his legs.

'The ... ...name Carl
Philipp ...

He h... ...McGahan.
McGaha...

'There ... ...rd of him,'
Mycroft ... ...own to statesmen
and journ... ...alike. He was – perhaps remains – his
master's valet; he is certainly his private secretary and
confidential agent. He is also the most dangerous man in
Europe.'

'Who is this Carl . . .'

'Philipp Emmanuel Guttman,' Mycroft prompted
him.

'. . . Carl Philipp Emmanuel Guttman's master?' asked
McGahan.

Mycroft lowered his voice.

'The Chancellor of the German Empire,' he said.
'Prince von Bismarck . . .'

Glen Petrie was born in Glasgow in 1931 and brought up in the Lake District. He saw military service in Singapore and Malaya during the 1949–51 Emergency (and was therefore one of Leslie Thomas's 'virgin soldiers') and was educated at Balliol College, Oxford, the University of Exeter, and London University's Institute of Historical Research. After teaching in London for ten years he became a full-time writer in 1977. He has published a biography of the Victorian reformer and feminist Josephine Elizabeth Butler and eight novels. His first Mycroft Holmes Adventure, *The Dorking Gap Affair* was published by Corgi in 1990.

Also by Glen Petrie

THE DORKING GAP AFFAIR

and published by Corgi Books

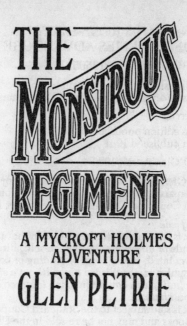

THE MONSTROUS REGIMENT

A MYCROFT HOLMES ADVENTURE

GLEN PETRIE

CORGI BOOKS

THE MONSTROUS REGIMENT:
A MYCROFT HOLMES ADVENTURE

A CORGI BOOK 0 552 13595 X

Originally published in Great Britain by
Bantam Press, a division of Transworld Publishers Ltd

PRINTING HISTORY
Bantam Press edition published 1990
Corgi edition published 1991

This book is set in 10/11 pt California
by Colset Private Limited, Singapore.

Corgi Books are published by Transworld Publishers Ltd.,
61–63 Uxbridge Road, Ealing, London W5 5SA, in Australia
by Transworld Publishers (Australia) Pty. Ltd., 15–23 Helles
Avenue, Moorebank, NSW 2170, and in New Zealand by
Transworld Publishers (N.Z.) Ltd., Cnr. Moselle and
Waipareira Avenues, Henderson, Auckland.

Printed in Great Britain by
BPCC Hazell Books
Aylesbury, Bucks, England
Member of BPCC Ltd.

For Michael

Chapter One

'I'm on my way to Knightsbridge, old chap. Care for a lift in my hansom? I mean when I've caught one, of course.'

They had met only that night over dinner. Mycroft Holmes put down the fellow's easy if unfortunate familiarity to the fact that he was a Yankee, and one of Irish extraction into the bargain. He took his hat and stick from the attendant.

'Most obligin' of you, Mr McGahan,' he replied. 'But the air will be wholesome at this hour of the night, and a walk will be beneficial. I haven't far to go, don't you know?'

Which was true enough. They had been attending the annual dinner of the Trustees of the National Gallery, Mycroft in his capacity as Honorary Treasurer to the Trustees, McGahan to report the occasion from the privileged position of a guest. The walk from the Trustees Suite at the Gallery to Mycroft's rooms at 73a Pall Mall would take no more than a quarter of an hour even at the leisurely dawdle which was his preferred pace. Even so, Mycroft would have welcomed a ride in a hansom, had he not felt an obligation to politely distance himself from Januarius Aloysius McGahan; it would scarcely be proper, he had decided, for one who was privy to much of Her Majesty's government's most sensitive information to be seen closeted with the distinguished foreign correspondent of the London *Daily News* and the *New York Tribune*.

Nevertheless, there was no avoiding stepping out on to the street together. Their breath turned to vapour as they did so. McGahan shivered somewhat pointedly, and turned up his collar in a way no gentleman would have done.

'Sure you ain't going to change your mind, Holmes?' he asked. 'The nights are turning cold now, and no mistake.'

He laughed self-deprecatingly, as if to let Mycroft know that he did not expect him to be taken in by this little ploy to get him on his own. Before Mycroft could express his displeasure at being pestered, there came an unexpected interruption. A small knot of people came marching round the corner from James Street. They were chanting; one or two held placards aloft which read, *The Bear Shall Not Have Constantinople!* and, *Britons Stand Fast With Brave Little Turkey Against Russian Tyranny!* A middle-aged woman came striding up the pavement clutching handfuls of pamphlets which she held out to Mycroft and McGahan. She was followed by a pleasant but anxious-faced young man whose chin had been wrapped in a thick angora comforter.

'Read about it, my friends!' the woman cried out in the tone of a seagull which refuses to be intimidated by a gale.

To Mycroft's astonishment, McGahan screwed up the pamphlet which had been thrust into his hand, and threw it into the gutter.

'Brave little Turkey, my eye!' he exclaimed. 'Haven't you heard what your Mr Gladstone had to say in Aberdeen the other day, about brave little Turkey?'

'Mr Gladstone is no true patriot!' the woman replied. 'The Queen has seen through Mr Gladstone – has seen through into the darkness of his heart!'

The young man took her by the arm.

'Come away, Mother,' he urged.

But she plucked it from him.

'You, sir!' she cried at McGahan, 'are an American! I've heard all about your *copperheads*! And your . . . *carpetbaggers*!'

'Mother!' the young man repeated.

McGahan watched them go to rejoin their group.

Without turning his head, he said to Mycroft, 'The *News* wouldn't print the half of the copy I filed from Bulgaria. And rightly, I guess: it wasn't the sort of story you'd want your wife or your baby sister or your parlourmaid to read. I saw three thousand dead bodies in one small village churchyard – mostly women and children. Your plucky Turkish allies had marched them into that churchyard. They had been bayoneted to death – not a bullet hole to be seen. But before they had been stabbed with bayonets, they had been forced by the Turkish *Bashi-Bazouks* to desecrate the icons and the crosses in the most abominable way. A Turkish officer who was with me told me it was so they would believe they would go to hell. He laughed as he told me. . . . Then they had been violated. Nobody told me that, but the signs were unmistakable.'

He sighed.

'Some of the stories I telegraphed back to London, I suppose my editors felt wouldn't be believed; perhaps they didn't believe them themselves. . . . There were many such churchyards, you see. Perhaps hundreds . . . I must say, I'm appalled at the way you Britishers seem to be ready to rush off to protect the Turks from the very people who wish to stop them from perpetrating these dreadful acts!'

He fell silent. Then he laughed again.

'My dear Holmes, you must take me for the most awful boor!' he said, 'ranting like this!'

Mycroft had been struck by the honest passion with which McGahan had expressed himself, a passion he would never have expected from a newspaperman.

'Not everybody close to the Government feels the way those people do,' he said. 'It is true that most are in sympathy with that sort of foolishness. . . .'

He waved his stick vaguely in the direction of the small huddle of people beneath the placards.

'. . . but there are one or two more perceptive intelligences seeking to act as restraining influences.'

He paused for a moment. Then he said, 'Will you take

a glass of brandy with me, sir – and a cigar?'

He waved his stick in the direction of a garish doorway across the street, under a stain-glass portico and fanlight.

'The James Street Divan,' he said. 'A respectable establishment as such places go.'

He held his stick perpendicularly above his head to indicate to the traffic on Margaret's Street that it should stop. Utterly confident in his own authority, he led McGahan across the street without looking either to left or right. Behind them, the knot of people with their placards had spotted a party of gentlemen spilling out of the Blue Posts Tavern and Music Rooms; they ran off down the pavement to accost them.

'When I was a kid in school,' said McGahan, 'the Christian Brothers tried to thrash into me a belief in a real, living devil. In those days, I just couldn't accept the notion that a loving God could allow the Devil to exist. After seeing what I saw in southern Bulgaria, I swear to you, Holmes, I now realize those stern-faced clergymen were right, and I was wrong.'

Mycroft stepped up on to the opposite pavement. As McGahan joined him, he said, 'I know for a fact the devil has been at play in the Near East, and that he has conceived a truly diabolic game—'

'You believe that?' McGahan interrupted him in astonishment. 'And you as close to the Government as you are?'

Mycroft came to a standstill. He turned to look him in the face, standing as close to him as his corpulence would permit.

'You are not to print one syllable of what I'm about to tell you,' he said.

'My dear fellow!' McGahan replied. 'Not a word, on my honour!'

They entered the divan. The air was thick and scented from a rich variety of cigars. The gaslight, filtered through orange and red leaf-shaped shades, cast a lurid glow over the gentlemen lounging on the velvet plush upholstery, the velour hangings and gilt-encrusted panels. Waiters in shirt-sleeves and turkish-towelling fringed aprons, with hair flattened and polished with pomade, glided between the benches, their trays held aloft, balanced on their fingers' ends. One of them showed Mycroft and McGahan to a red plush, circular ottoman with a luxuriant rubber plant growing up out of its centre. He took their order. Mycroft peered about him to ensure there was no acquaintance in the salon whose curiosity might be aroused, before taking his place beside McGahan. A dark-haired girl in a scarlet, short-skirted bustle-gown and 'military' pillbox hat, brought an assortment of cigars in a silver-plated humidor. She removed the bands from the cigars of their choice, clipped the ends, and held the taper for them to light them.

When their cigars were thoroughly lit, and brandy and seltzer had been brought, Mycroft sat back and crossed his legs.

'The devil I spoke of,' he said, 'bears the name Carl Philipp Emmanuel Guttmann.'

He heaved his bulk round to observe McGahan. McGahan looked at him and shook his head.

'There is no reason why you should have heard of him,' Mycroft continued. 'His name is unknown to statesmen and journalists alike. He was – perhaps remains – his master's valet; he is certainly his private secretary and confidential agent. He is also the most dangerous man in Europe.'

'Who is this Carl. . . .'

'Philipp Emmanuel Guttmann,' Mycroft prompted him.

'. . . Carl Philipp Emmanuel Guttmann's master?' asked McGahan.

Mycroft lowered his voice.

'The Chancellor of the German Empire,' he said. 'Prince von Bismarck. Six years ago, in the summer of 1870, there was no cause for war between the King of

Prussia and Napoleon III of France – not until Napoleon III was provoked by the Prussian government's publication of the Ems telegram. Guttmann drafted that telegram. One year later, Great Britain came within days of being humbled even more catastrophically than France. Disaster was averted and the incident kept secret—' Mycroft lowered his voice still further – 'only because, not for the first time, Guttmann had met his match.'

He pointed his forefinger at his own waistcoat button, in the region of his watch-chain.

'This Guttmann executes the orders of his master, Prince von Bismarck?' McGahan suggested.

Mycroft shook his head.

'He anticipates his master's wishes. Unnoticed because of his lowly origins and the menial position he ostensibly holds, he *creates* events which his Imperial Prussian masters can exploit. . . .'

'And you say he has been in the Balkans?' asked McGahan.

'With complete certainty, my dear chap. I have a friend on the Continent, a lady of the highest quality and breeding whose family suffered a terrible injury at the hands of this devil in human form. Because of this, she expends a part of her very considerable personal fortune on having a watch kept on his movements as he creeps about the world.

'In the spring of this year, she wrote to tell me that an acquaintance of hers had seen Guttmann taking a walking holiday in the Sanjak of Novibazar—'

'A *walking* holiday in Novibazar?' exclaimed McGahan. He could not prevent himself from laughing.

'Even the German enthusiasm for going on what I believe they call a *bummel* hardly explains why Guttmann should have chosen the most fly-blown and wretched of the Sultan's Danubian provinces for a walking holiday,' Mycroft replied. 'However, only three weeks after I had received this information from the lady

I mentioned, the Foreign Office received reports of uprisings among the Serbian minorities in Novibazar, Bosnia and Hercegovina against their Turkish masters.

'Shortly afterwards – towards the end of June – she wrote to tell me that another acquaintance, in fact a second secretary at the French legation in Belgrade, had spotted Guttmann in that city, apparently on a mission to buy peasant woodcarvings for a museum in Potsdam. Only a few days later, your own report was published in the *News* of King Milan of Serbia's request to the Tsar for military assistance against the Turks, and of the popular demonstrations on the streets of St Petersburg demanding that Russian troops should march against Constantinople.

'At the beginning of July, the lady informed me that an Austrian naval officer of her acquaintance believed he had spotted Guttmann on the Golden Horn in the company of two Turkish generals, surveying the Black Sea shore. A fortnight later, our own mission to the Sublime Porte sent the news that the Turkish armies facing the Russians across the Danube were to be provided with the latest Krupps field artillery and Nordenfeldt machine-guns.

'The last information which I received from the lady was in August. It was more troubled than the others I had received; it had clearly been written in a state of personal distress. It was sent from Bucharest: in it, she said that Guttmann was across the frontier in Bulgaria, staying as the guest of the German consul in the Turkish fortress-city of Plevna; she said she was terrified at the thought of the fate awaiting her fellow Christians in that unhappy country, and that she was praying daily for them. . . . You yourself saw the extent to which her fears were not idle ones.'

McGahan sighed deeply. He rolled his cigar between his fingers, and sighed again.

'The damnable thing was,' he said finally, 'that there was no rebellion against Turkish rule in Bulgaria. The Turks butchered thousands upon thousands of harmless peasants and their families in order to prevent an uprising which existed only in their imaginations!'

'Which had been introduced into their imaginations by Carl Philipp Emmanuel Guttmann,' said Mycroft.

'Why?' asked McGahan. 'What interest have his masters in stirring the Balkan provinces into war?'

'He intends provoking two great empires into a mutually destructive war,' Mycroft told him. 'King Milan of Serbia's call for Tsar Alexander to join him in an Orthodox Christian crusade against the Sultan, to avenge the martyred dead of Bulgaria, cannot go unanswered....'

'And you people are so besotted with the idea of the Russians as the big, bad bear,' said McGahan, 'and the Turks as plucky heroes, that you would rush to the Turks' rescue.'

'I'm afraid so,' Mycroft told him.

Every day, on his way back to his rooms from the Treasury, he saw the relays of orators on the steps of St Martin's-in-the-Fields, whipping up anti–Russian fervour in the crowds in Trafalgar Square.

'Will you be returning to the Near East?' he asked.

'The *Tribune* has asked me to go,' McGahan replied. 'I don't know that a London newspaper like the *News* would wish to print my despatches, given the state of public opinion over here – or that I have the stomach to report from the Turkish side, to tell you the truth.'

'The truth,' said Mycroft gravely. 'That is what I wished to speak to you about. We need to hear the truth – our public and its leaders need to have the truth thrust in their faces if we are not to plunge into disaster.'

McGahan had turned his head to reply when he glanced behind him. He lowered his head to look under the leaves of the rubber plant.

'Did you notice?' he asked Mycroft. He pointed. 'The fellow sitting behind us?' he asked. 'On the other side of this thing?'

'No,' Mycroft shook his head.

'Big fellow,' said McGahan. 'Broad shoulders. Hair *en*

14

brosse, like a straw stubble on a cropped field. Looked like a Death's Head Hussar or an Uhlan – something of the sort.'

Mycroft pulled himself to his feet as quickly as his weight permitted. He stared into the lurid gloom behind him. The far side of the circular seat was empty; he could see nobody whom he recognized among the lounging figures in evening dress smoking on the velvet settees about the walls.

'He seems to have made off quickly enough!' observed McGahan.

He saw the expression on Mycroft's face.

'My dear fellow! You look as if you've seen a ghost!' he said.

'I've seen nothing,' Mycroft replied.

He put his podgy flipper of a hand on McGahan's shoulder.

'Go back to the Near East,' he said, 'and report the truth.'

As he walked alone down James Street in the direction of Pall Mall and his lodgings, Mycroft wondered whether he had been wise to take Januarius Aloysius McGahan so completely into his confidence. Even more unsettling, however, had been McGahan's brief description of the man who had been sitting on the far side of their circular seat.

He told himself he was allowing himself to become possessed by bugaboos. Ever since the Dorking Gap business, police, revenue-men, and harbourmasters and their staffs had all been alerted to the possibility of Carl Philipp Emmanuel Guttmann's returning to England. There had been no report of any attempt on his part to land on these shores. Even more to the point, Princess Sophie Trubetskoy, who had kept him so well informed about Guttmann's travels in the Balkan states, would surely have known of his arrival in England. She had her agents in London as elsewhere: Mycroft realized he was

15

smiling to himself at the thought of Cyril, the black ne'er-do-well who had attached himself to Princess Sophie's English household. Cyril had served as his own valet during the Dorking Gap affair; he had been an impudent, amusing fellow, with all his wits about him. For several years afterwards, Mycroft had encountered him busking on the pavements of Piccadilly or the raw, new, Shaftesbury Avenue, performing his shuffling dance to the accompaniment of his own, peculiarly tuneless nigger-minstrel song – itself a piece of blatant impertinence. Then he had vanished. Secretly, Mycroft had missed him.

As he stepped out to cross the Haymarket, Mycroft noticed a closed four-wheeler drawing up further down the street, at the corner of the Haymarket and the entrance to Waterloo Place and Pall Mall. As he reached the pavement opposite, a talon-like hand grabbed at his sleeve.

'Steady on a moment, Charley! Feelin' good natured, is yer?'

He had been so deep in thought, he had scarcely noticed the small knot of 'gay' women who, in their swollen, old-fashioned crinolines, clustered like satiated moths under the lamplight. One of them approached him and he saw inside the weather-stained, yellow-stain peekaboo bonnet, the raddled, rouged face, and staring, kohl-rimmed eyes. Ill-fitting false teeth pushed her upper lip forward like that of a rodent.

'A shillun makes me ever so passionate, dearie,' the creature told him.

In disgust, he pulled his sleeve from her grasp. From somewhere behind her, one of her companions said, 'Don't be so bleedin' soft, 'Melia! That's Mr 'Olmes, that is. Only lives just round the corner.'

The first woman's face went a complete blank, as if he had vanished, had ceased to exist. He brushed her skirts aside with the end of his stick as he passed down the pavement. At the bottom of the Haymarket, the four-wheeler having picked up a fare, presumably, was turning about to make off down Cockspur Street towards Trafalgar Square. The hour was late and there was little or no traffic. As he left the small group of 'unfortunates' behind him and continued on his way to the upper end of Pall Mall, he could hear quite clearly the clop of hooves and the distinctive rumble of metalled wheels which gave the four-wheeled cab its familiar name of 'growler'.

He let himself into 73a Pall Mall. The gaslight in the hall had been turned low, but, as he thrust his stick into the large fake-oriental jar which served as an umbrella-stand, Mrs Turner came up from the kitchen. Her comfortably matronly figure was swathed in her quilted winter wrapper, and the thick brown hair under her cap, of which she was so proud, was a mass of curling papers.

'Why, Mrs Turner!' Mycroft exclaimed, 'You should not have stayed up for me!'

'I just thought you'd like a nice pot of tea when you came in, Mr Holmes,' she said, 'the night being so raw.'

'That is extremely thoughtful of you, Mrs Turner,' Mycroft told her.

In fact, it had been no more than he had expected.

From a pocket concealed in the depths under her wrapper, Mrs Turner produced an envelope.

'This came for you, sir – pushed through the letter-box not five minutes ago.'

He took it.

'A young woman brought it,' said Mrs Turner.

'Indeed?' asked Mycroft.

'It just happened as I was standing by the basement window,' Mrs Turner explained.

Which meant, of course, that she had heard in the silence of the small hours the click of female boots approaching on the pavement above the area outside the kitchen, and had gone to peer between the curtains.

'A young lady?' asked Mycroft.

17

'Couldn't see her face, sir, what with it being dark, and she wearing a bonnet. But I wouldn't say so. Could see she was young 'cause she was wearing her hair down, over her shoulders. I'd say she were in service myself. She had on a nice, well-made coat, but it looked like a hand-me-down, if you know what I mean, sir. And her boots were square-toed.'

Mycroft reached out and patted her upper arm.

'Well done, Mrs Turner!' he said. 'We'll recruit you into the Detective Police yet!'

'Oh, Mr Holmes!' Mrs Turner simpered roguishly.

He glanced down at the envelope in his hand.

'The young woman was certainly a messenger, and therefore almost certainly a domestic,' he confirmed. 'You see the quality of the paper – and the wafer?'

He drew it under his nostrils.

'Not a trace of scent or lady's *poudre-de-parfum*,' he went on. 'There is, however, a hint of tobacco – not Havana, however. Surinam, perhaps, and therefore Dutch.'

He held up the envelope so that she could see the superscription.

'Our correspondent is English,' he said. 'You see? The seven in 73 Pall Mall is uncrossed. He is also an autodidact.'

'Beg your pardon, sir?' asked Mrs Turner.

'A self-taught man, Mrs Turner. Or one taught to write from some well-loved book on his mother's knee. Do you see? This is neither the cursive script of the learned man, confident in his education, nor does it bear any sign of the board-school pot-hook. This hand was formed by studying printed books. So we have here a self-taught man who uses expensive writing paper, the employer of respectably dressed servants who indulges in inferior cigars. What shall we make of that, Mrs Turner?'

'I'm sure I can't tell, sir!' Mrs Turner replied.

She was too far gone in admiration for her brain to function properly.

'Come, Mrs Turner! You will never be appointed first

female detective-inspector of Great Scotland Yard if you do not make an attempt at deduction!'

But Mrs Turner could only giggle.

'The possibilities are limited,' Mycroft continued. 'We may have here some honest, unlettered artisan who has prospered by the design or modification of the machinery with which he works – there have been many such in our industrial age; or some successful performer of the popular theatre – a working-man who has achieved notoriety as a comic or singer of popular ballads in the new music-halls; or a member of the servant class who, by diligence and loyalty towards his employers, has risen to the position where he many send his inferiors on errands of his own, or who has achieved independence by become an agent for the provision of his fellow domestic servants . . . Let us see.'

There was no letter inside. Instead, Mycroft removed from the envelope, a yellow, printed playbill. Unfolding it, he read:

OLYMPIA THEATRE AND HALL OF HARMONY,
Victoria Street.
London's most fashionable Music-Hall.

Heading the bill was:

The celebrated *Champagne Charlie* in person!
Mr GEORGE LEYBOURNE!!
who will sing to you in person the patriotic ballad recently penned especially for him by Mr George Stratton and which has proved an instantaneous success throughout Her Gracious Majesty's United Kingdoms, Dominions, and Colonies:
'We don't want to fight (but by jingo if we do)' Assisting Mr Leybourne will be the talented Mr Cyril Prettyman the chocolate-coloured minstrel of Shaftesbury Avenue.

19

The name *Cyril Prettyman* had been heavily underlined. In the broad margin beside it, ringed, and in the same handwriting as on the envelope were the words, 'For two nights only'. Mycroft glanced at the dates at the top of the sheet. The first was the evening just past.

Prettyman? He had never heard Cyril call himself that. Presumably the rogue had invented it for the occasion. And had he himself sent the advertisement? Mycroft certainly wouldn't have put it past him to send one of his female admirers on a late-night errand through the streets of London's West End. On the other hand, the script was too precise, too pedantic for someone of Cyril's character. . . .

'A pot of tea would be most welcome, Mrs Turner,' he said.

For some reason, Mrs Turner seemed taken aback.

'Of course, Mr Holmes,' she replied.

He toiled up the stairs to his study. So Cyril had finally found his way from the kerb-edge to the boards of the theatre. That was not surprising. But that Mycroft should have been thinking of him for the first time for many months, only a few minutes ago as he was crossing the Haymarket; it was almost as if Cyril had materialized in response to his thought. Mycroft did not believe in coincidence. Coincidence was a word applied either to the will of an Almighty Providence, or to the contrivance of men; either way, it was meant. For this reason, he knew, despite his naturally inert disposition – the world was far too full of people rushing hither and thither for its own good – he would betake himself to the Olympia Theatre and Hall of Harmony the following night.

Prettyman, he thought; the vanity of the fellow passed belief. But who was responsible for sending him the flyer? Who wanted him to go to the Olympia to see Cyril? And for what reason?

Before turning up the gas in his study, he went to the window and looked up and down the street. There was only one vehicle – one sign of life – in the cold

20

desolation. A hansom was drawn up outside the Athenaeum Club, down from which a young clergyman was attempting to assist a large, spherical, and somewhat unsteady figure in the gaiters and canonicals of a bishop of the Church of England.

Chapter Two

'Good afternoon, Holmes.'

Mycroft woke with a start. He had dreamt that he was blissfully suspended in the stillness of the smoking-room at the Diogenes Club. Too late he reached across his desk to open one of the huge calf-bound ledgers which lay before him. He succeeded only in setting up a small cloud of dust.

Sir James Swarthmoor stood before him, with stick, hat and gloves in hand. Behind him, half a dozen junior Treasury clerks – younger sons of landed gentlemen, who had found no place in the Army or the Church and who needed a salary – craned to watch through the doorway to see why the Cabinet Secretary had come in person to speak with their older and senior colleague.

'Forgive me, Sir James. . . . A late night, don't you know? Trustees' Dinner at the National Gallery. . . .'

Mycroft would have heaved himself to his feet, but, by the time he had given the matter thought, it was too late for such a courtesy; it was a form of dilatoriness which had brought much trouble on his head when he had been a schoolboy. His junior colleagues were smirking at his discomfiture.

'To what do I owe the pleasure and privilege of this unexpected visit?' he asked.

'I need your excellent advice, Holmes.'

'You have heard that Carl Philipp Emmanuel Guttmann has returned to these shores?' asked Mycroft.

It was Sir James's turn to be taken by surprise.

'No. Have you? Have you heard from the Princess Trubetskoy again?' he asked.

Mycroft shook his head.

'He would not dare rear his head here!' Sir James continued. 'Not after the Dorking business. 'Her Majesty herself wrote to the Kaiser expressing her extreme displeasure at his activities, and declaring him *persona non grata*.'

'I perceive you have come directly from Great Scotland Yard,' said Mycroft, 'so I assume the matter at issue is a criminal one.'

Sir James glanced down at his boots as if to reassure himself that they had not betrayed his itinerary. He looked up again immediately. He leant across the desk, his hand on the parchment of the open ledger.

'Best if we talk somewhere else, Holmes. What do you say to a walk round the lake, eh?'

He straightened up, removed his hand from the ledger and dusted his fingers on his gloves.

'The sun will have gone down before we have crossed the Horse Guards,' Mycroft said doubtfully.

He had never adhered to the idea that physical exercise should be the accompaniment to serious conversation.

'The fresh air will keep our minds clear,' said Sir James.

Mycroft grunted. He pulled himself out of his comfortable leather chair, nonetheless. With a distinct sense of unease he followed Sir James out of his office, and down the length of the clerks' room to the gallery overlooking Downing Street and the Foreign Office. He knew that it was a serious matter that Sir James wished to impart to him; never before had the Cabinet Secretary come in person across from Downing Street to fetch him from his office. It was undoubtedly going to take up a great deal of his time. Worse still it might involve his travelling abroad, perhaps even a long and tiresome sea voyage, such as he had recently endured when he had had to deal with the unfortunate matter of Rear-Admiral Sir Loxley Jones and the Sultana of the Ruwenora Islands. The thought was profoundly unsettling to one who believed that civilization ended not at the Channel coast but at the

23

Inns of Court and Chancery Lane, and who was convinced that any breach of his daily routine meant a vertiginous descent into primal chaos.

'And how can you tell I have come directly from Great Scotland Yard?' asked Sir James, as they descended the stairs.

There was no surprise in his voice: only an academic interest.

'Very simply. The edge of the toe-caps and the insteps of your boots are freshly mired,' Mycroft told him. 'The pavements of Whitehall, the Horse Guards and Downing Street are swept. You would not have walked far at this time of day without taking a cab – not in pursuance of your duties. You must, therefore, have crossed Whitehall, a thoroughfare too broad for you to have obtained the services of a crossing-sweeper. . . .'

They had reached the bottom of the staircase leading to the Horse Guards Parade entrance to the Treasury. The porter recognized Mycroft; he assisted him on with his topcoat and handed him his cane, hat and gloves.

'There are only two places on the far side of Whitehall in the immediate vicinity,' Mycroft continued, 'to which you might have had recourse. One of them is the Cock Tavern where I myself was taking lunch not an hour ago. The other is Great Scotland Yard. . . .'

They stepped out into the chill brightness of the Parade.

'I have, indeed, been speaking to your old associate, Chief Inspector Grimes,' Sir James said.

'In which case,' Mycroft told him, 'I am not in the least surprised that you felt the need to come straight across to see me. In anything more subtle than catching a sneak-thief *in flagrante delicto*, Grimes's investigative powers are such as to leave confusion worse confounded. . . .'

'A moment, Holmes.'

Sir James touched his sleeve lightly. Footsteps and chattering voices echoed from under the arch separating Horse Guards Parade from Whitehall. Two families of

24

sightseers emerged into the dying sunlight, two husbands with their wives, with their children and governesses in attendance. Sir James and Mycroft stood aside to let them pass.

'Has your younger brother ever considered entering the service?' asked Sir James. 'He must have come down from Oxford by this time – he was at BNC, wasn't he? I remember you telling me he had an excellent head on his shoulders – you consulted him over the Dorking Gap business, did you not?'

'Young Sherlock has spent the past two years in Leipzig studying music under Joachim – the violin, you know,' Mycroft replied. Before Sir James had a chance to pass any comment, he added, 'I have attempted to point out to him that fiddle playing is scarcely the avocation of a gentleman. Now he writes to me to tell me that he has learnt all that the excellent Joachim can teach him, and that he is returning to this country to enrol as a student at St Bartholomew's Hospital in the School of Forensic Medicine.'

'Perhaps, unlike yourself,' suggested Sir James, 'he would positively like to assist the Detective Police in their pursuit of the criminal?' asked Sir James. 'Or has he ambitions to become a coroner?'

'He has expressed the odd notion of setting himself up in practice as a consulting detective,' Mycroft replied. 'He has always taken a morbid interest in the psychopathology of criminality. He assisted, you know, in the resolution of the mystery surrounding the past life of a 'varsity friend's father. The fact that it cost the parent his life, and that the son has had to go into exile on a tea plantation in Terai has not worried young Sherlock one whit. He pursues any end he sets himself with an obsessiveness amounting to monomania; it is in part, of course, the effect of a younger brother's jealousy of the powers of concentration and observation possessed by the elder.'

'He must cause you a great deal of anxiety,' said Sir James.

But it was evident to Mycroft that, now there was nobody within earshot once again, his attention had drifted elsewhere.

The sun was low over the trees of St James's Park; the light gleamed on the roof-tops of Buckingham Palace. The two families of sightseers had crossed the road to the park, and were trotting away towards Birdcage Walk. Mycroft and Sir James stood alone on the gravel expanse of the Horse Guards.

'Do you recall the case of young Louis Ponsonby?' asked Sir James.

Mycroft grunted. He prodded the ferrule of his cane into the gravel between his feet. Then he looked directly at Sir James.

'Last April, at Lord Dewsbury's seat in Hampshire – Caburn Towers. Found in the morning by the maid bringing up his hot water; gassed himself. Evidence given at the inquest that he'd been disappointed in love – killed himself for the sake of an actress or some such tosh.'

'Why do you call it tosh?' asked Sir James.

'Because that's precisely what it is! If I remember correctly, young Ponsonby had been seconded from his regiment to the Admiralty, and was travelling to Portsmouth on Admiralty business. He broke his journey overnight at Caburn Towers in order to pay his respects to Lord Dewsbury, an old friend of his father's. Now, a young fellow of his breeding and upbringing, if he were driven to take his own life on account of a young woman considerably beneath him in station, would have waited until he had completed the task entrusted to him by their Lordships of the Admiralty, before taking his life. He would then have done so in his own quarters, or at least in a hotel room. It is certain he would not have shown discourtesy to an old family friend by killing himself while he was a guest under his roof. It is quite unthinkable!'

'He did take his own life,' said Sir James.

'But not for love of a woman?' asked Mycroft.

'Not for the love of a woman,' Sir James confirmed. 'There *was* a young actress – a Miss Boardman, a Miss Florence Boardman. She was – still is, I suppose – a member of the Bancrofts' company at the Prince of Wales's Theatre. She gave evidence for us before the Southampton coroner. There had been a . . . an affectionate friendship between herself and young Ponsonby. . . .'

'But they had put it behind them?' asked Mycroft.

'Their mutual ardour was somewhat cooled, shall we say?'

'That was not what Miss Boardman testified under oath before the Southampton coroner, however,' Mycroft suggested.

Sir James sighed.

'Young Ponsonby was carrying sealed orders from the Admiralty to Rear-Admiral Sir Fitzroy Parkinson at Portsmouth. They were orders whose secrecy was of the utmost importance – the Admiralty's contingency plans in the case of an armed conflict in the Eastern Mediterranean area between the armed forces of Her Majesty and those of the Russian Emperor. He was granted permission – foolishly, we might think now – to break his journey in order to visit Lord Dewsbury. But who could possibly have supposed that there would have been any risk of his losing the orders at Caburn Towers? In any case, how could anybody have known that he intended to break his journey there? He did not know himself that he would be travelling down to Portsmouth until the afternoon he received his instructions – the afternoon of his journey. . . .'

'The Admiralty's sealed orders were stolen, nonetheless?' asked Mycroft.

'Yes. While the poor boy was dining with his host and hostess downstairs, somebody entered his bedroom, broke open the dispatch-box, and removed the sealed water-proof package containing Rear-Admiral Parkinson's orders. . . . That same night, he undressed, turned the gas

27

on for the fire and all the gas-mantels, and climbed into bed between the sheets to await death.'

'A most touching story,' said Mycroft.

If Sir James caught the hint of sarcasm in Mycroft's voice, he affected not to notice it.

'It was a pathetic business,' he agreed. 'But also a most grave matter for the Foreign Office. I need hardly stress to you, my dear Holmes, the gravity with which the FO viewed the possibility that the orders intended for our Eastern Mediterranean Squadron had fallen into the hands of the Imperial Chancery in St Petersburg.'

'Or into the hands of anybody interested in making matters worse between this country and Tsar Alexander?' suggested Mycroft.

'The matter was taken seriously enough for Lord Derby to take the first train out to High Wycombe, to the Prime Minister's place at Hughenden', Sir James continued. 'Lord Beaconsfield and he agreed that the public should know as little as possible regarding the true circumstances surrounding young Ponsonby's death. Apart from provoking a lack of confidence in Whitehall, any public revelation of the true cause of the tragedy would quite possibly have enflamed anti-Russian sentiment to a point where it could not easily be contained. The poor boy's father and Lady Ponsonby gave their consent to the fiction of an unhappy love affair between two young people of widely differing stations in life; and Miss Boardman agreed to play a part not in Mr and Mrs Bancroft's theatre, but on a wider stage for the sake of her country.'

'And to perjure herself in the process,' said Mycroft.

'That is too harsh, Holmes! There was no need for the young woman to tell a complete falsehood; only to make certain adjustments to the truth.'

'Lord Dewsbury's staff at Caburn Towers must be a wonderfully discreet one,' Mycroft observed. 'Was no alarm raised when Mr Ponsonby found that the Admiralty's orders were missing?'

'He discovered that his dispatch-box had been broken

into only when the family was retiring for the night, or even perhaps had retired for the night. It is the custom at Caburn apparently for one of the chambermaids to remain on duty on the guest-room wing until the last guest has finally retired and settled. It seems that young Ponsonby rang for her shortly after going to his room for the night. This young female said she found him in a state of some distress. He asked if she had noticed anybody going in or out of his room while he had been downstairs at dinner, or whether she had seen anybody she did not know by sight on that wing of the house. She told him she had observed nothing untoward, and asked if anything were the matter. He replied that it was nothing, and that she should leave him. Next day, she confessed to Lady Dewsbury that she had been sure something was badly amiss – I believe those were her exact words – but that she had not liked to press a young gentlemen like Mr Ponsonby. According to Lady Dewsbury, the maid was herself deeply distressed when she spoke to her – blaming herself for what had occurred, though nobody else did.'

'So, in fact,' said Mycroft, 'nobody knew that the Admiralty dispatch-box had been interfered with, and that papers had been stolen, until the next day. It is merely supposition that what was distressing Mr Ponsonby, when this young female found him, was the loss of the sealed orders for Rear-Admiral Parkinson.'

'My dear Holmes! What else should it have been?'

'A moment of melancholy at the thought of past happiness in the embrace of Miss Florence Boardman – however long past? A stubborn fragment of ill-chewed mutton in the digestive tract?' he offered.

'I fear you are being flippant, Holmes,' Sir James accused him.

'Not in the least, Sir James!' Mycroft replied, rebuking him. 'It is a matter for proper consideration. Why, do you suppose, did young Ponsonby do no more than summon a chambermaid to his aid before succumbing to suicidal despair? Why did he not raise the entire house? It was a matter of national importance was it not – the loss of sealed orders to the Naval Officer commanding the Eastern Mediterranean Squadron?'

'Perhaps he did not fully appreciate the full significance to the Nation of what had occurred,' Sir James replied. 'Perhaps he was aware only of the disgrace to himself. Perhaps he could not bear the thought of having to accept responsibility for what had occurred either before their Lordships of the Admiralty or an elder statesman like his host. . . . Perhaps he could not bear the disgrace he felt he had brought on his host.'

'And the maid? What of her? What sort of person is she?'

'A very respectable girl for her walk of life, according to Lady Dewsbury,' replied Sir James. 'Her name, as I recall, is Emily Richards. Her age, sixteen or seventeen – she had not been in service at Caburn for more than four or five weeks, but already the housekeeper was describing her as a most responsible and hard-working young woman. She had been sent down to Hampshire on approval from Mr Wellbody's – the new domestic agency in Margaret Street. She was most highly recommended. I myself sent Nuttall – Gilbert Nuttall, you remember? – down to Caburn to advise her on the evidence she should give to the coroner. He found her a most steady, intelligent girl.'

'Like Miss Boardman,' Mycroft suggested, 'she proved reasonably adept at making certain adjustments to the truth.'

'If you wish, Holmes. If you have to put it that way!'

'Tell me,' Mycroft asked, ignoring the note of irritation in Sir James's voice, 'was it this same female – Emily Richards? – who discovered Ponsonby's body the following morning?'

'No. Lady Dewsbury is most considerate towards her domestic staff. Any young female who has sat up half the night waiting for the guests to retire would not be expected to be up in time to carry hot water the following morning.'

30

'In everybody's anxiety to keep the truth of the matter from public attention,' Mycroft asked, 'was there any proper investigation into what had occurred?'

'Of course there was! Whatever did you suppose?'

'Tell me. Who executed it?'

'Your old associate – Chef Inspector Grimes of Scotland Yard.'

Mycroft grunted. He thought for a moment before asking, 'Did he find firm evidence of any criminality? I mean to say, Grimes is capable of that – even if his skill often falls short of identifying the criminal.'

'You are too harsh in your judgements, Holmes,' Sir James told him. 'He found clear evidence of an attempt to break in that night. A flower-bed below young Ponsonby's window had been disturbed. And there was evidence of an attempt to climb up the outside wall to the first floor – broken trellis, that sort of thing.'

'But no evidence of an actual entrance? Forced window latch? Broken pane?'

'There's no mention of anything of the sort in the Chief Inspector's report. But Grimes was absolutely sure of the evidence on the outside of the house.'

The shadows across the road in the park were lengthening. A lamplighter was making his way down Birdcage Walk, the light at the end of his pole faintly gleaming like a dim star above his head.

'Since he was engaged on Her Majesty's affairs of state – important affairs of state – I presume young Louis Ponsonby was armed. I mean, although he would not have been in uniform, he would have been in possession of his service revolver,' said Mycroft.

'Most certainly.'

'Let us suppose that he was so distraught by what he regarded as his breach of his superiors' trust,' Mycroft continued, 'that he was completely blind to the impropriety of doing away with himself while he was the guest of an old and honourable family friend. . . . In that extremely unlikely event, do you suppose that a gentle-

31

man, an officer of Her Majesty's Coldstream Guards, would go to the trouble of undressing himself for bed and then turning on all the available gas jets? Would he not put a bullet through his head and die a soldier's death rather than that of a love-sick draper's assistant? And would he not, at the least, leave a note exculpating his host and hostess from any responsibility for his fate?'

'If you do not believe that he did away with his own life. . . .' Sir James began.

'I do not. Not for a moment. Nor, I suspect, do you. A hypothesis comes immediately to mind. Louis Ponsonby never left the sealed orders in his room when he went down to dinner; that is based upon the presumption that he took his own life—'

'And upon the maid's statement to Lady Dewsbury,' interrupted Sir James.

'Let us assume this young female, Emily Richards, was telling the truth. . . .'

'We have no cause to suppose otherwise,' Sir James pointed out.

'Quite so. Let me continue with my hypothesis. Young Ponsonby keeps the package of sealed orders about his person at dinner. He returns to his room to find the Admiralty dispatch-box broken into, but no documents actually missing. Naturally enough he is concerned about it sufficiently to call the chambermaid, but not enough to disturb the entire household. Let us suppose that he retires for the night, placing the sealed orders with his service revolver under his pillows. Somebody enters the room – somebody who has access to a key, and who knows the precise geography of the room – somebody who has already attempted to steal the package and failed. They turn on the gas and retire. As soon as they can be certain that young Ponsonby is unconscious, if not dead, they return, turn off the gas, search for what they want till they have found it, then turn on the gas once more; it is possible that his death will be taken for suicide and there will be a delay in finding the loss of the sealed orders, or that what was indeed assumed will be assumed, that the papers were stolen during dinner and that he took his own life as a result. As for the disturbance of the flower-bed and the broken trellis – it is possible that the package was passed by somebody on the inside of the house to somebody on the outside. Or more likely, it was a false lead, deliberately placed to stop anybody from realizing that the package was still in the possession of somebody inside the house.'

'Are you suggesting that a member of Lord Dewsbury's household not only stole the package, but also murdered poor young Ponsonby?' Sir James asked in an appalled voice.

'That is the most feasible theory,' Mycroft replied calmly.

'Unthinkable! Quite unthinkable!' Sir James exclaimed.

But he stood silent for a moment. Then, as if seeking to avert such a possibility, he said, 'Not a soul knew, apart from their Lordships of the Admiralty, that young Ponsonby would be travelling towards Portsmouth that afternoon, still less that he would break his journey at Caburn Towers.'

'Have you ever heard the use of the term, a "sleeper", Sir James?' Mycroft asked.

Sir James thought and shook his head.

'Of course! You were good enough to tell me once,' said Mycroft, 'we do not employ a professional secret service.'

'Neither professional nor amateur!' exclaimed Sir James. 'It is not the British way, I hope.'

'In those less scrupulous states which do,' Mycroft continued, 'the term "sleeper" is used to denote an agent who has been put in place to remain there inactive and therefore unnoticed until, after what is frequently a considerable period of time, something occurs which will require him to go to work.'

'What a dreadful thing! And you are suggesting that there was such a creature lying in wait at Caburn Towers?'

'Caburn Towers lies just off the Portsmouth Road, or, if one takes the London, Brighton and South Coast Railway from London Bridge Station, it is no more than a half-hour's carriage drive from Emsworth Station. It is the home of an elder statesman distinguished in formulating our country's foreign policy; it is in the way of all important traffic passing between Whitehall and Portsmouth. What better place to employ a spy?'

Sir James shook his head.

'Oh, my dear Holmes!' he said wearily. He sighed. 'Is it possible that all that time there could have been an agent of the Second Section of the Russian Imperial Private Chancery on the domestic staff at Caburn? How much more of our plans, contingency and otherwise, is known to the Imperial Russian General Staff?'

'You should have consulted me on this matter many weeks ago, Sir James,' Mycroft told him. 'Indeed you should!'

Sir James gave him a curious look. In a voice which was almost apologetic, he said, 'It was not the Ponsonby affair I wished to consult you about.'

Mycroft raised his stick and stared up it into the darkening sky.

'You mean,' he said, 'that there has been a repetition of that unfortunate occurrence.'

'I fear so,' replied Sir James.

34

Chapter Three

The sky was like a vast dome set over an arena. It was not yet fretted with stars; the only star as yet visible was that on the end of the lamplighter's pole moving between the trees across the park. The air was growing more cold, defeating even Mycroft's habitual inertia. He lowered his cane to point it in the direction of the lake. The path around it was as deserted as in a dream. Sir James nodded his approval, and they walked on.

'Yesterday morning,' said Sir James. 'Rookworthy. At Vanderlys – old Lady Sowerby's place in Warwickshire. The maid bringing him his hot water found him dead in bed. Heart had stopped beating – that is all the local medical man could state prior to a thorough post-mortem.'

'*Evelyn* Rookworthy?' Mycroft asked. 'Lord Cormorant's youngest son?'

'Lord Derby's Parliamentary Private Secretary. Yes,' Sir James confirmed. 'They say he had a most promising future in politics.'

'And the papers that have gone missing?' asked Mycroft. 'What might they be?'

'They are the minutes of a discussion on the Bulgarian Question held at the Foreign Office between Mr Gathorne Hardy and Count Shuvalov, the Imperial Russian Ambassador. Rookworthy was travelling by railway to Liverpool; he was taking them to Lord Derby at his seat at Knowesley.'

'And, by coincidence,' asked Mycroft, 'he happened to ask Mr Gathorne Hardy if he might break his journey at Vanderlys?'

'Exactly. He left the train that evening at Rugby Junc-

35

tion,' Sir James confirmed. 'He had sent a telegram to Lady Sowerby announcing his intention of staying overnight at Vanderlys. It is only six or seven miles from Rugby; he intended returning there to catch the express train to Liverpool which leaves daily from Euston Square in the morning at half past eleven.'

'Who discovered that the minutes were gone?' asked Mycroft.

'Officers of the Warwickshire Constabulary.'

'A sturdy body of men, I daresay,' Mycroft commented dryly.

'As soon as the FO learnt of Mr Rookworthy's death,' said Sir James, 'the similarity to young Ponsonby's unhappy fate was remarked on. Before any further action was taken, a telegram was sent to Knowesley – Lord Derby immediately chartered a special and returned to Town – and the Warwickshire Constabulary were instructed to find the minutes and to return them to the FO. They could not find them. . . .'

They had reached the lake. They paused, Mycroft staring at the sky reflected in the darkening stillness of the water.

'There are several strange and interesting features in this case,' he observed, 'which, while they are not evident in the case of Louis Ponsonby, may throw light on it. Firstly – there is the fact that Rookworthy should have wished to break his journey at Vanderlys. One can fully sympathize with young Ponsonby's wish to break his journey at Caburn to pay his respects to Lord Dewsbury. But who, in full possession of his faculties, would wish to spend an evening and at least part of a morning with Lady Sowerby?'

'Holmes!' Sir James remonstrated.

'Come, Sir James! We have to apply a clear mind to this problem, untainted by false considerations of delicacy. The poor old thing may not be to blame for being the most tedious woman on this planet – ill health and so on, don't you know? But she is; it's an unassailable fact.

And one would quite expect a bright young sprig like the Honourable Evelyn Rookworthy to travel to Liverpool by way of Hereford or Norwich rather than risk having to spend a night at Vanderlys. I know that Lady Sowerby is – was – his great-aunt, and that he might have expected some benefaction from her will. . . . But even so, it is hard to imagine his actually asking his superiors for permission to break an important journey in order to visit her.'

'He did exactly that, despite what you say,' Sir James pointed out. 'In fact, I have been informed he has visited Vanderlys on a number of occasions during the past few weeks.'

'Secondly,' Mycroft continued, 'we may safely exclude Tsar Alexander's spies from our considerations.'

'Why?' Sir James exclaimed. 'They are the most obvious suspects, are they not? Let me say, Chief Inspector Grimes's people are carrying out the most rigorous investigation amongst the newly-arrived Russian-speaking Hebrews in Whitechapel and Commercial Street.'

'Then I say that they are wasting their time – not to mention the Nation's money – while letting the real scent grow cold. My dear Sir James, you must point out to the excellent Grimes the error of his ways with the utmost speed.'

Sir James paused before replying.

'Shall we walk a little?' he asked. As they strolled up the path towards the new and shining suspension bridge over the far end of the lake he remarked gently, 'I trust, my dear Holmes, your friendship with the little Princess Trubetskoy has not impaired your judgement.'

'Not in the least,' Mycroft snapped back. He recovered himself immediately. 'Any more than yours,' he continued in a more restrained manner, 'has been impaired by the popular anti-Russian hysteria whipped up by street-corner demogogues and the less responsible public prints.'

And yet Sir James's veiled accusation had found its

mark. Never for a single moment had he doubted the veracity of what Sophie Trubetskoy had written to him. He had never dismissed from his mind the notion that she might have been distorting truth in order to prejudice him in favour of her own motherland against the Turks, because the suspicion had never occurred to him in the first place.

Sir James's voice on the sharp afternoon air drew him from his cogitations.

'Who else but the Imperial Private Chancery in St Petersburg would wish to know HMG's response to Imperial Russian policy in the Eastern Mediterranean?' he asked.

Mycroft smiled to himself. 'It is strange, is it not,' he said in a kindly voice, 'how even to the most penetrating mind there may be something so obvious that it is allowed to stand without being considered? Take, for instance, the papers which Mr Rookworthy was carrying and which have disappeared. What would the Imperial Private Chancery in St Petersburg want with those? Are we seriously to suppose that HE the Imperial Russian Ambassador arrives at the Foreign Office in answer to a summons – invitation, if you like; it amounts to the same thing – without bringing an aide capable of recording the transactions of that meeting? So why should the Russians want minutes of a meeting which they would certainly have minuted for themselves? One might suggest they would be of interest to any of the Great Powers *except* the Russians. And if that is the case, does it not throw doubt on Russian involvement in the Ponsonby affair?'

'In that case, who would be your prime suspect?' asked Sir James.

Mycroft drew in his breath as if to sigh. He restrained himself from replying with complete honesty. Instead, he replied, 'As you know very well, Sir James, the notion of a prime suspect does not exist in English jurisprudence. But one must start one's investigations somewhere, so why not at the Turks? Unless you tell me that the Admiralty has already informed the Sultan of its future intentions, would not the Sublime Porte have a profound interest in the movements of Rear-Admiral Sir Fitzroy Parkinson's squadron in the event of the outbreak of war? Might not such knowledge be crucial in its consideration of its own policy towards the Russian Empire? Why not Austria-Hungary? The political situation in the Danube Basin is of the most vital concern with regard to the economy of the Habsburg dominions.'

'Or Berlin?' asked Sir James.

'No, Sir James. I will not be drawn. I merely wish to point out to you that it is very foolish to assume Russian guilt or even Russian involvement in these two very unhappy events. Such immediate – and I might add – foolish assumptions are a hindrance to proper investigation. It was most wise to keep them secret from the public. Vulgar displays of hysterics in the street over what is true is quite bad enough, without exciting them further by what is quite unproven – and, I daresay, false.'

'Very well, Holmes,' said Sir James. 'Despite your somewhat unkind description of Lady Sowerby, I should like you to go to Vanderlys to see what you can make of this dreadful business for yourself. I have spoken to Lord Derby on the matter, and to the Prime Minister. Your well-known prejudices regarding Prince von Bismarck and the foreign policy of Imperial Germany were discussed. But both Lord Derby and Dizzy are agreed, in view of your assistance at the Pitti Palace over Lady Kilgarden's unfortunate indiscretion, and, of course, in the Dorking Gap incident, that you are the man. And we have, needless to add, utter confidence in your discretion as regards particular matters.'

'I can't say that you have taken me by surprise,' Mycroft told him. 'The moment I saw you had come to the Treasury in person to search me out, I knew that my daily round was to be utterly disturbed, and my physical and mental well-being thrown into the hazard. When am I to leave for Warwickshire?'

'Tomorrow morning?' suggested Sir James. 'That same half past eleven Liverpool express from Euston Square Station which poor Evelyn Rookworthy was to have caught at Rugby Junction?'

'So soon?' asked Mycroft.

'I spared you from having to catch the Manchester Express at a quarter to seven this evening,' Sir James pointed out. Then he said, 'You do not employ a manservant, I believe.'

'No.'

'Then I suggest you obtain the services of a good valet, at least temporarily. Lady Sowerby will certainly expect any gentleman who is a guest at Vanderlys to bring his own servant.'

'I shall consider the matter,' Mycroft told him. Already he had decided that if he had to have a male attendant, he would see if he could not persuade Cyril to abandon, at least temporarily, his career on the stage.

As if he had read his thoughts, Sir James remarked, 'I don't have to impress on you that your personal attendant ought to be a fellow of reliability and discretion.'

'Of course! Of course, Sir James!'

They parted, Mycroft turning away towards the Duke of York's Steps and his lodgings at 73a Pall Mall.

Chapter Four

'I h-anticipates your lordship will be requirin' h-a box, h-if I'm not mistaken.' The theatre manager had swept across the foyer like a dowager under full sail. 'Business is brisk, my lord, there's no denyin' the fact of the case. Business is h-always brisk when Mr George Leybourne's name is top of the bill, h-of course. . . .'

He rubbed his hands in excess of scarcely controlled rapture.

'But Mr Stratton's new song, my lord!' he continued; 'h-it's that what's brought the nobility here. I expect it's that what's brought you here tonight, eh, my lord?'

His voice reverberated round the all-but deserted foyer. Mycroft regarded him with distaste. The fellow's nose was swollen and had the colour and texture of a ripe Gorgonzola, and there were candle-grease stains on the satin lapels of his tail-coat. From behind the heavy purple and gilt drapes which, down a short flight of stairs, separated the auditorium from the foyer, came a fierce drum-roll and clash of cymbals. Tumblers, Mycroft decided, inwardly groaning; tumblers and jugglers. But in what other company would he have expected to find Cyril?

'H-if your lordship would condescend to *share* a box, now – we might be h-able to find a place for your lordship h-even at this late hour. A wery good sittiation, my lord: stage-box right. No call to use h-opera-glasses to see the features of the young ladies on the stage, eh?' he winked. 'We has a wery sweet ballet, my lord – in the wery best of taste. . . . Your lordship will find there's h-only a couple h-occupying h-of the box – a wery respectable couple, I do h-assure you, my lord. . . . H-if your lordship would be so condescending as to give the young lady 'alf a sovereign. . . .'

Mycroft presented the enormously fat woman who had stuffed herself into the box-office with a half-sovereign. He had already noticed the dirty tankard and jug of stout she had barely concealed on the shelf behind the small window. Her ink-stained fingers relinquished the handle of the jug to take the coin. The manager gestured aside the attendant in his shabby livery; he led Mycroft up the stairs and round the passage with its red velvet, flock wallpaper and gilt-scrolled cornices, to the stage box. There was the sound of enthusiastic applause from inside.

'Jest in time, my lord,' said the manager. 'They're a-calling in the ballet-girls. Such a sweet lot of young females, all quaite new to the stage: your lordship will fall in love with one or two of 'em at the wery least, eh?'

He was about to open the door into the box when Mycroft laid his stick on his arm to stay him.

'Tell me,' he asked. 'There is a negro on the bill, is there not?'

The manager looked surprised.

'A nigger minstrel?' asked Mycroft. 'An acrobat of sorts?'

The manager shook his head.

'No, my lord. We ain't had a black-face act at the h-Olympia since the pantomime last March – *Robinson Crusoe*. Colonel William Stokeley's Alabama Banjo Band played the Cannibal King and his warriors. We ain't had nothing like it since.'

'I don't mean black-face,' Mycroft told him. 'I mean a genuine man of colour – a blackamoor.'

'Why bless you, no, my lord! We'd not have one o' your regular niggermen at the h-Olympia! We got to think of the ladies, my lord!'

He was scandalized. Mycroft lowered his stick and nodded, and the man opened the door of the box. Mycroft thought of turning away, of going back to the comfort of his own hearthside. But a certain curiosity drove him, now that he had come so far, to step up into the box. He was met by the stench, like an invisible wave, of cheap cigar smoke. Before him, beyond the curtain-framed arch of the box, limelights glared white on the chalk-stippled boards of the stage. From the gloom beyond the footlights, above a hubbub of conversation and clinking of glasses and pots, came the sound of slow handclaps and occasional shouts of 'Gerron with it!'

In the box, a small florid-faced gentleman with luxuriant gingery whiskers to make up for his bald, freckled pate, rose from his ormolu-backed chair.

'Pray make yourself comfortable – pray do, sir,' he addressed himself to Mycroft, and indicating three or four similar, empty chairs.

Mycroft glanced at the pleasantly plump, quite soberly dressed woman seated beside him.

'I trust I'm not intruding on your privacy,' he said.

'Not in the world, sir, Ay do assure you,' the woman told him. She waved a black-lace mittened hand in the direction of the chairs, and smiled. She was not in her first youth, but the roundness of her features kept them unlined.

The manager closed the door behind him; the click of the latch was like that of a prison cell. There was nothing for it, but to hang up his hat and coat on the pegs provided at the back, and to take his place, squeezing himself into one of the inadequate gilt chairs.

Across, in the wings on the far side of the stage, two lines of very young girls, some of them scarcely half-formed into womanhood, were holding hoops of paper flowers above their heads. The bandmaster in the pit below, a tall, angular man, sweating black dye from the curls which he had plastered on to his balding temples, raised his stick. The eighteen or so players who constituted the orchestra played a ragged but loud chord. The children raised themselves on their toes. As the music continued, they came out into the light, strutting their legs in wrinkled tights under short gauze skirts, the little wired-gauze wings attached to the backs of their satin bodices wobbling or drooping, and in no way suggesting the possibility of flight. They held their hoops high above their heads, showing the french chalk smeared on the bodices to hide the perspiration stains under their bare arms; some of them moved in time with the orchestra, all of them rapped the boards of the stage noisily with their frayed points, sending up little clouds of chalk dust. Their ability to dance to the music, or at all, was of little interest to a large section of the audience, who sighed, grunted, or sniggered its appreciation of what it saw. As they reached the climax of their encore, there was a tidal movement up the stalls and round the tiers of opera-glasses being raised. Despite what the manager had said about them being unnecessary, Mycroft's neighbour in the box had put a pair to his eyes.

'Such pretty little things!' whispered the woman, leaning across to Mycroft.

She glanced at her companion, then smiled directly at Mycroft.

'Affectin' – that's what they are,' she added.

From the reticule on her lap she pulled a tiny pair of mother of pearl opera-glasses on an ivory handle and watched through them.

The thumping of little feet landing heavily on the stage caused the whole box to vibrate. The little man beside Mycroft continued to watch avidly. The woman leaned over and offered her glasses to Mycroft.

' 'Ave a go, dear, if you ain't got none of your own! . . . . That's my watchword – " 'ave a go". You never know what you're missin' if you don't 'ave a go!'

She laughed softly. She was so close, he could smell patchouli on her breath. It was a perfume he particularly disliked. He drew away from her as far as his bulk and the restriction of his chair permitted.

'Thank you, no,' he replied firmly, making to push the offered glasses away. 'You are most kind. But I can see very well without.'

With a blare of trumpet, cornet, and trombone, and an

44

ear-splitting crash of cymbals, the dancers launched into their final, uncoordinated *jeté*, landing on the chalk-covered boards behind the footlights in an approximation of a curtsy. One girl with waist-length hair, skinny arms, and no bust to speak of, lost her balance and fell backwards, exposing to the gaze of pit and stalls the undarned holes up the inside legs of her tights and the crudely-stitched black seams of her satin gusset. The applauding audience crowed its approval of her: heavy swells in stiff, starch-polished shirt fronts, mingled with clerks and counter-jumpers in hideous checks, with pea-green bowlers perched on the backs of their bandolined heads. Some stood on their chairs the better to observe the dancers as they pranced off into the wings, cheroots clamped between their teeth. A few ran down to the orchestra-rail to examine the retreating children more closely, and to bawl out ribald invitations to meet them 'round the back' afterwards. As the girl who had fallen scrambled to her feet, leered and winked across the footlights, and ran off after the others, the applause died, and the band fell to tuning for the next act.

The forest-glade backcloth glided up into the darkness above the stage. Revealed behind it, and hanging slightly awry, was a sheet depicting an avenue of trees with, in the foreground, a fountain. A woman made her entrance from the wings to centre stage. Although Mycroft could see clearly the crow's feet about her eyes and the creases in her neck, shrouded though they were in powder, she was dressed in the short, calf-length skirts and high-button boots of a thirteen or fourteen year old, and was wheeling a child's hoop in front of her. As she came forward to face the audience, the expression on her face was the grotesque imitation of a guilty little girl who knows she must own up to something. Clutching the hoop against her skirts, she darted a bashful little smile over the footlights. A man's voice shouted out of the darkness, 'Come on, dearie! Tell your uncle all about it!'

45

at which there was a ripple of laughter from stalls and gallery. The singer waited, looking bashfully down at the footlights. The bandmaster raised his stick; the musicians began to play the sentimental introduction. The singer raised a finger to stop them and the music died out raggedly. As the audience murmured, she crouched behind her hoop at the footlights and whispered to the bandmaster, 'In E flat, *dumkopf*!'

As she stood up again, she maintained her simpering, sad little smile. But Mycroft had noticed the ferocity in her eyes, the cheeks flushing feverishly under her stage make-up, and the clammy sweat which plastered her hair on to her forehead and cheeks. She began in a quavery voice which picked up strength as soon as its little girl character was established:

> Mabel and I have been very best friends
> since together we first went to school.
> We keep no secrets from each other – it is
> always our golden rule.
> Until, that is, this afternoon, I was all by
> myself in the park. . . .

Aaah! The audience let out a sympathetic groan.

> . . . When down by the lake, at the foun-
> tain's edge, an old gentleman I did remark.

There were knowing cries of *Oho!* from up in the gallery, and more scattered laughter. The singer moved so close to the edge of the stage that she was over the footlights, and had she not been wearing short skirts, her petticoats would have caught alight. Mycroft could see past her straight into the wings on the opposite side of the stage. He could see the stage-hands at the ropes; as it was evidently fresh to the theatre, they were watching the performance.

An elderly stage-manager in his shirt-sleeves and wide paper cuffs, and clutching a bound and tattered sheaf of papers under his arm, was signalling instructions into the deeper recesses behind the scenery. Mycroft was able to make out in the gloom behind the limelights the form of a black or brown bear, the size of a man. At first, he thought the beast was wearing an old-fashioned frock-coat, nipped in at the waist; then, as he strained his eyes into the gloom, he could make out the rectangular epaulettes, and the rows of cartridge-holders stitched on either breast. It was a Russian bear, he realized, wearing an approximation of a Cossack officer's kaftan.

'I've always fancied older men . . .,' the singer was confiding archly.

To Mycroft's horror, the gentleman whose box he was sharing leaped up and, leaning over the parapet, shouted across the stage, 'Here I am, darling!' The singer stopped instantly and turned her head. She winked into the box. Amidst laughter, she turned back to the audience as if seeking its advice. She received it in abundance – largely from up in the gallery, and ranging from, 'Watch it, dearie! 'E's a wicked old devil, 'e is!' to a female chant of a public house ballad, 'Tell 'im yer got a 'eadache an' yer mother's stitched up yer drawers!' which cut discordantly across the accompaniment which the orchestra was struggling to continue. The singer appeared to come to a decision. She sent the hoop scudding into the wings where it was caught by a stage-hand, and to ribald cries of encouragement from all parts of the house, she came across to the box. The bald, ginger-whiskered gentleman leaned forward even further over the parapet, to cries from the gallery of 'Ooh, you wicked old reprobate, you!' and 'We knows your sort, don't you worry!' The woman who was with him leaned over to Mycroft and said, quite proudly, 'He's just like a little boy, he is! Never knows how to behave!'

In his efforts to reach out to the singer, the gentleman sent his opera-glasses clattering on to the stage. The singer crouched, picked them up and placed them on the velvet-topped parapet. But instead of addressing herself to him, she turned to Mycroft. She reached out. Mycroft turned aside in the hope of avoiding her touch, but she managed to pat his cheek with her finger-ends, so that he felt, albeit lightly, the scrape of her nails. He saw that the arch look of encouragement on her face was as fixed and artificial as her superannuated girlhood. There was a feral glassiness about her eyes which made him inwardly shudder.

With one hand resting on the parapet of the box, she faced the audience once again and continued singing:

> I've always fancied older men – it's my
> weakness, you might say;
> I might fall in love with a nice young boy,
> but not for more than a day.
> When this grey-haired man raised his hat to
> me, to play coy I could not endeavour,
> For he looked so distinguished, so man-of-
> the-world, I knew I would love him forever.

Despite his revulsion at her proximity, Mycroft's attention was caught by the bear waiting in the wings opposite. It had advanced to the very edge of the tab, and was staring out across the stage. It was its motion as much as anything which had caught his attention – not the heavy-rolling gait associated with a brown bear, but a sprung, long-limbed step, which was vaguely familiar.

'Imagine my distress!' The singer returned to centre stage. 'Oh, how was I to guess that. . . .'

She clasped her hands together and stared up at the back of the gallery with a look of ecstacy. The bandmaster raised himself on his toes and led the orchestra into the refrain:

> The gentleman by the lake was my best friend's
> father.
> The gentleman by the lake – oh, how was I to
> know?

48

> The old man by the water's edge was my best
>   friend's father;
> 'Twas my darling Mabel's daddy set my poor
>   heart all aglow . . .

The elderly stage-manager had grabbed the bear by the arm and was pulling him back into the gloom behind the tab. The bear was half-resisting, staring over its epauletted shoulder across the stage at Mycroft as if appealing to him.

Further behind, in the wings, another figure had appeared: a well-built man whose deportment alone conveyed the information that he regarded himself as a person of some eminence. He was dressed in cutaway tail-coat, open to reveal the union-jack waistcoat spread over his ample belly, kid breeches and Wellington boots, with an old-fashioned curly brimmed beaver hat on his powdered hair. For all that he never went to the halls, Mycroft knew immediately that this John Bull figure was the celebrated Mr George Leybourne. Mr Leybourne put his hand on the bear's shoulder, and the animal took his place quietly beside him.

On the stage, the singer was leading the audience in a reprise of the chorus – which was being bawled out with exaggerated emotion. At the end of the last line – ' 'Twas my darling Mabel's daddy set my poor heart all aglow!' – there was a roar of approval to which the singer curtsied, and curtsied, then curtsied yet again, this time blowing kisses in every direction before tripping young girl-like into the wings. The clapping and shouting continued, with cries for her to come on and sing a reprise. Mr Leybourne was standing beside her also applauding, and nodding to her to go back out on to the stage.

The bear was now standing behind the singer and Mr Leybourne. Mycroft saw that he was standing on his toes peering at him over Mr Leybourne's shoulder, and pointing upwards with his paw. He followed the direction of the paw.

He was being watched. From the *loge* at the end of the tier opposite and above where he was sitting there was a pair of opera-glasses directed not on to the stage, but on himself. He told himself that there was just the faintest possibility he could have been mistaken; cigar-smoke hung like a canopy above the stalls. The applause and shouting was rising to a crescendo. The singer was hesitating in the wings. The bear continued to prod his paw upwards signalling into the air. Staring sidelong, not wishing to be seen to be looking, Mycroft knew that there was no possibility of a mistake. He recognized with complete certainty the squarish head and heavy jowls.

He leaned over to the woman beside him.

'Madam!' he whispered.

But she was too engaged in clapping ineffectively her mittened hands, and calling 'Encore!' in a genteel squeak, to respond. As the glasses which were on him were lowered, he saw the eyes and knew he had been found out.

'Madam!' Mycroft whispered hoarsely. 'Your glasses, if you please!'

Having withdrawn from her, he tried to raise himself in order to reach over to her, but only succeeded in raising the chair with him, so tight was the embrace of the gilt-scrolled arms.

'Changed your mind, have you, dear?' she whispered back. 'I thought as that were a woman's pree-rogative!'

'If you please, madam!' Mycroft urged. The chair clattered under him.

She reached over, holding them out to him. 'Here you are, dear – only my little joke.'

He took them from her while she was still speaking, and held them to his eyes with both hands, ignoring the slender ivory handle. He took a moment or two adjusting them to his eyes. The *loge*-seat came into focus as if it were no more than five yards distant. It was empty.

He tilted the glasses upwards a little. A massive, tall shape was standing in the shadow of the curtains at the back of the *loge*. A narrow shaft of light shone up from the stage; it fell across the lower half of the face. Mycroft could see the ironic smile twisting the mouth: the smile of one who knew he was being observed and wished to communicate that he knew. There would be no amusement in the watery blue-grey eyes, however. Carl Philipp Emmanuel Guttmann's eyes only smiled at the accomplishment of some unspeakable act of wickedness. Mycroft lowered his glasses. Why? he asked himself. Why was Guttmann here in London, in the Olympia Theatre? It was not impossible, of course, for him to have evaded the Princess's spies. Had he himself walked into some sort of a trap?

The singer walked out once more on to the stage. She bowed then curtsied. For a moment she looked overcome by faintness as if she might fall. She recovered her poise instantly, and clasped her hands to sing once more.

Mycroft resumed looking at the *loge* opposite. No more than a minute could have gone by since he had the glasses fixed on the figure in the shadow. There was nobody there now – nobody behind the curtain, nobody in the empty chair. He dragged himself out of his own chair as if he were divesting himself of a garment. With the curtest of thank-yous, he returned the glasses to their owner. Turning his back on the turmoil beyond the box, he stepped down on to the passage and hastened as fast as his girth allowed to the stairs leading to the foyer. Below him, the foyer was deserted; a blind had been pulled down over the window of the box-office. Behind him, the riotous applause continued echoing from the auditorium; through it came the sound of the orchestra striking up an encore.

He descended the stairs. He noticed the guttering of the flames on the gas-mantels, as if they had been caught in a draught. He saw the newly-discarded programme on the foyer carpet, marked heavily by the heel of a boot. He hurried to the doors and went out into the cold air. He heard a persistent groaning. Turning, he found on the

51

top of the steps by one of the doors the foyer attendant. He had a worn, shabby overcoat slung over the shoulders of his old-fashioned footman's livery; he was crouched in the angle of the wall, his face pressed against the brick, his white-gloved hands clutched at his stomach. Mycroft grasped his shoulder.

'What's the matter, man?' he asked. 'What happened?'

'I only asked if he wanted me to call him a cab!' the man gasped. He groaned as if he were about to vomit. 'He tell me to step out of his way an' drove his stick into me gut, if you'll excuse the expression, sir.'

He looked up at Mycroft.

'There weren't no call for it, sir!' he said as if he were pleading with him. 'He drove his stick into me gut like he were going to shove it right through me!'

There were tears of pain dribbling down his cheeks.

'Which way did he go?' Mycroft demanded.

The man pointed in the direction of the new London Terminus Station at the western end of Victoria Street. Mycroft ran down the steps and out on to the pavement. There was only a scattering of people hurrying along the lamplit pavements, none of them bearing the least resemblance to Guttmann, and a couple of hansoms and a growler coming up the street from the station.

'Foreign gentleman, he were!' called the attendant.

'I know,' replied Mycroft, mounting the steps once more.

There was a cold wind blowing up the street from the direction of Westminster, to remind him that he had left his coat with his hat and stick in the stage box.

'Friend of yourn?' asked the attendant in a truculent tone of voice.

He had straightened up, but he was still clutching his stomach.

'That is no business of yours, my good fellow,' Mycroft replied.

He tossed half a crown to him nonetheless.

'Something with which to patch your bruise,' he

informed him as the man caught the coin with a quite surprising agility.

'Thank 'ee, sir. Much obliged to 'ee,' the man said, limping forward to hold the doors open for him.

Mycroft stepped back into the warmth of the foyer. The applause for the singer was just beginning to die down.

Guttmann would never have spent a casual evening in such a place; Guttmann whose musical skill and refinement of musical taste, more than any other single factor, had won him his unique place in the confidence of his master, the Imperial German Chancellor Prince von Bismarck, would surely regard an evening at the Olympia as an evening of acute suffering. There had to be some deliberate intention behind this astonishing encounter, and he would have to endure the remainder of the evening's performances in an attempt to find it out.

He went into the box. The clapping had died away. The brass and wind of the orchestra had launched into a martial strain. The bandmaster was swaying and waving his arms as if caught by a stiff breeze. The expression on his sunken features was intended to convey patriotic defiance.

The man and the woman in the box turned to greet Mycroft once more.

'Thought you'd seen enough already, old chap!' said the bald, ginger-whiskered little man with a laugh.

The woman waved him to the chair beside her.

'Been making a new little friend, have you, dear?' she asked. 'Well! You only live once, don't you?'

She held out her miniature opera-glasses to him. Mycroft pretended to notice neither the wave nor the glasses. He lifted a chair to the furthest edge of the velvet-topped parapet, squeezed himself into it, and fixed his gaze on the stage.

The bear in its Cossack kaftan trotted on its hind legs on to the stage and began to perform a shuffling dance – a dance Mycroft realized he had seen performed on the pavement of Shaftesbury Avenue. Immediately the applause turned to booing and cat-calling. A rotten apple

53

came soaring out of the darkness of the auditorium and splattered over one of the bear's rear paws. A raw egg splintered and splashed over the cockle-shell reflectors of one of the footlights and hissed and spluttered from the heat. Jeers, vegetable matter, and farthings and half-pennies were hurled at the unfortunate bear. Meanwhile, in the wings, a boy had appeared carrying a tray on which was a tankard and a black bottle. Mr Leybourne turned, filled the tankard from the bottle, drank the contents in a single draught, and wiped his lips with his glove. Returning the tankard to the tray, he signalled to the bandmaster. There was a drumroll and a clash from the cymbals. To the sound of 'Rule, Britannia!' played more enthusiastically than musically, the backcloth of the lake and fountain was rolled up into the ceiling, and a new sheet took its place. This portrayed the Widow of Windsor seated on Britannia's sea-girt throne, with a couchant lion lying beside her. Behind her rocky dais, borne on wavelets the shape of rose thorns, was the Royal Navy under full sail. There were tiny gun-flashes from the ports of the men-of-war, and puffs of smoke which billowed and eddied across the stage. The bear fell to the floor and died in a spectacular manner, to the cheers of the audience. A couple of stage-hands came running on to drag it away as a ferocious, metallic tarradiddle sounded on the drums of the orchestra, and a triumphant blare on cornet and trumpet. Applause soared, filling the house, as Mr George Leybourne came striding on through the gun-smoke. Without a moment's hesitation, he strode to the footlights, and with a voice whose richness and massive volume overbore the roar of applause, he sang out, 'We don't want to fight, but by jingo, if we do – eh, my brave lads?'

Shouting, clapping, footstamping, rose to a deafening pitch. Up in the gallery, men were climbing over the rail as if they were ready to launch themselves through the air in their desire to be led to war by Mr Leybourne, while their women-folk clutched on to them, dragging them back to safety.

From behind the tabs, sweeping round from either side, came two files of female soldiers carrying wooden rifles over their shoulders. They were very different from the previous *corps de ballet*; the gilt buttons on their scarlet tunics threatened to burst from off their maturely-swelling chests, and plump thighs shook inside their military-blue stockings. Behind them, union jacks unfurled and flapped down on either side of the Widow of Windsor, obscuring the Royal Navy on the waves behind her. The orchestra repeated the same phrase *alla marcia* over and over again, while the Amazonian army paraded round the stage behind Mr Leybourne, formed up behind him, and stamped their feet.

The woman in the box beside Mycroft was on her feet clapping her mittened hands as if she would never stop. Somebody shouted above the uproar, 'Let them Russkies hear you, Mr Leybourne!' A purple-faced gentleman, his face fringed with thick dundreary whiskers, had climbed on to his chair in the stalls. He was waving a huge cigar above his head as if it were a sabre, and was shouting, 'Let the Tsar hear you, George old boy! He'll wet his imperial breeches, eh what? Haw, haw, haw!'

George Leybourne smiled as benignly as a person at a christening. He raised his hands to still the tumult. The plump Amazons on either side of him stamped to a ragged halt. There was shushing all round the auditorium, and the noise died into a stillness broken only by a sudden clatter as one of the Amazons dropped her rifle. There was some laughter, but it was aborted by Leybourne raising his hand once more. Without turning his head to see which of his soldiers was the offender, with the orchestra he launched straight into the first chorus:

> We don't want to fight, but by jingo, if we
> do,
> We've got the ships, we've got the
> men – and we've got the money too!

We've fought the Bear before, by Gad! and
   while Britons shall be true. . . .

He paused for a moment, holding the audience's attention so completely that Mycroft could hear the creak of a
chair, before, swinging one arm, he pronounced in a
voice which bounced off the back wall of the gallery:

   The Rooshians shall not have Con-stantinople!

The orchestra crashed out the introduction once more.
The Amazon maidens marched to the edge of the footlights, and, stooping forward, thrust their chests out over
the heads of the orchestra to encourage the audience to
the greatest possible endeavour.
   'We don't want to fight . . . !' they chorused shrilly.
   The audience erupted into a pandemonium of enthusiasm as George Leybourne led them, conducting them
with both arms. The red-whiskered gentleman in the box
was leaning out, helping Mr Leybourne to conduct. The
woman, overtaken with emotion, had fallen back into her
chair and was fanning herself and crying, 'Oh, them
Rooshians! Whatever shall we do about them wicked
Rooshians?'
   The audience were on their feet, in the stalls, the tiers,
the gallery, stamping, clapping, yelling at the tops of
their voices,

   The Rooshians shall not have Con-stantinople . . . !

Staring through the reek and swirl of tobacco-smoke at
the mass of hectic, perspiring faces all screaming to go to
war against the Russian Empire – a din which congealed
in his ears – Mycroft looked to see if Carl Philipp
Emmanuel Guttmann had returned to preside over this
microcosm of a mindless Inferno. He heard through a
dullness of noise, as if from far away, a voice say, 'Mr
'Olmes, sir? It is Mr 'Olmes, ain't it?'

He paid it no attention until he felt a tap on the shoulder, and heard the woman beside him let out a scream. Standing in the semi-darkness behind his chair was the brown bear. Its head was tucked under its arm; on its neck was the head of a young black man. Mycroft stood up, struggling to divest himself of his chair. The woman's screams, unheard or ignored by everybody outside the box, turned to whimpering. The bald, red-whiskered gentleman had turned round. He was already on his feet.

'You've no business . . .,' he began bravely. 'No business comin' in here and frightenin' the lady . . . !'

Mycroft managed to free himself of the chair. He grabbed at the gentleman's arm to prevent him from attempting to strike a blow at the intruder.

'This fellow is known to me, sir . . . Madam,' he said to the woman who had sunk so low into the chair she was in danger of slipping on to the floor, 'I do assure you, you are in no danger whatever.'

The red-whiskered gentleman was still bouncing up and down and crying aggressively, 'Go away! Go away – back where you belong, do ye hear me, sir?'

Mycroft released his arm, interposing himself between the gentleman and the bear.

'I cannot imagine what you think you're about, you rascal,' he told the bear.

'Got somefink to tell you, 'aven't I, Mr 'Olmes?' the bear replied truculently.

Mycroft gave him a push.

'I'll join you outside,' he said.

He took down his hat and coat and picked up his stick from the back of the box. He stepped down into the relatively fresh air of the corridor. Pointing his stick at the bear's moulting chest, he said, 'I don't mind telling you, Cyril my good fellow, I have observed you in some extraordinary – not to say distressing – trappings from time to time. But this beats all. I'm scarcely surprised that the manager of this place refuses to acknowledge that you are employed here.'

'That's 'cause I'm not on his books, am I?' replied Cyril. 'Mr Leybourne, 'e pays me personal like.'

'Why did you come bursting in like that? You gave that poor female the fright of her life.'

'Fright of *her* life! Don't make me laugh!' Cyril told him. 'She knows me like her cousin twice removed. She's up at the back of the promenade most nights, trawlin' for gin-an'-peppermint with the rest of the girls. . . . I come round, even though it's my drinkin' time as you might say, 'cause I thought as you'd like to know there were a friend in the 'ouse tonight.'

'I saw him,' Mycroft replied. 'In fact, he left the theatre almost immediately he knew I had seen him.'

'Is that why you come 'ere, tonight?' Cyril asked.

'No. I came to see you, you young scoundrel. I did not even know Herr Guttmann was in London.'

'Thought as the Princess might 'ave told you,' Cyril said.

He looked quite disappointed. Mycroft shook his head. Then he said, 'You can take the ridiculous costume off. I have to go down into the country tomorrow. I need a manservant.'

'What? Like you did at Dorking that time, eh?'

'Something like that. Though it does not promise so much excitement, I am delighted to say. If you go and change into something which suggests you are linked, however tenuously, to civilized society, I shall explain your duties to you.'

'Can't do that, Mr 'Olmes, sir. Me and Mr Leybourne is billed for another h-appearance on stage tonight. Can't leave Mr Leybourne on 'is ownsome just like that.'

'Very well then,' Mycroft told him. 'You will come round to 73a Pall Mall first thing tomorrow.'

' 'Ang on a jiffy! What about my career on the boards then?'

'Is it your life's ambition to walk out on the stage every night and have half the vegetables of Covent Garden thrown at you?' asked Mycroft.

'Yer! 'course it is – for fifteen bob a week!' Cyril replied.

'I'll give you a guinea a week,' Mycroft told him.

Cyril clasped his hands together. 'Why, bless you, Massa sir!' he cried, rolling his eyes in imitation of a black-face minstrel. 'Lawdie bless you, sir!' He bowed and bobbed. 'Why, indeed, Massa – very first t'ing tomorrow mornin' jes' like you says, Massa boss!'

'And that,' said Mycroft, prodding him again with his stick, 'is quite enough of that!'

The applause for George Leybourne was still sounding across the deserted foyer as Mycroft stepped outside into Victoria Street. A fog had risen since he was last outside, drifting suddenly from off the Thames, up Horseferry Road and the Millbank Penitentiary. Even in the night there was a green hue in the darkness, as if it were the depths of the sea, and a cold dampness which clutched at the throat. The street lamps hung like orange orbs surrounded by drifting haloes of green. There was no sound of footsteps on the pavements, nor any sign of that almost invariable accompaniment of fog, link-boys with their naphthalene flares.

He looked for a cab, but though he could hear the sound of clopping hooves and the creak of wheels on the road, he could not make out in the swirling vapour any sign of lamps moving. He knew that he must nearly be opposite the entrance to Buckingham Row, his most direct route if he was to have to make his way home on foot. He stepped out on to the wet, sandy gravel of the roadway; it was as if he were stepping out into a desert. A hansom came trotting up; it was almost upon him when he heard the jingle of harness and the crunch of iron wheel-rims. The acetylene lamps gleamed like eyes through the fog. He raised his stick in the hope that it was not already carrying a fare, but it swept past him so close that he felt or imagined that it brushed his sleeve. A young man leaned out over the wooden apron and called back to him, 'Better watch out, old chap!'

Then it disappeared and was swallowed up immediately in the drifting mirk.

A row of flickering globes marked the public house at the corner of Buckingham Row together with the sound of laughter and the grinding of a barrel organ on the pavement outside. There was a hurricane lamp on the organ; in its livid glare stood a small group of rough-looking women in shawls and aprons, clutching pint pots in their reddened, swollen fists. In the glow of the public bar windows, Mycroft could see their menfolk silhouetted through the smoked glass. He crossed to the pavement on the further side of the Row in the hope of escaping the women's badinage. As he did so, a growler turned into the Row, and drew up some twenty yards in front of him. Thinking the cab-driver had recognized him as a potential fare, he hurried up to it through the drifting shreds of fog. The driver did not get down to greet him. Instead, the door was opened from the inside.

'Aren't you afraid of being garrotted, walking alone on a night like this, Mr Holmes?'

There was a woman inside the carriage. Her face was in shadow, but the voice spoke with the accentless perfection achieved only by a foreigner.

'You do not know me, Mr Holmes. But on a night like this, when there are so few cabs to be had, I am sure you will forgive my presumption in suggesting you permit me to take you to your destination. I had a friend who was attacked by garrotters on just such a night. He was almost strangled to death. . . .'

A sudden movement by the horse drew the carriage forward. Although it only moved a pace or two before the driver cried 'Whoa!' and applied the brake, it was enough to let the nearest streetlamp shed its light through the window on to the woman's face. She had her veil up; Mycroft recognized instantly the painted face of the singer from the Olympia Theatre. It was raddled with the febrile intensity of advanced sickness. He backed away in a fear so sudden he had no time to steel himself. He touched the rim of his hat between his fingers.

'Thank you, madam,' he said, 'it is most considerate of you. But I have to go such a short distance – and the exercise is, I dare say, beneficial. And since most of the way is within the purlieus of the Queen's Palace and St James's, I think there is little likelihood of my encountering garrotters, or any other sort of footpad. Good evening to you, madam – and once again, my thanks.'

Without waiting for any reply on her part he continued walking down the pavement. How in Heaven's name had she managed her performance on the stage, he wondered? Of course, theatrical people were accustomed to talk of Doctor Theatre, but he had not previously been sure of its efficacy.

The carriage came on after him. The woman was holding the door half open.

'Mr Holmes, are you quite sure you will not change your mind?' she called. 'It really is not a nice night for walking. The fog! One may hardly breathe!'

Mycroft kept on. The fog was in his throat, but he dared not cough. A ridiculous idea had come into his mind that somebody might leap out of the cab and seize him.

'Madam,' he called. 'It is most kind of you, but I must ask you not to persist in your solicitations. I wish to walk – in peace!'

'Very well then!' the woman shouted in an anger which sounded unnecessarily desperate.

She slammed the door. The cab-driver cracked his whip and the vehicle disappeared into the fog. From the end of the street, behind him, Mycroft could hear the sound of the barrel organ, and the raucous laughter from the public house. He found it reassuring. Instead of continuing down Buckingham Row to James Street, however, he turned into the yard of Emmanuel Hospital and, seeking the obscurity of the fog, returned to his lodgings by a devious route.

Chapter Five

'Mr Holmes!' Mrs Turner was not pleased. She wound the ruffled trim of her pinafore-apron round her fingers. 'Begging your pardon, Mr Holmes!' She did not sound as if she meant what she said.

Mycroft was sitting in his dressing-gown, by the freshly-lit fire. He was eating poached eggs on buttered crumpets, mopping up the yoke round the edge of his plate with evident satisfaction. The *Morning Chronicle*, which Mr Turner always ironed for him before leaving for work at the General Post Office at St Martin-le-Grand, was propped up against the teapot.

Without looking up, he said, 'I suppose, Mrs Turner, that there is some pressing reason for this unwonted matutinal agitation?'

She did not reply immediately because she did not understand what he had said. Taking advantage of her hesitation, he continued, 'I do not have to tell a person of your sturdy commonsense that it is a first and invariable principle of mental and bodily hygiene that a man be permitted to take his breakfast in an atmosphere of tranquillity . . . particularly when all he has to look forward to are the unspeakable rigours of travel on the London and North Western Railway.'

Not to mention, he thought but did not say aloud, having to endure, on arrival at Vanderlys, being entertained by a senile but garrulous *grande dame*.

'There's a blackamoor at the front door, Mr Holmes!' Mrs Turner protested. 'Says as you said as he were to come here.'

'Then he is telling the truth, Mrs Turner.' Mycroft

forked a final, yoke-moistened fragment of crumpet into his mouth, and dabbed his lips with his napkin.

'I've had to ask him to step inside!' Mrs Turner went on protesting. 'I couldn't let him stand on the step, could I – him being black as my kitchen range. I mean, what if the neighbours was to see a black man standing at my front door?'

'I'm taking him into my service,' Mycroft said.

He turned round in his chair to look at her. He saw the appalled expression on her face.

'Mrs Turner!' he exclaimed, taken by surprise.

'I'm sure Mr Turner and me have always tried to do our very best, Mr Holmes!' she said in a sulky tone of voice.

'Indeed you have, Mrs Turner,' Mycroft reassured her. 'But I can hardly deprive Mr Turner of your wifely ministrations by taking *you* with me into the country, now can I? . . . However pleasant that would be for me,' he added.

'Oh, Mr Holmes!' exclaimed Mrs Turner, putting her hand to her mouth to hide her smile of flattered embarrassment.

'The young man you have allowed to step inside, with your usual thoughtful consideration,' he continued, 'is the Princess Sophie Trubetskoy's servant – I'm sure you recall the Princess – I merely have him on loan, as you might say.' To consolidate his recovery of her good opinion of him, he added, 'Of course he should have used the area steps. Be sure I shall tell him to do so in future.'

'Thank you, Mr Holmes.' Mrs Turner smiled broadly.

Mycroft endeavoured to smile back. 'If you would be so good as to send the fellow up . . .,' he said.

'Of course, Mr Holmes. I'm sorry to have troubled you, sir, I'm sure.'

She followed Cyril back up the stairs and waited on the landing. In the study, Cyril glanced behind him, uncertain whether to close the door on her or not. His new-found familiarity with the theatrical world, Mycroft noted, had influenced his taste in dress. He was wearing a tight-waisted frock-coat, and trousers strapped under his boots, of a villanous dog-tooth check. His top-coat, which had a somewhat moulting fur collar, was slung over his shoulders, and he carried a light cane with what might have passed for a silver knob if it had not been both cracked and dented, and had crammed down on his tight black curls a peaked cap with a tassel which had almost certainly appeared as part of the student's costume in that fine old melodrama, *The Lyons Diligence*.

'A bowler hat would be more appropriate to your position,' Mycroft told him.

'What's wrong with this un?' Cyril demanded. 'Mr Leybourne give me this. 'Sides, I ain't got no bowler 'at.'

'Mr Turner's got a nice bowler 'at!' called Mrs Turner from the landing. 'A green un. Wore it when he went to the races – *when* he went to the races. He don't want it no more, though. Your blackamoor is welcome to it.'

'I wonder as what Mr Turner would say for 'isself,' Cyril remarked in a low voice. 'If asked, that is – which 'e ain't never goin' to be.'

'I'm sure Mr Turner's green bowler will answer very well!' called Mycroft.

Mrs Turner went to fetch it.

' 'Is favourite 'at, I shouldn't wonder,' observed Cyril. 'Full of 'appy memories of freedom an' the like, when it ain't full of 'ead.'

'Enough of that,' Mycroft ordered. 'Tell me. The woman who sang last night – the one in the little girl's costume, with the hoop. . . .'

'The one what sings "The Gentleman by the Lake," you means?'

'Yes, yes.'

'Jenny Miller's 'er name. What about 'er?'

'Or Jenny Mueller? She is surely German – from her accent.'

'Now you mentions it,' replied Cyril, with a great show of thought on the matter, 'she 'as a funny sort of an accent. Don't know nuffink about her – not really.

Keeps 'erself to 'erself, she does. No joshin' around with the other girls, an' that. Carriage come around an' collect 'er after every performance. Mr Leybourne reckons as she's a "plaything" – "bird in a gilded cage".'

'A "plaything"?' asked Mycroft.

'Female what treads the boards 'cos some swell's got it in 'is noodle to pay the management to let 'er 'ave 'er charnst on the stage. Come on, Mr 'Olmes, you knows the song! "She were only a rich man's plaything. . . ." '

'Think carefully, Cyril. Have you any reason to suppose that Miss Miller – or Mueller's – protector might be Carl Philipp Emmanuel Guttmann?'

Mycroft was gratified to see the look of surprise on Cyril's face.

'No,' said Cyril. 'Can't say as I 'ave. I mean, she's been on the past three nights – they took poor old Albert Correy an' 'is h-acrobatic pigeons off of the bill to make way for 'er. An' Mr Guttmann, 'e only come. . . .' His voice began to trail away '. . . last night.'

'Ah!' Mycroft called out. 'Here is the excellent Mrs Turner returned, and with the green bowler hat!'

Mrs Turner came in, arm and bowler hat out-stretched. Cyril surveyed it with distaste.

'Capital, Mrs Turner! Capital!' said Mycroft, taking it.

He removed the tasselled cap from Cyril's head and placed the bowler in his hand.

'You must permit me to reimburse you – or Mr Turner,' he said.

Mrs Turner simpered.

'That's quite unnecessary, I do assure you, sir,' she replied.

But he forced the coins into her hand. 'A bottle or two of Old Formidable – that is Mr Turner's preference, is it not?' he said.

'Thank you, Mr Holmes.'

'And you may find I have given you sufficient for a bottle of sweet sherry for your own drinking, Mrs Turner.'

'You are very kind, sir,' she replied. 'Mr Turner and I,

we'll drink to your very good health, sir.'

As soon as she was gone, and Cyril was about to express his frank opinion of the hat he was holding, Mycroft said, 'Do you know how I found out that you were appearing at the Olympia?'

'No, massa sir.'

Mycroft ignored the impertinence.

'Did you not send me a playbill? What I believe is known as a flyer? Advertising that you were appearing at the Olympia Theatre? At the hand of a young woman of the servant class?' he asked.

'I certainly did not, Mr 'Olmes!' Cyril looked bewildered, even indignant.

'And stating that you'd be appearing for two nights only?' asked Mycroft.

'Certainly not!' Cyril repeated. He added. 'Any rate, it ain't true. About me appearin' for only two nights – or it weren't until now! And I don't keep no company with servant girls, neither!'

'I shall have to go out,' Mycroft announced on a sudden decision.

'Thought you said as we was catchin' a train at Euston Square,' said Cyril.

'We shall take the quarter to seven train tonight,' Mycroft told him. 'Be back here at a quarter past five with your bag. . . . Properly dressed,' he added, tapping with his forefinger the green bowler hat Cyril was holding.

'I don't know about this, Mr Holmes. I really do not. Do you say you have made no appointment with Sir James?'

The Cabinet Secretary's Principal Private Secretary flicked Mycroft's calling card between his fingers. Then he glanced at it, though he was well acquainted with its owner.

'Most irregular!' he said.

'It is a matter of the utmost urgency, Mr Parrott, I do assure you,' said Mycroft. 'I have written – on the back of the pasteboard.'

The bright sunlight shone down from successive windows on either side of the wide stairwell. It gleamed bright from the pale cream paintwork of the walls, and concealed the portraits of successive prime ministers behind the reflected glare on the glass which covered them. There was a faint smell of fresh paint. The dark staining which had existed since the days of Sir Robert Walpole was all gone.

'Pray be seated,' said Mr Parrott.

As Mr Parrott went up the first flight of stairs, Mycroft eyed the delicate Queen Anne chairs with their gracefully curved, slender legs and fragile arm rests, and decided to remain standing. The liveried attendants in silk breeches and powdered wigs who stood at the entrance to the garden rooms stared past him as if he did not exist.

He had been standing there for five or ten minutes when he heard the sound of a door being opened on the landing above.

'Holmes! You are supposed to be on your way to Vanderlys by now,' Sir James called down.

'I decided that it was most important to speak to you, Sir James. Vanderlys can wait till tonight.'

'You had better come upstairs and prove your point.'

Mycroft followed Sir James up to the first landing, pausing only momentarily at the top of the stairs to regain his breath before following him into one of the Cabinet rooms. But for the huge desk-table by the window, it might have been, in its proportions and its comfortable, leather upholstered furnishings, the visitors' sitting-room at the Diogenes Club.

Sir James waved his hand in the direction of one of the armchairs.

'I daresay I have no need to warn you, Sir James,' Mycroft began severely, as he lowered himself comfortably into the seat, 'that in no circumstances should any Queen's Messenger or officer of the Admiralty or War Office carrying dispatches or memoranda be allowed to break his journey on any pretext whatsoever.'

'Instructions have been given to that effect,' Sir James replied.

He moved round behind the desk, and was about to sit down when Mycroft said, 'I shall tell you the reason.'

'Indeed?' asked Sir James.

He remained standing, his hand resting on the back of the chair. Mycroft stretched out his legs and crossed his ankles. He rested his cane between his boots as if it were a billiard cue resting on a bridge.

'Shall you tell me?' asked Sir James impatiently.

'Carl Philipp Emmanuel Guttmann is here in London,' said Mycroft quietly.

'The devil he is!' exclaimed Sir James. Then he asked, 'How do you know that?'

'I have seen him with my own eyes.'

Mycroft stared down at the ferrule of his cane.

'The fellow has the nerve of Beelzebub to come here after what occurred at Dorking Gap!' exclaimed Sir James. 'Are you quite sure?'

'Entirely so.'

Mycroft explained what had happened the previous night.

'It is my belief,' he concluded, 'that I was lured to the Olympia Theatre, and that a woman attempted to abduct me.'

'My dear fellow! Abduct you?' asked Sir James. 'To what end? And Guttmann. . . . Why should he have wished to reveal himself to you at a music-hall?'

'Vanity, Sir James. Pride: the *fons et origo* of all evil, even the most Machiavellian. I have frustrated his knavish tricks, if I may be permitted to use the expression, on two occasions now: in Italy, and again, in Surrey. It is not sufficient gratification for him to procure the downfall of this country; he must let me know he is doing so. He is a duellist. What satisfaction can be obtained from engaging in a duel if your opponent does not appreciate that there *is* a duel?'

68

He pressed his two forefingers together, resting them on his chin.

'He is, however, too faithful a servant of his master, Prince von Bismarck,' he continued, 'to invite defeat by showing his hand prematurely. We have to assume, Sir James, that the plot has reached the point of accomplishment, that the poisoned web has been spun.'

'Good gracious!' said Sir James. He sat down behind the desk. He stared at Mycroft in astonishment. 'You are sure you could not be mistaken? I mean, you told me no word was exchanged between you.'

'The negro saw him,' said Mycroft. He realized that Sir James was on the point of questioning Cyril's credibility as a witness. 'That boy is as sharp as a button, you know,' he added.

'The singer – Miller?' said Sir James.

'I suspect that her name is Mueller,' Mycroft told him. 'The German accent was unmistakable – the North German accent.'

'Perhaps,' said Sir James. 'But, my dear fellow, you have not suggested the least evidence that she intended to procure your abduction. You said yourself that she showed some interest in you when you were occupying the stage box. Could she not have taken you for a heavy swell – a . . . a . . . ?'

He waved his hands in the air.

'Sir James! I assure you, there was nothing in my manner which could have offered her the least encouragement. . . .'

It was Mycroft's turn to let his voice fail.

'Of course not!' Sir James replied. 'It is only that. . . .'

'Sir James, I beg you to have somebody from the Yard to trace her movements – to discover her activities outside the theatre.'

Sir James looked across at him. He sighed. Then he picked up a pencil and scribbled on the blotter in front of him.

'I will speak to Sir Philip Doughty,' he said. He finished scribbling the note, dropped the pencil, and sat back in the chair.

'I daresay you will have arrived at some hypothesis regarding the meaning of all this,' he said.

'You are acquainted with my reluctance to offer hypotheses, Sir James. It is not my way. . . .'

He lifted his cane from between his toes and laid it across his knees. Sir James said nothing. Perceiving that Sir James had no intention of coaxing him into a further reply, Mycroft proceeded: 'It is my conviction that Carl Philipp Emmanuel Guttmann is engaged in as bloody an enterprise, should it succeed, as any he has previously undertaken. I mean the embroiling of two great Empires, our own and that of Russia, not in the traditional playing fields of the Great Game – Afghanistan or the Punjab, or on the borders of Tibet – where the forces employed are few in number and the battlefields remote from public observation, but in a major European conflagration in the Balkans.'

'It is your serious belief that the present crisis in the Balkans has been stirred up in order to bring about a major Continental war between the Tsar's armies and ourselves?' asked Sir James.

'Exactly so. And already no less than fifteen thousand innocent Christian lives have been sacrificed in Bulgaria to that end.'

'To what end?' asked Sir James. 'I mean, to what final end?'

'Within the last few months we have seen how terrified of a renewed conflict with the German Empire the French government has been; they are prepared to pay almost any price to remain at peace. The Kingdom of Italy is racked with internal political and religious divisions. Austria-Hungary will do nothing which might encourage uprisings among her rebellious subject races. If Great Britain and Russia can be induced to maul one another to death, there will not be a great power left in Europe to challenge the hegemony of Prussia.'

70

'Holmes?' asked Sir James suspiciously, 'are you about to suggest that Guttmann is responsible for the deaths of young Louis Ponsonby and Evelyn Rookworthy?'

Mycroft did not reply.

'This is too fanciful by half!' Sir James exclaimed.

'Were my propositions regarding the Lady Kilgarden affair or the Dorking Gap business "too fanciful"?' Mycroft demanded. 'Was I wrong in my surmise as to what underlay the Sultana of Ruwenora's overtures of friendship with poor Sir Loxley?'

'Lord Derby wouldn't entertain it for a moment,' replied Sir James. 'He is entirely convinced of Russian involvement in the matter of young Ponsonby and Mr Rookworthy. Besides, he regards Prince von Bismarck as one of us – a landed proprietor of the old school.'

Mycroft grunted.

'Do you have reasons to support your hypothesis?' asked Sir James.

'Proposition,' Mycroft corrected him. 'There is a clear distinction to be drawn between "proposition" and "hypothesis". You will find it perfectly explained in Occam's *Opus Nonoginta Dierum*.'

'Very well,' Sir James humoured him. 'Proposition.'

'Wherever there have been outbreaks of conflict in the Balkan states,' said Mycroft, 'Belgrade, Novibazar, Bucharest, Guttmann has always preceded them. The Princess Trubetskoy has always let me know before the event occurred, that he was there.'

'Ah yes! Your little Princess! And did she inform you – in advance – that Guttmann was coming to London?'

Mycroft glanced down at his boots once more.

'No,' he said.

'Well. . . .' Sir James rose from his seat behind the desk. 'Perhaps her spies here are not as alert as those in Bucharest and . . .' he paused for a second, '. . . Novibazar.'

He had expected Mycroft to have presented weightier evidence in support of his case. He was clearly relieved; he could scarcely keep the smile from his lips.

'Has it not occurred to you, my dear Holmes,' he continued, 'that patriotism is not a virtue confined to these British Isles? That your little Princess may be motivated by something other than a simple desire to get even with a man she has every reason to detest?'

'You are surely not suggesting that Princess Sophie Trubetskoy is seeking to provoke conflict between Great Britain and the German Empire?' exclaimed Mycroft, genuinely astounded. 'Five years ago she helped to *save* this country from destruction.'

'She helped to save *you* from destruction,' Sir James replied. 'That is not quite the same thing. . . . Come Holmes! You have to agree that, from the point of view of Her Majesty's ministers, such a thing is perfectly possible. . . .'

'Reckoned as you'd be a-sendin' for the Princess,' said Cyril.

They were in the cab driving up Gower Street towards Euston Square. Mycroft shook his head.

'But you promised!' said Cyril. 'That time at Charin' Cross. Just as she were gettin' into the train. You said, any time you found as that Guttmann were gettin' up to no good, you'd send to 'er straight away. You did, you know!'

'I'm not paying you a very generous wage to be impertinent, young man!' Mycroft told him.

'Said you was going to, just the same!' Cyril said in a voice just low enough to be partially drowned in the rumble of the carriage wheels.

Chapter Six

With a regal wave of his stick, Mycroft dismissed the porters who sought to assist him with his bags, leaving Cyril to carry them, grumbling, down the sooty, fish-smelling ramp to the platform gate. A long-funnelled tank-engine had just drawn a train of north-bound carriages into the nearest bay. Steam and smoke swept like a gritty fog through the gate and the railings, obscuring the passengers who were passing through, and the ticket inspector in his booth alike. As Mycroft was arriving at the bottom of the ramp, a young woman – a girl of no more than sixteen or seventeen – passed him on her way up. He had seen her as he had approached, a figure shrouded in the smoke, standing as if waiting just outside the gate: a neat, strikingly pretty girl with forget-me-not eyes, and long, honey-blond hair falling from under her bonnet down over her shoulders. From her well-tailored coat, several seasons out of fashion with the fur trimming at the collar and cuffs showing signs of wear, he knew her to be a member of the servant class, a chambermaid or parlourmaid from some prosperous household. As she passed him by, she avoided his glance – not demurely, with eyes lowered, like any genteel young woman, but with eyes averted as if she were refusing to acknowledge his presence. Mycroft turned to look after her. He caught the smirk on Cyril's face, and glowered at him. Cyril gave the two modest-sized bags he was carrying a heave, as if the burden was very nearly too great for him to bear, and said, 'Remember 'the Princess, Mr 'Olmes? She 'ad ten porters to carry 'er luggage, she did!'

Mycroft ignored this remark and offered his ticket to the inspector at the gate.

'The young woman who was standing here just now?' he asked. 'Had she been waiting long?'

'She were here when I come on duty, sir. That were two hours since. Waiting for a loved one, I suspects. But he didn't turn up. Happens all the time,' he added gloomily.

Mycroft slipped a shilling into the man's hand, and passed through the gate. He left Cyril to place the portmanteaux in the van and to find a place in one of the third-class carriages. He himself found an empty first-class carriage. He had just arranged himself comfortably, when a young lady mounted the step and pushed herself and her fashionably voluminous skirts through the door. Behind her, amidst the steam rising from between the carriages, an elderly clergyman peered in from the platform. Behind him, a railway porter stood in attendance, with gaily striped and beribboned dress-shop and milliners' parcels heaped in his arms and concealing his face.

Mycroft opened his copy of *The Pall Mall Gazette* across his knees. The elderly clergyman said anxiously, 'Emily, my dear, the gentleman might wish to partake of tobacco. It is a smoking carriage, you know!'

That had been precisely Mycroft's intention. To that end, he had thrust his cigar-case into the swell of his waistcoat pocket; to that end, he had looked for a carriage with the legend, *Smoking*, frosted into the glass of the door window.

'I'm sure *I* shall not mind if he does,' replied the young lady brightly.

As she pushed past Mycroft to take the centre seat, beside him, the folds of her skirts swept the newspaper askew on his knees, and he had to snatch at it to retain possession of it. As she sat down, he found his arm submerged in a swelling breaker of red tarleton and white broderie anglaise; she did nothing to order her dress, and delicacy prevented him from extracting or even moving his arm.

74

She turned to him, raising her veil from her face as she did so.

'If you wish to smoke, sir, please feel entirely free to do so. I'm quite used to it. Dear Papa smokes like a chimney, and sometimes he lets me fill his pipes for him, don't you, Papa?'

'Emily!' the clergyman exclaimed in the gentlest of rebukes.

He had mounted the carriage step and was hanging on the hand rail, uncertain what to do. Behind him, the parcels in the porter's arms were beginning to tilt dangerously to both sides simultaneously. An untypical compassion for the clergyman's embarrassment inspired Mycroft to say to his instant regret, 'I had no intention of smoking when I took this seat, I do assure you, sir. Pray be at your ease.'

The elderly clergyman climbed aboard, followed by the porter and his load.

'Take care! Don't drop any of them!' the girl called out as one of the parcels slid from the porter's grasp and was about to fall on to Mycroft.

The clergyman turned round and caught it just in time. He helped the porter to place them up on the rack, then dismissed him with a threepenny piece. As the porter stepped down once more and closed the carriage door, the clergyman sat down at the opposite window to Mycroft. He leaned forward.

'I hope you will forgive my daughter, sir. . . .'

Mycroft raised a finger to prevent him from speaking further.

'There is no need in the world, sir. You see, I know you are about to tell me that the child has no mother.'

'Why, yes, sir. That is indeed the case—' the clergyman began to reply in surprise. He was interrupted by his daughter.

'My mamma died when I was only three. I have been brought up by governesses. That is why I do not always behave as I should. They were not always the ladies my poor papa supposed them to be – at first, at any rate. And governesses are *sui generis* – that's what Papa always says. . . .' She smiled across at her father, leaned forward and took his hand in her own. Mycroft seized the opportunity to extricate his hand from her skirts.

'Dearest Papa!' she said softly. Then, '. . . *Sui generis*,' she continued, releasing her father's hand and turning to Mycroft, 'such a dreary lot, are they not? Did you ever have a governess when you were young, sir?'

'Oh come, my dear!' the clergyman protested. 'We both liked Miss Stansfield exceedingly.'

'You did, Papa! That is, until. . . .'

'Perhaps these governesses,' Mycroft suggested hastily, not caring to be entertained by a recital of the fall from grace of the likeable Miss Stansfield, 'were not accustomed to the quiet of a country parsonage – one somewhat remotely situated in the western marches of Staffordshire, up on Wetwood or Ashley Heath, shall we say?'

Both the girl and her father were staring at him in wonderment. There was the sound from outside of doors being slammed, and the hiss of steam. The guard's whistle shrilled. Smoke billowed across the platforms, and the train began to move. For one brief moment, Mycroft caught sight in the obscurity of the dense, drifting vapour, of a tall, burly figure in the wide-brimmed, low-crowned hat of a clergyman. He was unable to make out the face or eyes; even so, he could *feel* in some strange manner that he had been observed – even seen through as if he had been discovered in some furtive, guilty act. He noticed that the clergyman sitting opposite him had also seen his colleague and had given him a little wave of the fingers.

'Forgive me, but are you acquainted with that gentleman?' he asked.

They pulled out into the darkness between the sooty brick embankments of Summerstown and into the tunnel heading northwards toward Wealdstone and Harrow.

'Why, no sir,' the clergyman replied. 'But he was of

great assistance to us in finding our way to the station and seeing us on to the train. Brothers in the cloth, I suppose one might say.'

'He told us he was to meet somebody on Euston Station,' said the girl. 'His wife's new parlourmaid who was arriving by train from the north.'

'And did he meet her?' asked Mycroft.

'We were just in time,' said the clergyman. 'The poor child had just come up from the platform when we arrived. I don't know how she would have found her own way across London. . . .'

'He told her to wait at the entrance,' the girl intervened, 'while he helped us to find a carriage on the train. Wasn't that very obliging of him?'

'Most obliging,' Mycroft agreed. 'Did this considerate gentleman tell you his name, by any chance?'

'He was a foreigner,' said the clergyman, 'which makes his act of kindness to us the more delightful. August, I believe he said his name was. He is Pastor of the Moravian Church in London.'

It was possibly true, thought Mycroft. One should always take care not to rush immediately to false conclusions.

The girl said with an eager smile, 'You have to tell us how you know the county *we* come from.'

'Emily, my dear,' her father chided her, 'he does not *have* to tell us!'

'It is a countryside,' said Mycroft, 'which must seem very wild, even haunted, to a genteel spinster lady who is accustomed to life in a town, however provincial.'

'You are not acquainted with Papa, are you, sir?' asked the girl in amazement.

Mycroft smiled at her, and shook his head. 'No, my dear. Your father and I have never met to my knowledge.'

'I hope you will forgive me if I seem as curious as my daughter,' said the elderly clergyman. 'But you appear to know a great deal about us.'

'Only the most superficial details, my dear sir,' Mycroft

replied. 'The conclusions which any one with moderate powers of observation might arrive at. The fact that this charming young lady has done a great deal of shopping in Town, yet you are unaccompanied by an older woman, suggests that you are a widower and she motherless. There is also the affection and understanding which, if I may be permitted to say so, is so clearly evidenced between you, and which suggests strongly that you are, in a manner of speaking, a couple in your own right – that your child has been something of a wife to you.'

'I'm afraid you must have also observed that I have made a poor hand at bringing her up,' said the clergyman.

'Not in the least,' Mycroft replied. 'A certain fearlessness of manner is not to be confused with impertinence.'

'You are most kind to say so,' said the clergyman.

But Mycroft had been thinking of somebody far from the enclosed compartment they were in.

'I am, in fact, the present incumbent of the Parish of St James-the-Less at Wetwood in Staffordshire,' the clergyman continued. 'Shall you tell me how you have come so close to us in your observation?'

'It is such a very simple matter,' Mycroft replied. 'I am almost ashamed to explain something which almost explains itself. First, there are your boots. Square-toed, sir, with two layers of toecap; the footwear of one who is more accustomed to country paths than clubrooms and ladies' drawing-rooms, eh? There are your daughter's parcels, and the clothes – new clothes – she is presently wearing. She came up to Town with you not only to keep you company on whatever business you were about, but also to replenish her wardrobe and linen presses. I suppose this shopping to have been fairly comprehensive. This argues not only that you rarely have the opportunity to go shopping, but also that you do not live within easy reach of a town of any size.'

'Such is indeed the case,' agreed the clergyman.

'There is the matter of your mode of speech. Your daughter's vowel sounds are those of the north – as are yours, but in your case there is evidence of a sojourn at one of our ancient places of learning, that, I fear, which is on the banks of the Cam. They do not indicate the far north, however – Manchester, or even Cheshire. Since you are travelling on the London and North Western Railway, rather than the Midland, or London and North Eastern, one can only assume that you are native of Staffordshire, and, in the case of your daughter, that she has spent her entire young life in that county. Then we have the evidence of your stick. . . .'

'My stick, sir?' asked the clergyman.

'Much may be learnt about a man through observation of his stick, sir,' Mycroft replied. 'There is, for instance, the denting in the ferrule of yours, which indicates its use on rough, country ways. There is the unevenness with which the tip is worn down, which indicates its owner's tramping on steep places. There are the teeth marks halfway down. It has frequently been carried by a dog both in time past and recently. The spacing of the teeth marks tells me that it is a large dog of a certain sort of breed – a mastiff, perhaps? Even a bull mastiff?'

He was gratified to hear a gasp from the girl beside him.

'You are a wonder, sir,' said the clergyman. 'A phenomenon, if you don't mind me saying so.'

'The evidence is there for anybody who wishes to see it,' Mycroft told him. 'Nobody has ever kept a bull-mastiff for its affectionate nature. Nor is it likely that a gentleman in Holy Orders, living alone with his young daughter, would retain such a beast in order to take part in the more barbaric of our country pursuits – bull baiting, dog fights, and the like. . . .'

'Certainly not, sir!'

'Quite so. Therefore one must conclude that you keep it to protect yourselves and your property. From this may be deduced the fact that your living is to be found in one of the wilder and more steep parts of a county not particularly well known for the wildness of its country.

79

Ineluctably one is drawn to the locality of Ashley Heath and Wetwood.'

'Do you know, sir?' said the clergyman. 'I believe the Almighty has bestowed on you a wonderful power of observation.'

'It may be so,' Mycroft agreed, humbly bowing his head.

'We did not come up to Town solely to let me go shopping,' said the girl.

'I did not suppose that you did,' said Mycroft.

He had hoped that the conversation was concluded.

'Papa wishes me to travel. Abroad, I mean. Next year my aunt, who lives in Town, is to introduce me into Society. Dear Papa would like me to travel first. To see the world, you know? Germany, Italy, all those places. So we had to go to find a suitable governess to accompany me.'

'Emily, my dear,' said the clergyman. 'I'm sure the gentleman does not wish to know about your future plans.'

Let her prattle on, thought Mycroft: as long as I may pursue my own train of thought. He contented himself with a reassuring smile directed at the clergyman.

'Travel is such a simple matter nowadays,' said the clergyman. 'What with railways and Baedekers, and the electric telegraph. And my daughter has led such a sheltered life, I feel she should see something of the wider world – though I must confess—' he gave a little, self-deprecatory laugh '– I do not know what I shall do without her for company.'

'You will do what you have always done, Papa,' the girl told him. 'You will go for long tramps along the hills, you will take tea with the Misses Harrison, and you will write your sermons.'

'I suppose I shall,' the clergyman sighed. 'Up the Rhine by boat, I thought,' he continued. 'I believe that is absolutely the thing nowadays. To Switzerland. And then on to Italy: to Florence. Have you been to Florence, my dear sir?'

Mycroft jolted himself awake.

'Yes, I am reasonably well acquainted with the city of Florence,' he replied.

'And is it a suitable place for a young lady to visit, would you say, sir? To spend a week or two.'

'In my opinion, sir,' replied Mycroft, 'all travel – particularly travel for its own sake – is unsettling both to mind and body. A constant procession of widely varied stimuli, passing by too quickly to permit comprehension or a proper psychical ingestion, can only provoke any existing tendency to neurasthenia in the impressionable young mind. And in the case of foreign travel, one must take into account the probability of encountering unhygienic quarters and greasy and indigestible foods. There is also the question of the company the young person may encounter – exerting influences which may be deplored by the responsible parent. . . .'

'Aha!' exclaimed the clergyman with a great show of discernment. 'One can see, my dear sir, that you have children of your own.'

'No, sir, I do not,' replied Mycroft.

'My papa has taken every possible care against my being over-stimulated,' said the girl, 'or falling into bad company. I am to have for my chaperone a veritable dragon of a governess. . . .'

'Emily dear!' her father protested.

'A Prussian dragon – or is it dragoon?' the girl continued.

'I'm sure Fräulein von Holz-zu-Birkensee will prove the most agreeable companion,' said her father. 'We have been most fortunate,' he turned to Mycroft. 'She is the young widow – so tragic – of a cavalry officer who lost his life in the late war, outside Paris. He left her in somewhat straitened circumstances so that, though she is of good family, she has been forced to earn her bread teaching her own language here, in England. . . .'

This seemed to Mycroft an unlikely account of her situation. The Imperial German government was considerably more generous in its pensions to the widows and orphans of its fallen warriors than was the Government of Great Britain. He said nothing, however.

'. . . She speaks excellent English and Italian,' the clergyman continued, 'and comes with the highest recommendations. She is just about to leave the employ of Sir Rinaldo and Lady Hornby; she has been in charge of their twin daughters.'

'That would be Colonel Sir Rinaldo Hornby, would it not?' Mycroft asked. 'Officer Commanding Royal Marines at Chatham?'

He was suddenly fully awake.

'Indeed it would,' the clergyman told him. 'I am led to understand that the Hornbys are to move to Malta; Sir Rinaldo is to take command of the Royal Marine establishment there, and Lady Hornby will go with him. The Misses Hornby will remain at the family seat in Dorset, in the care of relatives, so Fräulein von Holz-zu-Birkensee's occupation will shortly be done.'

Mycroft held his forefinger crooked against his closed lips.

'Most interesting,' he commented.

He remained silent for a moment.

'Are you acquainted with the Hornbys, may I ask?' said the clergyman.

Mycroft shook his head sharply; his train of thought was being disturbed. He lowered his forefinger.

'This Fräulein von Holz. . . .'

'zu-Birkensee?' the clergyman offered.

'Yes, yes!' Mycroft replied impatiently. 'You have offered her a position through private negotiation?'

'Why no, sir. Through the Wellbody Agency,' the clergyman replied. 'That is the cause of our visit to the Metropolis.'

'Did you say the Wellbody Agency?' asked Mycroft, 'in Margaret Street?'

'Why, yes, sir! The very same. I was told that the Wellbody Agency, though far from being an old-established firm – tried-and-true is my usual criterion –

has rapidly gained a reputation in the best circles.'

'So I understand,' Mycroft said thoughtfully. 'And this lady's position with you is to be of a temporary nature?'

'To accompany my child on her tour abroad, sir. I gather the Fräulein is not seeking another permanent post at present. In fact, she will return immediately afterwards to her home in Prussia.'

'Quite so,' Mycroft replied.

During the ensuing hour or so it took to reach Rugby Junction, he replied with the minimum that courtesy required to the girl's interminable chatter, and to the clergyman's desultory remarks. His mind was preoccupied with thoughts of the Wellbody Domestic Agency; the chambermaid, Richards, at Caburn Towers had been sent from Wellbody's. He wondered if he would find that a maid from Wellbody's had attended on young Rookworthy at Vanderlys before he died. But the theory to which he was drawn by following such a path was not to be contemplated. Even Guttmann, surely, would respect the sacred loyalty between master and domestic employee.

The train drew into Rugby Junction. The garish light from the station lamps shone through the rain-spattered windows. One or two porters on the platform signalled to passengers, and then ran, pushing their trolleys, to keep up with their clients' carriages as the train drew to a gradual halt. Mycroft heaved himself to his feet with an effort. The girl gathered in her skirts as he did so, not out of consideration, he noted, but smoothing them and inspecting them lest he had caused them some disarray.

He took his hat and stick down from the rack. A station attendant threw open the door and shouted in on a gust of cold, damp night air, 'Three minutes, ladies and gentlemen! You have three minutes to obtain refreshment and to make yourselves comfortable! Next stop Nuneaton, if you please!'

Mycroft was about to wish his erstwhile companions a safe journey, but was anticipated by the girl, who said to her father, 'I'm *so* glad we're not setting down here, dear

83

Papa, aren't you? I mean, it is so cold and windy out there, and so warm and snug in here.'

'Emily, my dear,' the clergyman began to reprove her.

Mycroft stepped heavily down on to the platform. He closed the door behind him, and stared through the rising steam to see if Cyril had retrieved the portmanteaux from the van.

'Three minutes!' the attendant was shouting as he strode along the carriages. 'Three minutes by the platform clock! Next stop Nuneaton!'

A half-dozen or so passengers from the third-class carriages were scurrying across the puddles in the wet stone to the station-house rooms. There was another strident, rasping voice calling out. This time it was, 'Papers! Evenin' papers!' and it came from a boy of twelve or thirteen with his eyes almost concealed beneath the chewed peak of an exceedingly greasy hat several sizes too large for his head. Under a dirty blue cotton railwayman's jacket which on him was almost a top-coat, he was sunk into a voluminous pair of moleskin trousers, rolled up about his ankles. A large but rather empty canvas bag was slung over his shoulder.

He looked up at Mycroft.

'Evenin' paper!' he roared.

His face was smeared with soot, and there were black gaps where two of his front teeth were missing.

'It's your last charnst, mister,' he announced. 'On'y got a couple left.'

'What is the paper?' Mycroft asked.

'*Rugby Evenin' Gatherer*, o' course,' the boy replied. 'Ain't no call for Lunnon papers on the down side 'cos all you gents got 'em already, see? My sister does the Lunnun papers, on the h-up side.'

'I certainly don't wish to read *The Rugby Evening Gatherer*,' Mycroft told him.

'Quite right, mister,' the boy told him. 'There ain't nuffink in it worf readin' – not tonight. It'll be different termorrer, though!'

A young, bareheaded gentleman stuck his head out of the window of the carriage next to the one which Mycroft had occupied.

'Here! You!' he called to the boy. 'Is there a Lamps on this station?'

The boy did not reply directly, but turned his head towards the station rooms and bawled in a voice which must have carried out into the town 'Farver! There's a gent 'ere wants Lamps!'

Mycroft saw that Cyril was coming up the platform, a portmanteau in either hand. A working man came trotting across the platform; he was wrapped in an oily apron with oily rags stuffed into the string about his waist, and in his oil-smeared hands he carried a can of oil and a small metal funnel. The newspaper boy called to him, 'H-over 'ere, Farver! Gent 's a-callin' for yer! 'Spec' it's smokin' wick or somefink . . .'ats my farver,' he proudly confided in Mycroft. ' 'E's in charge of all the lamps for the down trains.'

'Tell me, young man,' said Mycroft, 'since Rugby Junction appears to be something of a family business of yours. . . .'

'There's some troof in 'at,' the boy observed sagely.

'Which side of the station might I expect to find a carriage – a carriage waiting to take me in the direction of Warwick?'

The boy raised his arm above his head, pointing up to the apex of the blackened glass roof. He swung his hand in an arch to point to the opposite side.

'There!' he announced. 'Over the bridge, see.'

Cyril arrived. He dropped the bags at his feet. The boy turned to stare at him.

'You're a 'eeven, ain't yer?' he said, having given the matter due consideration. 'You're one of 'em *black* 'eevens wot we give our 'a'pennies for, in Bridge Street Sunday School.'

Cyril and he stared at each other. The boy turned to Mycroft.

' 'Cos there's two sorts of 'eevens,' he explained. 'There's 'em as lived in the olden days – Romans, they was called. And there's black 'eevens wot eats one anuvver – the sort you gives 'a'pennies for so as they can buy proper food, an bibles an' fings.'

'Cyril!' Mycroft exclaimed, because Cyril had raised his hand to clip the boy over the back of the head.

'One minute!' the attendant came down the platform shouting. 'One minute, if you please, ladies and gentlemen!' He directed his voice towards the windows of the station-house rooms. 'Next stop Nuneaton!'

' 'Ere!' said the boy. 'I'll give the 'eeven a 'and wiv the bags, 'cos I'm goin' to the h-up platform – an' I ain't got nuffink in my bag 'ardly.'

He picked up one of the portmanteaux. Before he set off leading the way up the steps leading to the bridge, he stuck his head into the carriage from which the gentleman had called for Lamps.

' 'Ere, Farver!' he shouted. 'Don't you go gettin' yoursel' a-carried off to Nuneaton again, or Muvver'll give yer what for even worser 'n last time!'

Mycroft and Cyril followed him up on to the bridge over the tracks. Cyril grumbled.

' 'E's only doin' it 'cos 'e thinks as you'll give 'im sixpence.'

' 'Course I am!' the boy replied. 'An' I bet you ain't such a' 'eeven yer works for nuffink, neither.'

'I suppose your mother is employed in the railway buffet,' said Mycroft, only half joking.

'Cor, bless you no!' said the boy. 'There's people as drops dead just lookin' at 'em samvidges in the buffet. My muvver's 'ead maid in the ladies' room. She bandolines the ladies' 'air. She says its a wonder 'ow many of the ladies rushes straight in to 'ave their 'air bandolined, soon as they gets off of the train – 'cos they don't want their loved uns seein' 'em lookin' a fright an' 'at. Susan – 'at's me sister, Susan – gets 'er 'air bandolined for nuffink, 'cos of my muvver. . . .'

86

But Mycroft had stopped paying him any attention. Below, through the bars of the rail, he looked down at the platform – the platform for trains travelling towards London. There was a four-wheeled trolley draped in black, and on it, similarly draped, was a coffin. With the two railway porters pulling the trolley was an undertaker, directing them, and on either side mutes of both sexes, the men with their staves and hats draped in black crêpe, the women in black bonnets with black veils spilling down over their shoulders. There were several gentlemen in the train of the coffin, their mourning less ostentatiously displayed. They were accompanied by a man who was not in mourning at all; his light brown bowler hat and caped ulster told Mycroft that he was an officer of the Warwickshire police force.

The north-bound train was on the move. There was the grunt of the engine and the grinding and hissing of pistons. Smoke belched upwards and enveloped the bridge. In the midst of the damp obscurity, Mycroft said to the boy, 'You told me just now that tomorrow there would be news worth reading in the pages of *The Rugby Gatherer*. What did you mean?'

He pointed through the smoke in the direction of the cortège he had just witnessed.

'Best cry of all, mister!' the boy grinned. ' " 'Orrible murder!", 'at's what it'll be. Ain't nuffink like a " 'orrible murder" to sell papers!'

'Who has been murdered?' asked Mycroft.

'Come on, mister! Can't tell yer that, now can I? You wouldn' 'ave no call to buy a paper termorrer if I tells yer! 'Tain't h-ethical an' 'at!'

Cyril was watching, a smile on his lips.

'I shall not be buying a copy of your unspeakable rag tomorrow,' said Mycroft. 'And I have here a shilling to prove it.'

He took the coin from his purse and held it up.

' 'At's different,' said the boy. 'If you ain't a-goin' to buy a paper anyway.'

'Who has been murdered?' asked Mycroft, still holding up the shilling.

'The Lunnon gent, it were. The one what were visitin' at Vanderlys Hall.'

'And how do they say he was killed?'

'Ooh!' said the boy, grinning with satisfaction. 'They says as it were a chambermaid wot done it – wiv a 'airpin stuck into 'is 'eart! They've h-arrested 'er an' took 'er off to the 'ouse of Correction in Warwick.'

'This maid – does she come from these parts?' asked Mycroft.

'Yer. . . .' said the boy. 'What, Ellen Brown? 'Course she does! Born an' bred at Vanderlys, she was. They do say as she were a nice, quiet sort of girl afore she did the bloodthirsty deed. 'Spec' now they'll 'ang 'er at Warwick. That's prime for sellin' papers – a hangin' 's better 'n the murder itself!'

Mycroft flicked the coin to him. The boy dropped the portmanteau to the ground and clapped it between the palms of his grubby hands. The smoke was dispersing. Looking down once more through the rail, Mycroft caught the eye of one of the mourners, that of Sir Ralph Dearing, Lord Lieutenant of the County of Warwick. Without waiting either for the boy or for Cyril, he moved with an alacrity quite foreign to his normal torpor, almost running down the steps to the platform. As he passed the coffin, he raised his hat to it perfunctorily. He went straight to the tall, corseted figure of the Lord Lieutenant.

'Why Holmes, my dear young chap!' the latter greeted him. 'Pleasure to see you again, m' boy. Complete waste of your time, though. As soon as the sawbones established it was a case of murder most foul, don't y' know? Quilt here had the bracelets round the culprit's wrists. Take my advice, m' boy. You accompany the earthly remains of poor Rookworthy back up to Town, what do y' say?'

'What I say, Sir Ralph,' Mycroft replied, 'is that if Mr Evelyn Rookworthy was indeed murdered for the papers he was carrying – as I was sure he had been even before I knew of the results of the autopsy – I am somewhat surprised that your Inspector . . . er. . . .'

'Quilt, sir – Chief Inspector,' said the small man in the bowler hat and caped ulster who was standing beside Sir Ralph Dearing.

'Exactly so,' Mycroft agreed. He continued to address Sir Ralph: '. . . that your Mr Quilt here should have immediately apprehended a local girl – one, indeed, if I understand correctly, from the Vanderlys estate, whose origins are known to everybody hereabouts. There must surely be servants at Vanderlys who are recent arrivals to this part of the country and who merit a certain scrutiny . . . . However,' he added with a magnanimous wave of his hand, 'I have not been sent here by Her Majesty's government to overlook the no doubt thorough investigations of Chief Inspector Quilt into a case of murder, but to undertake a preliminary enquiry into the loss of the Foreign Office's documents. . . . Will you be returning immediately to Vanderlys, Sir Ralph?'

Chapter Seven

In the carriage, Mycroft sat facing Sir Ralph Dearing and Chief Inspector Quilt of the Detective Branch of the Warwickshire Constabulary. The light from the carriage lamps shone obliquely on their faces, whitening them and emphasizing the disapproval in which they held him. The wind-driven rain scurried against the windows. Cyril had been ordered to sit up with the coachman, exposed to the elements. Mycroft could sense almost palpably the disapproval oozing through the wood and leather coachwork from that quarter. Occasionally the vehicle lurched down into a pothole and jolted up again, so that he wondered if Cyril would not be pitched into the road.

'Neither Sir James Swarthmoor nor Chief Inspector Grimes of Great Scotland Yard's K Division indicated that there was the least suspicion of the maid who discovered the body – the girl, Brown – having perpetrated the crime,' he remarked.

'The Chief Inspector here had not concluded his investigations when he telegraphed his preliminary report to the Home Office,' Sir Ralph Dearing replied stiffly.

It was not his corsets alone which caused the old fellow to sit so erect. He was an old cavalryman who had commanded a squadron of the Heavy Brigade at Balaclava, and, like a good commanding officer, was punctilious in his support of his subordinates.

'Of course,' Mycroft agreed. 'But a girl of sixteen, who had never been off the Vanderlys estate until she was removed in a police van to the Warwick House of Correction—'

'A hackney carriage, Mr Holmes.' Chief Inspector

Quilt was clearly offended by the suggestion that he lacked human compassion towards the accused.

'And hitherto of blameless character?' Mycroft suggested.

'A simple process of elimination,' the Chief Inspector replied. 'Your culprit could be a saint to all appearances. But when you've eliminated all those who could not have committed the bloody deed, and one – only one – remains, however improbable, that one has a *prima facie* case to answer before a Grand Jury. That is the lesson of the Road House murder, wouldn't you say, sir?' He looked to Sir Ralph.

The Lord Lieutenant nodded.

'Poor Inspector Whicher came a cropper, don't you know?' he said. 'Knew Miss Kent had red hands. Process of elimination; had to be her. But the rest of the world said, "Decent gel, blameless reputation," and all that. Now, she has confessed. But too late to save poor Whicher's professional career. . . . Still, it's a shockin' business this, at Vanderlys.'

The old soldier's chivalrous view of right and wrong came to the surface.

'. . . The girl's poor mother was in service at Vanderlys before her. Her father is still head stableman.'

'Unlikely business, wouldn't you say, Sir Ralph?' Mycroft persisted. 'Chambermaid, scarcely more than a child, never travelled more than a mile or two from Vanderlys, suddenly becomes the Tsar of Russia's hired assassin? I don't suppose she even knows her letters.'

'Mother is a lettered woman,' said Sir Ralph. 'Taught the child to read and write. Not a good thing among the lower order of servants, don't you know? It's of no practical use of 'em; only leads to mischief, in my opinion. . . .'

'The notion she's an agent of the Tsar, Mr Holmes. . . . Well . . . that's something your lot in London have dreamt up,' said Chief Inspector Quilt. 'We're simple folk, here in the country. We look for simple answers. There's no proof

91

whatsoever she stole government papers. . . .'

'Not even by a process of elimination?' asked Mycroft.

The carriage lurched and jolted violently. He grabbed at the strap to maintain his seat. The Chief Inspector fell into Sir Ralph's embrace.

'No call to be witty, Mr Holmes!' he snapped, as if Mycroft had been responsible for the state of the road.

He resumed his proper place.

'The unhappy deceased could have left the papers back in London,' he continued. 'Or in his railway carriage. There's no evidence he ever had them at Vanderlys.'

'That's true, you know, Holmes,' said Sir Ralph.

He dusted himself down as if contact with Chief Inspector Quilt had left an unwanted residue on his coat.

'It was your lot in Whitehall telegraphed us about these damned papers,' he continued.

'The Foreign Office papers were the cause of the Honourable Mr Evelyn Rookworthy's journey out of Town,' suggested Mycroft.

'But they were not the reason for his going to Vanderlys,' the Chief Inspector replied. 'Aha, Mr Holmes!' he tapped the side of his nose with his forefinger. 'Got you there! The unfortunate deceased had his mind on other things, in a manner of speaking.'

He leaned forward.

'The young female, Ellen Brown, may have been of hitherto blameless reputation. The same cannot be said of the unfortunate deceased. . . .'

He sat back in his seat, eyeing Mycroft in the lamplight to see what effect his words were having.

'Don't give me any pleasure to say such things of my betters,' he added.

'Had a taste for young females of the servant class, it seems,' said Sir Ralph. 'His father, Lord Cormorant, lui-même a un goût pour la boue, you understand? Quite deplorable! Takin' advantage, don't you know? Like shootin' at a sittin' bird.'

'Do I take it you're suggesting the young woman

92

stabbed young Rookworthy through the heart with a hairpin while defending her honour?' asked Mycroft.

'There's been a great deal of talk among the junior maids at Vanderlys about Mr Rookworthy's behaviour,' Chief Inspector Quilt replied. 'One or two were most reluctant to be alone with him – afeard to turn down his bed at night lest he be in his room, afeard to take up his hot water in the morning. That sort of thing.'

'You see what a confoundedly bad business it is, Holmes?' asked Sir Ralph Dearing. 'Only possible motive. Mustn't deny the young female justice. But her only possible line of defence is to blacken the ancient and noble name of Rookworthy. Dread to think of the effect it'll have on poor Lady Cormorant.'

Mycroft looked him in the eye.

'I wonder what effect the unfortunate business is having on the poor girl's mother – or father, for that matter. Honest, hard-working people both, I believe.'

'Of course. Of course!' Sir Ralph cleared his throat. 'But one takes account of breedin' – finely strung susceptibilities, don't you know? As with thoroughbreds, eh?'

The carriage lurched again and tilted as it turned away from the road. In the passing light from the carriage lamps, Mycroft saw dimly through the rain-spattered windows the iron bars and scrolls of a gate, and behind it, the narrow porch and gothic-arched door of the gatekeeper's cottage. The keeper, in a shiny oilskin cape, stood saluting, his fingers holding the rim of his hat from which the rain was spilling. As the carriage rocked and swayed on the neglected surface of the drive, Mycroft clutched at the strap with one hand while resting the other on the knob of his stick. He tried to sway with the movement of the vehicle, his ample weight acting as ballast.

'I understand your concern, Sir Ralph,' he said. 'Perfectly. But you may put your mind at ease on that particular account. Everything that you have told me merely reinforces what I already knew. I'm sure the briefest of investigation on my part will demonstrate that the young female, Brown, is not your culprit, and the motive for the crime will in no way be found to cast a stain on the escutcheon of the House of Rookworthy – except, of course, the fact that the Honourable Mr Evelyn Rookworthy might have taken a little more care for himself and the documents with which he had been entrusted.'

'By God, Holmes, I pray you are right!' said Sir Ralph.

A more than ordinarily deep pothole shot Mycroft upwards off his seat. He fell back with a gasp. It might have been the violence of the jolting that made the Chief Inspector utter something between a grunt and a snarl.

Chapter Eight

'Said as you were a gentleman really, Mr Prettyman, soon as I clapped eyes on you,' the little maid told him. 'Said to Mrs Arbuthnot, I did: 'e may be a blackamoor, but 'e's a gentleman if you asks me.'

She was standing beside where Cyril was seated at the table finishing his meal, so close that her sleeve was pressed against his shoulder.

'They do say as breedin' will out, eh?' he replied modestly.

The heat from the great open hearth at the end of the servants' hall, and the warm stew, had at last dissipated the chill of sitting on the roof of the carriage. The room had been the kitchen in the days of Cavaliers and Roundheads; it was as big as a coach-house, with a blackened ceiling which was almost invisible in the firelight and candlelight glow. The fireplace stood as high as a man. His fur-collared topcoat which had been drenched through and dripping steadily when he had at last dragged it off, now hung, circling gently and steaming, on one of the ancient but burnished spit-racks above the hearth. From across the flagged passage outside the door came the sound of bustling as the kitchen servants carried the supper dishes up to the dining-hall.

'You just pass me some of 'em lovely new potaties, sweetheart – to mop up the gravy wiv,' he said.

The little maid giggled.

'Ain't your sweetheart,' she said.

But she leaned across the table, maintaining the pressure of her sleeve against his arm, and drew the dish of potatoes up to his plate.

'Just h-anticipatin', darlin' ' he told her.

'Dunno what that means, when it's at 'ome,' she said, but it did not prevent her from giggling again.

He spooned seven or eight of the small potatoes on to his plate.

'Nah, there's a wonderful fing an' no mistake!' he said. 'New potaties in November!'

'Mr Hetherington grows 'em in the greenhouses,' the maid explained.

'Now where I comes from,' said Cyril, impaling two potatoes simultaneously on his fork and pushing them around the plate, 'Zululand, where I oughter be king if there was any justice, which there ain't – we grow new potaties all the year round, an' we don't need no green-houses nor nuffink . . . an' grapes,' he added. 'An' peaches. You'd like it where I comes from, you would – er – what's your name?'

'Florrie, Mr Prettyman.' She gazed at him with big wide eyes. 'Short for Florence. Flower—'at's what Florence means. Not many people knows 'at, but my friend Cicely read it in a book.'

She giggled again.

'An' a very pretty flower you is, Florrie, an' no mistake,' Cyril told her.

'Thank you kindly, Mr Prettyman,' she said.

And yet again she giggled. In time, thought Cyril, her giggling could become extremely wearing.

' 'Spect as it's been very tragical 'ereabouts,' he suggested. 'What wiv the 'orrible murder, an' your friend bein' carted away by the police an' all. She was your friend, was she, Florrie? That pore h-unfortunate girl?'

Florrie nodded solemnly. She even withdrew her sleeve from his arm, if only by an inch.

'She were a real pal, were Ellie,' she said, her voice gone all hoarse. 'One o' the best. Tell you something, Mr Prettyman; none of us girls think she done it!'

'An' I'll tell you somefink, Florrie my dear,' Cyril returned. 'My master is of the h-opinion she ain't the guilty party, neither!'

'Is 'at the truth? Is 'at the gospel truth, Mr Prettyman?'

'It does raise sartin complications, as you might say,' Cyril pointed out.

He shovelled several gravy-smeared potatoes into his mouth.

'Like, for instance,' he continued. He paused to chew for a moment. 'H-if it ain't your pal what committed the terrible crime – then it's got to be somebody else what's the guilty party, ain't it?'

'Oh lawks!' Florrie exclaimed. She clutched at her mouth.

'Still,' said Cyril, 'I'm sure you ain't the sort to go skewerin' a gent's 'eart wiv a 'airpin or nuffink, eh?'

She shook her head solemnly.

'Anyway,' she whispered. 'I ain't a upstairs maid.'

She lowered her hand and clutched her fingers in the lap of her apron.

'They says as this poor Mr Rookworthy 'ad an eye for the girls,' Cyril suggested. 'Not that it 'd be any consarn o' yours, you not bein' by way of a h-upstairs maid.'

'I ain't one for gossipin', Mr Prettyman,' Florrie answered. 'But none of 'em liked 'im. You can ask Annie or Rosie – they'll tell you.'

'Annie and Rosie?'

'Parlourmaids. They was scared of bein' anywheres by themselves with 'im. An' Maddy said as 'e 'ad more 'ands 'n one of 'em octopussies.'

She let out another involuntary giggle.

'Who's Maddy when she's at 'ome?' Cyril asked.

'Maddy Orchard. East-wing chambermaid she were. She 'ad a way with words, did Maddy. S'pose 'at's what done for 'er, likely. Mrs Arbuthnot dismissed 'er, without no notice, same mornin' as . . . what 'appened – you know.'

'My gentleman's room's on the East Wing,' said Cyril.

' 'At's where all the guest rooms is,' said Florrie.

Cyril took another mouthful of new potatoes.

'So this Maddy, what you're a-tellin' me about,' he said

with his mouth full, 'were takin' the 'ot water up to the East Wing, on the fatal mornin' as you might say, same time as the h-unfortunate h-accused?'

'No. That's it, you see, Mr Prettyman: Ellie were takin' up the 'ot water *for* Maddy. . . .'

'Go on, darlin',' Cyril urged her, 'you can tell me. 'Course my gentleman's goin' to find out 'bout it sooner or later.'

Florrie twisted her fingers against her lap. She lowered her voice.

'Maddy told Mrs Arbuthnot she weren't a-goin' to take no 'ot water up to Mr Rookworthy's room. 'Cos of what – well – the gentleman 'ad tried to get up to wiv 'er, last time 'e were 'ere! An' Mrs Arbuthnot said as either she took the water up or she packed her box an' went. So she went.'

'Florrie!'

'Ooh!' the maid squealed and jumped at the sound of the housekeeper's voice.

'You've got better things to do, my girl, than stand there pestering the life out of poor Mr Prettyman,' announced Mrs Artbuthnot.

'Just waitin' for Mr Prettyman to finish wiv 'is plate, Mrs Artbuthnot, if you please,' said Florrie.

'You'll give the poor man indigestion,' Mrs Arbuthnot told her. 'Go through to the back kitchen and help Cicely to hang up the pans – and then put away the cutlery.'

'Yes, Mrs Arbuthnot.'

Florrie scuttled out of the room.

'Very tasty stew, if I might make so bold, Mrs Arbuthnot,' said Cyril.

He sat back in his chair and let out a sigh of contentment.

'I'm not one for complainin',' he said. 'So you may take it as compliment when I tells you that the trouble wiv bein' a bachelor's gentleman, is the wittels. Now that there stew were a treat; the sort o' wittels as makes a man feel 'e's in a *real* family – know what I means, Mrs Arbuthnot? To one in my position, a stew what's as prime as 'at is h-ambrosia – h-unadulterated h-ambrosia, an 'at's my considered h-opinion, take it or leave it.'

'The secret, Mr Prettyman, is a drop of bottled beer in the gravy,' Mrs Arbuthnot confided in him. 'I've noticed as it's always very pleasing to a gentleman's palate.'

'An understandin' sort of a woman – 'at's what you is, Mrs Arbuthnot, an' no mistake! . . . You ain't got no h-objection to my takin' tobacco, 'as you?'

He drew a slim black Trichinopoly from his waistcoat pocket, and rolled it between his finger and thumb.

'I like the scent of a man's cigar after my dinner, Mr Prettyman. . . .'

She leant across the table for the candle, her generous bosom brushing the bare wooden surface, and drew it over to Cyril to light his cigar. He drew on it a couple of times, then relaxed back in the chair. He wished he could have rested his heels on the table top, but knew better.

'Bet my arrivin' 'ere set up a stir, eh, Mrs Arbuthnot? Bet your girls ain't a-seen nuffink like me afore!'

'I won't tell you a lie, Mr Prettyman. Seeing a heathen gentleman like you is bound to have its effect. But I reminded them of the words of our great Poet Laureate:

"How e'er it be, it seems to me,
'Tis only noble to be good." '

'A beautiful sentiment, Mrs A!' said Cyril. 'An' spoke beautiful, what's more.'

'Thank you, Mr Prettyman. . . . And I told them that just because your skin is black,' she prodded his shoulder with her forefinger, 'it don't mean you haven't got the heart of a true white man.'

'Never a truer word, Mrs A,' said Cyril.

He made himself comfortable in his chair.

'What's been h-on my mind,' he went on, 'is 'at 'ere you are, you've 'ad this 'ere dreadful 'appening, an' 'en you've 'ad to dismiss one o' your chambermaids for misbe'avin' hersel' over a gentleman. . . .'

He paused, waiting for her to interrupt him. She did.

'Not misbehaving herself, Mr Prettyman! Not as you'd call it misbehaving herself, precisely. More wilful disobedience, I'd call it. . . . A sad business altogether. I mean – she was a lovely girl, Mr Prettyman. And a reliable little worker, I'll give her that. But she wasn't from these parts; she was sent down from London. The trouble with domestics who don't *belong* here, is they have ideas of their own – and that's no good, Mr Prettyman, you have to agree. In a big establishment like here, at Vanderlys, you can't have a young female domestic telling you what she's going to do and what she isn't going to do, now can you?'

'It goes wivaht sayin', Mrs A,' Cyril agreed. 'An' when it's a matter of lookin' arter – or not lookin' arter – a gentleman – a noble gentleman! – what's a guest of the 'ouse, why, it's a h-abomination in my h-opinion, I don't mind tellin' you!'

'Mr Prettyman, I hope you won't take it as forward of me if I ask if you'd care to take a cup of tea with me in my parlour, and a slice of rich Dundee cake that I baked myself. The gentlemen and the mistress will be at table for another half-hour at least, so we may as well make ourselves comfortable.'

'I take that very kindly, Mrs A,' Cyril replied. 'It'd be most h-agreeable, I'm sure.'

'I can tell that, in spite of the colour of your skin, you're a gentleman, Mr Prettyman.'

Florrie had returned. She was carrying the silver cutlery in a wicker basket on her arm. She went to the sideboard opposite where Cyril was sitting, opened a heavy drawer, and began to place the silver in it. When she had finished, she pushed the drawer back into place with her hip. He noticed that she did not lock it. Not now, of course, he told himself, but before he and Mr Holmes left Vanderlys, there would be a time. . . . There must be so much silver in the baize-covered compartments of that swollen-bellied drawer that nobody would notice the loss of a desert spoon or two. . . .

Chapter Nine

'We're an old-fashioned house here, Mr . . . er. . . . We dine at . . . in the afternoon. But Mrs Arbuthnot has prepared a supper, I believe.'

Lady Sowerby stared from Mycroft up at Sir Ralph Dearing.

'Who is he?' she demanded in a loud whisper. 'I didn't invite anybody – I'm quite sure I didn't.'

'It is Mr Holmes, Lady Sowerby,' Sir Ralph told her. 'He is a friend of Sir James Swarthmoor.'

'Sir James? . . . Oh yes? . . . I suppose he's been sent because of this . . . er . . . terrible business. We shall go into supper, or Mrs Arbuthnot will be very cross with me.'

Sir Ralph offered her his arm and she took it. Mycroft walked a few paces behind them.

'Everybody thinks they have the right to be cross with me, Mr Horace,' she said over her shoulder Mycroft. 'It is because I have been ill, you know. So the servants all do exactly what they like.'

She was small, slender, and held herself proudly erect. Her wits might wander, and her face be as wizened as a winter apple, but authority and intelligence were still present in her, as hard as diamond.

'The late Lord Sowerby was old fashioned, you know,' she called over her shoulder. 'Didn't I have the pleasure of meeting you in Italy, Mr Horace?'

'We have only just met for the first time, Lady Sowerby,' Mycroft told her.

But she did not pay attention.

'One always has to say "the pleasure of meeting" some-body, don't you know,' she was telling Sir Ralph.

They were crossing a vestibule as broad as a stable

yard. They entered the dining-hall.

'When most people are not the least pleasure to meet,' she added. 'The late Lord Sowerby was Minister in Turin for many years. I expect that was how Mr Horner came to be introduced to me in Italy. One had to meet so many people, being married into the Diplomatic, you know? And I was far too young!'

She laughed.

'The Italians keep the oddest hours,' she said.

Some forty years previously, Lady Sowerby's father-in-law, the fifth Viscount, had had the hall restored. The Tudor ceiling had been raised to a gloomy vaulting in the early perpendicular style, from which sharp wooden finials pointed downwards like stalactites in a great cave. The stuffed heads of ibexes and chamois, mounted on shields set round the panelled walls, stared at each other across the spaces of the huge room, the firelight from the log fires at either end glittering in their glass eyes.

Three places had been prepared at one end of the long table. Behind each chair, a footman was waiting. Despite his corpulence, Mycroft moved nimbly enough to step between the chair at the head of the table and its attendant footman, to assist Lady Sowerby to her place. As she relinquished Sir Ralph Dearing's arm and sat down, she smiled flirtatiously at him.

'You have come to Vanderlys at the most dreadful time, I'm afraid, Mr Horace,' she told him, as he and Sir Ralph took their places on either side of her.

'Holmes, Lady Sowerby,' Sir Ralph corrected her. 'Mr Holmes is one of the Yorkshire Holmeses. He is a friend of Sir James Swarthmoor,' he repeated.

'Swarthmoor?' asked Lady Sowerby. 'Is he a Quaker? Quakers are all in trade, you know, Mr Horace. Don't receive persons in trade – it was a strict rule of the late Lord Sowerby's.'

She stared at Mycroft as if inspecting him.

'I have property in Yorkshire, Lady Sowerby. In the North Riding, close to Richmond.'

'No need to repeat what Sir Ralph has just said, young man!' she told him sharply. 'I'm not a fool, you know.'

One of the footmen ladled a thick soup into the dishes in front of them. She glared up at him.

'The servants all think I'm a fool,' she said directly at him. 'I've been ill, you see, Mr Horace.' She glared at the footman. 'They all think they can do exactly what they like!'

Sir Ralph pushed the decanter-rack in Mycroft's direction.

'The Burgundy is excellent,' he said. 'Lord Sowerby kept a remarkably fine cellar.'

'If the servants have left anythin' in it,' persisted Lady Sowerby.

She turned to Mycroft with a much softer expression on her withered face. He was in the act of removing the silver collar from the Burgundy decanter prior to filling his glass. Still holding the decanter, he turned to her.

'I used to speak four languages fluently, Mr Horner,' she told him. 'French . . . Italian . . . Greek? – No, that wasn't it! . . . Portuguese!' she concluded triumphantly. 'The late Lord Sowerby was Minister at Lisbon, do you see? Have you ever visited Coimbra, Mr Horner?'

Mycroft shook his head.

'You must make a point of doing so,' she told him, 'You are a young man. You still have your life in front of you.'

She sighed. Mycroft filled his glass, and replaced the silver collar round the neck of the decanter before setting it in the rack once more.

'I have always made a point of being good to my servants, Mr Horner. Even when the late Lord Sowerby was at Dublin Castle, I was the soul of consideration to my servants, and the Irish are the devil; so charming, so lazy, and so very treacherous. . . . Did you meet my husband at the Curragh, Mr Horner? He was a wonderful judge of horseflesh, you know. . . . Old Mrs Weevil used to say . . . Sir Ralph, do you remember old Mrs Weevil?'

Sir Ralph murmured his fear that he did not. It made

not the least difference; if Lady Sowerby had heard him, she gave no indication of taking the least interest in what he had to say.

'Old Mrs Weevil had never learnt her letters, but she was a wonderful judge of character.'

She kept her eyes fixed on Mycroft to ensure his close attentiveness.

'She used to say to me, the servants obey Lord Sowerby because they're afraid of him, but they obey you because they love you.'

'That is a wonderful compliment, Lady Sowerby,' Mycroft told her with an oleaginous display of sincerity. 'And richly deserved, I'm sure.'

Lady Sowerby searched his face acutely.

'If you're as clever as they say, Mr Horace, tell me why they are so cruel to me now?'

'Cruel, Lady Sowerby?' Mycroft asked.

'I'm sure Mrs Arbuthnot does her very best to manage the household as you would wish, Lady Sowerby,' Sir Ralph attempted to intervene.

But neither Lady Sowerby nor Mycroft paid any attention to him. Lady Sowerby reached over and grasped Mycroft's wrist in a frozen, talon-grip which sent a sharp pain shooting up his arm. There was a knowing leer on her face, as if she took pleasure in describing the misbehaviour of her servants.

'Oh, they can tell when they're in a good situation, Mr Horace. They know they can eat and drink of the best as long as they're under my roof. And they can do whatever they please when my back's turned.'

'It must be a cause of great sorrow to you, Lady Sowerby,' Mycroft earnestly told her.

'Yes, my dear. It is.'

'And the business of Evelyn Rookworthy,' he prompted her. 'A terrible thing. It must have been exceedingly distressing. . . .'

He saw the bewilderment in her face.

'Young Mr Rookworthy,' he suggested. 'Your great-

104

nephew. . . . Lord Cormorant's son,' he added. 'He was here, at Vanderlys, four nights ago.'

'So many people come and go, my dear,' she replied. 'Most of the time, I haven't the foggiest idea who they are. You'll have to ask Mrs Arbuthnot, I'm afraid. I've been ill, you know. . . . They take advantage of me.'

She released his wrist. Before he had time to withdraw his hand, she picked up a dessert spoon and struck him with it across his knuckles.

'I do not know who you are, sir!' she screamed. 'Coming here and asking me a lot of stupid questions! You're in trade, I suppose! They say you can't avoid meeting tradesmen everywhere, these days, thanks to the Marlborough House set. But I will not have 'em here, at Vanderlys!'

Sir Ralph had half-risen from his place, but Mycroft did not twitch a muscle. Nor did he take his eyes off Lady Sowerby. With a considered hint of anger in his voice he told her. 'My name is Holmes, Lady Sowerby. My family have held in freehold the manor of Halstead in the North Riding of Yorkshire, at least since the fourteenth century. I came here only because I was asked to do so by my friend Sir James Swarthmoor, who was long acquainted with the late Lord Sowerby, your husband. The purpose of my visit, which has put me to some inconvenience I may tell you, is precisely to assist you because of the misfortunes which recently have been visited upon you.'

The expression on Lady Sowerby's face melted.

'Really, Mr Holmes? It is most kind of you – so very kind! And so very thoughtful of Sir . . . er . . . the Quaker gentleman. I've always held the Quakers in high regard – such *good* people, don't you know? . . . But I can't imagine how you suppose you can help me. They are so very sly. They don't let anyone observe the wickedness they get up to; they wait until I'm alone. . . . It's because I've been ill, you know. . . .'

Mycroft glanced quickly at Sir Ralph Dearing. He had

resumed his seat. Mycroft looked Lady Sowerby straight in the face once more.

'You must give me an example of these tricks your servants get up to, Lady Sowerby.'

'Yes . . . yes, of course,' she replied. 'Well . . . when I am alone, I usually have my meals brought to my drawing-room on a tray. Would you believe it, Mr Horner? Those girls steal the food from off my plate when Mrs Arbuthnot isn't looking. Steal it, and gobble it up! *And* they laugh at me because they think I don't notice.'

Out of the corner of his eye, Mycroft saw Sir Ralph shaking his head, warning him not to believe all she said.

'Forgive me, Lady Sowerby,' he asked her, 'but can you remember if the chambermaid, Ellen Brown, is one of those who torments you in this way?'

It was a bow drawn at a venture. He fully expected her to tell him that she could not be expected to remember the names of all the servant girls at Vanderlys. To his surprise, she replied vehemently, 'Everybody is trying to tell me what a wicked girl poor little Ellen has been! I can't imagine for the life of me why! The very thought! Why, there have been Browns in service at Vanderlys since . . . since Domesday!'

Her fingers closed round his wrist again, to secure his attention.

'There was one girl, Mr Horner – oh, such a pretty, blue-eyed little thing, with the loveliest pale yellow hair, and a look as if butter wouldn't melt in her mouth. Not one of our village girls though. . . . I can't remember what she was called. Do you know what I caught her doing one afternoon?'

'Tell me, Lady Sowerby,' said Mycroft.

'I was having a nap upstairs. I woke up to find the child in my closet. . . . And what do you think she was doing? Can you guess, young man – they say you're so very clever! Almost as clever as the late Lord Sowerby. . . .'

She leaned her face towards him. Her breath smelled of cloves.

'And *he* wasn't as clever as he thought he was, Mr Horner!' she told him in a hoarse whisper, then laughed.

'You caught the girl in your closet, trying on one of your gowns, Lady Sowerby,' said Mycroft, firmly keeping her to the point.

'Ah, you *are* clever!' she exclaimed. 'But not quite clever enough! She was wearing my satin, and my little ballroom tiara – it is only paste, of course, worth no more than a couple of hundred – and she was admiring herself in my pier-glass. And do you know what else she was doing? . . .'

Her hand squeezed round Mycroft's wrist like a vice; her nails pressed into his skin.

'She was telling herself aloud how beautiful she was?' he suggested.

'Still clever. Mr Hornsey!' But still not quite clever enough!'

Her nails were biting into him so that he was afraid she would draw blood.

She was preening herself,' she went on, 'and singing – in German, Mr Hornsey – "*Ach, mein schön liebling! Ach mein liebste kind!*" '

She relaxed her grip on his wrist. He moved his arm away from her. He felt a sudden excitement. When she asked him, 'Can you believe that?' he could scarcely keep it out of his voice.

'Most certainly I can,' he told her.

'Huh!' she exclaimed. 'Nobody else can!'

It was almost as if she wanted him to believe that it was not true. She pointed at Sir Ralph Dearing.

'He doesn't believe me!' she exclaimed.

Sir Ralph smiled condescendingly. He was about to say something when Lady Sowerby went on, 'I have been ill, you see, Mr Horace. There are times when I don't know whether I've seen something, or whether it has just been put into my poor head. I used to be able to speak four languages – Italian . . . and Portuguese . . . and. . . .'

She counted them on her fingers.

Signor Cavour told me how clever I was – the late Lord Sowerby was Minister to the Court of Turin, you know. But gentlemen don't care for clever women, do they? So it's best to say nothing. . . .'

After supper, when Lady Sowerby's personal maid had helped her up to room for the night, Sir Ralph Dearing took Mycroft up to the Elizabethan Long Gallery. There, under the watchful eyes of generations of Sowerbys, staring from dark-stained canvases in the dim candlelight, they strolled up and down, smoking their cigars.

'It's best to disregard everything the poor lady says, I'm afraid,' Sir Ralph remarked. 'Mrs Arbuthnot assures me that the story of the maids helping themselves from her plate is complete nonsense. As for the maid who was supposed to have been in her closet, trying on one of her gowns – Mrs Arbuthnot assures me that she was a perfectly well-behaved girl, sent down from London with the highest recommendations; she was certainly not the sort of girl to – well – behave in the manner described by Lady Sowerby.'

'People whose minds wander, Sir Ralph,' said Mycroft, 'do not *invent* experiences. They fragment them, or misplace them in time. I am not disposed to dismiss anything Lady Sowerby has told us as untrue. I expect she has seen servant girls picking at food which she has left on her plate. It is a frequent practice among the lower class of maid; after all, the food they find there is likely to be of a superior quality to that they receive in the servants' hall.'

'And can you draw any conclusions from what she told you?' asked Sir Ralph.

'If you mean hypotheses?' asked Mycroft. 'The answer is no. But most certainly, I have arrived at one conclusion: that we are embarking on very deep waters here, Sir Ralph – deep indeed!'

Chapter Ten

'I hope the appalling old beldame takes her breakfast in bed,' remarked Mycroft.

He stood at the window, his trousers pulled up over his flannel combinations, his braces dangling against his legs. Outside, rain-soaked garden terraces spread away under a heavy grey sky, to a fringe of noble elms and an endless vista of rolling parkland. A wide, gravelled path swept round the wing from the carriage drive at the front of the house. From it, a steep grassy bank climbed to the base of the wall indicating that the present wing had replaced the curtain wall of the medieval fortifications.

'They was layin' a tray, downstairs,' replied Cyril, who was by the washstand stropping Mycroft's razor. 'Very fine silver coffee pot, an' silver egg-cup with silver chasin', all round it.'

'You speak like an auctioneer's clerk,' Mycroft told him. 'Or a fence's,' he added.

'Mr 'Olmes!' Cyril expostulated. 'That ain't fair! Ain't fair at all!'

Mycroft ignored him.

'The grounds are open from all sides,' he observed. 'There is nothing to stop somebody standing below the window here to receive a package dropped to them. They would hardly be observed unless a gardener was early at his work. I don't suppose the sturdy Dogberrys of the Warwickshire constabulary searched the ground with any thoroughness.'

'Not when they got a h-opportunity to persecute poor workin' girls what can't defend theirselves,' Cyril replied. 'Busies is the same everywhere, if you asks me.'

He rolled up his shirt-sleeve, poured hot water into

Mycroft's bowl, and tested it with his elbow in a flamboyant gesture of expertise.

'In any case, the question is merely of academic interest,' Mycroft remarked, chiefly to himself.

He left the window and ambled to the washbasin. Cyril was holding the open razor. He rolled his eyes in true black-face style.

'Massa will be wantin' a chair?' he said. Mycroft glared at him.

Cyril whipped a Turkish towel over his arm.

'Yes suh! Massa suh!'

He made to fetch the Windsor chair which stood at the foot of the bed. But as he moved from the washstand, Mycroft expertly removed the razor from his hand.

' 'Ere! Mr 'Olmes!'

Cyril sounded quite hurt.

'I'll feel a great deal safer shaving myself, you young scoundrel,' Mycroft told him. Before Cyril had a chance to reply, he continued, 'Am I correct in supposing you regard the girl, Ellen Brown, as guiltless of the foul murder of Mr Evelyn Rookworthy?'

'She's as h-innocent as what I am!' Cyril replied.

'Innocent indeed!' commented Mycroft.

'That ain't fair at all, Mr 'Olmes!' Cyril told him.

Holding the razor downwards between his fingers, Mycroft began lathering his face.

'And on what do you base this presumption of innocence?' he asked through the soap. 'Is it bred of a simple prejudice against the English constabulary – the envy of the civilized world, may I point out? Or is it a song sung by the sirens of the servants' hall?'

'Dunno what that means,' said Cyril. 'You ain't 'alf one for saying fings long-winded like. Just like one of 'em old actors you are, sometimes – the sort what never say nuffink for 'emselves when they can let Shakespeare do it for 'em.'

He propped his back against the wall beside the washstand so that he was facing Mycroft.

'Tell you one fing, though,' he went on, as Mycroft lifted the razor to his throat. 'None o' the girls thinks she done it. 'Cos it's stupid, see? Don't make no sense.'

Mycroft ran the foam off the razor on to his finger, then washed his finger off in the basin.

'Go on,' he said.

'You ever stabbed a man, Mr 'Olmes?'

Mycroft lowered the razor.

'Certainly not, you young dog!' he said.

'Well, I been brung up in a different school 'n what you was,' Cyril told him with sententious frankness. 'The school of 'ard knocks, if you takes my meaning.'

Clearly, thought Mycroft, Cyril had no notion of schooldays at Fernyhurst, on the bleakest and remotest of north Yorkshire moors, with 'Flogger' Marchmain as headmaster.

'It's a messy business if you ain't been h-instructed in the art of killin',' Cyril continued. 'Ain't as easy as people thinks. I mean, there's the ribs, for one thing. An' the very idea of a young female what's knowed for bein' kind an' gentle, an' what's allus been good as gold, stabbin' a feller to the 'eart wiv a 'airpin! Well! I asks you! It'd take 'em Busies to believe it, I'm telling you!'

Mycroft looked at him and nodded slightly before finishing scraping the lather from his cheeks.

'Any road,' Cyril continued, thus encouraged, 'the poor kid weren't expectin' no trouble when she went up to Mr Rookworthy wiv 'is water—'cept the other girls' talk. I mean, it were the girl what were given 'er notice who were supposed to take the water h-up to 'im. That Maddy Orchard. Told Mrs Arbuthnot she weren't a-goin' to do it, 'cos of 'at Mr Rookworthy makin' h-advances to 'er on a h-earlier h-occasion. So Mrs Arbuthnot takes the water-jug from 'er 'an shoves it into poor Ellen Brown's 'and, like.'

Mycroft laid down the razor.

'So this girl – Maddy Orchard, is it? – was summarily dismissed . . . ?'

'Packed off, bag an' baggage to take the first train back to Lunnon. . . . "We can't 'ave young females," Cyril imitated Mrs Arbuthnot's aspiring-genteel accent, "decidin' what chores they're a-goin' to do, an' what they h-ain't. Not 'ere at Vanderlys!" '

Mycroft stared at him, the residual patches of shaving soap drying on his jaw.

'This young female . . . Maddy Orchard. Was she, by any chance, a very pretty girl – with pale yellow hair and blue eyes?'

'Yes, Mr 'Olmes. Leastways that's more or less 'ow Mrs Arbuthnot described 'er. Does it mean somefink?'

'She was here, at Vanderlys at the time of the killing,' said Mycroft, 'but had been sent away before the police arrived.'

'So *she* couldn't 'ave done it, could she?' said Cyril with heavy irony. 'Stands to reason – some people's reason.'

Mycroft rinsed the soap from his face. He took the Turkish towel from Cyril to dry himself.

'I shall speak to Mrs Arbuthnot,' he said. 'Bur I think you should prepare for an immediate return to London. I don't believe there is anything to be served by staying here.'

'Not even savin' poor Ellen Brown from the noose?' Cyril asked.

'There'll be time enough for that when we have saved others from dying – possibly tens of thousands,' Mycroft told him.

'The scrambled eggs and kedgeree are to your liking, I hope, sir.'

'Entirely, Mrs Arbuthnot. And the devilled kidneys are beyond praise. . . .'

'Most gentlemen who visit here are kind enough to tell me they enjoy my devilled kidneys for breakfast,' said Mrs Arbuthnot.

'Quite,' Mycroft prevented her from complimenting herself further. 'And if you would send this excellent fellow to fetch more hot water for my coffee. . . .'

He crooked his finger in the direction of the liveried footman, who took the hot-water jug and departed. Mycroft watched his retreating back.

'Now, Mrs Arbuthnot,' he said. 'I have asked you to step in here while I break my fast because I wish to ask you a few questions about the chambermaid you had cause to dismiss, the morning poor Mr Rookworthy was found murdered.'

'Yes, sir?'

'I do not normally combine breakfast with making enquiries of this sort, you understand? Nothing is more conducive to an attack of dyspepsia than breaking one's fast in anything but an atmosphere of Trappist calm.'

'I'm sure you're right, sir.'

'You may sit if you wish, Mrs Arbuthnot.'

He waved a flipper-like hand at the chair on the opposite side of the table. Mrs Arbuthnot stiffened.

'No, thank you, sir. Very kind of you, I'm sure. But I know my place.'

'Very well. As you wish.'

Refusing to be discomfited, he scooped a portion of scrambled egg and kidney on to his fork and devoured it. Halfway through finishing his mouthful, he said, 'How long was this girl – Maddy . . . Magdalen? . . . Orchard – in service here at Vanderlys?'

'She came down from London just into the New Year, sir.'

'She has been here these past ten or eleven months then. And you have had every opportunity to get to know her, I suppose. I imagine you are a very acute judge of those who are in employment under you here.'

'I don't believe Lady Sowerby and his Lordship, before he passed over, have had any cause for complaint on my account, sir.'

'I'm sure not, Mrs Arbuthnot. One only has to speak with you for a moment or two to appreciate your worth. . . .'

'Very good of you to say so, sir, I'm sure.'

'Yet it took you ten – eleven – months to discover the truth about Maddy Orchard's true character.'

'For the whole of her time here, except for that very last morning, the girl gave complete satisfaction, sir.'

'So that her direct refusal to obey one of your instructions came as a complete surprise?'

'Yes, sir. And no. I know that sounds funny sir, but it's the truth.'

'I believe you, Mrs Arbuthnot. But I would like you to explain, if you will.'

'I didn't like the girl from the start, sir. I've always prided myself on being scrupulously fair in my dealings with my inferiors. Especially the younger maids. I mean, they do have their ups and downs, sir – their little moods from time to time – I'm sure you know what I mean, sir. And it's a bad housekeeper who doesn't know how to take them into account. But I never did trust that one – I don't know why. I mean, she never did have any moods, never showed any temperament or anything like that; and she was always most conscientious in her work. . . .'

'Too conscientious, perhaps?' asked Mycroft.

'It was like she was pretending all the time. A bit sly. But it wasn't anything you could put your finger on exactly.'

' "She was a great observer," ' suggested Mycroft. ' "And looked quite through the deeds of men." '

'Yes sir. Something like that.'

The footman returned with the hot water. Mycroft thanked him gravely and gave him permission to retire. He rose to his feet, went to the silver chafing dish on the sideboard, and spooned a second helping of scrambled egg and devilled kidney on to his plate.

'She was about sixteen – seventeen? – years of age?' he asked.

'I suppose she was, only she behaved like she was quite grown up,' Mrs Arbuthnot replied.

Mycroft said down again, and applied himself to the food in front of him.

114

'Did you ever hear her speaking German, Mrs Arbuthnot? Just a few words? A phrase? No more than that.'

'Why, no, sir! Maddy came from one of those new charity children's homes. They train them up for domestic service. They don't teach them foreign tongues or geography or any fiddle-faddle of that sort.'

'Tell me. "They" – who brought her up – were they nuns, did she tell you?'

'She wasn't a Roman, sir; I can tell you that! I wouldn't employ a Roman – not here, in Vanderlys! But now you mention it, she did say they were sisters, some kind of sisters. I didn't pay much heed, to tell you the truth.'

'Wantage?' Mycroft suggested. 'The Wantage Sisters?'

'I believe, now you mention it, sir – that was what it sounded like.'

'The Wantage Sisters are an order of Benedictine nuns owing obedience to the Church of England,' Mycroft told her. 'They have a house of refuge and training for young Magdalen penitents at Wantage, in Berkshire.'

'A young Magdalen!' Mrs Arbuthnot exclaimed in horror. 'Here at Vanderlys! And she came with the highest recommendations!'

'Not a Magdalen, Mrs Arbuthnot,' Mycroft told her. 'Something worse, I fear. As for the recommendations – you have yourself said what a good little worker she was . . . . Perhaps you would cast your mind back to that dreadful morning. Can you remember what the girl, Maddy, was about immediately before the act of defiance which lost her her place here?'

'Certainly, sir. Before taking up the hot water to the bedrooms, she always went up to the mistress's room. It was her particular duty to go in without waking the mistress, to see if her fire was still in, or if it needed rekindling.'

'But, if she did her duty properly, Lady Sowerby would remain unaware of her presence in the chamber?'

'That is so, sir.'

'And how long would you expect her to take over this particular task?'

'It would depend on whether she needed to relay the fire and light it again.'

'Quite so, Mrs Arbuthnot. But since I am not in the habit of laying fires. . . .'

'Forgive me, sir. She would be upstairs ten minutes to a quarter of an hour.'

'Where is Lady Sowerby's chamber? I mean, in relation to the guest rooms in the East Wing?' asked Mycroft.

'It's on the same floor, sir; hard by. The mistress has a suite of rooms. The entry is just off the Long Gallery at the eastern end.'

'In effect, almost next door to the guest rooms? A walk of a few seconds only?'

'Yes, sir. There's a short passage way, then just round the corner on to the East Wing.'

'And, of course, you procured this Maddy Orchard's services from the Wellbody Agency, in Margaret Street, Westminster.'

'Why, yes, sir!' Mrs Arbuthnot exclaimed in surprise. 'I know it's a newly-established firm, but Mr Woodnutt, Lady Sowerby's legal adviser from London, told me how reliable it was.'

'Mrs Arbuthnot, I shall be leaving for Town immediately with my servant.'

'Immediately, sir?'

'I am not a policeman, Mrs Arbuthnot. There is nothing more for me to do at Vanderlys. The damage has been done here. It is my duty to prevent the same and much worse occurring elsewhere. I would be grateful if you would be so kind as to have a vehicle brought round to take me back to Rugby Junction.'

As Cyril climbed into the gig after him, a maid standing in the gateway of the stable yard called across the drive, 'Goodbye, Mr Prettyman!'

'Mr Prettyman?' asked Mycroft, looking at Cyril.

'Why not, Mr 'Olmes?' Cyril replied. ' 'Ad to 'ave a proper name for the theatre, didn't I? Thought as Prettyman suited me very well. . . . Thought I'd 'ang on to it – for a bit, anyrate.'

They jolted off down the drive.

'Brown, is it?' asked Mycroft of the sturdy but weary-looking man huddled in his waterproof cape behind the horse.

'It is, sir,' the man replied, in a tone which conveyed that he did not welcome being addressed.

'You need have no fear for your daughter, Brown,' Mycroft told him.

'That'll be for a judge and jury to decide, I reckons,' Brown replied.

'Her case will go no further than the Grand Jury,' said Mycroft.

Brown looked away.

'That's more 'n any of us have the power to tell,' he muttered at the horse's rump.

'Don't let your natural grief make a fool of you, man!' Mycroft informed him. 'I'm telling you, and I'm personally acquainted with Lord Chief Justice Coleridge.'

He turned to Cyril.

'A music-hall singer with a German accent,' he said. 'A German governess. A chambermaid who preens herself in front of her mistress's mirror, talking to herself in German.'

'What do you make of it, Mr 'Olmes?' asked Cyril.

'I say that Carl Philipp Emmanuel Guttmann has returned with the evillest intent, and that his creatures, his familiars, are everywhere emerging from their lairs to do his bidding.'

'Then I says, beggin' your Massaship's pardon,' Cyril told him, 'that it's time you kept you solemn word, an' you told the Princess. That's what I says, an' you can take it or leave it.'

'And I'll thank you to mind your own confounded business!' Mycroft replied.

117

Chapter Eleven

'This is a trifle incontinent in you, Holmes!' Sir James expostulated. 'I can't speak with you now! I'm having lunch with the Home Secretary.'

'All the better,' Mycroft replied. 'The Home Secretary is the very man we need.'

They were standing at the foot of the stairs of the Carlton Club. Voices rang down from the vaulted landings above as gentlemen made their way from smoking-rooms and library to the dining-room.

'Why are you not down in Warwickshire?' asked Sir James.

'I have only just returned from Vanderlys,' Mycroft replied. 'I went straight round to the Cabinet Offices, only to be informed that you had come on here. Sir James, I beg you to consider: I would not have disturbed you at this sacred hour if it had not been a matter of the utmost urgency.'

'You have discovered something?' asked Sir James.

'I have every reason to suppose Colonel Sir Rinaldo Hornby to be in danger of his life.'

'Colonel Hornby? Colonel Hornby is at his seat in Dorset with his family,' said Sir James.

'He is shortly to leave for Malta with Lady Hornby – to take command of 2nd Brigade, Royal Marine Light Infantry, I presume,' Mycroft told him.

'Good God, man!' exclaimed Sir James. He glanced up and down the corridors leading from the spacious hall-way of the club. 'Wherever did you learn that?'

'From an elderly and perfectly innocuous clergyman who was travelling with his equally innocuous but insufferable young daughter to his parish in

Staffordshire. He intends to take on the German governess presently in Lady Hornby's employment, as a chaperone for his daughter when Sir Rinaldo and Lady Hornby embark for Malta. The German woman is to accompany the child on a Grand Tour of Germany, Switzerland and Italy. . . .'

He lowered his voice.

'Sir James, I would be failing in the responsibilities you have laid upon me if I did not warn you most earnestly that I am convinced this governess is a spy, and very possibly a potential assassin.'

'Holmes . . . !' Sir James warned him.

'A spy like the spy who was lying in wait for young Ponsonby at Caburn Towers, and for Rookworthy at Vanderlys. Not spies employed by the *Deuxième Bureau* of the Russian Imperial Private Chancellery, but creatures of our old friend Carl Philipp Emmanuel Guttmann. . . .'

'Look, Holmes,' Sir James told him. 'Dick Cross is waiting for me upstairs. I really must not keep the Home Secretary waiting a moment longer. Let me tell you that yesterday morning, after you mentioned that you had seen Guttmann at the Old Olympia, Victoria Street, I telegraphed Berlin. I thought it exceedingly unlikely he would dare to show his face here in England after his *débâcle* over the Dorking Gap business – and I *am* taking into account the affair of Sir Loxley Jones and the Ruwenora Islands. I received a telegram in reply from our Embassy, last night. It appears Herr Guttman was attending the Prince von Bismarck, four days ago, at a boar shoot on the Bismarck estates at Varzin; he was seen there by Lord Odo Russell in person.'

'I would not detain you on a frivolous matter, Sir James!' Mycroft gulped for breath. 'I am not a frivolous person, as you well know. I tell you it is my belief that, unless we act the very moment Sir Rinaldo Hornby receives his written movement orders, he might as well be receiving his death warrant.'

119

Sir James Swarthmoor looked about him uncertainly.

'Very well, Holmes,' he said with a sigh. 'I see we must talk further. Let you return to your lodgings across the street. I'm sure you wish to refresh yourself after your railway journey. With your permission, I will join you over there as soon as I may.'

'Do not leave it too late, Sir James,' Mycroft told him, 'both with regard to Colonel Hornby's health, and because I intend to go to the theatre again, tonight.'

'To the theatre again?' asked Sir James.

'To the Prince of Wales's Theatre, lately known as the Old Dust Hole, off Tottenham Court Road. I propose to have a brief word with Miss – or is it Mrs? – Florence Boardman, one-time friend to poor young Louis Ponsonby.'

'I was *not* mistaken! I can assure you, gentlemen: the presence of Carl Philipp Emmanuel Guttman is not something I could ever be mistaken about.'

Sir James Swarthmoor and the Home Secretary, Mr Richard Cross, were seated either side of Mycroft's study fire. Mycroft was at the bookcase which occupied the entire wall between the door to the landing and his bedroom door. He was holding the Continental *Bradshaw* in his hand, his finger marking the pages containing the timetable for trains between the Hook of Holland and Berlin.

'It might very well be intended that I should *appear* to have been mistaken,' he added. 'But it is perfectly possible for Guttman to have been at the James Street Divan three nights ago, and to have been shooting wild boar with his princely master the previous day, at Varzin.'

A gust of wind rattled the window sash.

'A winged Mercury,' he added, 'could scarcely compete with our modern railway systems and our cross-Channel steam packets. . . . I'll tell you something else,' he continued as he replaced the *Bradshaw* in the bookcase. 'I know who the maid at Vanderlys was – this so-called

Maddy Orchard. Her real name – and I am sure I am not mistaken – is Abigail Rodgers. . . . Aha! I see that name strikes a chord, Sir James!'

'The little between maid, at Ranmore Hall above Dorking Gap?' Sir James asked.

'A farmer's daughter, twelve or thirteen years old,' Mycroft explained to Mr Cross. 'Who became Guttmann's willing and adoring creature. . . . I warned you then, Sir James, if you let her go after the Dorking Gap affair to be trained into service by the Wantage Sisters, you would find her exercising her precocious talent for intrigue as an upstairs maid in some great house – and as C. P. E. Guttmann's agent.'

'And are you suggesting that this young woman is a murderess, Mr Holmes?' asked the Home Secretary.

'I am certain that the unfortunate chambermaid at Vanderlys, the village girl, Ellen Brown, is not,' Mycroft replied. 'Have you ever stabbed anybody, Home Secretary?'

'Certainly not!' replied the astounded Mr Cross.

'It is employment for a skilled person,' said Mycroft pontifically. 'The rib-cage, that sort of thing, don't you know? It requires somebody who has been instructed in the art. . . .'

'And you are suggesting that there is such a domestic, trained to murder, in Colonel Hornby's household in Dorset, biding her time?' asked Mr Cross.

There was a tap at the door, and a rattle of crockery. Mycroft opened it to admit Mrs Turner bearing a tea-tray. Maisie, the general maid, followed her, carrying a silver-covered dish large enough to contain a Christmas goose.

'I thought as the gentlemen might care for a pot of best Ceylon, the afternoon being as nasty as it is,' said Mrs Turner, putting the tray down.

She took the serving dish from Maisie, and put it down beside the tea things. She removed the lid.

'I know Mr Holmes likes muffins for his tea, well

buttered,' she said. 'So I brought some extra.'

'That is very considerate of you, Mrs Turner,' Sir James told her.

'Your housekeeper looks after you very well, I see, Mr Holmes,' said Mr Cross.

Mrs Turner curtsied slightly.

'I do my best, gentlemen,' she said.

Mycroft nodded. 'Thank you, Mrs Turner,' he said, with only the slightest hint of impatience.

Mrs Turner left the room, driving Maisie in front of her by prodding her with two fingers between the shoulder blades.

'I can see that you have nothing to fear from *your* servants, Mr Holmes,' said Mr Cross. 'But it's an abominable business, if you are right in your surmise. It is hard to contemplate anything more damnable than treachery in a fellow's very own household!'

'It is something no ordinary, honest man would even conceive of,' said Sir James. 'A trained regiment of murderous domestic servants!'

Mycroft nodded.

' "A Monstrous Regiment of Women," ' he quoted. 'But we have learnt, have we not, Sir James, that there is nothing so evil that Guttman would not conceive of it, if it served the interests of his master, the Prince von Bismarck, and the State of Prussia?'

'One can possibly imagine such black treachery being dreamed of in the winter darkness of the Russian steppe,' observed Mr Cross. 'Your Muscovite is covered only by a very thin veneer of civilization. But your Brandenburger is a Protestant as we are, a sportsman, a lover of hearth and home!'

'Your Brandenburger is also an ironmaster, a weaver, a merchant,' pointed out Mycroft as he began to pour the tea. 'His industries are the fastest-growing in the world. He needs raw materials and he needs markets. His country is a barren one; he needs grain. He sees our Empire as a rival to his; he sees the Tsar's Empire as a potential source of supply. Nothing would suit him better than a cataclysmic, mutually destructive war between Russia and ourselves. The result would be a Prussian world hegemony.'

'My dear Mr Holmes!' exclaimed Mr Cross. 'That is to suggest that civilized nations behave like beasts in some primeval jungle!'

'There was a moment, Home Secretary,' Mycroft told him, 'when Guttman believed that I was forever his helpless prisoner. It was then he explained to me his view of Prussia's destiny – much as I have just related it to you.'

He pushed the dish of muffins in Mr Cross's direction. The Home Secretary shook his head vehemently, as if the very thought of consuming muffins was an act of indecency. Sir James took one, murmuring, 'One would not want to offend the excellent Mrs Turner.'

Mycroft took a muffin in either hand, and sat down facing the fire.

'The burden of our present policy is based on the Russian threat on the North-West Frontier,' said Mr Cross, 'and on our lines of communication with India. It would be hard to persuade either my fellow Cabinet members, or indeed public opinion, that the Tsar would not welcome war with Turkey so that he could exert a stranglehold over the Eastern Mediterranean.'

Mycroft was in the act of biting into one of his muffins. He leaned forward, letting the crumbs spill down his chin on to his waistcoat.

'It would be equally hard to persuade me,' he said, 'that a Russian agent murdered Evelyn Rookworthy in order to obtain papers whose contents were not only already known to Count Shuvalor and his aides at the Imperial Russian Embassy, but of which Ambassador Shuvalov was actually co-author. They were the one set of papers dispatched from the Foreign Office in which a Russian spy would take not the least interest. The person who took them knew nothing of their contents, and probably cared nothing. It is transparently clear that what is being perpetrated here is a peculiarly malignant form of mischief-making – and one which would scarcely favour the interests of Imperial Russia.'

'You have to admit, Home Secretary,' Sir James told Mr Cross, 'Holmes here presents an appallingly convincing case – particularly in the light of the Dorking Gap and the Ruwenora episodes.'

'Both of which exemplified my greater clarity of perception than that of most members of the government of the day,' added Mycroft. 'Not to mention my intervention in the case of Lady Kilgarden and the Papal Nuncio.'

'Quite so!' said Sir James quickly.

Mr Cross stared into the fire, his lean, sensitive face creased in bewilderment.

'The Prussians are our traditional allies,' he said. 'Our Imperial dynasties are linked by marriage. We uphold the same virtues. . . .'

He sounded like a husband who has just been informed of his wife's infidelity. Mycroft consumed one muffin and started on the other.

'There *was* the Dorking Gap affair, Home Secretary,' Sir James reminded Mr Cross.

'We were in opposition then, of course,' said Mr Cross. 'But I understood that the Chancellery in Berlin apologized for that little episode – explained that there had been some confusion in the chain of command between the then Crown Prince Friedrich and von Moltke's staff. Besides which, the police and customs officials at all out ports and harbour railway stations have been ordered to keep watch for the least attempt on the part of Herr Guttman to enter this country. I understand his physical presence is easily recognizable. . . .'

He tailed off, hesitated for a moment, then said, 'See here, gentleman! If Mr Holmes's hypothesis is correct – that there is some Machiavellian scheme devised by Bismarck and the Prussian General Staff and engineered by this fellow Guttman, a plan to draw the British and

Russian Empires into armed conflict in the Near East – it would mean that our own Foreign Office has been misdirecting our policy with regard to the Eastern Mediterranean for the past eighteen months! It would mean that the shrewdest heads in the FO *and* the War House are wrong!'

He paused again. Mycroft finished his second muffin. He drew a large bandanna handkerchief from out of his breast pocket and wiped his mouth and fingers. He thrust it back again into his pocket, thought for a split second, then turned and picked up a third muffin from the dish on the table behind him.

Mr Cross shook his head.

'Why!' he exclaimed. 'The Mediterranean Fleet is anchored in Besika Bay, ready to sail up the Dardanelles into the Bosphorus the moment the Russian fleet moves out of its Black Sea bases. We have two transport vessels dispatched from Calicut to Valetta to carry the 2nd Brigade, Royal Marine Light Infantry, together with two batteries of Royal Marine Artillery, to join the fleet as soon as Colonel Sir Rinaldo Hornby is sent out to Malta to take command. . . .'

Again he tailed off. Mycroft nodded. He finished most of his mouthful before he spoke.

'Suppose Sir Rinaldo were to be assassinated at his home in Dorset, and his embarkation orders were stolen, together with the sealed orders which go with them,' he suggested. 'Taking into account the present climate of opinion regarding our relations with Imperial Russia.'

'War would be unavoidable,' Mr Cross said quietly.

'*Vox populi* – ever an undiscriminating organ – would not be inclined to wait in order to find out whether the assassin was an agent of Tsar Alexander's *Deuxème Bureau* or of the Imperial Chancellery in Berlin,' said Mycroft. 'That would be the true *casus belli*, would it not? And your colleagues, Home Secretary? Are they baying for Muscovite blood?'

'I shall tell you in strictest confidence, gentlemen,' Mr

Cross replied, 'neither Dizzy nor Lord Derby, nor myself, regards war against one of the Great Powers with the slightest equanimity. The truth is, in spite of the music-hall song, we may have the money, but we do not have either the men or the ships to sustain a major campaign, nor could we raise them without also raising taxation to an unacceptable level.'

Mycroft finished his muffin.

'Another cup of tea, gentleman?' he asked, wiping his fingers once more.

He gathered in the cups, and refilled them.

'May I offer my services in a single capacity?' he asked. 'One which is not affected by whether you accept my opinion of what is occurring or not.'

He passed a tea cup to Mr Cross.

'Will you ensure, when orders *are* sent to Colonel Hornby in Dorset, that it is I who bear them to him? I do not care to travel, you know; it unsettles the nervous system quite dreadfully. Nor do I care for the country; it is perfectly apparent that *homo sapiens* is intended by nature to be a gregarious animal – *in multitudine, solitudine*, don't you know . . . ?'

He passed a cup to Sir James.

'. . . But for the moment, it is the only thing I can think of which will answer,' he concluded.

Mr Cross scratched his head. 'I cannot for the life of me,' he said, 'understand how anybody as conspicuous as this fellow Guttmann could enter and re-enter this country at will!'

Cyril was sent from his place in the kitchen to procure a cab to carry Mr Cross back to the Home Office. Sir James Swarthmoor took his leave at the same time, charming Mrs Turner by calling his thanks for the excellent pot of tea down to the kitchen basement. Mycroft stepped down on to the pavement, in spite of not having a coat to protect him against the bitter wind. He let the Home Secretary climb into the four-wheeled growler, but held Sir James back for a moment.

'For God's sake, Sir James, prevent anybody but myself from taking Colonel Hornby's orders into Dorset,' he said.

'You may depend upon it, Holmes,' Sir James replied, and patted his shoulder.

Mycroft shivered in the cold.

'I would be greatly obliged if you were to come to the Old Dust Hole with me tonight' he said, as if it were an afterthought.

'My dear fellow! I was hoping to spend an evening with my wife,' Sir James replied. 'She sees little enough of me, these days!'

'I would like you to witness any conversation I might have with Miss Florence Boardman,' Mycroft told him.

Sir James looked at him.

'Very well,' he agreed. 'If you think it necessary. But mark you, there'll be no making a night of it, eh?'

'I assure you, Sir James,' Mycroft replied stiffly. 'It is not my practice to "make a night of it" if I can possibly avoid doing so. Shall I call for you across the street? I shall have a cab here at seven.'

He waited only until the growler was moving away from the kerb before stepping back into the house, out of the wind. So it was that he did not notice the huge, heavily-built clergyman standing in the doorway on the opposite pavement, with a prayerbook tucked under his arm, and empty, watery blue-grey eyes watching intently from under the broad rim of his black clerical hat. . . .

Chapter Twelve

The billboard set up on the pavement under the portico roof and lit by a line of fluttering gas-jets overhead, read;

> Sir Edward Bulwer Lytton's celebrated drama in five acts
> THE LADY OF LYONS: or LOVE AND PRIDE, in which Mr Parfitt will appear in the role of *Melnotte* and Mrs Boardman as *Pauline*.
> Also: THE DEADLY PLANK: or THE DUMB SAILOR BOY, a comical drama in one act, in which Mrs Morgan will dance *The Sailor's Hornpipe*.

Sir James Swarthmoor rapped the lower half of the billboard with the end of his stick.

'*Plus ça change,*' he observed.

Mycroft turned away from paying off the cab-driver. In fact, everything about the Old Dust Hole had changed, apart from the all-pervading smell of fried fish which floated out of the alleys surrounding the theatre. Ever since Mrs Marie Bancroft had inherited it, it had become a model of theatrical gentility. Two attendants in royal blue coats with black frogging stood on the top step, on either side of the painted-glass swing-doors. One held a broom with which he flicked away the least sign of mire on the steps; the other was responsible for chasing away street arabs begging under the pretence of holding horses and opening carriage doors. A steady stream of respectably dressed men and women, some with their adolescent children, were descending from carriages and entering the theatre: an audience quite unlike the raffish battalions at the Old Olympia. Mycroft with Sir James after him joined them, passing through the swing-doors into the mahogany-panelled, brass-railed foyer. In the sudden warmth, the smell of fish was exchanged for a no less pervasive odour of cheroot, patchouli and eau-de-cologne from the groups gathered round the cloakroom maids and the wholesomely pretty programme-sellers.

Mycroft stared around him. An effeminate-looking young man was gazing down from the balustrade of the upstairs foyer. He was in black evening-dress, and half his face was concealed behind a curtain of well-groomed chestnut hair. He caught Mycroft's eye, and came running down the curved staircase, making his way with easy familiarity through the audience going up.

'Mr Holmes, is it not?' he asked. 'Mr *Mycroft* Holmes?'

Mycroft acknowledged that it was indeed he.

'If you would be so good as to come with me, Mr Homes,' said the young man. 'And this gentleman?'

'Sir James Swarthmoor is accompanying me,' Mycroft told him. 'He will be with me in my box as my guest.'

'Of course, sir,' said the young man. 'But I understand from the note brought by your negro servant that you wished to have a word with my mother – Mrs Squire Bancroft. Both of you gentlemen?'

'If your mother has no objections, Mr Bancroft,' said Mycroft.

'None in the world, I'm sure,' the young man replied. 'This way, if you please.'

They followed him up the stairs.

'My father is appearing in the principal piece tonight,' he explained. 'He prefers to act in the older pieces, don't you know? What is it Mr Hardcastle says in the Goldsmith piece? "I love everything that's old; old friends, old times, old manners, old books, old wines," and in my father's case, old plays. . . . Here we are . . . Mother? Here is Mr Holmes, with a friend, Sir James . . . er . . . Swarthmoor,' he concluded with a flourish.

He threw the lock of hair back off his face and stood

aside. Mycroft led Sir James into a small parlour just off one side of the upstairs foyer. It was furnished as if it were the parlour of any prosperous bourgeois household in St John's Wood or Maida Vale, with tasselled velour drapes over the window and mantelpiece and table, with daguerrotypes and framed sepia-toned photogravure portraits crowding every surface, with bowls of coral arrangement and plaster fruit, and a coal fire blazing oppressively in the small hearth. It was here that the most distinguished members of audiences at the Old Dust Hole came to pay their respects to its proprietress when she was not gracing the footlights.

'Mrs Squire' was sitting at one end of the padded *chaise-longue*, the upper half of her torso rising from an oceanic upheaval or ruched taffeta and black lace edging. Her neck and bared shoulders were covered in a film of white powder as if they had been exposed in a flour mill. There was the faintest glow of rouge on her cheeks, and her eyes had the glistening penetration accentuated by a carefully applied rim of kohl about the lids.

'Ay've seen yer somewhere!' she announced, the rich theatrical diapason of her voice swelling to fill the tiny room.

Her remark was addressed to Sir James.

'Ay'm blessed with a famous memory for names and faces, don't ye know!' she added.

She looked Mycroft up and down.

'Niver seen you, young man!' she told him. 'He ain't your son, by any chance?' she asked Sir James. 'No, of course not!' she answered herself. 'Silly of me, eh?. . . . You're Mr Holmes?' she asked.

'I am Mycroft Holmes,' claimed Mycroft. 'This is Sir James Swarthmoor.'

'Name don't mean anything,' said 'Mrs Squire'. 'But the face – that's different! Politics, ain't it? "Political Portraits" in *All The Year Round* – that's where Ay've seen it?'

'It is possible, Mrs Bancroft,' Sir James replied.

130

' "Mrs Squire", if you please! Everybody calls me "Mrs Squire". . . . Take a seat, pray. Be comfortable. . . . Not you, young man!' she exclaimed, pointing her closed, ivory-handled fan in Mycroft's direction.

The chairs by the *chaise-longue* were of the Queen Anne style, with spindly, curved legs and delicately carved, scrolled backs.

'The Windsor over there will answer very well.' She waved her fan in the direction of the window, as far removed from the fireside as the small room allowed.

'He's too fat, d'ye see?' she told Sir James as if he was indeed Mycroft's father. 'Ain't fair on the 'osses! . . . The note brought bay your nigger-man said you wished to conduct an interview with Flo Boardman. Fain upstandin' young fellow, your nigger-man. Ever considered putting him on the stage, Sir James? He'd do famously as the Nubian Prince in *Sardanapalus*, or the Moor in *Timour the Tartar*. . . .'

'The negro is Mr Holmes's servant, "Mrs Squire",' Sir James told her. 'And it is Mr Holmes who wishes to speak with Mrs Boardman. I am merely accompanying him.'

'Is that so, Sir James?'

Mrs Bancroft turned to peer over the back of her *chaise-longue* into the draughty shadow where Mycroft had obediently placed himself.

'Ay regard mayself as standing *in loco parentis* to may young ladies, Mr Holmes,' she told him. 'It is may experience that an affectionate friendship struck up between a young female player and a gentleman invariably – in . . . variably, Ay say! – leads to un'appiness. The Sweet Swan says it most eloquently in the Danish play, don't you know?

"These blazes, daughter, givin' more laight than 'eat, are no true fire." And Ay don't mind telling you, since all the world heard of it, that poor Flo Boardman took it very 'ard when Mr Ponsonby discarded 'er!'

'It is precisely about her friendship with Louis Ponsonby that I wish to speak to her, "Mrs Squire",' Mycroft told her.

'Can't permit it, gentlemen!' Mrs Bancroft said. 'Not

131

fair on poor Flo, don't ye know? Took it very 'ard – very 'ard indeed. First rate little actress, she is – the *dearest* creature. And just as she were makin' a good recovery from the way that wicked, wicked boy 'ad treated 'er, she was persuaded – quaite against *may* advaice, Ay promise you – to give evidence at the inquest on 'im, down in 'Ampshire. Ay tell you, Ay've given 'er the part of Pauline Deschapelles in the Bulwer Lytton piece to take 'er maind off 'er misfortunes, and—' she lowered her voice without reducing its carrying power '—'er 'and off the sherry bottle. It was my own role, you know; dear Sir Edward commended may playin' of it – said Ay came nearer to it than Mrs Faucit, and it were written for 'er, don't ye know?'

Sir James glanced back across the room at Mycroft. Mycroft was sitting with his finger crooked on his lips. He shook his head slightly, then lowered his finger.

' "Mrs Squire", you said, if I'm not mistaken, that young Louis Ponsonby *discarded* Mrs Boardman,' he remarked, 'and that he was "a wicked, wicked boy". But that, surely, was not as it was given out to the world? Indeed, the case as it was reported was clean to the contrary.'

'Holmes!' Sir James tried to interrupt him.

'No, Sir James,' Mycroft insisted. 'I know that the indelicacy of my line of questioning offends your gentlemanly feelings – and it does you credit. But I must know the truth. "Mrs Squire", will you tell me the cause of Louis Ponsonby's discarding of Florence Boardman's affections?'

Mrs Bancroft was both taken by surprise and impressed by Mycroft's evident air of authority.

' 'E dayrected *'is* affections to another quarter, Mr Holmes.'

'It was ever thus,' said Mycroft gently.

'No, it was not, Mr Holmes! Ay say it was not!' Mrs Bancroft replied, raising her arm in a dramatic appeal to Heaven. 'If may poor Flo's rival 'ad been a Duchess, or even a city merchant's daughter, one maight have understood it – not forgiven it, maind you, but understood it. But an 'ousemaid! A common skivvy!'

'A housemaid in the service of Lady Dewsbury, at Caburn Towers?' asked Mycroft.

'Exactly, Mr Holmes. Not even a respectable sort of gel, either! A gel without family, who owed 'er position entairely because of Lady Dewsbury's charitable feelin's – a gel from the Females' Penitentiary at Millbank.'

'Recruited through the Wellbody Agency in Margaret Street, I daresay,' suggested Mycroft, 'and a most conscientious worker – a "treasure" is the expression, I believe.'

'That is more than Ay know, Mr Holmes – or care to know,' Mrs Bancroft told him.

'We are greatly obliged to you, madam,' Mycroft gravely told her, rising from his chair. 'There is no need to trouble Mrs Boardman. Let us hope that success in her dramatic role and the approval of discriminating audiences will prove a restorative to her wounded spirits . . . . Come, Sir James. We have found all we could have hoped to have discovered here.'

As they drove in a hansom down Tottenham Court Road and the new Shaftesbury Avenue back to Pall Mall, Mycroft observed, 'The monstrous regiment, do you see?'

'It is a theory, certainly. But a shocking one,' said Sir James. 'Are you so certain of it that you are willing to adopt it as a working hypothesis?'

'You know the maxim of my medieval exemplar, William of Occam?' asked Mycroft. ' "*Entia non sunt multiplicanda?*" which one may justifiably if somewhat freely translate as, "Why seek for a multiplicity of factors if you have already arrived at one which is perfectly satisfactory?". . . Young Ponsonby did not break his journey at Caburn to pay his respects to his father's old friend, any more than young Rookworthy went to Vanderlys to be bored to tears by his great-aunt. It was

133

the most shopworn of all impulses which made them act so irresponsibly: sexual infatuation. We have heard – indeed, I suspect we *know* – that Maddy Orchard or whatever her name is, is a remarkably good-looking young woman, and we may safely presume that the house-maid at Caburn was not unattractive. I have no doubt whatever that the governess at Colonel Hornby's Dorset seat, 'Fräulein von Holz-zu-Birkensee' though Prussian and a member of a somewhat more elevated if still despised profession, will also prove to be what I believe is known in modern artistic circles as a "stunner".'

'If you are right, Holmes,' said Sir James, 'this is atrociousness beyond the bounds of infamy, beyond the savagery of the most primitive human societies. There is no place, even in Dante's Hell, for one who so deliberately desecrates the holy trust which exists among the members of an Englishman's household, be it in cottage or in castle.'

'It is Carl Philipp Emmanuel Guttmann's strength,' said Mycroft, 'that his imagination operates in a primal chaos beyond anything which the mind of a Christian gentleman can conceive of. It is the dreadful reality which Princess Sophie Trubetskoy had to face over the death of her beloved sister.'

He twisted himself round to face Sir James, his bulk forcing Sir James to back up against the inside wall of the vehicle.

'Be sure that no papers are sent from the Admiralty or any government office to Sir Rinaldo Hornby, unless I carry them,' he said. 'I cannot state it with too great an urgency.'

Mrs Turner was in wait for him as he let himself into 73a Pall Mall.

'There's been a clerical gentleman asking for you, Mr Holmes,' she told him.

'Do you mean a gentleman in Holy Orders?' asked Mycroft as he dropped his stick into the oriental hallway jar.

'From St Thomas's Hospital,' Mrs Turner told him 'A big, foreign gentleman. Not Church of England, but not a Papist, neither – I can always tell one of them. He said it was urgent: said he'd been sent by a woman who's lying very sick in the fever ward. Said she's got something weighing very heavy on her mind which can only tell to you, and she ain't going to make a peaceful end until she's got it off her chest!'

'Did this clergyman leave his card – or a name?' asked Mycroft.

'He said he was the. . . .' She paused to collect her thoughts. 'The Moravian chaplain . . . ?'

Mycroft nodded. 'That is a German Protestant church, the Moravians,' he explained. 'And this woman – does she have a name which you can recall?'

'Well . . . it sounded quite English to me, Mr Holmes. Jenny Miller, I think he said it was. . . . Mr Holmes! Whatever are you! . . .'

But Mycroft had plucked his stick out of the jar, and was bolting out of the front door and down the steps into the gaslit street.

'Stop, man! Stop!' he shouted to the driver of the hansom which had brought him home and which was now setting off through the evening traffic in the direction of Waterloo Place.

Waving his stick imperiously above his head, and with a complete disregard for his own safety and the oaths of passing drivers who had to pull their beasts' heads over to avoid him, he pursued it down the centre of Pall Mall until he had attracted the cab-driver's attention and had brought the vehicle to a halt – to the considerable inconvenience of the driver of a brewer's dray which was going in the direction of St James's, and that of a family brougham which was travelling in the opposite direction.

Chapter Thirteen

The cab passed under the west front of Westminster Abbey, its towering carved façade and great rose window shrouded in the fog which was seeping up from the river and drifting between the dismal orbs of the streetlamps. As it turned into Parliament Square, the lights of St Margaret's and the Houses of Parliament seemed to hang like a myriad disembodied Jack o' Lanterns in the damp cloud. On the corner of George Street, a small group of men and women stood huddled about a watchman's brazier. In their arms they clutched signboards and posters on poles which read, *Tsar Alexander is the Anti-Christ*, *True-hearted Britons stand shoulder to shoulder with gallant little Turkey* and *Death to Russian tyranny*.

The cab drove out over the foggy expanse of Westminster Bridge. The smell of decaying sea-drift was deathly cold across Mycroft's face. The giant wrought-iron caryatids supporting the gaslight orbs on either parapet appeared, then disappeared behind drifting, ragged clouds. Behind him, as the cab approached the embankment on the farther side, an invisible Big Ben struck ten o'clock.

He got out in a side alley at a narrow doorway.

'That's the way into the fever wing, Guv,' the cab-driver told him. 'But they don't let no visitors in. Not that I ever 'eard of.'

He looked down at the coin Mycroft had put into his hand and was agreeably surprised.

'Want me to stay, Guv?' he asked, 'Case they don't let you in?'

'Be off with you, man!' Mycroft replied.

He mounted the step and pulled at the bell-chain. Even without touching it, he sensed through his glove the cold river-damp on the wall. The door was opened by a heavily-built man in a peaked cap and porter's overalls.

'What do you want?' he demanded without the least trace of civility, let alone deference.

His face was a mass of pock marks.

'I wish to be admitted – as a visitor,' Mycroft informed him. 'I was sent for on behalf of a female patient who is in danger of death.'

'Only fever doctors use this door,' the man replied. 'Them and the layers-out.'

'My good man,' Mycroft told him, tapping him on the button of his overall jacket with the knob of his stick, 'I am not in the habit of attending fever wards at this time of night for my amusement. It is, moreover, damnably cold out here. So, if you would be so good as to. . . .'

He was about to push the fellow aside with his stick when a nursing sister appeared out of one of the side rooms on to the whitewashed, dimly lit passage.

'What do you want, young man?' she demanded. 'This door is strictly private.'

She came marching down the passage, her boots ringing on the well-scoured stone flagging. As she came under the light of a naked gas-jet burning from one of the rusted iron mantles set in the wall, Mycroft saw that she was a large, swarthy woman with a shadowy moustache. She wore the distinctive hodden grey gown, creaking starched apron and tightly gophered cap of a senior sister of the Nightingale Nursing Institute. A steel-rimmed pince-nez was suspended on a bootlace ribbon round her neck. She plucked it from her prow-like bosom and clamped it on to the bridge of her nose.

'I was sent for by the chaplain appointed by the Moravian Church to St Thomas's,' Mycroft told her, looking her straight in the face.

'Pastor Schumacher?' the nurse enquired.

'My housekeeper took the message. I was not at home.'

He took his card from his pocket and, holding it between two fingers, presented it to her.

'My housekeeper, a most reliable woman, informed me that this foreign but nevertheless reverend gentleman wished to let me know that a woman patient here in the fever ward, a Jenny Miller or Mueller, was *in periculo mortis*, and would not rest easy in her conscience until she had spoken with me. I would be grateful, Sister, if you would take me to her with all possible speed; if you keep me standing out here much longer I have no doubt you will have to admit me as a patient suffering from the tertian ague.'

'I am customarily addressed as Matron, young man. . . .'

'And I, Matron, am customarily addressed as Mr Holmes.'

He took his card back and pocketed it.

'Now we have exchanged appropriate civilities,' he continued, 'perhaps we may proceed?'

The matron did not move.

'This is Mrs Jenny Miller, I suppose,' she said. 'A singer in the halls, I believe. . . . I have to tell you, Mr Holmes, that it is the custom when any chaplain in this hospital feels that it is appropriate for a relative of the patient to be brought to the bedside for him to inform the appropriate members of the medical staff first – in the case of Mrs Miller, myself. Pastor Schumacher, a most punctilious gentleman in all respects, has not mentioned your name to me.'

She exuded *petit bourgeois* suspicion: 'What, precisely, is your relationship to the patient, Mr Holmes?'

'My position, Matron – there is no relationship between us whatsoever—' Mycroft replied, 'is that of investigator. I am here in my capacity as an agent of Her Majesty's government. I have reason to suppose that what Mrs Miller, or Mueller, wishes to tell me may prove to be a matter of grave importance, and I must ask you not to obstruct me any further in the pursuance of my duty.'

For the first time, the matron looked unsure of herself. She even glanced over her shoulder at the porter behind her. She said to Mycroft, 'The patient is in the tertiary stage of her fever, Mr Holmes. It is most irregular to allow anyone who is not a member of the hospital to approach a patient in so virulent a state of infection. . . .'

She turned to look behind her again.

'Ah! Dr Feldman, if you would be so good as to spare us a moment of your time!'

A young house-surgeon was crossing the passage behind her, and was about to disappear behind a green baize door. He was collarless; his shirt-sleeves were rolled up to his elbows, and his waistcoat was unbuttoned.

'Dr Feldman, this young man insists he must speak with the female patient, Miller,' said the matron.

Mycroft was pleased to note that the doctor, despite the dark hair receding from his lean forehead, was several years younger than himself.

'I'm afraid, Doctor, the word is indeed "insist",' he said. 'I was sent for by Pastor . . . ?'

'Schumacher,' prompted the matron.

'. . . But my instructions are from Number 10, Downing Street. My business concerns a matter of national importance. You may send to the Cabinet Office if you wish.'

He held out his card a second time.

'But for the moment,' he added, 'I would be much in your debt if you were to permit me to step out of this confoundedly raw night air.'

Dr Feldman glanced at the card without actually reading it.

'Of course,' he said, stepping aside to admit Mycroft into the gloomy, whitewashed passage. 'Close the door, Millichip, there's a good fellow.'

The porter did as he was bid, and clattered away down the passage.

'Mr—' Dr Feldman began. He glanced at the card again. '. . . Holmes. Matron has explained to you the

139

present condition of the woman, Miller, has she?'

'She has told me that the patient's fever has reached the tertiary stage – that is the crisis point, is it not?' Mycroft replied. 'In which case, there is every likelihood the next stage will be the coma vigil, followed by death.'

'I perceive you are not entirely ignorant of medical matters, Mr Holmes,' remarked Dr Feldman.

'I have read Alwyn on *The Diagnosis and Treatment of Contagious Diseases*,' Mycroft replied. 'The standard work in medical schools, I believe. For my general enlightenment, of course; at no time did I ever consider professing Medicine.' He cleared his throat. 'So it is of the utmost importance I see the patient, Miller, while she is still capable of speech.'

'Very well,' Dr Feldman replied. 'She is in Mary Seacole, is she not, Matron? Perhaps you will accompany us?'

'Very well, Doctor,' the matron replied.

She went into a side room from which emanated a smell of ammonia and carbolic. The blue flame of a bunsen lamp burned on a dispensary shelf. The matron lit a candle-lamp from it, and placed the glass funnel over the new, brighter light before bearing out into the passage. Mycroft was able to see the weariness under the young doctor's eyes.

'I cannot impress on you too strongly,' said Dr Feldman as they proceeded up the passage to the steps at the far end, 'the absolute need to avoid any physical contact with the patient. If there were any such contact at this stage, and I were to let you back out on to the streets, I would be behaving as irresponsibly as the Ottomen of the Middle Ages who launched plague corpses into Crusaders' castles and thus set off the Black Death.'

They went up the steps and entered a labyrinth of whitewashed passages and dun-coloured doors. They passed tiny, cupboard-sized dispensaries, sluice-rooms and privies whose stone floors were smeared with the white traces of lime-based disinfectant. Everywhere reeked of chemicals, carbolic, and sealing-wax. Once, they had to stand with their backs pressed against the whitewash as two porters, swathed in soiled white flax aprons, rattled a wooden four-wheeled trolley past them; on the trolley, under a blanket, a body lay still as a corpse – only the insistent groaning gave evidence of a consciousness isolated within its own suffering. Occasionally, a nurse passed by carrying a candle-lamp, who bobbed a slight curtsy to the doctor, lowered her eyes demurely, and murmured, 'Good evening, sirs. Good evening, ma'am,' before carrying on.

A second but much broader flight of steps led up to a wide, vaulted landing. A tall window looked out on to a wall of fog, shreds of which crept about the panes fingering them as if searching for a way in. Beams of yellow light glowed dimly from the lamps on the Thames Embankment below. A big rectangular double door stood facing the head of the stairs. Beside it, there was a large white notice with black lettering:

Mary Seacole (Fever) Wing.
Unauthorized entry strictly forbidden.

Above the door and lodged in the tympanum was the large stained wooden plaque of an earlier generation, which read:

Lord, if Thou wilt, Thou canft make mee
clene.

Matt Ch 8 v 2.

A nurse was just inside the door, at a table bearing a sheaf of papers and a paraffin lamp. She was as burly as a dock labourer, and had a vast, crocheted woollen shawl wrapped about her to keep out the river-cold, which all but concealed her uniform.

'Good evenin', Doctor,' she whispered.

'The patient, Miller,' said the matron. 'This gentleman wishes to speak with her.'

'Miller?' asked the nurse. She eyed Mycroft up and down. 'She's been took through to Isolation.' She nodded down the length of the huge ward. 'She'll be a gonner by first light, I reckon.'

'Is she in a condition to speak?' asked Dr Feldman.

'To speak? Yes,' the nurse replied. 'To listen? Well, that's something else altogether, ain't it?'

'It is imperative that I make an attempt to communicate with her, at least,' said Mycroft in a low voice.

Dr Feldman nodded.

'We shall go on through to her,' he told the nurse.

The nurse held out a hand to Mycroft who dropped his gloves into his hat and passed them to her. He retained his stick.

'Beggin' your pardon, sir?' asked the nurse. 'But are you Mr 'Olmes? Mr *Mycroft* 'Olmes?'

'I am.'

'The poor creature bin askin' for you, sir. Several times, she has.'

Mycroft glanced at the matron. He nodded.

'Thank you,' he replied.

They passed on down the cavernous ward, between the rows of wooden cots, each with its tiny night-light flame flickering in the gloom like a Jack o' Lantern. From all sides came groans, occasional cries, and the babbling of feverish delirium. Nurses in starched head-dresses and aprons moved like white wraiths from cot to cot; where Mycroft, the matron, and Dr Feldman passed them, they bobbed polite curtsies. A chaplain in Geneva bands, a slight young man with prematurely greying hair, was stooped over one of the beds. He was holding the woman-patient's hand between his own and murmuring reassurance to her. At the end of the ward, by the farther door, a young nurse in the uniform of the Nightingale Institute was sitting on a three-legged stool beside a child's cot. Dr Feldman stopped.

'Little Rosalie?' he asked.

The young nurse rose and curtsied. 'Yes, sir,' she replied.

'You should be asleep,' Dr Feldman told the child. 'You won't get better if you don't go to sleep.'

'I can't sleep, if it please you, sir,' the child whispered.

'It does not please me, little Rosalie,' Dr Feldman replied.

'Begging your pardon, sir,' the nurse intervened. 'But she's been ever so much calmer since the reverend gentleman spoke a few words of comfort to her, haven't you, Rosalie?'

'Yes, sir,' the child whispered. 'He were ever so nice! He tell me Jesus is coming to see me soon. . . .'

She turned her head. Above the door hung a large oil painting only partly visible in the gloom; a sentimental, pre-Raphaelite Jesus with long silken hair over his shoulders and a sparse, silken beard, was standing facing out into the night from the doorway of a well-lit church. His arms were outstretched in welcome. The lettering on the cracked gilt of the frame read:

> The Good Shepherd welcomes His sheep into
> the Everlasting Fold.

Dr Feldman laid his hand on the child's forehead.

'I expect he will come very soon,' he said. 'And then you can have a long, peaceful sleep, eh?'

'Yes, sir,' the child whispered.

'Stay with her, nurse,' he said.

The nurse curtsied again. 'Yes, sir,' she said.

'It won't be long,' Dr Feldman said.

The matron had taken a key from under her apron. She unlocked the door and held it open. As Mycroft and Dr Feldman passed through into the short passage beyond, Dr Feldman said, 'Who is that nurse, Matron? I've not seen her in here before.'

'Just another student sent up from the Institute for a spot of night duty, I expect,' the matron replied.

'Sorry task, watching over a dying child,' said Dr

143

Feldman. 'She doesn't look much more than a child herself.'

The matron closed the door.

'They all have to face up to it at some point in their training,' she said.

The only light in the Stygian blackness of the passage was the light from the matron's candle. It flickered wildly inside the glass funnel. The passage was very short, and ended in a brick wall. On one side were two doors, from behind the nearest of which came a steady sound of groaning only broken by the occasional piteous cry. On the other side, a wooden trolley with its blanket covering stood waiting. The cold air reeked of carbolic and disinfectant. The matron opened the first door; Mycroft followed Dr Feldman through. There were three cribs set against the walls of the bleak, bare room, only one of which – the one opposite the door – was occupied. There was a single narrow window set high, out of reach, like that of a condemned hold.

The matron went over to the crib which was occupied.

'The doctor's come to see you, Miller,' she said. 'He's brought the friend you've been asking for.'

Dr Feldman took the lamp from her. He held it so that flame lit the woman's face. She was staring fixedly upwards. Her lips moved. They were as cracked and parched as summer earth. Her teeth were encrusted in dried mucus; her hair, tangled and matted, clung to her forehead and cheeks.

'He has returned?' she rasped without moving her eyes from the ceiling above her head.

Mycroft recognized instantly the wreckage of the face of the woman who had sung at the Old Olympia and who had accosted him from her carriage in Buckingham Row.

'He has come to speak to you, dearie,' the matron told her in a perceptible softening of her tone of voice.

An acidic smell of urine rose from the woman's body which caused Mycroft a sudden lurch of nausea. Dr

Feldman took a wooden spatula from his waistcoat pocket. He used it as a pointer.

'Note the extent of the *pitechiae*,' he said as if addressing a group of medical students; 'clearly visible to the naked eye, even in this light.'

He indicated the mass of tiny eruptions, like a mulberry stain on the woman's lower cheek and jaw.

'There will be an even more extensive display on the surface of the mammarian glands, and, of course, in the skin creases between the genital region and the hip. It marks where subcutaneous bleeding is infected with a *leucocytus*.'

He straightened up and looked directly at Mycroft.

'A visible, moving contagion, Mr Holmes,' he said, 'seeping under the skin. A contagion of death-dealing proportions. Until *rigor mortis* has her in its grip, this woman is a bomb of lethal infection. No plague-rat of the Neapolitan sewers presents as deadly a threat to the city in which it lives.'

There was no indication in the woman's ravaged features that she could hear or understand what was being said. Her expression was one of dull apathy. Mycroft noticed that her pupils were reduced to pin-points. But the cracked lips were moving again. He forced himself to overcome his revulsion so far as to stoop over her to listen to what she was trying to say.

'*Es dunkelt schon* . . .,' she creaked, '. . . *mich schlafert: muss in halt weitergehen*.'

Dr Feldman looked at Mycroft and shook his head.

'Nonsense, I'm afraid,' he said. 'Something about it getting dark. Otherwise. . . .'

He shrugged his shoulders.

'She says that it is getting dark,' Mycroft told him; 'that she wishes to sleep, and that it is time for her to take her leave of us. . . . She is speaking in *Schwabisch*,' he explained.

He stooped over her again. Speaking in carefully enunciated German, he said, 'Fräulein, I am Mycroft

Holmes. I have come here because you say that you wish to tell me something of the utmost importance.'

Dr Feldman gripped his arm in an attempt to draw him back. Mycroft wrenched it free.

'No! No!' he insisted.

Again he bent down over the woman.

'Fräulein Mueller? What is it you have to say to me?'

The woman whispered again, the words formed on the rasp of her throat: 'Mycroft Holmes? I tried to fetch him. He is too clever. It was not my fault, I swear it!'

There was a sudden knock on the door behind them. Mycroft turned immediately, fearing a trap. The matron opened the door. A nurse was in the passage outside.

'Nurse Redfern! You have no business—' the matron began.

'If you please, Matron,' the nurse said. 'It's little Rosalie Mottram. She's been left all alone, and she's crying fit to break one's heart.'

'Left alone?' exclaimed the matron. 'Where's the girl from the Institute?'

'She just picked up her lamp and left, if you please, Matron. Didn't say a word to nobody.'

'To *anybody*, Nurse Redfern? She did not speak to anybody!'

'No Matron.'

'This new generation of girls!' the matron exclaimed to Dr Feldman. 'They've been so sheltered at home – never encouraged to face up to unpleasantness, that's the trouble. . . . We had better report her to the principal at the Institute. What's her name?'

'Don't know, Matron,' said the nurse. 'Never seen her before.'

'Never seen her before?' exclaimed the matron. 'But you only came across from the Institute yourself a month ago!'

'Yes, Matron. But I never seen her before, I promise.'

'A moment, Mr Holmes, if you please,' said the matron. 'We had better see to the poor child. She can't be left alone just now.'

146

'I'll come with you,' said Dr Feldman. 'Don't approach the patient if you please, Mr Holmes. I shall be back in a moment.'

He rushed out, followed by the matron. The nurse hesitated at the door, uncertain whether she was supposed to stay with Mycroft or follow the others. She elected to follow the others back to the main ward.

Mycroft turned to look at the patient. Behind him, the door swung to; he heard the clatter of the iron latch as it closed. As he spun round to look, he heard a grating sound as of a large key being turned in the lock. He put his hand to the latch to try it. As he did so, the silence of the cold, dark room was shattered by an unearthly-sounding scream which filled the confined space. Again he spun round. What he saw filled him with such horror that he had to ask himself if the strain and restless activity of the past three days had not brought on nightmare delusions. It seemed, in the flickering darkness, that the woman was hanging in the air, looming above him; her eyes were sparks of luminous red; her arms, outstretched to enfold him, were shrouded like wings in the folds of her white hospital nightgown.

'Herr Guttmann!' she screamed at him. 'You did not tell me I was going to my death! You never told me *that* was part of your plan!'

She stepped down from the bed on to the stone floor.

'You did not tell me I would die, Herr Guttmann!'

She sounded like a snake hissing through gravel. Mycroft struggled to open the door. He was seized with the futility of trying to explain that he was not Carl Philipp Emmanuel Guttmann. Instead, filled with a panic of which he was not in the least ashamed, he cried out, 'Dr Feldman! Help! . . . Dr Feldman!'

The door did not yield a fraction. The shouting seemed to be absorbed into the thick stone of the walls.

'You swore there would be time enough to cure me!' the woman croaked.

She staggered slightly, but she was approaching across

the floor. She was near enough for the smell of her incontinence to enter his nostrils. She was reaching out for him, her sleeves trailing like ragged cerements on a living corpse. An overwhelming disgust was added to his terror, almost paralysing him. He realized that she could not see – that she was searching for him. He edged along the wall, out of her way, but also separating himself from the door. He grasped at his stick, holding it by the end so that he could use the silver knob to club her with, if necessary. He had never struck at anybody or anything with physically injurious intent, except at the occasional bluebottle with a rolled-up copy of the *Morning Post*. He was not at all certain he could do it.

'When I failed the first time,' she whispered, 'you said there was time for a second attempt!'

Her voice broke through the gravel into a wail: 'I don't want to die, Herr Guttmann! I never wanted to die!'

The ghastly, shrouded figure with its sweat-lacquered face turned to follow Mycroft. It was staring at him, stabbing him with its tiny red, glaring eyes. As he backed further along the chill, damp wall, there came a rattling at the door.

'Mr Holmes! Let us in!' the matron was shouting imperiously. 'Let us in!'

'Let us in, Mr Holmes!' shouted Dr Feldman. 'For God's sake, unlock the door!'

For a moment, Mycroft could not speak. Inexorably, the shrouded figure was following him round the circumference of the room.

'The door is locked on the outside!' he called back, finding difficulty in raising his voice sufficiently.

'On the outside?' called the matron in a stuff-and-nonsense tone.

'Somebody locked it on the outside!' Mycroft repeated.

There was a muffled sound of consultation outside. It was followed by a creaking of starched apron hurrying off down the passage.

'We will have it open in a minute!' Dr Feldman called. 'In the mean time, be very careful!'

'The woman is on her feet?' Mycroft called. 'She is following me!'

'She is on her feet?'

Again the note of disbelief; why did everybody have to repeat what he said, Mycroft wondered desperately. The woman was very close now; her face, which seemed to hang in the darkness, had twisted itself into an expression of cloying devotion.

'I never refused you, Herr Guttmann,' it whispered. 'I've always been willing to do anything, haven't I? Save me now!'

Her narrow fingers slipped out from under the shroud-sleeves. They reached for the silk lapels of his coat like multiple pincers.

'I did my best for you, didn't I, Herr Guttmann? Your *klein Jenni* did her very best. . . . It wasn't her fault! . . .'

Her mucus-encrusted mouth attempted to twist into a smile. Mycroft could almost feel the touch of her nails. He retreated. Suddenly his back was pressed against the foot of one of the unoccupied cots. He raised his stick in the air. There was no help for it – he would have to strike now.

'Save me,' she grated, 'and I'll try again, I promise! I'll do anything for you; you know I'm your. . . .'

She stopped abruptly. Her hands dropped. Mycroft saw that the red pinpricks of light in her eyes were gone to dullness. She swayed forward. He lowered his stick, and was just in time to squeeze himself clear of the cot as she fell forward, dead-weight. Her chin caught the wooden board of the cot. He heard the click of her spine at the base of her skull. She hung grotesquely from the end of the cot, suspended between her chin and the balls of her feet. Behind him, there was the sound of a key turning, and the rattle of the door-latch. Now he was safe, his mind seized control once more, lucid as ever. He did not wait for the matron and Dr Feldman to speak as they came in.

'She did not touch me, nor I her,' he said. 'The young nurse – the pupil – you have not seen her?'

'She left,' said the matron. 'You heard what Nurse Redfern told us.'

She sounded as if she were not entirely certain Mycroft had not locked himself in.

Dr Feldman went straight to the body.

'It was your pupil-nurse,' said Mycroft, 'who locked the door on me. The pupil-nurse whom nobody knows, and nobody has ever seen before. She left the little girl's bedside it is true. But she left it to come through to the next room – which is empty, is it not?'

He went out into the small passage. He threw open the door into the neighbouring room. It was an unlit pantry: mops hung from hooks; pails were stacked, with scrubbing brushes and kneelers, on the floor.

'She hid in here,' he called to the matron, 'and when she heard you go to the ward, she came out, closed the door on me, locked it, took the key, and left. . . . Which means, Matron, that she cannot have gone far. Not yet!'

Without ceremony, and with as much speed as he could muster, he rushed away, down the main ward to the exit, pausing only so long as was necessary for him to snatch up his hat and gloves from the table. By instinct rather than calculation, he found his way down the stairs, down the bare, whitewashed passages and through the dun-coloured connecting doors, until at last he was in the side alley. The fog wreathed round him. In the short time he had been in the hospital, it had become more dense; it crept into his nose and throat, making him cough.

Guided by the vague outlines of the buildings on either side, and the glow from gaslamps on brackets at the corners of the narrow streets, he found his way back to the Embankment. Above him loomed the great black iron span of Westminster Bridge behind drifting curtains of fog, the yellow light from the lamps on its parapet diffused into dulled shafts of light in the hovering damp. A woman of uncertain age, in a shabby, coat, several of whose buttons were missing, and with a black boa slung round her neck, stood leaning against the wall at the foot of the steps leading up to the bridge. She stepped forward as Mycroft approached.

'Feelin' good-natured, are you, Charlie?' she called.

She reached for his sleeve. 'Bet you're the passionate sort, eh? I can always tell. . . .'

As he drew away from her and mounted the first two steps, her tone of voice changed.

'Sixpence for me lodgin' – that's all I'm askin', sir.'

He stopped.

'You shall have a shilling if you tell me the truth,' he said. 'Has anybody else passed this way within the last ten minutes or so? The truth, mind you!'

She stared at him, uncertain if the truth would be enough to obtain a shilling from him.

'Not really, sir,' she said. 'Bein' truthful, like you says.'

'What do you mean by "not really"?' he asked.

'One of 'em nurses come by,' she replied. 'From St Thomas's. Goin' to the nurses' 'ome, other side of the bridge, I suspects.'

'A *young* nurse?' asked Mycroft.

The woman sniggered. 'Younger 'n me, if that's what yer fancies,' she said.

'Don't be impudent, woman!' Mycroft snapped. 'This girl went through here? Under the bridge?'

'No, she didn't, now yer mentions it,' the woman replied. 'Thought it were a bit funny like. I mean, usually they goes under the bridge along here, 'cos its quicker. But this one went the way you're goin' – up the steps *on to* the bridge.'

Mycroft took a shilling from his purse. He was placing it in the woman's ungloved palm when a man's voice called from above their heads.

'Take your pleasure while you may, Mr Holmes. . . .'

Mycroft looked up. He saw the tall, broad-shouldered figure against the parapet of the bridge; the face was

151

hidden in obscurity, but the head was haloed in the wide, black rim of a clergyman's hat. Behind it, cast by the diffusion of the gaslight in the fog, loomed a gigantic shadow like some massive carrion-eating bird awaiting its prey.

'A fortnight, Mr Holmes. . . .' The voice with its slight hint of a Teutonic accent, echoed against the fog and the invisible surface of the river. 'The fever is merciful. Like your British Justice. It allows a fortnight's grace between sentence and execution.'

'I'm proof against you, Guttmann!' Mycroft called back. 'I wear the full armour of light!'

The figure was gone. Laughter came echoing back, borne across the shrouded river.

Mycroft ran up the steps, taking them two at a time. He had to clutch at one of the iron caryatids to support himself at the top. Gasping to regain his breath, the inhalation of cold, moist air gave him a pain on the chest. Before him, the broad expanse of the bridge spread silent and deserted for as far as he could see in the fog.

Chapter Fourteen

The room into which he was shown was more of a small, chintzily-upholstered parlour than an office; there was nothing in its furnishings of a lawyer or broker's place of work except, perhaps, for the delicately-wrought walnut escritoire set in the window-bow overlooking the busy traffic of Portland Street – and that only because it bore more than its appropriate burden of papers and cardboard folders. Beside it, half-screening it from the visitor's view, was a large, potted aspidistra.

'Set you down, Mr Tennerby, sir! Set you down and make yourself comfortable.'

The occupant waved his hand in the direction of an armchair vividly covered in one of the new Grosvenor Gallery prints.

'Will you take a glass of sherry, sir? Or tea?'

'Tea, if you please,' Mycroft replied.

He lowered himself into the chair. He found it difficult to suppose that the strange, fashionably Japanese style of the upholstery was designed to support anything as gross as the human posterior.

'A fancy, sir, with sugar-icing? Or toasted muffins? Gentlemen usually prefer something a little more substantial with their tea than a fancy, or cucumber sandwiches finely cut, don't they?'

'Muffins would be most agreeable,' Mycroft replied. 'I must tell you, Mr Wellbody, you have a wonderful way of making your visitors feel at home.'

'Aha! Not Mr Wellbody, I fear, Mr Tennerby, sir.'

The man swept the swallow tails of his coat aside and sat down in the armchair opposite to Mycroft, holding the crease of his trousers as he did so.

'Mr Wellbody is Mr Wellbody deceased, alas! And has been, these past three years. My name, sir, is Partick, at your service. And may I thank you for your *very* kind remark. Most condescending of you, sir.'

He reached forward and tinkled the little bell which stood on the occasional table beside him.

A minute or so passed before a maid entered silently, a comely, upright, and fresh-faced young woman in her late teens or early twenties, dressed in neat black bombazine and immaculately white cap, apron, and streamers. She bobbed to Mr Partick whose hands fluttered back into his lap.

'Promptness, Cooper! Promptness, alertness and loyalty are the female domestic's three Graces, are they not?'

'If you say so, sir,' whispered the maid.

'Oh, I most certainly do say so. And you, my dear, were just a tiny bit less than prompt in answering my summons. . . .'

'Sorry, I'm sure, Mr Partick, sir.'

'We learn from our errors, do we not, Cooper? And I'm sure Mr Tennerby will agree that your appearance is very trim and clean.'

She had been looking down demurely. She glanced towards Mycroft. For a fraction of a second her expression changed and her lips parted slightly. Mycroft looked directly at her.

'Most commendable,' he said.

The maid immediately lowered her gaze. 'Thank you kindly, sir,' she murmured.

'The tea-tray, if you please, Cooper.' Mr Partick appeared to have noticed nothing out of the ordinary, Mycroft remarked to himself, or he would certainly have rebuked the maid for it. 'And a dish of toasted muffins for Mr Tennerby – and the usual fancies, of course.'

'Thank you kindly, sir.'

Without raising her eyes again, she bobbed in Mycroft's direction.

'An attractive young thing,' said Mr Partick, as she went out. 'A country girl, as you will have observed – for you *are* an observant gentleman, if I may make so bold. She is a child who wishes to better her prospects. One of my spies noticed her – she was the merest slavey, sir, a drudge in a railway hotel in Surrey. We removed her here – it is our practice when one of our spies sees a likely servant – to train her, even educate her – I'm sure you would agree, sir, *educate* is the appropriate word, into a new incarnation as a parlourmaid.'

'You clearly take a fine, old-fashioned pride in your profession, Mr Partick,' Mycroft told him. 'And "old-fashioned" is a compliment I do not bestow lightly, don't you know.'

'You really are *most* condescending, my dear sir!' exclaimed Mr Partick. 'And how *very* kind of you to use the word "profession". You cannot know how gratifying it is for one in my position.'

'You are, I take it, the actual proprietor of this establishment?' asked Mycroft.

'No, Mr Tennerby. That is not an honour I can lay claim to. When the firm was in Croydon – when Mr Wellbody passed over to the Other Side – I had hopes, unworthy though I am, of stepping into the shoes of that good man. I had not realized, however, the extent to which, in his last days, he had been raising capital with a view to expansion and to moving to premises here in Margaret Street, in the fashionable heart of the Capital.'

Nothing ventured, nothing gained, Mycroft decided. He did not often feel so uncertain; he could not prevent himself from clearing his throat.

'At least one may say,' he remarked as casually as he could manage, 'that in the heart of Westminster, there is one firm at any rate which has not been made vulnerable to foreign interests – that is truly English – even in these days of commercial recession!'

Mr Partick sighed.

'I trust, as the managing director of Wellbody's that I

can say we retain a truly English sense of values,' he replied. 'But honesty compels me to admit that the capital which enabled us to remove from Croydon to these premises, and on which our present modest fashionable success is based, was invested by a small group of merchant gentlemen in Westphalia. I may say, however, I enjoy as much independence in the day-to-day running of the firm as if I were indeed its proprietor. I believe I may say, I enjoy the completest confidence of our investors.'

'A confidence which, I am sure, is very well merited, Mr Partick,' Mycroft told him.

'Mr Tennerby, you really are so very kind!' exclaimed Mr Partick.

If he had detected any double edge to Mycroft's compliment, he did not show it.

'Would it be the services of a valet, a gentleman's personal attendant, you are seeking?' he asked.

'By coincidence,' Mycroft replied, 'I'm enquiring after a chambermaid.'

'Gentlemen do require chambermaids from time to time,' Mr Partick assured him emolliently. 'Gentlemen from the country, in Town on business, are frequently commissioned by their wives to procure female servants.'

'In my case,' said Mycroft, 'it is my housekeeper who has conscripted me to this task.'

'And unmarried gentlemen, one soon learns in this business,' said Mr Partick with a smile, 'are invariably anxious to please a good housekeeper, eh, sir?'

'Very true, Mr Partick,' Mycroft agreed. 'A good housekeeper is indeed worth her weight in gold.'

The door opened, and the maid returned, bearing the tea-tray.

'Ah, thank you, Cooper! A most welcome sight, I always say.'

The maid put the tray down on the occasional table. She spread the silver tea service and the Crown Derby cups and saucers.

'There is one particular girl on your books, Mr Partick,' Mycroft told him. 'She left her previous position four or five days ago. She was dismissed, I believe, but under circumstances which do her more credit than otherwise.'

'Indeed, sir?' asked Mr Partick.

The maid unfolded the wooden cake-stand and stood it within Mycroft's reach.

'An old acquaintance of mine,' said Mycroft. 'To be completely frank with you, Her Majesty's Lord Lieutenant of the County of Warwick, Sir Ralph Dearing, brought this poor child's predicament to my attention. It appears that rather than permit herself to be subjected to the unwanted attentions of a young nobleman, she refused an order which would have meant her being alone with the young man – in his bedchamber, don't you know? Of course, the housekeeper had no alternative but to send her packing immediately. . . .'

'The muffins, Cooper,' Mr Partick told the maid. 'Next to Mr Tennerby, if you please. And remove the lid, just in case there is a trace of butter on the handle – Mr Tennerby does not want grease on his fingers. Good girl! . . . Mr Tennerby, sir! Pray forgive me. . . .'

'Of course, Mr Partick,' Mycroft replied. 'Your concern in instructing this young person in her duties only does credit both to yourself and this establishment.'

'Sir, you are so exceedingly kind! So indulgent, I hardly know how to thank you! . . . Pray do continue what you were saying before I so rudely interrupted you.'

'According to Sir Ralph,' Mycroft went on, 'the girl had given complete satisfaction up until the moment of her sudden mutiny – as she would have done, being, as she was, a young woman from Wellbody's.'

'So extraordinarily kind!' murmured Mr Partick. 'Pray help yourself to a muffin, sir. . . . Cooper, my dear child, I am sure we shall need some more hot water.'

'My housekeeper has been dropping more and more open hints that she would like the services of a good,

157

hard-working girl as chambermaid,' Mycroft said as Cooper left the room. 'Almost to the point of nagging, don't you know?' he added amiably. 'When Sir Ralph mentioned what had happened, and that the girl had been sent from Wellbody's into Warwickshire, I decided to call upon you. The thought occurred to me that I might supply my inestimable housekeeper with a good worker while at the same time providing a situation for the unfortunate child who, one may presume, is presently without a character.'

He bit into a muffin. Mr Partick leaned forward from his chair.

'Do you know, sir,' he said, 'what a pleasure it is to encounter a gentleman who displays so Christian a concern for the misfortunes of a complete stranger? What a beautiful place the world would be if all gentlemen were governed by such charitable impulses! I am quite sorry to have to inform you that we found the girl, Orchard, another situation immediately – though not, I fear, as a chambermaid. She had to content herself with the position of general kitchen help in the household of a country gentleman in somewhat reduced circumstances – one of those sad cases where a family is anxious to maintain its landed property and thus its social position without the funds adequate for the purpose. It is a shame, really. I am sure the situation you would have provided would have been more advantageous. But at the time, we could only regard her as being fortunate in finding any position.'

Mycroft finished his first muffin. He dusted the crumbs from off his fingers.

'But what kindness!' said Mr Partick. 'What a lesson in Christian compunction you have provided us with, and no mistake!'

Mycroft reached for another muffin.

'Almost sufficient to parallel your own generosity, Mr Partick,' he said.

'*My* generosity, sir?' Mr Partick asked.

'There are not many agencies of the standing of

Wellbody's which would undertake to set young females from a refuge for Magdalens on the path of honest domestic toil,' said Mycroft, taking a bite from his second muffin.

'Oh dear, Mr Tennerby! You have discovered our guilty secret,' said Mr Partick, simpering.

The maid returned with a fresh jug of hot water.

'The girl, Orchard, confided in one of her colleagues below stairs at Vanderlys, it would appear,' Mycroft said.

'Remarkable ladies, the Wantage Sisters,' said Mr Partick. 'It is a privilege, you know, my dear sir, to be of some small assistance to them in their work of reclamation and redemption. Unfortunately, not all families are prepared to receive a reformed Magdalen into their midst.'

'I would be most interested to know where the girl, Orchard, is now,' Mycroft said, as casually as he could.

Mr Partick shook his head.

'At the risk of giving offence, Mr Tennerby, sir: that I must not tell you!'

Mycroft swallowed the remainder of his second muffin.

'Confidentiality is the watchword of Wellbody's,' Mr Partick continued. 'I would go further. I would say, confidentiality is the *synonym* for Wellbody's. You do appreciate the need, I'm sure, sir. . . . That will be all, Cooper. You may leave us.'

Yet again the maid bobbed, first to Mr Partick and then to Mycroft. As she left, Mycroft removed the rubble of his muffin from his lips with his handkerchief.

'And that young woman?' he asked. 'I daresay she would suit my housekeeper very well.'

'Spoken for, Mr Tennerby,' Mr Partick replied. 'As surely as if she were a property with a sign up marked, "Sold"! In a fortnight's time she goes to the home of a teacher of mathematics at one of our ancient houses of learning – a gentleman in Holy Orders – he lowered his voice – with a particular *penchant* for young women with long hair. And, it has to be admitted, Cooper has a *very* fine head of hair. . . .'

Mycroft took his leave, having arranged to return to Wellbody's the following week to be shown several aspiring chambermaids. Mr Partick saw him to the head of the stairs leading down to the Margaret Street entrance, and remained leaning over the banister looking down until he had stepped out into the fading afternoon light. He was standing on the step, surveying the street for a hansom to take him back to Pall Mall, when he heard a girl's voice barely audible above the clatter and rumble of the traffic, calling.

'Mr 'Olmes! . . . Mr 'Olmes!

He looked over the rail down into the basement area, surprised to hear the sound of his proper name. The girl, Cooper, had stepped out from the kitchen. She was clutching a fringed blanket shawl over her neat servant's uniform, against the raw November air.

Mycroft stepped down on to the pavement. The maid mounted the area steps. She glanced fearfully about her. Through the iron railing, she said, 'I can tell you where Maddy Orchard is, Mr 'Olmes!'

'How do you know who I am?' Mycroft asked.

'You stayed at the Whiteposts Hotel in Dorking,' she said. 'You had a black servant – black as the ace of spades. Long time ago, it was, but I remembered you, didn't I? I was working in the kitchens there.'

Mycroft took out his purse. She glanced at it.

'You will tell me where Abigail Rodgers is now?' he asked. 'It *is* Abigail Rodgers, is it not – this Maddy Orchard . . . ?'

The maid nodded emphatically.

'Where is she?' he asked.

'Place out in Norfolk,' said the maid. 'It's called Prior's Fairing. She's got a sittiation at Fairing Manor, I think it's called. And that's all I knows.'

'Thank you, Cooper.' Mycroft took out a half-crown.

'But,' he said, 'in return for this, you are not to tell Mr Partick my true name. Do you understand?'

'Yes, if you please, Mr 'Olmes. I promise.'

He gave her the half-crown.

'Thank you very kindly, sir,' she said, slipping it into the pocket under her apron.

Mycroft saw a cab approaching from the direction of Mortimer Street. Raising his stick, and defying the rest of the traffic proceeding to and from Oxford Street to run him down, he stepped out into the street to stop it. The girl on the area steps turned her back to the railing. She looked up to a second-floor window. Mr Partick was looking down at her. She nodded to him. He smiled slightly, and nodded back.

Mycroft sat at his own hearthside, a teapot keeping warm on the hob, an empty cake dish on the table beside him. *Stanford's Gazetteer of England and Wales* was open on his knee; *Bradshaw* lay beside the cake dish.

Cyril stood by the window. He was looking down at the street below with something like a wistful expression on his face. He had a pair of spoons between his fingers and was rattling them against the knuckles of his other hand, accompanying himself as he sang softly:

> All dem darkies am a singin',
> Singin' to de ole banjo.
> All de bells in Heben am ringin'
> To hear dem darkies singin' so.

Mycroft had been too intent in his researches to notice Cyril's performance. When he did, it was as if to realize that he had been suffering from a headache for the past half-hour.

'Be quiet, man!' he growled.

Then he noticed the silver, rat-tailed spoons in Cyril's hand.

'And where, pray, did you acquire those?' he

161

demanded, pointing at them.

Cyril looked down at them.

'Me father's, weren't they!' he said. ' 'is royal regalia, what 'e smuggled out of Zululand so Shaka didn't steal it off of 'im, see?'

He rattled them on his knee.

'They bear an uncanny resemblance to a set of dessert spoons I happened to notice at Vanderlys,' Mycroft told him.

Cyril's face assumed the pained look of a schoolboy accused of flicking an ink pellet when the usher's back is turned.

'Dunno as 'ow you can say such a thing, Massa sir!' he said.

'Without much difficulty where you are concerned, my lad.'

'I never stealed nuffink off of you!' said Cyril. 'Now 'ave I? 'Ave I? Go on! Say it!'

As if tho truth of the statement absolved him automatically from all other delinquencies.

'We are going into Norfolk tomorrow,' Mycroft told him. He shuddered at the thought. 'We'll need warm clothing and stout boots. No doubt it will be exceedingly cold and exceedingly damp.'

'Why are we goin' there?' demanded Cyril.

'Because that is where Abigail Rodgers has gone – alias Magdalen Orchard.'

Cyril clicked the silver spoons on his thigh.

'An' what do you suspecks she's h-up to, Mr 'Olmes – if I may ask?'

'Nothing,' Mycroft replied. 'I do not believe she's up to anything. I surmise Herr Guttmann has "withdrawn her from circulation" to coin a phrase; or, in the vernacular favoured by your theatrical colleagues, she is "resting".'

'Why 'ave we got to go h-into the country, then?' Cyril demanded.

'Because, if I am right in my surmise, Herr Guttmann will be elsewhere,' Mycroft told him, 'and I may be able to persuade her to make a full and frank confession while he is not there to stiffen her resolve. I have done it before.'

'Yer – but that were five years ago, when she were still only a kid,' Cyril pointed out. 'She'll be a bad 'un in 'er own right, now, I reckons!'

'That may well be true,' Mycroft agreed. 'But remember, my boy, what Dr Johnson said: the knowledge that one is to be hanged in the morning, concentrates the mind wonderfully. In Abigail Rodger's case, the belief that we know enough to hang her may be sufficient to persuade her to speak to me. If she does, it may save all of us a great deal of trouble.'

Cyril made no reply. He clicked the spoons on his thigh again.

'All them darkies,' he reprised in a thin, abstracted voice, 'am such a happy lot!'

He stared down from the window at the pavement below.

'Should've sent for the Princess to 'elp us,' he muttered, as if he were animadverting to himself.

Chapter Fifteen

The little train chugged slowly across the dismal marshland wastes under a bleak grey sky. Seagulls circled where fields reclaimed from estuary floods had been brought under the plough. On the occasional low hillock, once an island, farm buildings of flint stood amongst bare oaks and elms. The train stopped and steamed noisily at small country stations apparently for the sole purpose of allowing the station staff, a solitary figure in the brass-buttoned navy blue coat and braided cap of the Norwich, Cromer and East Anglian Railway Company, to converse with the engine-driver and his mate. All the stations on the branch line between East Barsham, where Mycroft and Cyril had spent the night at the Bull Hotel, and Brancaster Staithe were called Creake: South Creake, Abbots Creake, North Creake and Creake Burnham.

After Creake Burnham, the prospect only increased the melancholy that invariably threatened Mycroft when he was out of walking distance of the Diogenes Club and 73a Pall Mall. Now they had almost reached the sea, where dunes turned to grass-fringed sodded mudbanks by the autumn rains were the only barrier between the empty flatlands and the North Sea tides, and the off-shore wind rattled the ill-fitting carriage windows in the splintered door frames.

As Mycroft and Cyril stepped down on to the wooden planks of the unsheltered platform at Brancaster Staithe – the only passengers to do so, though several empty metal milk churns were thrown out of the van behind them – the bitter sea wind embraced them like long-anticipated loved ones. No sea was visible over the railed fence which was itself almost concealed in a tangled neglect of furze, bramble and rank grass: only a limitless expanse of mudflats. There was nobody on the platform even to receive the milk churns. When they made their way through the tiny station-house to step out onto the village street, they found the station-master cum porter and ticket-collector huddled over a tiny grate in his office, with a small blackened frying pan containing two sizzling rashers of bacon and a pork sausage. A chipped enamel mug containing thick black tea stood on the hob plate.

'Bain't normal-like for a soul to get off a down train,' he explained his neglect of his duties. 'Not till the women-folk come back fro' Norwich market. Not this time o' the year. . . . Now ye'll just be pardonin' me for a moment,' he added.

He took down an enamel plate from a shelf, looked at it, blew at it, then wiped off the more stubborn dirt with his sleeve, before placing it down on the hearthside floor. He transferred the bacon and sausage on to it with the aid of a large clasp-knife and a twisted fork.

'Now, measters,' he said, leaving his meal to keep warm, and rising to his feet.

He noticed Cyril for the first time.

'Well I'll be danged!' he explained. 'And what 'eathen part do 'e come from?' he asked Mycroft. 'African, I suppose, or somewheres about them God-forsaken climes.'

He took the tickets as Mycroft rebuked him with, 'My servant and I have both come from London, and. . . .'

Cyril, however, was not to be done out of one of his own extensive repertoire of replies.

'Zululand,' he interrupted Mycroft; 'Where them as is rude enough to stare at people is put into a pot an' boiled wiv carrots an' taters, an' sage an' onion to give 'em flavour.'

'Would you be so good as to direct us on our way to Prior's Fairing?' asked Mycroft.

'Prior's Fairing?' asked the railwayman. He pushed his

cap back off his grizzled hair and scratched his skull with oil-blackened fingernails. 'Well! I never heard tell of a gentleman wantin' to go there, this season o' the year, neither.'

'Or Fairing Manor?' asked Mycroft.

'Ye'll have to take the ferry, down the foreshore, yonder, if old Tom's a-willing. That's when the tide be in, o' corst. Prior's Fairing be on Scolt Head Island. No great distance, I suppose – and there's folks hereabouts'll walk it, low tide, but that bain't for strangers, bearing in mind, like, the quicksands and the currents. The currents is mighty treacherous, specially this time o' the year. Carry away many a good fellow – aye, and lass – anybody'll tell 'ee. Corst, there be nobody out there to hear un if un gets into trouble? Un jest sinks down an' down an' down into a clammy wet grave – aarch!'

The railwayman, like the Fat Boy in *Pickwick*, Mycroft decided, had a propensity for trying to make people's flesh creep.

'And Fairing Manor?' asked Mycroft.

'Be about two mile, three mile, down the island from Prior's Fairing. Doan't get many going there this time o' year, I can tell 'ee. Summer, now. That's different, like. Pertikally when 'Is Royal 'Ighness is stayin' at that new 'ouse what 'e's 'ad builded near Sandringham. Then all the nobses – beggin' your pardon, measter – goes over to Scolt. There's plenty to see, for a scholard, that is. Fairing Manor, and there be the lighthouse them Romans builded in the old days. Jest a few stones now – but it' surprisin' the number o' gentry go acrorst to see un! Mind 'ee, un'll have to look sharpish if un's a goin' to the old manor an' back to Prior's Fairing. Old Tom'll have to catch the same tide to bring 'ee over again. Otherwise un'll have to stay till 'morrer arternoon for Tom to go over for ur – that's if 'e's willin' o' corst, corst old Tom bain't allus a willing fellow, like!'

'Is there a halfway decent inn at Prior's Fairing?' asked Mycroft.

'Dunno as a gentleman like 'ee'd call it decent or half-way decent, measter,' the railwayman replied. 'There be *The Dish o' Lampreys*, kep' by Mrs Rigg.'

'We shall have to forgo clean linen tomorrow morning, I fear,' declared Mycroft, as he and Cyril faced the clean sea wind which whipped up the village street from the foreshore at the farther end.

'Huh!' said Cyril, for whom the notion of being without a clean collar the following day was the least of misfortunes. 'And what's a lamprey when it's at 'ome?'

Mycroft was suddenly confronted by a small but gaping hole in his self-protective omniscience.

'A king of England once died from eating too many of them,' he answered evasively.

' 'Spect they're a sort of shrimp or whelk,' Cyril suggested gloomily. 'Lots of people die of eatin' shrimps an' whelks an' such. Or they get such a pain in their bellies they wish as they could die.'

They trudged the remainder of the way down to the beach in silence. They crossed the sandy, grit track at the bottom. On either side, banks of bleached shingle strewn with seaweed stretched down to the wet sands and tiny rivulets and shell-bottomed pools left by the ebb-tide. Seagulls wheeled and glided and cried on the wind. On either hand, breakwaters of rotting timber baulks, some draped with nets, partitioned the shingled beach.

They spent two uncomfortable hours in a smoky taproom, the cynosure of all and every wandering eye, until old Tom, the ferryman, with the aid of several pints from a barrel labelled 'Old Redoubtable', and the promise of a sum over and above the fare prescribed by local by-laws to provide himself with quantities of a similar restorative on the other side, was persuaded that there was sufficient draft of water in the estuary mouth for the crossing to Scolt Head Island to be a feasible proposition. Although it was no more than two o'clock in the afternoon when they set out across the estuary channel the grey wrack of the clouds reflected in the ragged crested, heaving waters made it seem to Mycroft, huddled in his plaid-caped greatcoat in the stern, as if the daylight was already fading. Cyril, for his part, did not look as if he cared whether it was day or night. Sitting in the prow as it rose and fell, occasionally leaning out over the gunwale and then crouching back again, he was totally pre-occupied with his own physical sensations.

The crossing took half an hour. The four or five miles length of Scolt Head Island was, for the most part, a strip of mudflat and marsh as desolate as the mainland shore of which, some centuries previously, it had been a part. Here and there, the monotonous landscape was broken by a clump of ancient woodland. The western point, where stood the village of Prior's Fairing, was thick with great, low oak trees shaped by the wind. From their midst rose the squat, grey tower of a Saxon church, and the smoke from cottage chimneys.

The ferryman brought the boat round into the tiny harbour – a semicircle of stone cottages standing back from a low sea wall. He moored the boat at the flight of seaweed-slimy steps. Stepping up on to the stone plat-form at their foot, he helped Cyril out of the boat. Ignoring the damp, Cyril slumped down on the bottom step, propping his face in his hands. Several of the older islanders were at their favourite occupation: leaning on the harbour wall, and philosophically smoking their clay pipes. Wonderment was written on their weather-beaten, leathery faces as they surveyed him. Cyril did not notice them, or if he did, could not bring himself to care; there was no trace of the King of the Zulus left in him.

Mycroft managed to heave himself on to the tiny quay. Although it felt as if it were rolling and pitching under his feet, he steadied himself, and even managed a sympathetic, 'Come lad!' and a helping hand to Cyril. At the top of the steps, he took out his purse and paid the ferryman double his due.

'You shall return for us tomorrow on the afternoon tide,' he said.

Old Tom looked at the coins in his palm as if he were counting them one by one.

'Oh aarh?' he said, as if he were undecided. Then he said as if to himself, 'If weather suits, maybe.'

Mycroft asked for *The Dish of Lampreys*. One or two of the ancients removed their pipes from their mouths and pointed, grunting, with the wet, broken stems down a lane leading away from the bay, under the bare branches of the oak trees. The inn was a small place consisting of two low-beamed Tudor cottages knocked together. It faced the church across a green on which stood a weather-beaten maypole. There were only two bedrooms for guests. Mycroft left Cyril in one of them, lying prostrated on the four-poster bed, to be ministered to by the amiable, portly widow, Mrs Rigg, who was the proprietress. She for her part seemed well gratified at having so exotic a creature under her charge; one which, Mycroft supposed, would provide her with matter for conversation at least until the arrival of summer brought its crop of visitors to the island. When he asked her if she knew of an honest man with a horse and trap or gig who would take him to Fairing Manor, she shook her head and looked at him in bewilderment.

'Bain't be nothin' o' that sort on Scolt,' she said. 'Only the lamprey-netters' carts.'

'Then it seems I must walk,' said Mycroft with what he hoped sounded like a note of buoyant optimism.

'I hopes you woan't take it amiss, measter, if I enquires if you be one o' them gennelmen from Cambridge University?'

'Cambridge was never my 'varsity, madam,' Mycroft replied stiffly. 'My sole concern is to pay a call on Fairing Manor.'

If anything, the air on the village road had become rawer. He wrapped his woollen comforter round his throat.

'Ye'll find your way easy enough,' Mrs Rigg told him. 'The path goes straight down crorst the wetlands. But it's

169

a fair step. Ye'll not be back afore dark.'

Living in such barbarous parts, the woman clearly had no idea of the customs of gentlefolk: that the family holding Fairing Manor would certainly place a vehicle and groom or coachman at the disposal of a visitor, even a stranger, to return him to his inn.

He set out. The outskirts of the village also marked the end of the barren shelter of the winter trees. A rough cart track, straight as a rule could make it, stretched out between unfenced dykes into a flat, boggy desolation of sand and deep muddy gullies, interspersed with low dunes of coarse grass. After a mile or more of discomfort underfoot and harsh monotony all about him, he passed a gate to a fenced side track which led to a low mound some fifty yards away on which stood a blackened, weather-worn triangular gibbet, a warning set up under an earlier penal system to smugglers and other malefactors.

He stumbled on, his boots slipping and squelching into the rain-softened ruts of the track. A thin, icy drizzle drifted in on the east wind, with a texture on his exposed face more like wet material than particles of moisture. He looked behind him, but the distant edge of the wooded headland had disappeared behind a grey, twilight mist. Shreds of cloud were drifting in front of him, obscuring the path ahead. In his solitude, and the emptiness all about him, he tried to find the comfort and spiritual ease which was the Grail enshrined in the silence of the Diogenes Club. But as the sea-fog closed in about him, he began to become aware of noises, and not the reassuring, muffled noise of traffic in Pall Mall. These were quiet, unexpected, sounds: the suck and plop of mud; the sound of his own breath; and spasmodically the splash, splash, splash of footsteps wading some short distance behind him, on the far side of the dyke to the left. Several times, he stopped. There was silence. Then there would be the occasional plop from the mud, like the sound of a frog. Then silence again. Not until he set off walking once more would he hear the evenly-spaced splash of watery footsteps.

At one point he noticed that the dyke on the left-hand side of the track was covered to become a conduit, enabling him to step off the path into the rank meadow. The mist drifted about him, moistly caressing his cheek. The sound of wading feet stopped. He took only a few paces before, on glancing over his shoulder, he realized that if he pressed any further on to the meadow, he might lose his way altogether. Just then, in a sudden rent in the mist which enclosed him, he saw in the grey swirl of damp, indistinctly, the shape of a strange, lean, scarecrow figure on high, spindly legs like some enormous stick insect. It was hurrying with a peculiar, stiff, strutting motion, away from him.

He hurried back to the path. A most distressing, abject sense of panic was beginning to take its hold. It occurred to him to turn back: there was something about Mrs Rigg's physical amplitude and comfortable manner which reminded him of Mrs Turner, of brass scuttles filled with shiny lumps of coal, and of muffins generously buttered; there could be little doubt that the pot-room of *The Dish of Lampreys* would afford a brandy of sorts, and seltzer, even in these God-forsaken parts. But he was now much nearer Fairing Manor than Prior's Fairing. There was nothing for it but to hurry on.

At first, as he continued, there was only silence in the mists, broken by the sucking and plopping where the track was no more than a causeway across the mudflats. Then the steady splash of wading began again, this time further away. He hurried on, stumbling once or twice and almost falling. The lines of the poet, Coleridge, kept singing over and over again, possessing his poor brain:

> Like one, that on a lonesome road
> Doth walk in fear and dread,
> And having once turned round walks on,
> And turns no more his head;

171

> Because he knows, a frightful fiend
> Doth close behind him tread.

A horrid thought came to him, exacerbating the sense of panic he was struggling to resist: that he might fall and wrench his ankle, and have to lie there in the mud to await whoever was coming after him – or nobody at all, ever. Which was, of course, wholly unworthy, as he knew Cyril would not desert him.

At last, as his heart had begun to pound – not fatally, he hoped, though the thought occurred to him that shock compounded with physical exhaustion and the pestilential nature of the damp air might very well prove sufficient to bring his life to a close – he saw the shapes of massive, rugged oak trees looming before him. On either side, the marsh reeds and coarse knot grass turned to a lush green meadow grass. Against one of the old, bare oaks leaned the rusted remains of an old-fashioned wheeled recoulter. The track became an avenue – the wreckage of what had been a handsome carriage-drive, on which grass and weeds all but covered the gravelled surface.

There was no sound now, save his own footfall. Before him there appeared in the mist the broken remains of a fine, eighteenth-century gatehouse. One of the ornamental gates was propped against the inside wall; the other hung crazily from rusted hinges. The pinnacle-finials on either side of the gatehouse roof were chipped and blunted. As Mycroft passed through, the sudden slap and flapping of wings almost against his ear gave him a start. Whatever it was flew away cawing into the all-enveloping cloud.

He realized the truth. He cursed himself for having ignored his usual practice of retiring to the Diogenes's library and consulting its copy of *Black's Interesting Localities* before setting out. Had he walked into a trap, as he had done at Dorking, he wondered? As he had very nearly done at St Thomas's. And behind him on the wetlands, between him and the inn at Prior's Fairing, was the scarecrow figure on its long, insect legs. He stepped off the curved drive into a maze of neglected laurel bushes, bramble and dripping tree-branches. He moved cautiously under cover, pushing between the soaking vegetation, following the curve of the drive so far as he could see it in the increasing gloom of the fog. He wished Cyril were with him.

The house, steep-roofed, jagged and gabled, loomed up before him. There was nothing for it but to cross the open drive to the front steps under the broken portico-roof. As he approached it, Mycroft saw the ivy clambering the walls and creeping over crumbling sills into the broken windows. As he stared upwards, he saw the blackened, jagged roof-beams reaching through broken patches of tile into the drifting moisture. The steps were littered with roof-tiles and stone rubble; he mounted them cautiously, watching for a piece of masonry or timber to drop down on him. He was caught on the horns of a dilemma which he recognized from other occasions – his inclination to husband with the greatest care his mental and physical resources, coming into conflict with his strong sense of curiosity. He was absolutely certain that Abigail Rodgers, or Magdalen Orchard as she now called herself, was not lurking in the ruins of the old house. He was equally certain that somebody else would be – Guttmann himself, perhaps. C.P.E. Guttmann would never have contrived a simple wild-goose chase; it would not have made sufficient demands on his ingenuity to cause him any gratification.

The main doors were ajar. Mycroft pushed them open to let in both himself and the little light which remained. There was no need for the latter; there was as much light inside as out. He saw before him in the gloom a spacious hall with a large oak double staircase leading up to a panelled gallery. The stairs, like the steps outside, were littered with debris. He looked up. The fog was descending through the open roof far above. As he peered around

173

him, at the massive, carved fireplace, now draped in thick dusty cobwebs which fell from the mantel and hung festooned over the great iron firedogs, at one or two of the large portraits which still hung askew from the walls, their subjects concealed from view by a heavy coating of dust, his gaze arrived at one of the alcoves behind the great staircase, at the lean, sprawling figure on one of few remaining chairs, his head and shoulders propped drunkenly against the broken wainscot panelling. The man's coat was draped loosely over one shoulder; the shirt-sleeve was rolled up off the other arm, almost to the shoulder, and a physician's rubber tourniquet was tied tightly about the forearm. A morocco case, shaped like a pencil-box, lay on his knee. As Mycroft watched as if in a trance, the man limply struggled, employing a drunkard's fierce but scarcely adequate concentration, to take from it a small bottle, open it with the help of his teeth, stand it upright in the case, pick up a hypodermic syringe from the silk-lined compartment next to the bottle, and fill it from the bottle. He lifted it to examine its contents. As he did so, the lean, sensitive, Grecian face became visible to Mycroft, even though the hoods were lidded drowsily over the normally sharp eyes.

'Sherlock!' he exclaimed in horror. 'In God's name! What are you about?'

Chapter Sixteen

'Be so good as to stand off for a moment,' Sherlock told him in a thick weary voice, quite unlike his normally brisk manner of speaking. 'The light in here is bad enough without. . . .'

He did not bother to complete the remark. He lowered his eyes to search for a raised vein in his forearm. Approaching carefully, Mycroft was able to see with a twinge of disgust, even in the gloom, the tiny scars and puncture marks on the naked hairless skin. Sherlock slid in the point of the needle and depressed the small piston with his thumb. Then he slipped the syringe out of his arm once more, leaving behind a tiny bead of blood. Mycroft was forced to cling on to the edge of one of the broken flight of stairs beside him for fear he would faint. Sherlock replaced the syringe in the morocco case with long, faltering fingers. He lay back on the chair with a dreamy expression on his face. He sighed deeply and waited.

'Ah!' he said at length. 'Better. So much better! The pain is dissolving – drifting away.'

'What in Heaven's name are you inflicting on yourself?' asked Mycroft.

'Anaesthetic,' Sherlock murmured. 'For the most confoundedly dreadful headache ever suffered by man.'

'You appear,' Mycroft told him, 'to suffer frequently from such headaches.'

The result no doubt, he thought to himself, of Sherlock's unhealthy enjoyment of the music of Meyerbeer and – infinitely more likely to induce disorders of the brain – that of Wagner.

'You grow observant, my dear brother,' Sherlock told

him. 'A first-rate intellect you have always possessed. But it has not always been allied to the simple toil of observing detail.' He sighed again, and closed his eyes. 'The liquified distillation of the coca leaf,' he continued. 'I have been told by Dr Ludwig Rotwang of the Leipzig Allgemeines Krankenhaus that, taken in a 10 per cent solution, it is the perfect answer to morphine addiction.'

He opened his eyes again, and smiled gently up at Mycroft.

'It is also perfectly harmless,' he continued. 'Certain tribes of Amerindians take it all the time – orally, of course. It is their principal sustenance – and their religion. Extremely convenient for a hunting people; a religion which, for once, genuinely sustains the believer.'

'Sherlock!' Mycroft exclaimed, genuinely shocked by his brother's seeming flippancy.

'Oh, my dear old chap!' Sherlock mistook him. 'I have never become addicted to morphine, I assure you. Nor do I inject a ten per cent solution. Seven per cent is perfectly adequate for my needs.'

Mycroft carefully removed the case from Sherlock's lap and slipped it into his own pocket. Sherlock sat utterly limp; Mycroft could not be entirely certain he realized that it had been taken out of his possession.

'And who,' Mycroft demanded, 'is this Dr Rotwang who believes one can use a narcotic as an antidote to a narcotic?'

Sherlock shook his head slowly from side to side, still smiling like an amiable drunk. He held up his face once more, his eyes wide open.

'What do you see, old fellow?' he asked.

'A young fool!' Mycroft replied, 'who is on his way to becoming a drug fiend.'

'My eyes, Mycroft. Look into my eyes. What do you see?'

'Your pupils?'

'Exactly. And what is the state of my pupils?'

'They are dilated,' said Mycroft.

176

He knew what Sherlock would ask next.

'And what is the effect on the pupils of the administration of a narcotic drug?' Sherlock did ask.

'It causes them to narrow,' he replied.

'Excellent, my dear Mycroft. From which we may adduce, may we not, that the distillation of the coca leaf, when taken intravenously, is not a narcotic but the antidote to narcosis.' His voice suddenly turned gloomy. 'I was subjected, against my will I may say, to a powerful narcotic before being brought to this confoundedly dank and wretched place. From the symptoms, chiefly a headache which threatened to explode my skull, I would say it was a dangerously strong solution of tincture of gelsemium. I don't usually indulge myself with cocaine in surroundings such as these, but it did seem the only answer. Where are we, by the way?'

'Scolt Head Island,' Mycroft replied. 'Off the southern shore of the Wash. This is Fairing Manor – the ruins of Fairing Manor.'

He had no intention of telling Sherlock of his mistake.

'Scolt Head, eh?' said Sherlock. 'My poor friend, Victor Trevor, used to speak of it. A wonderful place for the study of marine ornithology, I believe.'

Night was falling, as well as the fog rolling in through the broken roof. Mycroft realized he could scarcely make out the expression on Sherlock's face.

'Who brought you here,' he asked. 'Where from? And how?'

'No idea. Drugged, you know – rather obviously, I would have thought. Gelsemium muddies the brain like nothing else in the pharmacopoeia: that's why I woke up here with the most deafening headache. I was put to sleep in Leipzig, in my own small study in the Wallensteinstrasse; do you know, I was foolish enough to submit to hypnosis? Fortunately, the fellow who injected gelsemium into me did not realize that I kept that compact little case you took from me in my coat pocket. I did drift into consciousness on several occasions, but only to pray I might fall back into unconscious again, I felt so dreadfully ill. All I can tell you is that it seemed as though I was being carried down a long, garishly lit tunnel walled with iron sheets, and positively reeking of machine oil.'

'A ship hold?' suggested Mycroft.

'No. A tunnel. The walls were curved like the sides of a conduit, my dear fellow.'

The possibility entered Mycroft's head, if to remain only for a second, of a tunnel stetching from the shores of Holstein to the Wash along which the armies of Imperial Germany might march into the least defended part of the English coastland.

'Are you able to walk?' he asked.

'I'm very weak,' Sherlock replied. 'A few paces. No more. My mind is growing clearer with every moment. My headache is entirely gone. But I am confoundedly weak.'

'We must find a more concealed spot than this,' Mycroft told him.

He glanced back at the doors. Fog and darkness had invaded the hallway to such an extent that they were no longer visible.

'I was tricked into coming here,' he added. 'I'm afraid you are the bait which is laid to trap me. And I was followed the two or three miles from Prior's Fairing.'

He described the strange figure he had seen in the sea fog.

'A fenman, that's all,' said Sherlock dismissively. 'It is the practice of inland fishermen on the wetlands to walk on stilts. The poor fellow supposed, I daresay, that the only person who would be walking along the island on an afternoon like this would be a poacher after his nets. Or he may have been a poacher who took you for the law. Either way, it is most unlikely he represented any darker purpose. I'm afraid, my dear Mycroft, I am to be the cause of your spending a damp and exceedingly uncomfortable night in this inhospitable place. Even if I had my strength and my full complement of wits about me, we could hardly venture into this foul obscurity. On the other hand, you may console yourself with the thought that whatever strange campaign you are engaged upon at the moment – of which, I presume, I am the hapless victim – we may be quite sure we are safe from your enemies. They are no more capable of penetrating the fog than we would be. So make yourself as comfortable as you can. Help yourself from the brandy flask I perceive you are carrying in your inside hip pocket, under my syringe-case, and indulge in one of those appalling *vaguera* cigars which, I do assure you, are infinitely more calculated to harm one's constitution than cocaine in a 7 per cent solution.'

Mycroft took out his flask, removed the cup and poured a generous finger of brandy into it. He offered it to Sherlock who shook his head.

'One restorative is sufficient,' Sherlock said.

Mycroft sat down on the foot of the staircase.

'I shall smoke a cigar for recreation's sake,' he said. 'I shall then explore what may be done by way of light and a fire. There must be materials here for both, and in ample quantity.'

He placed the cup on the step beside him, took a cigar from his case, bit off the end, and lit it. He felt better with the first few puffs.

'Tell me whose mesmeric skills you submitted yourself to,' he said. 'I must say, you appear to have behaved rather more foolishly than even you are accustomed to.'

'He claims to have been acquainted with you.'

'I daresay,' said Mycroft. 'Since he was engaged in a plot to have me come here and find you.'

'In Florence,' said Sherlock. 'When you were engaged on your study of Vincenzo Galilei and the Camerata Fiorentina. I believe he was then studying to become a Jesuit priest at the Villa San Girolamo in Fiesole.'

'An Irish gentleman – if one may stretch the word a little? About the same age as myself' said Mycroft. 'Who

179

acted as some sort of spiritual adviser to the Countess Kilgarden, while she lived in Florence.'

'James Moriarty,' Sherlock nodded. 'One of the very few men I have ever met whose intellectual grasp and whose range of knowledge and interest is as great as my own – *our* own, I should say.'

'A dangerous man,' said Mycroft. 'Didn't you perceive that immediately?'

'Genius is an unstable commodity,' Sherlock replied. 'One recognizes it in oneself, my dear chap. That is the true justification for . . . taking. . . .'

He waved his finger at the pocket in which Mycroft had placed the syringe case.

Mycroft grunted and coughed. The cold fog had mingled in his throat with his cigar smoke.

'You may be right,' he admitted. 'You may very well be right. About genius, I mean. One cannot condone this.' He patted his pocket. 'And this erstwhile Jesuit, James Moriarty?'

'Like myself – and wholly unlike you, my dear old chap,' Sherlock told him, 'he is quite restless in his pursuit of intellectual activity. One notices how his face oscillates from side to side like that of a lizard searching for insect prey. He cannot keep still. I suppose most ordinary people might find something quite repulsive about his manner. . . .'

'Lady Kilgarden did not,' Mycroft interrupted. 'She found him entirely fascinating. And so, I fear, did you.'

'Oh Mycroft! His mind!' Sherlock exclaimed. He had gradually become his usual animated self. 'He had not been in Germany more than a few months when his *Treatise on the Binomial Theorem* won him an associate professorship in Pure Mathematics at Vienna!'

'A mathematical genius!' Mycroft interrupted again. 'The most unstable type of genius – abstract, devoid of moral context or sympathies. And what was your point of contact with this exceedingly dangerous individual?'

'My developing interest in forensic medicine, which you know about. . . .'

'And regret,' said Mycroft.

Sherlock ignored this, third, interruption.

'Moriarty was engaged on a book, *Grundriss der Arzneimittellehre*, which will revolutionize our attitude to the drugs which act on the nervous system,' he said. 'And he has a particular interest in those drugs which arrest the process of putrefaction in the human body.'

'And he persuaded you to assist him in his researches?' asked Mycroft.

'Exactly,' Sherlock replied.

This time it was Mycroft who sighed heavily, and not with contentment.

'That is sufficient explanation as to why I find you in this condition, I suppose,' he said. Then he added in a burst of impatience, 'Didn't your fascination with the subject he was pursuing allow you scope to make any enquiry as to the man himself?'

'You know me, my dear Mycroft. I have a perfect talent for single-mindedness. He claimed acquaintanceship with you, and knew something of your work with regard to the Papal Nuncio at the Palazzo Pitti and the unfortunate and indiscreet Lady Kilgarden – did you, by-the-by, have some slight romantic attachment to the lady . . . ?'

'You certainly do not know *me*, if you could entertain such an absurd supposition for a moment!' Mycroft exclaimed.

'And, in any case,' Sherlock continued, 'as Gustave Flaubert has remarked. . . . Do you read Flaubert, by the way? *Madame Bovary*? There are the most splendidly detailed accounts in *Madame Bovary* of the effects of arsenical poisoning! Quite remarkable for a work of fiction. . . . Anyway, as Flaubert has remarked, "*L'homme n'est rien – l'oeuvre, tout*".'

'If you had thought to consult me,' Mycroft told him, 'regarding what must have been obvious to a person as observant as yourself – that this was an association fraught with risk – I could have told you from what little I know of the man Moriarty, that *l'oeuvre*, if not *tout*, is certainly indicative of *l'homme*. He comes from a land-owning Irish family – they have property in Waterford, I believe – with a tradition of rebellion. There are, of course, rebels, even in Ireland, who maintain their treasonable opinions with a degree of honour and principle. There are also those who embrace the rebel cause because it gives them scope to indulge a Machiavellian love of intrigue and a pathological taste for murder. One such is James Moriarty. It was he whose mental grasp of the principles of chemical science made him responsible for the extraordinary explosive device which, nine years ago, blew out the wall of Clerkenwell Gaol, destroyed an entire street, and killed or injured for life forty-five innocent people, most of them women and children. As a result of police enquiries, he fled to Italy, where he went to ground by enrolling as a student with the Society of Jesus at Fiesole. They, of course, were happy to welcome so brilliant an intellect – and devious a character – into their midst. No doubt they encouraged him, perhaps even ordered him, to become the *confidant* of the exiled Irish Countess of Kilgarden. The Jesuits have little love either for Pope Pius IX or for King Victor Emmanuel, and no doubt they saw in the Countess's indiscretions with the Papal Nuncio at the Pitti a splendid opportunity to embarrass both Pope and King to their own advantage.

'Carl Philipp Emmanuel Guttmann, who was with the Prussian legation to the Pitti at the time, grasped immediately the embarrassment that could be caused to our own government by exploiting the scandal which was likely to break at any moment. At the same time, he appreciated that in James Moriarty there was an agent with a peculiar aptitude and taste for causing misery and confusion, placed in a situation where he could do so to the greatest possible effect.

'Fortunately for the maintenance of friendly relations

between the House of Savoy and the British government, I too was in Florence at the time. As a result of my endeavours, I daresay James Moriarty decided that he had had enough both of Holy Orders and of Italy, and retired with his new paymaster to safety north of the Alps, little guessing that he would meet there my foolish young brother.'

'I wonder what device was employed to bring you to this unpropitious spot, my dear fellow,' said Sherlock with only the faintest hint of malice.

For a moment, Mycroft was about to rebuke him. He thought the better of it. He smoked his cigar in silence for a minute or two.

'I came in search of somebody,' he said. 'But not you. I was far from expecting to find you.'

He spent the next five or ten minutes explaining what had been happening. When he had finished, Sherlock said, 'This murderous young female – you know where she really is?'

'I fear she has been sent to Seacombe House, in Dorset, the home of Colonel Sir Rinaldo Hornby and his family,' Mycroft replied.

'Where the Prussian governess is already in place?' asked Sherlock.

'Guttmann knows that I am on his trail,' said Mycroft. 'He must make no crass mistake as he did over Rookworthy at Vanderlys. And when the dastardly crime is perpetrated, he will have to ensure that there is clear evidence of Muscovite guilt. I believe that *he knows that Colonel Hornby's movement orders are about to be issued* and that he intends going into Dorset in person to supervise whatever mischief he has afoot. . . .'

'While supposing that you,' Sherlock interposed, 'being the good, responsible elder brother you are, would feel bound to take me home to Halsteads instead of following him to the Purbeck coast.'

'Or hoping that, by delaying me in my pursuit of him there, the fever which he believes me to have contracted from the woman Mueller will have become much more deadly in its contagious effect by the time I reach Colonel Hornby and his household. . . .'

He broke off and listened. There was the sound of voices and feet trampling on gravel, borne through the fog.

'Friends,' said Sherlock. 'Enemies would make far less noise.'

Mycroft stepped out into the hall. A familiar voice called from outside, 'Hey, Massa Sahib! . . . Anybody at home? . . . You at home, Massa Sahib, sir?'

Globules of orange light glowed through the damp, illuminating thousands of tiny beads of moisture.

'Here!' Mycroft called. 'Cyril, you impudent rascal! Over here!'

Boots clattered invisible up the debris-strewn steps. The flicker of the naphthalene flares could now be seen, sending curious rays and casting strange reflections on the fog. Faces emerged through the drifting obscurity: Cyril's, and those of four or five islanders. One of the latter, an old fellow, powerfully built, in a tattered peaked seaman's cap, with a fringe of white beard round his leathery features, said, 'Ye've got Japhet yonder to thank that ye bain't been left to catch yer death of rheumatics or worse!'

A small, wizened little creature, in a ragged winter coat tied with fisherman's cord about his waist, and a moth-eaten woollen cap drawn down to his eyes, appeared through the fog. He was carrying a pair of ancient stilts on his shoulder. He bowed, and grinned. He had one tooth in his head and spittle running down his unshaven shin. He laughed.

'Japhet may not have no more 'n one 'his five wits,' said the old seaman. 'But he knows better 'n to go wanderin' strange places on a night like this, doan' 'ee, Japhet?'

Japhet nodded and bobbed his head up and down.

'Oh aye! Oh aye!' he said grinning and grinning again.

'Pair on ye, be there?' exclaimed the old seaman.

He glanced at Cyril, who shook his head, then raised his eyes to Heaven suggesting that it was all beyond his understanding.

'This gentleman is my brother,' said Mycroft. 'He was brought to Scolt Head earlier today.'

The old seaman looked at his fellow. The naphthalene flare-light played on their expressions of puzzlement and disbelief.

'Bain't seen no boat today fro' mainland shore,' said one. 'Save old Tom and the ferry. You was on that, Measter,' he said to Mycroft. 'But not that un!'

The others murmured agreement. As he looked at their creased, leathery faces regarding him with disapproval, he felt tempted to tell them that Sherlock had come by tunnel from Germany. It would have produced no greater disbelief than that they were already displaying.

'Yon didn't walk,' said the old seaman. 'Croost the sands?'

'Nay! He didn't that!' agreed another. 'He'd a been a dead man, an' no misteak!'

'I could not have walked.' Sherlock spoke for the first time. 'I am not well.'

'P'raps yon has the fever!' said one of the islanders. 'I's heard o' cap'ns puttin' passengers ashore when they 'as the fever.'

'Aye! Aye!' grinned Japhet, nodding.

'Best carry 'im back to Mrs Riggs,' said the old seaman. 'He can't be left here.'

'Aye! Aye!' Japhet repeated, bobbing his head.

Back at *The Dish of Lampreys*, Cyril yielded up his room to Sherlock. A bed was made up for him on one of the high-backed settles by the tap-room fire. That night, after he had seen Sherlock safely to bed, with Cyril's help, Mycroft himself retired. He blew out his candle, but for an hour or more he found that he was too tired to sleep. There was the anxiety about what was happening in London and Dorset – Guttmann would not have

185

decoyed him away to no purpose. He was haunted by the question of how Sherlock had been brought to the island. The image of a tube-shaped, iron-walled tunnel possessed his imagination, refusing to yield to sleep. How had Guttmann come and gone from England at will, when he was watched for as an undesirable alien? Had he used this extraordinary tunnel? It began to madden him; it became so visible in the darkness, in his imagination, that he debated with himself whether to light his candle once more.

He was reaching for his matches when he heard a furtive scuffling on the ancient, narrow staircase at the end of the low, timbered corridor outside. Never having been one to meet trouble halfway – the sort of trouble which was physically threatening, at any rate – he pulled the bedclothes up round his nose, and lay there listening.

Voices were whispering. He heard Cyril's voice quite clearly.

'Now, if you was a-talkin' 'bout my dad,' he was saying. 'It'd be different. My dad 'ad ten wives, 'e did. Cos of 'im bein' a king, see. An' each of 'em 'ad their own 'ouse, like. Only where I comes from, we calls 'em 'uts.'

'Bet as 'ee has un or two lady friends, eh?' whispered Mrs Rigg's voice. 'On'y 'ee doan' call 'em wives, eh, you wicked black devil!'

'One at a time 's allus been my rule,' Cyril's voice whispered. ' 'Cos I'm naturally the considerate sort. 'Bout people's feelings, if you knows what I mean.'

'Ooh, you wicked fibber!' came Mrs Rigg's voice hoarsely. 'I's heard 'bout you black uns, an' how wicked passionate you is!'

The boards creaked past the door of Mycroft's chamber. The creaking turned a corner. There came a whispered 'Ooh!' followed by a trailing wisp of delighted laughter.

Mycroft closed his eyes and fell into the soundest of sleeps.

Chapter Seventeen

The following afternoon, Mycroft left Sherlock with Mrs Rigg. It was obvious that, alert though his mind was, he was in no physical condition to be brought to London; nor would the rooms in Montague Street which Mycroft had rented for him on his coming down from Oxford, be aired and made ready for him. It was quite late by the time the small local train brought Mycroft and Cyril back to East Barsham, nevertheless Mycroft had no intention of staying there overnight. Instead, he sent Cyril to fetch the bags from *The Bull* and caught the evening train to Norwich. He reconciled himself to passing the night in the modified discomfort of a first-class carriage, and took the milk-train back from Norwich to the Eastern Counties Railway Terminus at Liverpool Street.

He intended proceeding immediately on arrival to Margaret Street in the hope of catching the egregious Mr Partick unprepared, as well as the trainee parlourmaid, Cooper, with the idea of intimidating them into revealing the truth so far as their paymaster had revealed it to them. From there, he decided, he would go to directly to Sir James Swarthmoor at the Cabinet Office.

Stepping down at Liverpool Street, bleary-eyed in the first pallid light of a winter morning, he realized from the paucity of cabs, the emptiness of the platforms, the newspapers on the trestle-stalls, and, as he went out on to the forecourt, the pealing of bells from the City steeples, that it was Sunday. There was a solitary growler parked against the kerb, its horse munching in a canvas nosebag, its driver standing on the pavement a few paces away, warming his hands at a glowing brazier placed at the station entrance by a City charity for the benefit of railway company porters. Wellbody's would be closed and deserted; Sir James would have retired into the bosom of his family at his new, Italianate villa, built on Ramsgate's West Cliff overlooking Pegwell Bay. For all the unaccustomed sense of urgency which threatened to possess him, there was nothing for Mycroft to do but to order the solitary cab to bear Cyril and himself to 73a Pall Mall.

He comforted himself with a hot bath, a change of clothes, and the most ample breakfast Mrs Turner could provide. He then proceeded to St James's, Piccadilly, to attend sung matins in a setting by Thomas Tertius Noble, a composer who, though modern, made no attempt to elevate those of a susceptible disposition into an unhealthy religious exaltation. Nor was the Rector's sermon calculated to whip up his fashionable congregation into a spiritual zeal unbecoming in members of the Established Church. He preached on the text of Jesus's saying, that it was easier for a camel to enter the eye of a needle than for a rich man to enter the Kingdom of Heaven.

'Did the Saviour mean quite literally what He said?' the Rector pleaded. 'And if he did not, are we to suppose that the Son of God was guilty of uttering an untruth?'

Mycroft found that his eyelids were drooping. Like everybody else in the congregation, he regarded his material situation as comfortable rather than *rich*, and the question, therefore, as academic.

'Of course we are not!' the Rector laughed at the absurdity of his own proposition. 'When we say that we escaped from something "by the skin of our teeth", we are telling the truth; but we do not mean anybody actually to believe that we escaped by the skin of our teeth! Oh no . . . !'

Mycroft sank into a deep, luxurious slumber and did not wake until all around were lustily singing the final hymn, 'Glorious things of Thee are spoken!' He dragged himself to his feet, and joined in.

He stepped thankfully down into the raw air of Jermyn

Street, pausing in the porch only to thank the Rector for a most edifying discourse. He then proceeded to the St James's end of Pall Mall, and the Diogenes Club. There he enjoyed an excellent lunch in solitude – there were single tables only in the dining-room since it was an article of faith of the founders of the club that social intercourse, always a doubtful pleasure, was a positive distraction from the enjoyment of good food and wine. After lunch he withdrew into the smoking-room for a cigar and several brandy and seltzers taken in a meditative calm broken only by the gentle and comforting hiss of the seltzer bubbles.

In the privacy of his deep-winged porter's chair, and sipping occasionally at his second glass, his processes of thought began to become more lucid. There was a double game being played out – of that he was now quite certain. There was the Great Game: the game of rival Empires, with a new and ominous player, Imperial Germany, threatening to break the time-hallowed rule of Balance of Power. There was also the private duel between C.P.E. Guttmann and himself: a game in which he, since the Dorking Gap incident, following on by the business of Rear-Admiral Sir Loxley Jones and the Sultana of the Ruwenora Islands, held the victor's laurels. In either case, there was no more dangerous loser than the man with the intellect of a genius, the johnny-come-lately arrogance of the Prussian, and the moral sense of a scorpion. At the same time, such a double game provided the murderous complexity that Guttmann relished, that was virtually his sustenance. He must try to examine the state of play from Guttmann's point of view.

It was most unlikely that Guttmann had discovered that, almost miraculously, there had been no physical contact between himself and Guttmann's poor dupe in St Thomas's Hospital. Guttmann must surely believe that he, Mycroft Holmes, was in the process of becoming an ever more virulent walking bomb of contagion – with no more than ten or eleven days to live. What pleasurable satisfaction Guttmann must have derived from the thought of his enemy finding his younger brother lying sick and drug-ridden in that remote spot; from imagining him embracing him, perhaps even physically carrying him to some place of warmth and comfort, only to realize that not only was he, Mycroft, dying, but that in his heedlessness he was the cause also of his brother's infection and death. It would scarcely affect the outcome of the Great Game, the game of Empire; it was merely an arabesque, a baroque ornament to a more general cruelty involving tens of thousands, perhaps millions.

And now, sickened both in mind and body, a general plague-bearer maddened by increasing pain and delirium, it was intended he should rush down to Dorset, to Sir Rinaldo Hornby's seat of Seacombe House. It had always been Guttmann's intention that he should endure his final agony there, watching helplessly in the anguish of his final fever as the fleets and the armies of Great Britain and All the Russias plunged into the vortex of a Balkan Armageddon.

'Damnable!' he cried out aloud. 'More than damnable!'

And he thumped one of the arms of his porter's chair with such ferocity that his brandy glass jumped and clinked against the drum-shaped humidor containing his cigars. There was a moment's absolute stillness during which Mycroft realized that the voice reverberating round the stillness of the smoking-room was his own. Then came a whispered call for an attendant. There was a longer pause, during which the silence was broken only by the slight murmur of a pencil being applied to paper. A waiter came to Mycroft's chair, bearing a silver tray on which was a single sheet of club writing paper discreetly folded. Mycroft took it.

'Sir,' he read, 'you should feel most horribly ashamed of yourself. I myself was proposed for membership of this club on the recommendation of my medical adviser, as the place of resort best suited to someone of a nervous disposition. . . .'

Mycroft endorsed the note with the single word, *Peccavi*, and signed it with a flourish, *M. W. Holmes*. As the waiter returned it, its author received it with a muffled snort. Mycroft, however, remained unmoved. Even as he had been countersigning the note, there had been vouchsafed to him a sense of certainty which he found both satisfying and soothing to his unwontedly ruffled intellect. He settled back comfortably into the obscurity provided by the leather wings of his chair, and waved his unlit cigar to attract the attention of one of the waiters. The fellow took a taper from a side table, lit it at one of the gas-mantles, brought it over and stood waiting until Mycroft had lit his cigar satisfactorily. He then withdrew a discreet distance before extinguishing the taper between his finger and thumb. There was a gentleman lounging on a chesterfield not far from where Mycroft was sitting; he had fallen asleep with his copy of the *Observer* spread over his face and chest. While not actually snoring, he was breathing deeply so that the edges of the newspaper's pages fluttered and rattled slightly. Returning the extinguished taper to the sidetable, the waiter stepped over to the sleeping gentleman. Taking a pin from the lapel of his own jacket, be bent over the recumbent figure and with the utmost delicacy secured the offending pages together without disturbing him.

Mycroft signalled once more to the waiter.

'Would you be so good,' he mouthed rather than whispered, 'as to fetch from the library Black's *Interesting Localities*?'

The waiter nodded in acknowledgement and silently left the room. Once again Mycroft lay back in his chair. He no longer had the least doubt that C.P.E Guttmann, having plotted with such ingenuity the form and place of his, Mycroft's demise, would wish to observe it with his own eyes. He was certain that Guttmann, in some form, in some disguise, would be there in Dorset, to play out the end-game.

*

191

The next morning, Mycroft left 73a Pall Mall at nine o'clock. With him in the hansom went Cyril armed with a short cane whose pear-shaped knob was loaded with lead.

'They calls 'em knobkerries where I comes from,' Cyril declared knowledgeably.

Mycroft grunted.

'In Seven Dials?' he suggested.

Cyril ignored the gibe. 'My farver, 'e 'ad 'ole regiments what carried these,' he said.

He struck his own palm with the weighted handle. It gave off a satisfactory smack.

'Only in case of absolute necessity,' Mycroft warned him.

Cyril grinned.

'Yass, suh, Massa-Boss!' he said.

'None of that, if you please,' Mycroft told him. 'I'm in no mood for your impudence.'

The hansom put them down in Margaret Street, opposite Wellbody's. Mycroft told the driver to wait. Across the street a little girl in a soiled, faded mob-cap was sitting by the basement area of Wellbody's, her bottom squeezed between the railings. She was playing in desultory fashion with a rag doll. Her mother, a youngish woman in shawl and clean apron, was standing at the foot of the steps leading to the front door. The outer door was closed, indicating that the premises were not yet open for business.

Mycroft crossed the street to her.

'They open late, surely,' he said.

He noticed that the flounce of her petticoat under her tidy skirt was black with grime, and that her boots, though clean, were split. As she turned her face to him, he saw that it was careworn and tear-stained.

'He said he had a position for me, sir,' she replied. 'Me and my little one slept in a doorway, last night. Oh, sir! What is to become of us?'

She raised her eyes to the first floor. Mycroft followed

her gaze. The window above the door was filled with a large sign which read:

'FOR SALE. Apply Winterspoon and Barlow.'

Across it was pasted a strip of paper with the legend.

'Sold by private negotiation.'

Mycroft nodded across the street to where Cyril was waiting by the cab. As he walked round the corner into Portland Street, Cyril joined him. They looked up to the window of what had been Mr Partick's office. A workman in a rough white apron, with a dusty paper hat clamped down on his head, was chipping the glass pane with *Wellbody's* embossed on it out of the frame.

'Is Mr Partick there, by any chance?' Mycroft called up.

The workman lifted the glass into the room, then leaned out.

'Mr Partick?' Mycroft repeated.

'Nobody 'ere of that name, guv'l!' the man called down. 'There's a Signor Viviani.'

'Who is Signor Viviani?' asked Mycroft.

'Madame Viviani's 'usband!' the workman called down.

He evidently had pretensions as a Shakespearean clown.

'Want me to go up there an' give 'is 'ead a thump?' asked Cyril in a hopeful tone of voice.

'Be quiet!' Mycroft told him. 'Who is Madame Viviani?' he called up.

'Ladies' Modes,' the workman replied. 'Capes and mantles, a speciality. Grand Openin', week on Wednesday.'

'Can you tell me where Wellbody's is removed to?' asked Mycroft.

'Dunno, guv'l! Dunno as it's moved anywhere. We come 'ere this mornin' thinkin' as we're goin' to 'ave to 'elp 'em move to new premises, like. Even brought the van. But they'd vanished, lock stock an' barrel! Not that I'm complainin'l!' The workman pointed down at Cyril.

'Your muvver the bleedin' Queen of Sheba, then?' he asked.

'Queen of the Zulus!' Cyril called back. 'An' my farver were King of the Zulus! Bet you don't know 'oo your bleedin' farver was!'

'Enough of that!' Mycroft rebuked him.

They returned round to the front of the building. Before crossing over to climb aboard the waiting hansom Mycroft went over to the young woman who had joined her little daughter by the area steps.

'This place has been bought by a Madame and Signor Viviani as an emporium of ladies' fashions,' he told her. 'They are to open a week next Wednesday. It is possible they may require the services of a shop-maid? I suppose. In any case here is something towards shelter tonight for you and your little girl.'

He put a guinea into her hand. She looked at it.

'God bless you, sir!' she said. 'Oh, God bless you!'

The tears in her eyes were unaffected. The little girl tugged at her mother's apron.

'Can we get somefink to eat now, Ma?' the little girl demanded with the tyranny of childhood.

'Buy something for yourself, my dear,' Mycroft told her, giving her a sixpence.

The small, grubby fingers closed over it so fast, he felt he had scarcely escaped with his hand intact.

He returned to the hansom. '10 Downing Street!' he called to the driver.

The driver flicked open the roof-hatch.

'Begging your pardon, sir. But did you say what I thought I heard you say, sir?'

'What did I say?' Mycroft asked, closing the wooden apron doors over his knees.

'10 Downing Street, sir?'

'That is where I wish to go – and quickly, cabbie!'

'Right away, sir!' the driver replied in an awed tone.

'Deuce take it, Holmes!' Sir James Swarthmoor told him.

'The orders *had* to be dispatched. They wouldn't wait until you returned from some wild-goose chase into the Fens. The Russkies might have stormed Scutari by that time!'

'Wellbody's Agency has closed down.'

'Wellbody's?' Sir James exclaimed in astonishment.

'Lock, stock and barrel,' said Mycroft. 'Leaving not a wrack behind.'

'What significance do you attach to that?' asked Sir James.

They were sitting on opposite sides of the Cabinet Room table. Mycroft leaned forward.

'Can't *you* see?' he asked. 'It has served its turn – or rather, Guttmann's murderous turn. The game is all but over. And you have allowed some nincompoop, some idiot of a youngest son whose parent bought him a commission to keep from making a fool of himself at home, who just happened to be orderly officer of the day at the Admiralty building, to take Sir Rinaldo's orders down to Dorset . . . !'

Sir James sighed heavily.

'I understand your concern, Holmes,' he said. 'But do you seriously suppose the Russkies are going to postpone their march on Constantinople because Mr Mycroft Holmes has chosen to spend the weekend in Norfolk? On the other hand, they might postpone it if they know that Her Majesty's government is taking the threat of war in the Near East seriously. In any case, it was the good judgement of my Lords of the Admiralty that Sir Rinaldo should sail from Southampton with Lady Hornby by the afternoon tide next Friday for Valetta, and that, leaving Lady Hornby in Malta, he should proceed immediately to take command of the Royal Marine contingent with our ships presently anchored in Besika Bay. It is the usual practice on such occasions to allow the poor fellow a few days' notice. . . . At my request, the movement order, together with sealed orders both for Sir Rinaldo and for Admiral Parkinson at Besika, were taken by an officer of whom even you, my dear Holmes, would approve.'

'Who might that be?' asked Mycroft.

'Major Edwin Barnaby, of the 21st Lancers.'

'Barnaby is a first-rate fellow – loyal and brave to the utmost degree,' Mycroft agreed. 'But one would hardly describe him as an intellectual luminary – no match for one of Guttmans's skill. Was he warned?'

'I myself told him frankly what had occurred with young Ponsonby and with Rookworthy,' said Sir James. 'Besides which, he knows that we have placed our own agent among Sir Rinaldo's servants.'

'I thought you had once told me that Her Majesty's government regarded it as dishonourable to employ a secret service,' said Mycroft.

'A volunteer,' said Sir James. 'Dedicated, discreet, and as intelligent as you would wish.'

'I know of nobody in the latter category save myself,' said Mycroft.

He sat back in his chair.

'At least we are safe for the moment,' he said. 'I shall travel by the South Western Railway to Dorset tomorrow, taking the noon train. Perhaps you could have one of your people send a telegram to Seacombe House asking Sir Rinaldo to send a groom to fetch me from Wareham station. Guttmann, or his agents, will not strike until I am there, do you see?'

'Why ever not?' asked Sir James. 'I thought you feared the opposite.'

'Because I have come to understand his diabolic scheme. There are aspects of it I have not yet had the opportunity of grasping: how he manages to slip in and out of this country, evading your watch on the ports and the railway termini; how he proposes to make it appear that the Tsar's agents are responsible for whatever is to occur at Seacombe. But of one thing, I am absolutely certain: *I* am the weapon he has devised for the destruction of Sir Rinaldo.'

He explained what had occurred at St Thomas's Hospital.

'You mean that he believes you are the carrier of this pestilence?'

'He believes that I will rush down to Seacombe in one last desperate bid to save my Queen and my country from rushing into a disastrous war,' said Mycroft. 'His satanic pride demands that we should have an encounter, face to face.'

He leaned forward across the table as far as his stomach permitted.

'I suggest, Sir James, that you have Chief Inspector Grimes, or Sergeant Gregson – the task should not be beyond his limited capabilities – go to Wetwood in Staffordshire, to interview closely the incumbent of the parish of St James-the-Less and his daughter. It was from him that I learned of Sir Rinaldo's likely removal to take command of the Royal Marine contingent in the Eastern Mediterranean, and of the Prussian governess he employs.'

'You are not suggesting that this parson and his daughter . . .,' Sir James began.

Mycroft lifted his outstretched palm to stop him.

'I don't believe the Vicar of Wetwood is a Prussian spy,' he replied. 'In fact I am perfectly certain he is quite guiltless of any treasonable intent. "Guileless" would probably be the appropriate word if my own observation was correct – as I am entirely sure it was. But where C.P.E. Guttmann is involved, nothing happens by chance; I'm sure he intended that I and this honest cleric should meet when we did, in the manner we did. It should be Grimes's or Gregson's task to discover how it was contrived. . . . May I suggest that you employ the telegraph to inform me of the results of their enquiry. I shall be found, as from tomorrow evening and until Friday at the least, at Seacombe House. I suppose the nearest post office with a telegraph machine will be Corfe Castle.'

197

Chapter Eighteen

The final stage of the journey, on the Southampton and Dorchester Railway, was uncomfortable and painfully slow. Heavy rains during the past two days and nights had caused flooding over Holton Heath, closing the toll road from Poole to Wareham. The train stopped between East Holton station and West Holton so that people stranded in their carriages and carts at the Holton tollgate, could scramble up the embankment to continue their journey by train to the station nearest their destination. When Mycroft stepped down on to the rain-swept exposure of Wareham station, looking for Cyril to join him from the third class carriages, the platform lamps had already been lit, and were guttering in their sooty glass funnels, and the lampman with his pushcart was hurrying from compartment to compartment.

'Holmes, my dear old fellow! You must have had the most dweadfully uncomfortable journey, don't you know!'

Major Barnaby stepped out from the shadow of the station-house gate. He was in the blue-black frogged coat of the 21st Lancers' undress, with a peaked cap pulled down over his eyes against the wind and rain. Five years had passed since Mycroft had last seen him – on another wintry railway platform, at Charing Cross. His moustache had grown heavier, his dundreary side-whiskers more luxuriant. He slapped his riding switch under his arm, and extended his hand. Mycroft took it less than enthusiastically.

'And you, you young scoundwel! Let me shake you by the hand m' boy!' he said to Cyril, embracing him warmly. 'Don't suppose they'll have seen any of your sort in these parts, eh?'

Mycroft prodded Barnaby with his stick.

'What are you doing away from your charge, sir?'

'Here! I say, old chap!' Barnaby protested.

He pushed Mycroft's stick away.

'I've bwought two charges with me to accompany you back to Seacombe,' he said. 'Damned pwetty charges, too!'

He waved his switch in the direction of the station forecourt.

'Their mama and papa will be deuced worried, don't you know, if we don't take 'em – and you – back to Seacombe at a bwisk canter!'

'Didn't Sir James tell you you were not to take your eyes off Sir Rinaldo and the sealed orders?' Mycroft asked.

Without deigning to reply, Major Barnaby led them through the small station-house. Against the pavement outside stood the Hornby family brougham, its polished leather and burnished brass gleaming in the lantern light, the two perfectly-groomed horses pawing the cindered ground under their hooves. Behind it, and tethered by the rein to the rail of the rear outside seat, was an equally well-groomed mare saddled and bridled for riding. The coachman, in his old-fashioned multi-caped coat, extricated his knees and legs from under the canvas apron which protected them, and swung down from the carriage. He saluted Mycroft with his whip, examined Cyril with faint astonishment, and proceeded to remove the rough blankets which he had thrown over the horses' backs.

Barnaby placed his hand on Mycroft's arm.

'Word in your ear, my dear fellow,' he said. 'Colonel of Woyal Marines is perfectly capable of lookin' after himself, eh what?'

'Against C.P.E. Guttmann?' asked Mycroft.

'Anyone, old chap,' Barnaby replied with absolute certainly. 'In any case, left my colleague in charge, don't you know?' And he winked at Mycroft. 'As for the sealed orders – have 'em on me . . . always! Day and night.'

He patted the coat-pocket against his thigh with his switch. It gave off the sound of a paper parcel being struck. Mycroft glanced about him.

'For God's sake, man!' he exclaimed.

'Don't intend givin' 'em to the Colonel till I've seen him aboard at Southampton on Friday, don't you know,' Barnaby explained. He lowered his voice. 'Keep a shooter loaded in the other pocket. Don't mind tellin' you, I intend usin' it on the first person tries dippin' for the orders, be they man, woman, babe in arms, or clerk in Holy Orders, eh?'

'Have you, or anybody else, noticed anything suspicious – out of the ordinary – since you arrived at Seacombe?' Mycroft asked.

'Not a thing, old chap,' Barnaby told him. 'Soon as I heard you were on the case, and Sir James told me about poor young Ponsonby and young Rookworthy, I told myself – just the adventure for you, Edwin Barnaby, old fellow! Keep the old shooter oiled and loaded, don't you know; and the eyes peeled for some sweet young actress, eh, or a buxom serving-wench with murderous intent. There's been nothin' of the sort, dammit. Quiet as the gwave. Perhaps your arrivin' 'll stir things up!'

The coachman had lowered the carriage step and was holding open the door.

'You climb up on top, feller-me-lad,' Barnaby told Cyril. 'Keep Mr Lewis company.'

Cyril was holding a portmanteau in either hand and a box under his arm. He threw them one by one up on to the roof. He looked at Mycroft. He had an aggrieved expression on his face.

'Do I 'ave to?' he demanded. 'I 'ad to sit out in the rain last time – when we was gone to Rugby.'

'Dash it, my boy!' Barnaby told him. 'Can't sit inside

200

with the young ladies. Wouldn't be at all the thing. Fwighten 'em to death, don't you know!'

A girl of fifteen or sixteen, with freckles and a snub nose, stuck her head round the open door.

'Major Barnaby!' she called. 'When *are* we going home? Henrietta-Louise says she's got. . . .'

'Arabella!' came a shrill cry of indignation from inside the carriage.

The coachman at the step offered a look of weary resignation.

'She says,' said the girl leaning out of the door, 'she's got. . . .'

'Arabella!' came a second, even more indignant cry.

'. . . pins-and-needles-in-her-b-t-m!' said Arabella very quickly. 'Yes you did!' she shouted back into the carriage. 'So don't you pinch me or I'll tell Fräulein when we get back, and she'll make you stand under the stairs!'

Arabella's head disappeared inside the carriage. There came another scream, more loud than the first two, and a cry of, 'I *will* tell Fräulein! I will! I will! I will!'

Mycroft breathed in deeply.

'My dear Barnaby,' he said, 'I can see why you prefer to be up in the saddle. I wonder you did not bring a spare mount. We could have talked on the way.'

A girl's head appeared round the door once more. For a second, Mycroft thought it was the same head; then he saw that though it was snub-nosed and freckled, it was less round than the first.

'Where's the cannibal king?' it demanded. 'Major Barnaby! You promised there was going to be a cannibal king!'

Cyril had mounted halfway to the coachman's seat. He swung out from the iron stirrup.

'Here Ah is! Ah is de Cannibal King – yessah Missee!'

He rolled the whites of his eyes and flashed his teeth. But what made him a truly terrifying spectacle, Mycroft decided, was his pea-green bowler hat and vivid dog-tooth check trousers. He wondered how he had come to be so distracted by events that he had allowed Cyril to travel in such outrageous garments.

'You're not a cannibal king,' said the girl. 'You're just Mr Holmes's negro servant.'

But she said it with a certain lack of conviction, and Cyril, as he swung himself up on to the seat and pulled the canvas apron up to protect himself against the wind and rain, showed no sign of having heard her. To his own astonishment, Mycroft heard himself say, 'I daresay his father ate a missionary or two.'

The girl retreated before him as he mounted the step into the carriage. She sat beside her sister; both of them stared at him as he took his place opposite them, facing the direction of the horses, removed his hat and placed it on the seat beside him, and rested his hands on the knob of his stick. He looked from one to the other. As the coachman closed the door, their faces were shadowed inside their bonnets.

'I flatter myself I have taught the son a better respect for the cloth,' he told them.

There was the faintest hint of a giggle from the shadows. Mycroft indicated with a wave to Major Barnaby through the window that he was ready to begin the final stage of the journey. The carriage heaved as the coachman mounted, then they swung round and out of the station forecourt.

'Forgive me, young ladies,' said Mycroft. 'You appear to have the advantage of me. You know who I am, but I. . . .'

The rounder-faced of the two girls said, 'I'm Miss Hornby. My sister is Miss Henrietta-Louise Hornby.'

'I was given to understand,' said Mycroft, 'that you are twins.'

'We are!' Miss Henrietta-Louise replied promptly.

'I was born first!' Miss Hornby replied, almost as quickly.

'*She* won't admit we're *real* twins,' said Miss Henrietta-Louise.

'I was born ten minutes before she was!' said Miss Hornby.

Mycroft glanced out through the window. The brougham was labouring up the hill from the station into the high street of Wareham town. Candles and oil-lamps were being lit in the shop windows. They passed the cross roads which was the centre of the small town, and descended with a squeal of brakes to the bridge across the River Frome. As they did so, Major Barnaby rode up abreast of the carriage, stooped in the saddle, and looked in. Mycroft gave him what he hoped was a baleful glance. Beyond Barnaby was what appeared to be a very decent inn; Mycroft felt a pang of regret for a fireside seat, an ample steak-and-kidney pudding with gravy, and a pint of mulled claret. He sighed. The twins sat staring through either window at the darkening landscape.

They drove over the ancient stone bridge and splashed along the causeway across the water-meadows on the far side of the Frome.

'Mamma didn't want us to come to meet you, Mr Holmes,' said Henrietta-Louise. 'Stop fidgetting, Arabella!' she added.

Arabella Hornby had been flicking up and down one of the tassels which fringed her velvet paletot. She scowled and continued flicking one small tassel after another.

'Mamma was afraid the causeway would be flooded,' Henrietta-Louise. 'She was afraid we might have put up in Wareham, at *The Swan* – without any of the maids to look after us!'

'But you came all the same,' Mycroft pointed out.

'We *think* Mamma was under the impression Fräulein was coming with us. Only, Major Barnaby said he thought it would be more comfortable if she didn't because of you being – well – rather big, don't you see?'

Mycroft stared out at the wide, eerie desolation of Stoborough Heath. On the edge, against the dying light, reared the long, high ridge of the Purbeck Hills which separated the coastal region from the mainland like an earthwork thrown up by Titans.

'Anyway,' said Henrietta-Louise. 'Fräulein didn't want to come. She wanted to chat with Papa.'

Arabella stopped playing with her tassels. Still staring sulkily at her knees, she said, 'Fräulein is always chatting with Papa.'

'No, she isn't!' Henrietta-Louise contradicted her. 'Not always.'

'Tell me,' asked Mycroft. 'What do Fräulein von Holz-zu-Birkensee and your Papa talk about when they have these chats?'

'Mil-it-ary matt-ers!' replied Henrietta-Louise. She put her hand to her mouth and pretended to yawn. 'Papa says she knows as much about mil-it-ary matt-ers as most gentlemen do. He actually *likes* talking to her – golly gosh!'

She put her hand to her mouth again and pretended to yawn even more deeply.

'Her father was a major in the *Potsdamer* Grenadiers,' said Arabella, 'and her husband was killed in action against the French at the Battle of Gravelotte – wherever that might be.'

Mycroft stared out of the window at where the heathland stretched into the furthest distance, toward the Frome estuary and Brownsea Island. It was more forbidding even than the Fenlands, because of the dense stretches of black broom and fern which concealed the rush-strewn mires in which man or beast might sink noiselessly, slowly, without leaving a trace behind.

'Have you visited Dorset before, Mr Holmes?' asked Henrietta-Louise, sounding almost grown up.

Mycroft shook his head.

'It's quite horribly dull!' Arabella told him.

'Except for Lord Eldon at Edgecombe,' said Henrietta-Louise, 'there's absolutely nobody one can be At Home to who doesn't live *miles* away. And he's so *dreadfully* old!'

'I wish,' said Arabella, 'that we could go to

204

Southampton with Papa and Mamma, on Friday. But there's nobody else going.'

'Except Whitlock,' said Henrietta-Louise. 'And Major Barnaby, of course . . . and Claudine, with Mamma. . . .'

'Claudine?' Mycroft asked.

Claudine Lebrun,' explained Henrietta-Louise. 'Mamma's new maid. She's French. Major Barnaby brought her specially to look after Mamma on the voyage.'

'There's one blessing,' said Arabella. 'Fräulein von Holz-zu-Birkensee will be going with them.'

'Going with them?' asked Mycroft. 'Are you sure?'

'Only as far as Southampton. She'll be changing to the London and South Western Railway there. She's meeting a parson's daughter in London; Fräulein is going to be her governess on a trip abroad. I'm glad I'm not going to Europe all by myself with Fräulein – I can't imagine anything more *dire*.'

'I expect the parson's daughter will be as dull and boring as she is,' said Henrietta-Louise. 'They'll be dull and boring together, all over Europe.'

'I expect Major Barnaby's attitude to Fräulein von Holz-zu-Birkensee is somewhat different to your own,' Mycroft suggested.

He experienced a certain repugnance at encouraging the twins to gossip. It went entirely against his usual principles. His actions, however, had to be dictated by circumstances.

'Major Barnaby doesn't care for her a tiny bit,' said Arabella.

'Major Barnaby is a *real* soldier,' said Henrietta-Louise. 'He likes talking about horses, and riding.'

'In any case,' said Arabella, 'Major Barnaby is spoony about Claudine.'

'Don't be so stupid!' Henrietta told her off. 'How can he be spoony about her? She's only a servant!'

'Amy said she saw them spooning on the path through Dead Man's Wood,' said Arabella.

'You shouldn't repeat what servants tell you about

205

people!' Henrietta-Maria replied. 'Unless it's about other servants. You shouldn't even listen! It's very wicked!'

'Claudine's very pretty,' Arabella persisted. 'I might feel spoony about her if I were a man.'

The horses were beginning to toil uphill. Looking out of the window, Mycroft could see nothing but sheep cropping a fern-covered bank. Stooping down, however, and looking upwards, he could see, uprearing and jutting from the crest of the great grass and fern-covered mound, a massive ruin of towers and battlements reaching up into the broken western sky, and looming over them. He realized that they were arriving at Corfe Castle.

'She isn't pretty,' Henrietta-Maria was saying scornfully. 'She's too old – she must be at least twenty-seven. You can't be pretty when you're twenty-seven. You can be beautiful. But she's certainly not beautiful. As Papa says, her looks are all wrong!'

'No, they're not!' Arabella replied.

'Yes, they are!' said Henrietta-Maria.

Mycroft continued to look wearily out of the window. The road had suddenly become more steep as the horses laboured to draw the carriage up and round the foot of the castle mound. They were entering the village, low, single-storey cottages built so sturdily they seemed themselves to be outcrops of living stone. On the opposite side of the road to the castle, the parish church, surrounded by weathered gravestones, was standing on a more modest mound.

'She has dark brown hair,' said Henrietta-Louise. 'Almost black, like a Chinaman's. . . .'

'It isn't black like a Chinaman's!' exclaimed Arabella. 'A Chinaman's hair is black like Indian ink – and it's all shiny like grease. Claudine's hair isn't in the least greasy, even though she's a maid. . . .'

'And her eyes slant like a Chinaman's . . .,' said Henrietta-Louise.

'No, they don't!' exclaimed Arabella. 'They're blue!'

'They still slant!' said Henrietta-Louise. 'Chinky-chink-chink-chink!'

And she put her fingers to the corners of her eyes and lifted them. Then she saw the expression on Mycroft's face, and lowered her hands immediately. She looked guilty and awkward. She gave Arabella a sidelong glance, but Arabella was playing with the tassels on her paletot once more.

Mycroft pointed his finger at Henrietta-Louise.

'This woman is twenty-seven, you say? You are sure?'

Henrietta-Louise stared at him. She nodded.

'Yes sir. I heard her tell Mamma so.'

'She has dark hair – in curl?' he asked.

'Yes, sir.'

'And high cheekbones?'

He indicated the bone structure with his fingers on his own florid features.

'And blue eyes – very striking blue eyes?' he asked.

'Yes, sir.'

'She is slim. She could almost be taken for a boy?' he asked.

'I don't know, sir. . . .' Henrietta-Louise's voice had almost sunk to a whisper.

Of course, Mycroft thought; she had never seen her in anything but the full petticoats and skirts of an upstairs maid.

Arabella looked up, one of the tassels twisted round her finger.

'Do you know Claudine Lebrun, Mr Holmes?' she asked.

'I believe I do,' he replied.

He raised himself to his feet. With the knob of his stick he rapped on the small hatch above the twins' heads. It slammed open.

'Yes, sir?' the coachman called in.

'Halt immediately, if you please! I wish to set down!'

'Here, sir?' the coachman asked in surprise.

'Here, sir! This minute, sir!' Mycroft replied.

'But Mr Holmes . . .,' Arabella looked at him in complete astonishment.

Henrietta-Louise stared in equal bewilderment.

The carriage came to a standstill. Mycroft did not wait for the coachman to get down. He opened the door and, without waiting for the steps to be lowered, jumped heavily to the ground. Barnaby was riding some yards ahead. He swung his horse about and returned. They were at the end of a street of low stone cottages. Immediately in front of them, the open, drizzle-swept heath stretched away into the diminishing twilight.

'Major Barnaby! If you would be so good as to dismount!'

Barnaby dropped lightly from the saddle. His face, framed in his cavalry cap and whiskers looked comically apprehensive. Mycroft, aware that the twins were watching from the open door of the brougham, indicated with his stick that he and Barnaby should step a few paces out on to the heath. He glanced up and motioned for Cyril to drop down to join them.

'You brought the Princess Trubetskoy to Seacombe House!' he exclaimed.

'Haw! Haw! Haw!' Major Barnaby laughed. 'You found out our little secret then, eh? Makes a vewwy fetchin' lady's maid, I must say!'

Mycroft turned to Cyril.

'*You* know nothing of this, I hope, you rascal!'

'Nuffink of what, Mr 'Olmes?' Cyril asked.

'Princess Sophie! At Seacombe House, disguised as a maid!'

Cyril looked caught between utter astonishment and equally utter delight. Mycroft realized what was in his impudent head: that, for the first time he and the Princess, to whom he was devoted, would meet on equal terms socially.

As they stood facing one another, the rain gathered and dripped from the rims of their hats.

'Sir James Swarthmoor knows of this?' asked Mycroft at last.

'It was Sir James who suggested I should bwing Sophie down here,' Barnaby replied.

'She must leave instantly!' Mycroft exclaimed. 'At the first possible moment! If necessary, you must take her back to London – even better, to your mother's place at Farnham. . . . The stupidity of it!'

'I'll take 'er, Mr 'Olmes!' Cyril volunteered eagerly.

'Be quiet, man!' Mycroft ordered. 'I must think!'

After a few moments of silence broken only by the dripping of the rain, he placed a reassuring hand on Barnaby's sleeve, he said, 'Forgive me, my dear fellow. You weren't to know. . . .'

'She's in danger?' Barnaby asked.

'She is in the greatest possible danger. So are we all. So are the fortunes of this country,' said Mycroft. 'I will tell you. She is here in Dorset for only one reason – because Guttmann planned that she should be here. That is why I am here, and this black scoundrel, and maybe, my dear, rash young friend, you as well. In his diabolic scheme he intends this as his killing ground on which he will destroy us all. But Sophie Trubetskoy is more essential to his main plan than any of us – even myself if it is possible for you to believe it. It is true he means that I should be the unwitting – and unwilling – instrument of Colonel Sir Rinaldo Hornby's death. But when I came to understand that, I could not see how he was going to ensure blame would be laid on the Russians – and it is essential in this instance that there should be incontrovertible evidence of Russian responsibility. But with Sophie Trubetskoy in the house, disguised as a servant (and we have seen the parts played by upstairs maids in the cases of Louis Ponsonby and Evelyn Rookworthy), the Russian connection will be established. She will be made to appear an agent of the Imperial Chancery in St Petersburg – and since we are all known to be her friends or associates, we will be depicted at best as dupes, at worst as accomplices.'

'You don't mean spies, do you, old chap?' asked Barnaby. 'Sophie, and me – and you . . . and even him?' He pointed to Cyril. 'Spies? Wussian spies?'

'Me?' asked Cyril. 'A Russian spy?'

He guffawed loudly.

'Russia's greatest poet had a negro grandfather,' Mycroft told him.

Cyril stopped laughing.

Mycroft continued, 'I must return to the carriage. We have to reach Seacombe House as soon as possible. Whatever happens to us, one thing is absolutely certain: the sooner, and the further we have the Princess away from there, the less the chance Guttmann has of embroiling this land of ours in another stupid and bloody war in the Near East.'

Chapter Nineteen

Major Barnaby wiped the moisture off his saddle with his sleeve, and mounted with practised grace. Mycroft and Cyril walked the short distance back to the brougham.

' 'Ow d'yer fink 'e got 'er to come to this 'ere miserable part of the world?'

'Cyril glanced at the bleak, lowering expanse of Corfe Common and shuddered.

'Thus is demonstrated the clear distinction between cunning,' Mycroft replied, 'which you, my dear fellow, possess in ample quantity. And intellectual capacity. . . .'

He stopped at the open door of the carriage. Lowering his voice, he continued, 'Having followed Guttmann's progress through the Balkan kingdoms and observed his activities, it was the most natural thing in the world for her to have followed him to London. No doubt she arrived at her apartments in Bruton Street at about the same time as I set off on my jaunt to Norfolk. . . .'

'*We*!' suggested Cyril. '*We* set off!'

Mycroft ignored him.

'. . . as Guttmann intended I should. The first person to welcome her to Town – was . . . ?'

'The Major?' Cyril asked, glancing up the road at the gleaming rump of Major Barnaby's mare.

'Of course,' Mycroft told him. 'Emotional attachments – even of the . . . er . . . intermittent kind – take precedence over friendship. And the Major, being presently attached to the War House, was only a stone's throw from Bruton Street. For Sir James, when he saw that there was no preventing my Lords of the Admiralty from sending Colonel Hornby's orders into Dorset, Major Barnaby was the obvious messenger: brave, resolute,

a bit of a fool, perhaps, but not a young one. And since
. . . our friend . . . was in Town, and even Sir James is
scarcely capable, in view of her family's history of Siberian
imprisonment and her own exile in Nice, of seriously
supposing her to be the Tsar's agent, there was a team
already prepared. . . .'

'Hurry up, please do, Mr Holmes!' Henrietta Louise
called from the interior of the carriage. 'I'm cold!'

'And I'm *freezing*!' exclaimed Arabella, as if, even in
this, some element of competition was required.

'A moment, ladies!' Mycroft replied.

There was a slight kerfuffle inside the carriage, and a
giggled mimicry of his 'Ladies!'. Mycroft touched Cyril's
lapel with the knob of his stick.

'You may be sure that if I appreciate what has happened with only the least information,' he said, 'C.P.E.
Guttmann would have known it would happen, and has
acted accordingly.'

Cyril had assumed an expression which was intended
to convey profound concentration.

'So 'e *will* be 'ere, Mr 'Olmes? Or 'ereabouts?' he asked.
'He looked at the dismal landscape and shivered.

'You may be certain of it,' Mycroft told him. 'Even
though our bold Major claims that he has noticed nothing
out of the ordinary. So keep your eyes peeled and your
ears open, my lad.'

He gave Cyril a pat on the shoulder. The coachman
had lowered the steps, he noticed. It was just as well, he
decided. He had felt badly jarred jumping down on to the
road without them. The act of pulling his weight through
the carriage door, wearied as he was by continual
travelling, could have had a very deleterious result. He
fell back into his seat opposite the twins with such force
that the carriage shuddered on its steel springs.

The carriage toiled on across the wilderness, then
climbed gradually to the top of a high ridge and proceeded along its summit. There was a smell of the sea on
the draughts which blew round the doors and windows

as they turned to descend the far side. There was a rough wooden sign-post at the roadside. In the glow from the carriage lamps, Mycroft read:

> Worth Matravers, 1½.
> Seacombe House, 1.

The descent was into parkland consisting of a steep-sloping valley. On either side loomed the dark shapes of high bushes and scattered tall trees. Finally, they turned on a wide circle of gravel, and drew up under a well-lit porch. A footman came down from the open front door to lower the step and to assist Mycroft from the carriage. A handsome woman in her mid-twenties was standing immediately under the portico lamp. She was on the tall side, held herself rigidly erect, was plainly but neatly dressed, and had her straw-blond hair in two plaits wound on each side of her head. She inclined her head slightly as Mycroft entered, and murmured 'Good evening, sir,' in accented English. Her attention was reserved for the twins.

'Miss Hetty? Miss Bella? Come here this instant? This instant? Do you hear me?'

She raised her voice in such a way that each sentence, even each phrase, sounded like a question, whether it was one or not. The girls stepped down from the carriage.

'You told your dear mother I said I will come with you, when you knew I said nothing of the kind – what do you mean by that?'

The footman took Mycroft's hat and stick, and began to help him to remove his topcoat.

Henrietta-Louise said, 'Major Barnaby told us he would look after us, Fräulein. Didn't he, Arabella?'

Mycroft heard the clink of Barnaby's spurs as he entered the hall. The footman laid Mycroft's coat on the hall table and went to assist Barnaby. The governess was saying, 'You know very well a gentleman does not *look after* young ladies of your age – not without the assistance

213

of another, older lady! Whatever will people think? And not only of you! Of me, who lets you go wandering' – she pronounced it 'vann-dering' – 'with a soldier! Of poor Major Barnaby, too!'

Barnaby smiled at Mycroft.

'My weputation in Wareham,' he said quietly. 'Wuined – in tatters, don't you know?'

'But that is nothing, girls! Nothing compared to the wickedness of telling lies to your poor, dear mother . . . !'

'If you please, sir. The Colonel is in the library. . . . If you would be good enough to come this way, sir.'

From the man's bearing and his facial character – that acquired look of experience and authority which is to be found in the faces of most veteran soldiers when they regard themselves as being on duty – Mycroft knew that he was being addressed by Colonel Sir Rinaldo Hornby's orderly, for all that he was in civilian clothes.

Sir Rinaldo was standing halfway up the wheeled spiral stepladder designed to provide a platform on which one might browse among the books on the top-most shelves. He had resting on one arm an *octavo* volume of palladian architectural elevations. He presented a contrived picture of pursuing an interest to which the newcomer's arrival was incidental. It was not, however, a pose he was, by temperament, capable of maintaining.

'You are, of course, welcome to my home, Mr Holmes,' he said without lifting his head.

His accent was clipped, economical, no-nonsense. He closed the book and replaced it in the shelf.

'You had a comfortable journey, I trust?' he asked.

'As comfortable as one might have expected, thank you, Sir Rinaldo,' he replied.

'Which means, not at all comfortable, eh?' said Sir Rinaldo, without the hint of a twinkle.

He got down from the stepladder.

'Well! It's nothing to do with me,' he went on. 'I didn't ask for my house to be invaded by some blethering idiot of a cavalry major – who, may I say, does not regard me as a fit person to hold the sealed orders entrusted to me by the Admiralty! Nor did I ask for Lady Hornby to be spied on by some flighty, half-Tonkinese French maid. . . .'

He let his monocle fall from his eye.

'Half-Tonkinese?' asked Mycroft.

'It isn't your doing, by any chance?' Sir Rinaldo demanded.

'Very far from it,' Mycroft told him quietly.

'It's a damned insult!' Sir Rinaldo exploded. 'A half-caste, by God! A Chink with curly hair and blue eyes; some Frog subaltern's by-blow. And that's the kind of gel some chair-bound desk-wallah at the War House regards as a fit companion for my wife! And now they've sent you! – No personal feelings involved, of course – mustn't misunderstand me, my dear fellow. But, deuce take it!— having to send Lewis and the brougham out on an afternoon like this, not to mention the wretched horses! And for what? What *do* they imagine you're going to do here that I couldn't do for myself?'

Mycroft did not reply immediately. Two things occurred to him. First of all, it was perfectly obvious that Sir Rinaldo was more uneasy than he made out. Secondly, on a small, baize-covered Hanoverian card-table in the centre of the room stood a silver-chased cigar box; he recognized the design on the bands, *Romeo y Julietta*. As a result, he was experiencing a profound craving for tobacco.

'You've been informed of the fate of young Ponsonby and Rookworthy?' he asked.

'Some damn' fool nonsense about being murdered by chambermaids acting as Russian spies!' Sir Rinaldo replied. 'Lady Hornby hasn't employed a new servant for over a year – except for the blue-eyed Chink we've had forced upon us, of course.'

'I should say, from what you have told me, Sir Rinaldo . . . .' Mycroft gazed evenly at him, '. . . that you are going to find that my first act on arriving here suits your own inclinations entirely.'

215

'Indeed, sir?'

Since Sir Rinaldo gave no indication of inviting him to take a seat, Mycroft settled himself into a comfortably upholstered mock *Louis Quatorze* chair.

'You may regard me as something of a benefactor,' he said with defiant ease of manner. 'Since I propose to remove Lady Hornby's unwelcome personal attendant and send her packing straight back to London. I propose, moreover, that she should return to London in the care of the equally unwelcome Major Barnaby.'

Sir Rinaldo was taken by surprise. He sat down himself, on an upright chair at the card-table.

'You have authority for this, Mr Holmes?'

'I have authority to do anything I deem necessary to ensure the safe departure of you and Lady Hornby for Valetta, with the dispatches for Rear-Admiral Parkinson.'

'But Major Barnaby presently holds those dispatches in his own keeping!' said Sir Rinaldo.

'I shall take personal responsibility for them,' Mycroft told him. 'Until you step aboard ship at Southampton, you need not give them the least thought.'

'May I ask you why you are taking this somewhat surprising line of action?' asked Sir Rinaldo.

'Because there is no reason why you and Lady Hornby should be embarrassed by the presence of three strangers in your house during your last few days of furlough from your military duties . . . when only one is required, namely myself,' he replied with an air of sweet reasonableness. 'I wonder if I might be permitted to take tobacco?' he added.

'Of course. If you wish,' Sir Rinaldo replied. He screwed his monocle back into his eye. 'Have one of these,' he muttered, pushing the cigar box across the table.

'Most kind,' said Mycroft taking one. He nipped off the end between finger and thumb, then, taking out his own box of vestas, lit it. Sir Rinaldo watched.

'When do you propose they should leave?' he asked.

Mycroft drew on the cigar and exhaled the blue smoke. 'Immediately,' he said.

'They might as well remain here,' said Sir Rinaldo.

The monocle magnified the pupil of his eye so that one side of his face stared fish-like at Mycroft.

'Damn it, man!' he forced a laugh. 'It's only a matter of three days!'

'Three days too many,' said Mycroft. 'As you yourself guessed, it was a blunder on the part of some idiot of "a chair-bound desk-wallah", sending them here. Their presence here puts both them and us in the greatest danger. Without them, there is virtually no danger.'

Sir Rinaldo shook his head in an expression of exasperation. Mycroft drew on his cigar again.

'I shall be entirely open with you, Sir Rinaldo,' he said.

'Pray do!' Sir Rinaldo exclaimed.

'Entirely' was perhaps a little strong. But Mycroft intended to tell something of the truth.

'The young woman who is acting as Lady Hornby's personal attendant is a lady of the highest quality and very considerable personal fortune – a Russian noblewoman, in fact. Her facial appearance is the result of Tatar ancestry. She is indeed half-French; her mother is a French aristocrat of the highest rank; her father was Russian of ancient Boyar lineage. She lives with her mother in the South of France, having spent her childhood with her parents in a Siberian prison; she has no cause to love the Tsars. It is for that reason that Whitehall thought her a suitable person to watch over you and your wife. As for Major Barnaby: he is a very gallant and resolute gentleman, as I have good cause to know personally. He is also the lady's friend, and constant companion when she chooses to reside at her London address.'

Sir Rinaldo continued to hold him in his half-fish stare. His monocle stayed in place but his mouth had dropped open.

'The mistake – I would go so far as to call it a very

grave blunder,' Mycroft continued, '– perpetrated by your "chair-bound desk-wallahs", is their failure to appreciate that if anything should happen to you while this Russian lady is under your roof, it will be immediately assumed – by the journal-reading public if by nobody else – that the lady is an agent of the Tsar's government. It is not merely that she risks being taken for a Russian spy; that is a triviality compared to the certainty that it would be exploited as an immediate *casus belli* between Great Britain and the Russian Empire.'

'Forgive me if I appear a little dull, Mr Holmes,' Sir Rinaldo said. 'But am I to understand that you are saying that the real danger comes from those who wish to provoke war between this country and Russia?'

'Exactly so. You are far from dull, sir,' Mycroft told him.

Sir Rinaldo removed his monocle from his eye and slipped it into his top waistcoat pocket. He took a cigar for himself, and lit it.

'I would always do my duty to the best of my abilities,' he said. 'But I don't mind telling you, Mr Holmes, in strictest confidence of course. . . .'

'Of course, Sir Rinaldo.'

'. . . the thought of my lads and a battalion or two from India going into action against the Russkies with only a rabble of murderous Bashi-Bazouks to hold our flanks fills me with no enthusiasm whatever. From what I've heard the Russkies are a damn sight better trained and equipped today than they were in the Crimea. *And* they'll think they're fighting a crusade – nothing like a crusade to make men fight like devils, eh?'

'We shall exchange confidences, sir,' Mycroft told him. 'I am here, as you know, on the authority of Sir James Swarthmoor – and, which perhaps you don't know, with the full knowledge of the Prime Minister and Lord Derby. There is known to be in this country one of the most efficient and dangerous agents of a foreign government; the principal object of his attentions at this moment, is yourself, Sir Rinaldo. I don't know if he is here, on the Isle of Purbeck, in person yet; I would expect him to be no great distance away. And if he is not, he will have one of his underlings watching you.'

'I know of nobody who could possibly be a foreign spy . . .,' began Sir Rinaldo. 'Damn it, sir! Seacombe – and Worth Matravers. . . . Everybody knows everybody else's business. The cleverest agency on earth couldn't place a spy in this part of Dorset without him being detected immediately!'

He stared at Mycroft, searching his face.

'I would not have gone to the trouble of coming here, sir,' Mycroft told him, 'had I not known with absolute certainty that you, and with you, the Nation itself, are in grave danger.'

Sir Rinaldo breathed in deeply.

'Very well, sir,' he replied. 'Sir James Swarthmoor appears to believe you to be a sound sort of chap – a square abacus man, as they say.'

He stood up and went and gave the bell-pull a smart tug.

'No point in wasting a moment, eh? We'll have the lady and her cavalier as far as Wareham tonight, at the very least.'

'It would be best,' Mycroft agreed. 'Major Barnaby knows my mind on this.'

The door opened and Sir Rinaldo's orderly came in. 'Sah?' he asked.

'Ask Major Barnaby if he would be so good as to join us here, Whitlock,' Sir Rinaldo told him.

'Sah!'

'In my opinion,' Mycroft suggested, 'it might be no bad thing if the lady and Major Barnaby were to leave here unremarked – by as few people in the house as possible, and by nobody outside.'

'You mean, so that the real enemy may show his hand?' asked Sir Rinaldo.

'Exactly,' Mycroft replied.

'Unfortunately we only have the one way out,' said Sir

Rinaldo. 'Too dark now, of course – but in daylight, you'd see that we're enclosed between two steep ridges, going down to the shore. Different in the saddle: one can ride on horseback up on to the ridge. But for a lady – hard going, don't you know?'

'This lady was born in the saddle,' Mycroft told him. 'She'd ride any of your people into the ground, I'd lay money on it.'

Major Barnaby came in. Mycroft wearily pulled himself to his feet.

'The governess is out of earshot?' he asked.

'Busy punishin' the gels for insubordination,' Barnaby grinned.

'What's that?' asked Sir Rinaldo. 'Been playing up the Fräulein, have they? That is one thing I cannot abide. Playing up one's inferiors. I don't care if it's my own daughters or anybody else – it's not to be borne. If it weren't for Lady Hornby's finer sensibilities, I'd have those two gels thrashed – that would make women of 'em. And the Fräulein's the woman to do it. Told me the other day, her father was still thrashing her when she was seventeen, and she's a fine-looking woman, the Fräulein!' Then he added, 'It was a bad day for England when they abolished the Bridewell floggings. They'll be abolishing field punishment next, you mark my words!'

'Vewwy true, sir,' Barnaby agreed. 'I've said the vewwy same thing, myself.'

Mycroft raised an admonitive finger to silence him.

'Barnaby,' he said. 'As I remarked on the road, we must have the Princess away from here with all speed. We are most fortunate in that the Colonel is a most shrewd and perspicacious gentleman. . . .'

He glanced quickly at Sir Rinaldo, who tweaked the ends of his side-whiskers with becoming modesty.

'He has suggested that in order to quit Seacombe unobserved you should do so in the saddle, cross-country,' he went on. 'For my own part, I recommend that you make, not for Wareham, but Dorchester. It is further, and therefore there is less likelihood of a watch having been set. The Colonel has very wisely pointed out that if we can have you and the Princess away from here unnoticed, it will confuse our enemy and make it more likely he'll show his hand.'

'It's a dreadful night!' Sir Rinaldo observed.

'That won't worry the Pwincess,' Barnaby declared with a touch of possessive pride. 'She has all the pluck in the world, don't you know!'

'You have a groom you can trust – implicitly?' Mycroft asked Sir Rinaldo.

'My fellow will go with you to Dorchester,' Sir Rinaldo told Barnaby.

He did not bother to ring. 'Whitlock!' he shouted. 'Come, damn your eyes!'

The orderly came in immediately.

'Eavesdrops,' Sir Rinaldo explained to Mycroft. 'Soldier-servants no different from the civilian sort. The difference is, Whitlock will keep his mouth shut about what he overhears – won't you, my lad!'

'Sah!' shouted Whitlock.

'You will send Mr Crashaw to me, immediately, do you understand? You will then proceed to the stables – without telling anybody – *anybody*. You will saddle up The Duchess and Black Prince – side-saddle on Black Prince, you understand?'

'Sah!'

'For yourself, you will take the roan mare – damn it, if I can remember what she's called. You are to accompany Major Barnaby here, and a lady, to Dorchester tonight, as soon as possible, as quickly as possible. You need not return with the horses till tomorrow. You will take all further orders from Major Barnaby. And remember – you say nothing of this, not a word, or I'll have your lips rivetted and you can talk through your arse for the rest of your days!'

'Sah!'

'Send Mr Crashaw!'

'Sah!'

As the orderly left, Sir Rinaldo turned to Barnaby.

'Cigar, Major? Before you take your leave, eh?'

Barnaby took one and rolled it between his fingers before lighting it.

'Whisky and soda, gentlemen?' asked Sir Rinaldo.

As the three of them stood smoking and drinking, Crashaw, the butler, appeared. He was a stooped, silver-haired man, with a smooth, port-infused complexion. An old retainer, Mycroft saw instantly; it was apparent from the fact that he had obviously, regularly, and probably with a certain moderation, applied himself to the family decanters, and had been tolerated in doing so. It followed that his entire world was that of Seacombe and the Hornby household.

'Crashaw! Be so good as to tell. . . .' Sir Rinaldo paused fractionally, '. . . the Mistress's new gel, Lebrun, to come to us here.'

'Very good, sir. . . . Begging your pardon, sir,' said the butler.

'What is it, man?'

Sir Rinaldo appeared to regard a slight edge of impatience in his voice to be necessary to get the best out of his servants.

'Annie and Rosie, sir. They've locked themselves in the back pantry, sir. They say they're afraid to come out because of the blackamoor.'

'The blackamoor?' Sir Rinaldo looked puzzled.

'My man, Sir Rinaldo,' Mycroft explained. 'Most reliable fellow. I'd go further – the sort of chap you could go tiger-shooting with.' He turned to the butler. 'And born and bred a London cockney, whatever he's telling 'em below stairs. Would you please tell him I want him up here?'

'Yes, sir.'

When the butler was gone, Sir Rinaldo said, 'This agent, Mr Holmes: which government employs him?'

'No government, Sir Rinaldo,' Mycroft replied. 'That's

the damnable thing. I have no doubt he regards himself as a devoted subject of the Kaiser. . . .'

'Ah!' Sir Rinaldo exclaimed.

'But Carl Philipp Emmanuel Guttmann's true loyalty is to his master, the German Chancellor, Prince von Bismarck. He was, for many years, von Bismarck's personal valet and musician. In that capacity, he performed tasks for his master which von Bismarck as a *Junker* and true *herr* would never have performed for himself; one may say that he anticipated his master's unspoken wishes with unerring accuracy.'

'So this enemy of ours is no more than a servant?' asked Sir Rinaldo.

'Oh yes! A great deal more than a servant,' Mycroft replied. 'He is a genius in his own way; but a genius of the most dangerous sort. He is one who is devoid of the least scrap of moral sense save his perception of his master's interest. Though he may not realize it himself, his is the pathology of the homicidal maniac who has harnessed his lunatic appetite to an agency beyond himself – in the same way the Dominican Friars of the Spanish Inquisition harnessed their pathological love of inflicting pain to the service of the Pope.'

'And you believe he is here?' asked Sir Rinaldo.

'Here, or on his way here. You may depend upon it.'

'What is this Princess's part?' Sir Rinaldo glanced at the library door, as if she might enter and overhear him. 'How the deuce does she come to be playing the agent's role?'

'She is C.P.E. Guttmann's implacable foe,' Mycroft explained. 'She is determined to frustrate his diabolic schemes wherever he may practise them. It is the governing principle and satisfaction of her life. Seven years ago, her elder sister, a beautiful and noble lady who was married to a most distinguished Russian diplomat and scholar, placed herself in the unfortunate position of being blackmailed by Guttmann – the blackmailer's threat being the destruction of her husband's career and reputation. The lady resolved her hideous predicament by taking her own life, thus placing herself beyond the monster's clutches. The Princess rightly regards her sister's death as murder. . . .'

'Worse than murder, damn it!' Sir Rinaldo exclaimed. 'Blackmailing a lady by threatening her husband's reputation? It'd be deuced hard to think of a fouler crime than that!'

'The expression of your feelings is exactly what one would expect from an English gentleman,' Mycroft told him. 'I myself cannot think of a worse offence. . . .'

He glanced at Major Barnaby who shook his head in agreement.

'But there is one which is almost as bad,' said Mycroft.

'Almost as bad?' asked Sir Rinaldo, as though such a thing defied credulity.

'The deliberate placing in gentlemen's households of domestic servants,' said Mycroft, 'for the express purpose of spying, stealing documents, and if necessary, murder.'

He paused to let his words take effect.

'Now that may not seem to be as heinous, but in my opinion it is worse in its effects; for it undermines the trust, the loyal affection, between master and man – or maid – which is the cement holding together the fabric of any well-ordered society, whether here in England, or in farthest Cathay.'

His statement was greeted in silence. At length, Sir Rinaldo took his cigar from his mouth, tossed back his whisky, and said, 'The most disgusting thing I've ever heard. Disgusting!'

He shook his head.

'That is what happened at Caburn Towers, Lord Dewsbury's place,' said Mycroft. 'And at Lady Sowerby's place, Vanderlys.'

'Disgusting!' Sir Rinaldo repeated. 'Past belief! Couldn't happen here. . . . Where's that damn' fool Crashaw got to, blast his eyes!' he exclaimed as if he wished to drive so distasteful an idea from his imagination.

224

He went to the bell-pull and tugged it.

'*Anno domini*, I suppose,' he said. 'There's a cottage for him down by the bay, when he finishes here. Keep the poor old chap out of the cellar, I daresay; have to lay down his own wine, eh?'

He laughed. Then: 'Where do these servant-spies come from, Mr Holmes?' he asked.

'An agency,' Mycroft replied. 'An old-fashioned family business which was acquired and brought into London's West End with Prussian money.'

'There! You see?' said Sir Rinaldo. 'We have no need to go to a London agency for our domestics – all sound healthy Dorset gels. Not much brains – who wants skivvies with brains, eh? But plenty of staying power, and steady as they come, what?'

Mycroft drew on his cigar. He examined the length of ash on the end with proprietorial interest.

'Fräulein von Holz-zu-Birkensee?' he asked quietly. 'Not a Dorset girl, surely?'

Sir Rinaldo laughed again.

'Confound it, Mr Holmes! She's been with us these past two years. One of the family, almost. Comes in here and chats with me about military history – which is more than my wife has ever done! Splendid gel!'

'Where did you find her?' Mycroft asked. 'Two years ago.'

'I don't know, damn it!' Sir Rinaldo exclaimed. 'Goodbody's? Wellman's? Goodman's?'

'Wellbody's of Margaret Street,' said Mycroft, 'the agency to which I have just referred.'

'Forgive me, sir,' said Sir Rinaldo. 'But I cannot believe it anything so shocking of Fräulein von Holz-zu-Birkensee. She is the daughter of one Prussian officer and widow to another. She is governess to my children. She leaves here on Friday, at the same time as Lady Hornby and myself; she is taking up employment with a Staffordshire parson.'

'She is to meet the parson's daughter in Town,' Mycroft replied, 'in order to accompany her – but not the parent –

across the sea to Germany, and from thence to act as the young lady's chaperone on a continental tour. It is the safest way she could leave our shores when she has played her part on behalf of her true employer – which is neither you, sir, nor your Staffordshire parson, but Carl Philipp Emmanuel Guttmann. Somewhere in Europe – in the *calle* of some Venetian stew, or the tavern quarter of Florence's *Oltrarno*, if her standards are compatible with those of her evil genius – she will lose and desert the poor child she is supposed to be protecting, and return to Berlin alone. . . .'

'Mr Holmes, I am not altogether a poor judge of character. . . ,' Sir Rinaldo had begun, when there came a tap on the door. 'Come!' he shouted.

The old butler came in.

'Where the devil have you been all this time, Crashaw?' Sir Rinaldo shouted at him.

'Very sorry, sir,' the butler replied. 'But we can't find Lebrun anywhere. Mrs Burnside has sent to her room and to the drawing-room, sir. And Jim's been out to the stables, because she had a great fancy for looking at the horses did Lebrun. She's nowhere to be found.'

'It's true as I live, Mr 'Olmes!'

Cyril had come in. He glanced at Crashaw.

'The maids is 'avin' a laugh about it,' he said grimly. 'Sayin' as 'ow she took off 'cos their manner's too rough for " 'er ladyship" – that's 'ow they puts it, the stupid cows!'

'Cyril! Mind your manners, sir!' Mycroft told him.

Cyril's genuine indignation brought forth an equally honest apology: 'Very sorry, gentlemen, I'm sure. Run away with meself.'

'Do you think that could, in fact, be the truth, Mr Holmes?' asked Sir Rinaldo. 'That she found the ways of the servants' hall too strange for one of her quality?'

'Mycroft had just opened his mouth when Major Barnaby exclaimed, 'Certainly not! The Pwincess has put up with a lot worse than the servants' hall here, I'll be bound!'

'She would have spoken to Major Barnaby,' said Mycroft. 'They are friends of some years' standing. Besides, she knew from the Major that I was arriving. Why should she expose herself willingly to the wind and weather of your heathland when her most sure and certain friends in England would shortly be about her?'

'The maids are still searching, I hope?' asked Sir Rinaldo.

'Yes, sir,' Crashaw replied. 'Mrs Burnside has sent them looking in the cupboards and presses upstairs.'

'Have the men search the gardens and the out-houses,' Sir Rinaldo. 'Send one of 'em down to the pagoda.'

'Yes, sir!'

There was a rustle of silks. Lady Hornby came in, a pretty, plump women in the full, flounced gown and jet black ringlets which had been fashionable ten years before – of course, Mycroft was reminded, through his rising anxiety, fashion would be ten years behind Town in this desolate part.

'They say Claudine's gone missing!' she exclaimed. There was a childishness in her voice which she had once cultivated to charm potential husbands, but which had now become natural to her. ' 'Melia says she's run away or something!'

She stared about her at the men, who did not reply. She saw Cyril.

'Ooh!' she said. 'You're the black one they're all talking about, ain't you?'

'Crashaw!' Sir Rinaldo ordered the butler, who withdrew.

'Is it true, Rinny?' Lady Hornby asked her husband.

'I fear so, my dear,' Sir Rinaldo replied.

'But she's such a sensible girl! And so clever! She quite frightened me with her cleverness!'

'Have you the orders the Colonel is to carry to Rear-Admiral Parkinson?' Mycroft asked Major Barnaby.

To his intense relief, Barnaby drew a waterproof packet from the inside of his coat.

'Let me see them.'

He noticed the expression on the faces both of Sir Rinaldo and Barnaby.

'By the authority vested in me by Her Majesty's Ministers of State . . .,' he recited, holding out his hand. 'You will all stand as far back as will ensure you cannot read the contents.'

There was an escritoire standing against the wall farthest from the hearth. To it, he took the package. He lit the candles in the wall brackets with one of his own vestas. His feeling of relief drained away. Controlling his voice as best he could, he said, 'The package has been tampered with. The seals are broken . . . very carefully broken apart so that one would not notice it at a casual glance.'

He was aware of the eyes of those gathered about the hearth on his back. He untied the string, picking broken fragments of wax off the knots as he did so. Behind him was silence. He unfolded the waxen paper. There was no need for him to unfold the quarto pages of vellum inside. He could see that they were blank.

He buried his face in his hands. The patient silence of those behind him was almost comforting. He lifted his head again. Without turning round, he said, 'Too late! The trap has been sprung.'

Chapter Twenty

'Candles, sir?' Crashaw asked.

It was after midnight. For four hours, every available man on the home estate had searched in the pouring, winter rain, the gardens, the park as far as the bay shore, and the east and west ridges to the cliff edges. Colonel Sir Rinaldo Hornby, with Mycroft and Major Barnaby beside him, all equally drenched, stood on the portico step in the rain-streaked light of the lanterns held by the small crowd about them. He thanked the men for their readiness to turn out on such a night, and bade them bear his apologies to their wives and families for having so disturbed their hearthside ease. A flogger and disciplinarian he might be, Mycroft observed, even as he himself wished the rain would stop dribbling out of his hair and down under his collar, but he was the sort of commander who would win the utmost devotion from his men.

'In the library, thank you, Crashaw. You need not wait up for us: we shall take them as we require them.'

'Thank you, sir.'

'And now, my stout-hearted, lads,' Sir Rinaldo turned back to the small crowd, 'we shall all meet together at church tomorrow. . . .'

He paused to pull the turnip-watch from his waistcoat pocket, under his cape.

'Today, lads!' he exclaimed. 'Today morning!'

There was a ripple of laughter – a break in the tension of the evening's grim search.

'And so, goodnight to you all, and once again my heartiest thanks to you.'

There was a general murmur of 'Goodnight, maister',

'Goodnight, Squire,', 'Goodnight, Colonel'. Sir Rinaldo led Mycroft and Major Barnaby back into the house.

He had explained over dinner that it was the pleasant custom on the Seacombe estate, when he was called to active duty, for all the people who could do so to gather at the parish church of St Nicholas, in Worth Matravers, to pray with the family at a short act of worship, and to bid him God-speed. They had discussed over the dinner-table whether, in view of what had happened, it would be appropriate to hold the service as planned, the following day. Mycroft had expressed the view that most certainly the service should be held; that there should be no mention of the discovery that the Admiralty's sealed orders had gone missing, and that the household should behave precisely as if a new domestic had gone astray. Now, as they returned to the library, Sir Rinaldo observed, 'It will be remarkably convenient, eh? All our people there: organize 'em into search parties. We can beat the estate and the shore from Tilly Whim to Chapman's Pool. Cliffs are as full of holes as a Gorgonzola cheese.'

'It is, of course, for you to decide, sir, what action is best,' said Mycroft. 'As the senior and most experienced tactician and leader of men – not to mention the position you hold here at Seacombe. . . .'

He cleared his throat, and hoped that exposure to the elements was not bringing on a chill or, worse still, an attack of pneumonia. Given the appalling shocks, strains, and general fatigue imposed on his system over the past few days, he did not suppose he had any strength left to resist the debilitation caused by a fever. It would be ironic, he thought grimly, if Guttmann's monstrous scheme to lay him low with pestilence should be over-taken by death from 'natural causes'.

'. . . But if you would permit me to offer advice . . . ?'

'Yes. Yes, sir! That is why you been sent here, is it not?' Sir Rinaldo replied impatiently.

The three of them sat wearily round the library table.

The rain beat against the casement-windows; in the warmth from the log fire, the steam rose from their damp clothing.

'Brandy and seltzer's the thing,' Sir Rinaldo pronounced.

The decisive way he said it allowed for no disagreement. Not that Mycroft felt the least inclination to refuse the invitation.

'There will be no need of further search parties,' Mycroft said.

Sir Rinaldo had gone to the decanters on the sideboard. He turned round.

'What d'ye say, sir?' he asked, as if he had just been addressed by a more than normally stupid subaltern.

'There are certain factors which have become quite clear to me,' said Mycroft, wishing he had held his peace until his host had poured the drinks. 'Carl Philipp Emmanuel Guttmann is here, on the Isle of Purbeck somewhere. He will not wish to compromise himself by physically harming the Princess – that is not his way, if he can avoid it, and on this occasion it is not in the interests of either himself or his princely master. In all probability, if we act with subtlety and restraint, he will himself lead us to her. He has reason to believe that I am mortally ill, and that any moment now I will start to show the signs. . . .'

He raised his hand to prevent interruption.

'If I am indeed ill, gentlemen, I assure you that it will be the result of a chill caused by exposure to your Dorset weather – and it is possible to take certain immediate steps to prevent any such misfortune.'

He tried to avoid too obvious a glance at the decanters on the sideboard. It was just sufficient, mercifully, to remind Sir Rinaldo of what he was about. Mycroft waited until he had completed the task and had rejoined them at the table before continuing.

'I shall endeavour to create the impression tomorrow that I have indeed taken the contagion he believes he has visited on me,' he continued. 'Gentlemen, I urge you, if you wish all to be well, not to reveal this charade of mine to anybody – anybody at all.'

'Because,' Major Barnaby suggested with unwonted timidity – he had been silent since the discovery that the sealed orders were missing – 'this Guttmann fellow couldn't wesist comin' out of hidin' to watch you in your last agonies, eh, Holmes?'

'You see, Sir Rinaldo?' Mycroft asked. 'Major Barnaby knows the ways of this villain, as I do.'

He reached across the table to put his hand comfortingly on Barnaby's sleeve.

'So don't you go following young Ponsonby's example, eh, old chap? We shall need you. More than that, the Princess will need you.'

Barnaby tried to raise a smile of gratitude.

'I'll tell you this for your comfort,' Mycroft told him; 'C.P.E. Guttmann is not in the least interested in the contents of those orders. I don't suppose the German Kaiser or the Prince von Bismarck is either. What they seek is that our people should find them in the possession of someone they will later take to be a Russian agent – a female posing as a servant. If Guttmann is to succeed in provoking hostilities between ourselves and the Russian Tsar in the same way he succeeded in provoking war between the German allies and France six years ago, the Princess Trubetskoy must be discovered by our people alive and in possession of the orders, preferably attempting to leave our shores. He will, moreover, wait until the last moment before placing the orders in the Princess's possession. It would be best, from his point of view, that she should not know that she *is* in possession of them. After all, it would never do for her to walk into Great Scotland Yard, shall we say, and give them over into the care of the police. In my view, he will put her in possession of the orders as one might prime a bomb – at the last possible moment.'

'Damn it, man! Surely you are not suggesting we do

nothing?' exclaimed Sir Rinaldo. 'With the Admiralty's orders to Sir Fitzroy Parkinson gone missing. . . . To be ready by anybody, don't you know?'

Mycroft smiled. The brandy and seltzer was having its gentle effect.

'Sir Rinaldo,' he said, 'you know better than either of us that you don't go hunting the tiger by creating as great a hoo-hah as if you were putting up pheasants.'

Sir Rinaldo looked sourly into his glass. But he nodded.

'So what *do* you propose we should do?'

'The Dorsetshire constabulary are a sturdy body of men, I daresay.'

'Reliable enough,' Sir Rinaldo replied without enthusiasm. 'But in a matter of this importance. . . .'

He tailed off.

'Unperceptive with regard to finer details?' Mycroft suggested. 'Not entirely capable of creative imaginative leaps where logical progression fail, eh?'

'Don't know what you mean entirely,' Sir Rinaldo replied. 'They're solid countrymen.'

'Quite so,' Mycroft agreed. 'Just the sort we need, don't you know?'

'Eh?' asked Sir Rinaldo.

'Inform the constabulary at Wareham that you've lost some valuables . . . silver? – that's something they'll understand. Give 'em a description of the Princess, tell 'em she's a maid recently arrived from London, that almost certainly she has a male accessory speaking with a slight German accent. . . . And that you have reason to believe they are still here, on the Isle of Purbeck. The point is this, my dear sir. It is just possible Herr Guttmann does not understand the geography of Purbeck. He will know that it is not a true island. He may not have appreciated that it is walled in by Nine Barrow Ridge to the east, and Purbeck Hill to the west, and that there are only two roads off the island – the Studland road, by Ballards Down, and the Wareham road past Corfe Castle: any other way and he will head into the marshes on Middlebeere Heath or Stoborough Heath. Even if he crosses them, there are only three railway stations he can head for – at Wool, East Coke and Wareham. It will be a simple task, even for Dorsetshire policemen, to seal off the district.

'But it is my convinced opinion that he will attempt to leave by sea. This coastline, after all, has always been known as a haunt of piracy and smuggling, and for good reason, as you yourself said: it is riddled with coves, bays, creeks, and as many holes, tunnels and caves as a lump of Gorgonzola. I would not be in the least surprised if Guttmann does not intend to create the idea that the Princess is attempting to be taken off by sea. For this reason, when you send your man with a message to the Wareham police, I would like him, if he is a trustworthy fellow, to send a message for me by telegraph, to Sir James Swarthmoor at the Cabinet Office. If he does so, we will have enough revenue sloops and naval cutters patrolling off shore to ensure that from Lulworth Cove to Old Harry Foreland, a coracle could not set out to sea without being intercepted. What do you say, Sir Rinaldo?'

Sir Rinaldo sighed heavily.

'How do you suppose the papers were removed from Major Barnaby's possession?' he demanded.

Barnaby, who had been showing signs of returning to life, lapsed once more into an expression of deepest misery.

The question had not been one which had bothered Mycroft much.

'If one applies the intellectual method advocated by the great Schoolman whose disciple in philosophy I have come to regard myself,' Mycroft replied; 'I refer, of course, to Occam's Razor – in approaching any problem, particularly deep matters, one cuts away everything that is irrelevant to the actual solution to the problem. The problem in this case, is to frustrate the abominable schemes of one whom one may justly describe as an enemy to everything that is decent, honest, and noble in human society. Fräulein von Holz-zu-Birkensee is a petty creature, who exists as far as we are concerned only as the instrument of the Power which wields her. It may be that she has been spiritually seduced by him – there are many such. It may be that she is in thrall to him because of some hold he has over her – I mean blackmail. But for us, she has no existence apart from him, who placed her here.'

'Placed?' Sir Rinaldo demanded.

'I have known of a case,' Mycroft told him, 'where such a person was in place for as many as five years, gaining the trust and friendship of all about her, before the occasion arose for her to betray them.'

'What a vile thing!' Sir Rinaldo exclaimed. 'I cannot believe . . . !'

'It *is* hard for an Englishman to conceive of,' Mycroft agreed. 'Which is why the Government of this country will not employ such methods. It is not the British way, thank God!'

'Have you evidence, sir?' Sir Rinaldo demanded. 'Evidence which will convince a British jury?'

'Your scepticism does you much credit,' Mycroft returned a soft answer. 'At this present, sir, I do not. But I believe you will find before you leave for Southampton that Chief Inspector Grimes and Sergeant Gregson of Great Scotland Yard will have accumulated just such evidence. . . .'

Major Barnaby was holding his hand up like a school-boy. Mycroft and Sir Rinaldo both turned to him.

'I believe I can tell you the occasion the Fräulein took the papers, gentlemen,' he told them.

Neither Mycroft nor Sir Rinaldo said anything. But they remained silent. Barnaby wriggled uncomfortably in his chair.

'It was the day before yesterday,' he said. 'Lady Hornby had been out walkin' – down to the bay – with the Pwincess in attendance. She told the Pwincess to take her cloak and bonnet up to her closet. I saw the Pwincess

235

on the stairs. I wished to speak to her: I wanted to know how she was gettin' along, don't you know? Playin' her part, and all that. I went into the closet with her, and . . . well. . . .'

He wriggled a bit more.

'We was embwacin', and that sort of thing. First time we'd been pwivately together for – I don't know how many months – years. . . . Oh, deuce take it! Holmes knows how it is between the Pwincess and me! . . . And I'd taken my coat off. . . .'

He stopped and stared miserably first at Sir Rinaldo and then at Mycroft.

'Please continue, Major,' said Mycroft.

'Fräulein von Holz-zu-Birkensee disturbed us,' Barnaby went on. 'Told us Lady Hornby was comin' up . . . . Tewwible situation, don't you see? Only the one way down. The Fräulein took me to her woom to wait till Lady Hornby had gone. Only, I left my jacket behind and the Fräulein said she would fetch it. It had the orders in the pocket, only I was so embarrassed I didn't think of it. She came back with my jacket about a quarter of an hour later. Said Lady Hornby had come up too quickly, and she'd had to thwow it behind the window-seat curtains in the passage. At the time, I felt most awfully gwateful to the Fräulein. . . .'

'I don't suppose Lady Hornby had so much as set foot on the stairs,' Mycroft told him in quiet rebuke.

'That's what the Pwincess said,' Barnaby replied. 'But I thought. . .' He gave a little shrug. '. . . she must have gone up to another room, don't you know? Natural assumption to make and all that wot!'

'Deserve to be cashiered, Major!' Sir Rinaldo declared.

'Can't be helped now,' Mycroft interceded for him. 'Barnaby may still prove a very useful ally.'

'Do my level best, damn it, I will!' Barnaby affirmed wretchedly.

'And not a hint to Fräulein von Holz-zu-Birkensee that anybody suspects anything,' said Mycroft. 'She may be of

more use to us at liberty and off her guard than otherwise
.... Well!' he said, finishing his last drop of brandy and
seltzer. 'Let's go up and have a good night's sleep. I hope
and trust that tomorrow will prove to be an exceedingly
busy day.'

'Let us hope your advice proves sound,' Sir Rinaldo
told him.

' "Tis the sport to have the engineer," ' quoted
Mycroft, ' "hoist with his own petard". . . . There is just
the possibility – no, by God!' He slammed his closed fist
on the table. 'More than a mere possibility – that such
will prove the case with Guttmann!'

Chapter Twenty-One

There was a cold, low sunlight shining on one of the high, bald ridges that reared up on either side of the parkland running down to the sea. The sea itself was visible, from Mycroft's window, as a glittering patch of silver beyond the edge of the park, hemmed in by the high chalk cliffs that marked the end of the ridges. Mycroft was standing in the bow of the window allowing Cyril to straighten the fall of his tie, though he had no great confidence in Cyril's ability at the finer points of a valet's tasks.

'You will accompany me to church this morning,' he told him.

'To church!' Cyril exclaimed. 'I h-ain't been to church since I gone to the Jacob's Wharf mission for my Christmas dinners!'

'I suspected as much, you scoundrel,' Mycroft told him.

' 'Ave a 'eart, Mr 'Olmes!' Cyril pleaded. 'H-us Zulus ain't never been churchgoers – seein' as we ate up all the missionaries too quick for 'em to baptize us, see?'

'You are to come to church with me,' said Mycroft, 'to carry my prayer-book, as is expected of you as my valet.'

'Oh, Mr 'Olmes! Church is wicked borin'!'

'I know. That is why it is good for you. If it were diverting, it would be a self-indulgence, not a spiritual exercise. Apart from that, I may very well need you. I believe we are about to reach the climax and end of our adventure.'

'Shall I bring that stick what you give me yesterday?' Cyril asked.

'As long as you promise faithfully not to use it unless I tell you to.'

'You know you can trust me, Mr 'Olmes!'

'Do I? How much of the household silver have you taken already?'

'Mr 'Olmes! I ain't took nuffink!'

Mycroft went downstairs to breakfast as Fräulein von Holz-zu-Birkensee was herding the twins upstairs.

'You must look very good for church!' she was saying. 'You must not sit down when you have put on your gowns, or you will crease them, and that will never do!'

Being in front of her, the twins were noiselessly imitating her speaking. The effect, thought Mycroft, was that of a pair of demented gophers gnawing at their food.

'Good morning, ladies!' Mycroft said to them as he passed them. '*Gute morgen, Fräulein,*' he said to Fräulein von Holz-zu-Birkinsee.

'Good morning, Mr Holmes,' the twins chorussed, just loud enough to drown their governess's greeting. 'Hope you had a pleasant night,' they added more raggedly, and giggled as if they were eight year olds rather than fifteen or sixteen.

'*Schnell, damen! . . . Schnell!*' the Fräulein shooed them on impatiently.

As he reached the newel-post at the bottom, Mycroft gripped at it. He uttered a deep groan which owed its conviction largely because its author's hearty dislike of amateur theatricals was in conflict with the need he felt to give a dramatic performance while the governess still had time to report it to her true employer. He dredged out his favourite property, his large bandanna handkerchief and, continuing to clutch at the newel-post, mopped his perfectly dry brow with the other. He groaned again. He wondered whether to attempt to give the impression that the strength in his legs was draining away, but decided that it would only cause him to resemble the protagonist of Mrs Leo Hunter's 'Ode to a Suspiring Frog'.

One of the twins came to his rescue.

'Oh, Fräulein!' she called brightly. 'I do believe poor Mr Holmes is not feeling himself.'

'Mr Holmes?' Fräulein von Holz-zu-Birkensee called. 'Mr Holmes?'

Painfully, and with great effort, Mycroft turned to look up at her.

'It is nothing, my dear,' he said with commendable lack of conviction. 'A chill – a slight fever – brought on by exposure to the elements last night.'

He clutched the bandanna to his forehead to conceal the total absence of perspiration or even the merest flush of his complexion. He managed a dry cough.

'Oh dear!' said Fräulein von Holz-zu-Birkensee, making no effort to come down the few stairs to where he was standing.

Then she said, 'Girls, take Mr Holmes's arms and help him to the morning-room sofa while I go to fetch your dear papa.'

For a moment, Mycroft saw straight into her eyes, saw the cruel malevolence in them. The woman was gloating – but not at his imagined fate. She intended that the two young girls should come into close physical contact with him and should catch the pestilence from him.

As if to confirm this belief she said, 'I expect dear Mr Holmes would like you to kiss him better.'

'The fit is passing, my dear Fräulein,' he said, releasing the newel-post.

He gave his brow a final wipe with the bandanna, and sighed deeply.

'My regrets, ladies,' he said. 'Truly, it was nothing.'

'You must take care of yourself, Mr Holmes,' said Fräulein Holz-zu-Birkensee. 'Mustn't he, girls? . . . Quick now, or we *shall* be late!'

Crashaw came to the foot of the stairs. He was holding a silver tray. On it was a large, limp yellow envelope.

'It has been brought by trap from the post office at Wareham, sir,' the butler explained. 'The man is waiting in the kitchens, should you wish to send any reply.'

'Thank you, Crashaw.'

Mycroft took the envelope and tore it open. Major Barnaby came out of the dining-room.

'Sir James?' he asked in a near whisper.

Mycroft nodded.

'Would you be good enough to wait just a moment, Crashaw?' he asked.

He went with Barnaby into the dining-room. Sir Rinaldo was sitting there. Mycroft held up the envelope.

'Close the door, Barnaby,' he said. 'There's a good fellow.'

He sat down at the table, next to Sir Rinaldo. He tore open the envelope and drew out the flimsy enclosure, spreading it over the place before him. Sir Rinaldo rose.

'May I help you to some kedgeree, Holmes?' he asked. 'Kedgeree and some scrambled egg?'

Mycroft raised a flipper-like hand.

'One moment, I beg you!' he said abruptly, concentrating on what was before him.

Sir Rinaldo sat down again, none too pleased, and waited. A few moments later, Mycroft looked up.

'It is,' he said. 'exactly as I thought.'

He glanced across to Major Barnaby and then to Sir Rinaldo. Disregarding their looks of enquiry, he rose heavily from the table.

'Pray indulge me for a further minute or two,' he asked. 'There is paper and a pencil in the library?'

'Of course,' growled Sir Rinaldo.

'Obliged,' said Mycroft. 'I will join you again in a minute or two.'

He returned in five or six minutes, rubbing his plump hands together, and apparently oblivious of the chill emanating from Sir Rinaldo.

'Kedgeree and scrambled egg!' he exclaimed, resuming his seat. 'Most satisfactory!'

Sir Rinaldo gave him a glance which would have reduced a Royal Marine adjutant to incontinence, but he got up from the table just the same.

'And a couple of slices of that handsome cold ham, if you would be so kind, Sir Rinaldo!'

Mycroft hoped that Sir Rinaldo was capable of the imaginative leap from 'a couple of slices' to four or five. To Major Barnaby, he confided, 'Not a symptom – not a hint of a cold. A miracle, eh? after that wetting last night!'

He watched Sir Rinaldo carve three slices from the ham – a compromise between irritation and the demands of hospitality.

'As you will have observed,' he remarked, 'this morning, I received a telegram from Sir James Swarthmoor. I took the opportunity of the presence here of the telegraph boy to send off a brief report and request that a watch should be set over the appropriate harbours with their railway stations between here and London, over the Waterloo Street terminus, and that the offshore waters between Poole and Portland Bill should be closely patrolled both by day and night.'

'You are very certain of the trustworthiness of the telegraph boy!' Sir Rinaldo remarked.

'My experience of servants of the General Post Office,' Mycroft replied, thinking of the excellent Mr Turner, 'leads me to believe that they are an admirably trustworthy body of men. In any case, I wrote my instructions to Sir James in Latin – the Latin of Boethius rather than that of Cicero, more obscure to the generality, don't you know? – So I think it improbable the honest fellow will make much of it. Particularly since his honesty is proofed in gold – the gold sovereign I bestowed on him with my admonition that he should see my message despatched with all speed.'

Sir Rinaldo's chill began to dissolve.

'You are a man of admirable decisiveness, Holmes,' he said, carving a fourth slice of ham and placing it on Mycroft's plate.

'I'm sure you have just described yourself, sir, to perfection,' Mycroft replied.

Sir Rinaldo thawed completely. Passing the filled plate to Mycroft, he remarked, 'Kind of you, sir. Very.'

As he loaded his fork with ham, covering it with scrambled egg, Mycroft remarked, 'You wish to know what it is the Cabinet Secretary wished to communicate to me, I daresay.'

He stuffed the forkful into his mouth. Without waiting to demolish it completely, he continued, 'It was despatched by Sir James Swarthmoor, of course. But the information is provided by the worthy Sergeant Gregson of the Detective Police at Great Scotland Yard.'

He paused to chew.

'Let's hear what he has to say!' Sir Rinaldo urged.

'Very well. Gregson went into Staffordshire for the express purpose of interviewing Fräulein von Hotz-zu-Birkensee's future employer – the Vicar of St James-the-Less at Wetwood. His purpose was to discover how the good vicar came to have the Fräulein recommended to him.'

There was another brief interval, as he attacked the kedgeree.

'Excellent!' he exclaimed. 'Beyond praise! Your military duties have taken you to India, I dare to suggest, Sir Rinaldo.'

'You are perfectly correct, my dear Holmes.'

Mycroft pointed his fork in the direction of the still-crestfallen Major Barnaby.

'Let me tell you, Barnaby. The only households where you may enjoy kedgeree perfectly prepared are those of old India hands, eh Sir Rinaldo?'

He scooped up another forkful, then dabbed at his lips with his napkin.

'It will surprise nobody who is aware of the system I apply on these occasions, that the results of Gregson's enquiry are exactly as I supposed they would be. On the day the reverend gentleman and his daughter attended at Wellbody's offices in Margaret Street, they found there was present with Mr Partick, the senior manager and

243

executive director of the firm, another clerical gentleman, a minister of the German Moravian Church – a Pastor Gustav-August von Holz. When Pastor Gustav-August, as he prefers to be known, heard what were the Vicar of Wetwood's particular requirements of a governess, he pointed out that he had a niece, an excellent young lady of *junker* antecedents, tragically widowed in the late unpleasantness between France and Prussia. This niece was governess in the household of Colonel Sir Rinaldo Hornby, Royal Marines, but, by happy chance, was seeking another position almost immediately. She was, moreover, perfectly qualified to accompany a girl such as the vicar's daughter, on a tour abroad. The business was arranged to everybody's satisfaction, and when it had been concluded, by another happy accident, Pastor Gustav-August was able to give the vicar and his daughter a lift in his own conveyance to Euston Square. He turned to them. 'There you have it. As for the rest, it is clear that he had had my movements shadowed for the past several days. It was a simple matter to calculate the train I must take, and then to lead them to the very carriage in which I was travelling. Almost *too* simple for this diabolical Pastor.'

He finished the food on his plate, and embarked on toast and marmalade.

'I met C.P.E. Guttmann in the role of Pastor, the other night,' he observed. 'On Westminster Bridge. Like any strolling player, he had to display himself to me – he needs his audience. There is no need to flush him out. He will soon make another appearance. What will it be this time, I wonder?'

He thrust the piece of toast into his mouth. With a total disregard for table manners, he continued with his mouth full,

'A Dutch sea-captain put into Brownsea perhaps? . . . No! I have it! A physician! A fever-doctor fortunately visiting in the vicinity of Worth Matravers and Corfe Castle just in time to attend me in my final illness.'

He swallowed his food, shrugged his shoulders, and said, 'He has to make his appearance very soon. He knows he has only forty-eight hours before you, Sir Rinaldo, and Lady Hornby depart from these shores.'

When they had finished breakfast and had retired to their chambers to make their final preparations, they all gathered once more for the short journey up to Worth Matravers, and St Nicholas' Church. On the carriage-drive in front of the house the servants were piling into two wagonettes. Fräulein von Holz-zu-Birkensee and the twins had already climbed on board the brougham. One of the grooms was assisting Lady Hornby to mount the step. Sir Rinaldo, Major Barnaby, and Mycroft with Cyril in attendance, were all standing under the portico. It had been decided that Sir Rinaldo, with Major Barnaby, should accompany the brougham in the saddle, and that Mycroft should ride inside with the family. This had met with whispered but quite audible objections from the twins, who clearly regarded the Major as the more amusing – or persecutable – travelling companion.

'There's just one thing has occurred to me. . . .'

Barnaby gave Mycroft a very uneasy glance.

'Yes?' Mycroft asked. 'What is it?'

'Yes, man!' Sir Rinaldo butted in. 'Speak if you're going to, damn it!'

'Supposin' . . . I mean to say, I don't know if this is damn' stupid. . . . But just supposin' Guttmann thinks he's in a bit of a tight spot, don't you know? And he decides to use the Pwincess as a hostage – you know? Thweatens to cut off her ears . . . or kill her . . . that sort of thing. . . .'

There was a silence almost as awkward as Barnaby's manner.

'I'd thought of that,' Mycroft lied solemnly. 'Didn't want to discuss it for the very good reason that there is only one line of action any of us could take in the circumstances – as patriotic Englishmen!'

He looked at the others.

'The way of Regulus,' he said. 'To put Queen and Country before any other consideration.

'Yer!' said Cyril unexpectedly. 'But Regulus went an' got *isself* killed, didn't 'e? I mean, 'e didn't just sit an' let a lady-friend get killed for 'im, did 'e?'

'What do you know about the history of the Punic Wars?' Mycroft demanded.

'Nuffink,' said Cyril. 'Never 'eard of 'em.'

'Well then! Hold your tongue!'

'It's true though, ain't it?' Cyril muttered angrily.

The carriages parked round the rain-sodden, mud-patched area of grass and duckpond which passed for the village green in the tiny village of Worth Matravers. The cluster of thick-walled grey stone cottages around the green was dominated by three buildings: St Nicholas' Parish Church and the parsonage, both of which were sheltered among ancient trees, and the *Square and Compass* inn which stood alone, some little distance away, surrounded by a hedge.

A straggling procession of villagers together with families from nearby farms on the Seacombe estate was making its way up the village and under the church-yard lych-gate under the bare, forked branches of the trees. The household servants, dismounting from the wagonettes, mingled with them, greeting members of their families who lived in the parish. Without waiting for the rest of the family, the twins jumped down from the brougham and, followed by Fräulein von Holz-zu-Birkensee, ran up the churchyard path and into the church porch. Sir Rinaldo, who was still in the saddle, shouted after them, 'Watch your manners, girls!'

But they took no heed of him whatsoever. He jumped down, and went to the carriage where Mycroft was assisting Lady Hornby down on to the road.

The sexton of St Nicholas was waiting for Sir Rinaldo, standing under the lych-gate roof, a worried expression on his face.

'Beggin' your pardon, Colonel, sir,' he said, touching his forehead with his finger crooked. 'But Parson's been called away to Salisbury.'

'To Salisbury?' exclaimed Sir Rinaldo. 'Whatever for? Why didn't he tell us at the house, eh?'

Lady Hornby was on her husband's arm. She turned to Mycroft.

'The living is in Sir Rinaldo's gift, you know,' she lisped in her childish voice 'As it was in my father's before I was married.'

'Summons from the Bishop, sir,' the sexton was saying. 'Summat about a complaint, I did hear. Summat about Court of Arches or some such – I doan't rightly know, sir, but 'twas the sound on it. Mrs Sabine gone with him. They say as a messenger come last night from Blandford.'

'Without my being informed?' said Sir Rinaldo.

'Summons was most urgent, they do say, sir,' replied the sexton. 'Like 'twas summat to do wi' the law, an' tha-at.'

'Who,' asked Mycroft, 'has the cure of souls in the parish now?'

'Ah! You mean while Parson Sabine's gone, do 'ee, sir?' asked the sexton. 'Why it be the parson as has been staying wi' Parson Sabine, these past three days. Foreign gentleman, Parson August his name be. You knows 'im doan't 'ee, Colonel, sir? Says as he's own uncle to the young lady as looks after Miss Arabella and Miss Henrietta-Louise. . . .'

'By God!' Sir Rinaldo threatened to explode.

'What's the matter, dear?' Lady Hornby enquired.

They had been joined by Major Barnaby.

'He's a damn' cool customer,' he said. 'You have to allow him that!'

'We must do nothing rash,' said Mycroft.

'Does this "Parson" August fellow intend taking the service this morning?' Sir Rinaldo demanded of the sexton.

'Bain't be nobody else, sir,' the sexton replied. 'Not

unless we sends over to Kingston, to Reverend Allberry, or to Langton, to Canon Stockbridge.'

'Whatever is the matter, dear?' Lady Hornby asked again. 'It's a pity we can't have *dear* Mr Sabine. But we can have a pleasant little service, whoever takes it. And the servants do so appreciate it!'

'My dear!' said Sir Rinaldo, 'You have not the foggiest idea what you are talking about!'

'No, dear,' Lady Hornby agreed.

'Let him take the service, Sir Rinaldo,' Mycroft urged. 'Let us do nothing to suggest there is anything out of the ordinary, hard though it may be. Remember, Guttmann does not yet know we have discovered the loss of the documents. We need him to lead us both to them and to the Princess. I beg you, sir. Be advised by me.'

'Very good, Holmes,' Sir Rinaldo told him. 'Until now, you have shown you know what you are up to—'

He broke off. Obviously, thought Mycroft, his soldierly instinct rebelled against circumspection of this kind. With Major Barnaby, he followed him and Lady Hornby into the church.

The walls of the narrow nave, between the tall lancet windows, were whitewashed, so that they shed a pallid light in the November gloom. They were broken by brass plates and plaster hatchments commemorating members of the Weston family into which Sir Rinaldo Hornby had married in order to acquire Seacombe House and its lands. At the east end of the nave, an uneven chancel step under a rudimentarily carved stone archway led to a crooked, half-timbered chancel. Most of the pews were filled with villagers; many of the men in clean smocks, the younger women in white muslin under their heavy worsted coats. They rose to their feet as they saw Sir Rinaldo and Lady Hornby coming in through the south door.

The twins, under the supervision of Fräulein von Holz-zu-Birkensee, were handing out hymn books. The Fräulein in person held one out to Mycroft; he shook his head, indicating that Cyril, immediately behind him was carrying his prayer-book, which included *Hymns Ancient and Modern.*

'But Mr Holmes! The girls and I have been keeping this one especially for you!' the Fräulein said, with a heavy Teutonic winsomeness. 'Haven't we, girls?'

'No, we haven't!' said Henrietta-Louise.

'Nobody said anything about it to me!' said Arabella. 'Not that that's surprising.'

Mycroft took the worn hardboard-bound hymnal. As he went with Major Barnaby to take his place in the second pew, behind that of Sir Rinaldo and Lady Hornby, he noticed the sheet of sickly lavender-coloured paper folded in it. He squeezed into the pew, then heaved himself on to his knees, following the example of his host in front of him. Hassocks, together with the width of pews, were designed peculiarly by the Established Church to ensure that its members remained in wakeful discomfort when they were in the act of praying. The rest of the congregation followed the example of their betters. He was aware, however, that Cyril behind him had remained in a mutinously sitting position.

He drew out the paper and unfolded it.

> My dear Holmes, he read: I hope you appreciate the finer feelings I displayed in effecting a meeting between yourself and your talented young brother before you are, as some of your compatriots like to put it, 'raised to Glory'. You will be pleased to know that your dear friend, Princess Trubetskoy, is under my protection, and is entirely safe so long as you pass from this 'Vale of Tears' (what a treasury of euphemisms you English employ to mask the reality of Death!) with tactful quietness and dignity – particularly quietness, since Death (let us call it by its own grim name) is, alas, rarely attended with dignity.

I am sure a sensible and intelligent fellow such as yourself will comprehend perfectly what I mean.

Yours, till we meet in a better place,
Carl P.E. Guttmann.

Even as he was reading, the congregation rose once more to its feet. He passed the lavender-coloured note to Major Barnaby beside him. He heard the hiss of Barnaby's intake of breath. The organ at the back of the church sounded, somewhat insecurely as if the boy operating the bellows had not quite got into his stride, the first phrase of the opening hymn. The congregation took up the familiar melody in hearty voice, with happy disregard for the meaning of the words:

> God of our life, to Thee we call,
> Afflicted at thy feet we fall;
> When the great water-floods prevail,
> Leave not our trembling hearts to fail. . . .

Fräulein von Holz-zu-Birkensee came hurrying up the aisle with her two charges, and bustled them into their parents' pew. As she took her place beside them, she glanced a singularly cruel and knowing smile at Mycroft, turning her face away so quickly that he was left with the feeling that his mind might be playing tricks on him.

Through a side-door into the tiny transept on the opposite side of the nave, a small figure entered and took her place on an upright chair just below the narrow choir stalls. She wore a hodden grey cape over her coarse, striped housemaid's gown and starched white apron. Her hood was thrown back to show her long straw-yellow hair falling gleaming over her shoulders from under her white linen mob, in a manner forbidden to any lower servant from a decently-managed household. Her forget-me-not blue eyes met Mycroft's, and she too smiled. It was the girl he had noticed at the ticket gate on Euston Station; it was Abigail Rodgers alias Maddy Orchard –

five years older than when she had been Guttmann's child-ally and worshipper at Ranmore, overlooking Dorking Gap. Now she was a beautiful young woman, there was no gainsaying it; a murderously beautiful young woman. He wondered how many more of Guttmann's acolytes were seated in the congregation around them.

> Great God of our salvation, Thee . . . bawled
>   the congregation;
> We love, we worship, we adore;
> Our refuge on time's changeful sea,
> Our joy on Heaven's eternal shore.

The sexton entered first from the vestry, in a crumpled surplice, with a black wand surmounted by a small, silver cross in his gnarled and horny hand. After him and towering over him, came a huge and impressive figure creaking in a stiffly starched surplice topped with the white, furred hood of an Oxford Master of Arts. The stubble of cropped, blond hair above the absorbed, prayerful expression on the face, presented a curious effect of power. There were surely members of the congregation who took him for a bishop at the very least – and a bishop of quite monstrous authority.

He turned on the chancel step to face the congregation. As he waited for the loud, ragged, 'Amen!' which concluded the hymn, to die away, he stared impassively with his dreadful, vacant, watery eyes, at the west window beyond the dangling bell-ropes. Mycroft had expected a glance in his direction: of leering triumph, of amusement, of conspiracy, or even merely to establish his presence. None came; it was as if Guttmann were subsumed into his role as Parson Sabine's *locum tenens*.

Guttmann raised a white-surpliced arm. In faultless but German-accented English, he pronounced, 'In the name of the Father, the Son and the Holy Ghost. Amen.'

251

The congregation sat down. Out of the corner of his eye, Mycroft was aware of the maid, Abigail Rodgers, sitting staring at her master with a look of mesmerized adoration. Nothing had changed in that direction, he decided, since those summer days at Dorking Gap. How many times would Guttmann have to betray her, to leave her to her fate, before she realized the monstrosity of the evil which had seduced her? Or was that what was meant by the damnation of a human soul – the loss of any ability to eschew evil, even when that evil caused hurt to yourself as well as to others?

'Dearly beloved brethren,' the Guttmann-pastor intoned. 'As you may have heard, your father in God, Mr Sabine, has been called quite suddenly to Salisbury, to attend your Bishop. Before he left with Mrs Sabine, he asked me if I would stand in his place this morning, to lead and preside over your prayers for the safety of your good squire, Colonel Sir Rinaldo Hornby, and for Lady Hornby, before they set out on their voyage to what may become – dear God, forbid! – a seat of war. . . .'

There was a rustle of surprise through the congregation. The capital might be afflicted with war-fever, but it had not yet affected the honest yeomanry of East Dorset. Guttmann was determined to spread that infection, thought Mycroft, like any other.

'Permanence,' Guttmann pronounced, 'is the symbol amongst those of us who have not yet shaken off our raiment of flesh for the garments of Immortality, of Eternity. . . .'

He was looking at nobody, Mycroft noticed – as if he were blind with self absorption, like Lucifer in the Ninth Circle of Dante's envisaged Hell:

> . . . If he were beautiful
> As he is hideous now, and yet did dare
> To scowl upon his Maker, well from him
> May all our misery flow.

*

'And Permanence,' Guttmann was continuing in his strange, sing-song intonation, 'is what is so admirably expressed in those lovely words of your English hymn,

> God bless the squire and his relations,
> And keep us in our proper stations.

But Holy Scriptures also tell us, *Here is no abiding city*; we must accept that there will be partings, and there will be bereavements. In a word, we must accept that your beloved squire, like those of my own dear homeland, may be taken from you to do his duty towards his sovereign as a soldier – and perhaps to fall and suffer painful death in the performance of that duty. . . .'

'Damn it, sir . . . !' Sir Rinaldo's voice rang through the church.

Mycroft had noticed the whitening of Sir Rinaldo's knuckles as he gripped the front of the pew. He had noticed also the unhappy bewilderment on the face of Lady Hornby at the Guttmann-pastor's extraordinary performance. But stronger then either of these was his realization of the pleasurable satisfaction in his role that Guttmann was enjoying behind the appalling vacancy of his eyes.

Sir Rinaldo had to be stopped. At this juncture, nothing must prevent Guttmann from continuing his charade. Mycroft rose to his feet. He uttered what he hoped would be a dreadful cry of physical distress. In fact, he realized, it sounded more like the honking of a performing seal at the sight of a fresh herring. It was sufficient, however, to cause both Sir Rinaldo and Lady Hornby to turn round. He pulled himself to his feet, dragged out a large red pocket handkerchief and dabbed at his forehead as he squeezed himself out of the pew on to the aisle. Then, with what he hoped sounded like a suspiring groan, he pitched himself forward to fall prostrate on to the ground. Around him, he heard the gratifying clatter of footsteps on pew gratings, and gasps of astonishment and concern. Opening his eyes without lifting his head, he saw the lace edge of a surplice only inches from him. He raised his arm weakly. In a desperate voice, he cried out, 'Get back, all of you! Typhus! In God's name, get back!'

He heard the footsteps retreating a short distance around him. He heard Fräulein von Holz-zu-Birkensee ordering the twins to keep their distance. He croaked out a second time, 'Typhus! Beware!'

To his dismay he heard one of the twins – he thought it was Henrietta-Louise – say, 'He's pretending – just like you do, Arabella. Only he ain't half as good at it as you!'

Then he heard Sir Rinaldo say, 'How dare you, young lady! Just you wait till we are back at the house!'

And then, further away, the Fräulein adding, 'And you know very well you do not say "ain't" but "is not", you wicked thing!'

The surplice and the polished boots below it had not moved. For a moment Mycroft wondered if Guttmann was of the same opinion as Henrietta-Louise. He pretended to have fallen into a swoon. The voice of Guttmann, close to his ear, murmured comfortingly.

'I shall pray for you, Mr Holmes. We shall all be praying for you.' The voice moved even closer so that Mycroft thought he could feel the bristled lips brushing his ear. 'And I am sure little Abigail will add her prayers to mine,' it whispered soothingly.

Chapter Twenty-Two

Major Barnaby and Cyril assisted Mycroft to his feet. As he leaned on them with virtually his entire weight, he saw through half-closed eyes Sir Rinaldo approaching him to assist them in their unequal task.

'No!' he croaked out. 'You have your duty to Her Majesty to consider!'

And he made a tolerable pretence of trying to wave him away with a hand too weak to accomplish such a task.

He noticed that Guttmann was also maintaining his role. Still wearing his surplice and Oxford academicals, he went before the brave little cortège who were assisting Mycroft back to the Hornby's family brougham, clearing the crowd of yokels who were clustered, gawping, in the porch and down the churchyard path.

'Colonel!' Mycroft called softly.

Sir Rinaldo bent down.

'Do nothing to let the fellow know you have found him out!' Mycroft whispered. 'I implore you!'

'If you say so, sir!' Sir Rinaldo agreed grudgingly.

'It is of the gravest importance!' Mycroft appealed to him.

He gave it the authentic ring of a dying man's final instruction. The pretence of being ill was extraordinarily close to the reality, he was discovering; he wondered if there was a valetudinarian lurking in everybody's psyche.

Cyril was gasping with the effort of supporting him.

' 'Ere!' he whispered. 'Can't yer take some of the blessed weight on your own feet?'

Guttmann himself opened the carriage door and lowered the step. Cyril and Major Barnaby heaved

Mycroft up into the carriage. Mycroft tumbled face forward on to the cushions. Cyril climbed in, ostensibly to make him comfortable.

'Is our friend still there?' Mycroft whispered.

As if to answer his question, Guttmann said loudly, 'You have only to send for me, when he has need of spiritual comfort. I shall remain in the parsonage to await your call.'

Mycroft felt the carriage rock to and fro. For a moment, he was afraid Guttmann had climbed in behind him. Then he heard Major Barnaby say, 'It's all right now, old chap. He's going back up to the church.'

He heaved himself round to look at his companions, without sitting up. The door was still open. Sir Rinaldo was framed in it, standing on the step.

'Listen to me carefully,' Mycroft said. 'Carry out my instructions to the letter. Sir Rinaldo, is *your* fellow a man you'd take on a tiger-hunt?'

'Whitlock?' Sir Rinaldo asked. 'I'd trust him as my loader anywhere.'

'Very well,' Mycroft continued. 'I want you to place him under the Major's command. . . . Barnaby? Bring your mount a little way out of the village, and then return here on foot with Marine Whitlock – do you understand?'

'Yes, Holmes.'

'You will take up a place of concealment so that you may watch anyone's movement in or out of the parsonage – you understand?'

'Yes, Holmes.'

'Should Guttmann leave, or that creature, Abigail Rodgers, you are to follow them to find out where they go. You will leave the marine to watch in your place. The parsonage must be watched the entire time, do you understand?'

'What about me, then?' demanded Cyril.

'Be quiet,' Mycroft told him. 'We have no time to lose . . . . Whether you find yourself following Guttmann or the girl Abigail, Barnaby, you may be sure of one thing: they will be tolerably certain they *are* being followed. At best they'll try to lead you off the scent. At worst, they'll try to lure you to some form of destruction – on to a cliff-top that is crumbling into the sea, or up to the top of a broken staircase, something of that sort. So take the greatest of care, and remember that they are both as cunning as serpents. The aim must be to discover where they are holding the Princess – or, if they have her in the parsonage, which I very much doubt, where they will take her in order to incriminate her.'

'By Gad, sir!' said Sir Rinaldo, 'You are a loss to Her Majesty's armed forces, I don't care who knows it!'

'Not C.P.E. Guttmann, if you please, Colonel,' Mycroft replied. 'But I am flattered, sir, I assure you. And now, perhaps, you had best take me back to Seacombe, where Cyril here will attend me on my death-bed. . . . And Barnaby? You will receive no further instructions from me except by Cyril's hand, is that clear? . . . Now, if you get down, and Guttmann is still watching us, I suggest that the shedding of a manly tear or two might be appropriate – not to say affecting.'

Major Barnaby and Marine Whitlock took it in turns to watch. They lay on tarpaulin capes above the parsonage. Meadows and heath stretched several miles to the cliff-tops of St Aldhelm's Point where stood the ancient sailors' chapel and a cluster of low, single-storey coastguards' cottages. From the concealment of bracken-covered hill-ocks, and with the aid of a spyglass lent to them by Sir Rinaldo, they could observe both front and back of the house, the path between the church and the lych-gate, and the path to the rear of the church which led to a stile over the churchyard wall and the public way across the fields, over the downland ridge to the neighbouring village of Kingston.

Barnaby envied Marine Whitlock. Scarcely had the

latter taken up his post when he produced a stained clay pipe and asked permission to take tobacco.

'I hopes as you don't find the odour of "Ship's" offensive, sir,' he said politely.

'Of course not, my good fellow,' Barnaby told him. 'Smoke away – as long as you don't give away our position, eh?'

'Obliged to 'ee, sir.' And the raw air was filled with the comfortable aroma of freshly-lit tobacco.

There was no reason why Barnaby should not have taken out one of his cheroots and lit one, except that, somehow, smoking would have seemed an indecent self-indulgence given his desperate anxiety and sense of remorse regarding the possible fate of the Princess.

It was almost two o'clock in the afternoon, and they had been there since noon – Barnaby had begun to wonder what they should do when the light failed, as it would in two or three hours' time – when Marine Whitlock beckoned to him.

'Begging your pardon, sir!'

He held out the spyglass to him.

'There, sir!'

Following the direction in which the man was pointing, Barnaby focused the glass. He saw, in the clearest definition, Abigail Rodgers crossing the churchyard to the stile. She was wearing the hood of her grey cape up over her head, covering her long yellow hair, and was carrying a thick bundle, of clothes perhaps, or blankets, under the cape. But, as she mounted the stile, there was no mistaking her for anyone else. He watched fascinated, and was glad that Marine Whitlock could not know what he was seeing, as she lifted her apron and gown and displayed her black-stockinged calves under the white flounce of her petticoat, to bestride the top rail of the stile. As she did so, she turned to look about her. For a single moment, in the magnification of the glass, her eyes seemed to meet his; but there was no sunlight – it was impossible that she should have detected him.

'She's grown into a deuce pwetty gel, deuce take her!' he exclaimed.

The thought struck him that, once again, he had proved what a weak cavalier of Princess Sophie's he was. He wished he could have swallowed back his words.

'The foreign gentleman's maid, would that be, sir?' asked Marine Whitlock.

'It is,' Barnaby replied. 'First clapped eyes on her when she was a child. She was wicked as Satan then, and she's wickeder now, I'll be bound! . . . Here!'

He hoped the little speech redeemed himself in his loyalty to his mistress. He handed back the spyglass.

'I must see what villainy she's up to. I'll have to leave the foreign gentleman to you, my dear fellow. I'll be back as soon as I can.'

He picked up his cape and threw it over his shoulders. He made his way as fast as he could across the rough meadow-land, taking a direction parallel to that taken by the girl. There was little enough cover on the windswept heath stretching towards the cliffs. As he approached her more nearly, following the seaward path she was taking, he was forced to adopt a semi-crouching position, and to hug the hedgerows. She came to a halt now and then in order to move her bundle from under one arm to under the other. When she did so, she would look all about her as if to see if she were overlooked. Once or twice he was afraid she might have caught sight of him, and remembered what Mycroft had told him about how she, or Guttmann, would know they were being followed. The idea embarrassed him.

She began to descend the slope of the heath where a steep, narrow valley path led down from Worth Matravers to the old, abandoned quarry workings on the cliff shelves, known as Winspit. As she did so, it became easier for him to follow her without exposing himself to view. The steeper the path, the more it twisted and turned. Huge fallen rocks provided cover, and the singularity and confined nature of the path meant that the girl could only go the one way.

Cautiously, he rounded the corner where the quarry

shelf overlooked the sea. There was a harsh, blustering wind, and the great breakers smashed against the lower cliff wall, hurling their white crests splashing and foaming, to ebb off the shelf floor before the next breaker struck. Clutching at an edge of rock, he watched as the girl picked her way along the shelf between the broken rocks, holding a course as close to the wall of the upper cliff as she could. There were broken buildings on the shelf, with roofs open to the grey, ragged sky: tool-sheds, stables for truck-drawing ponies, and quarrymen's huts; the sea-spume ebbed and flowed between them, leaving a wrack of seaweed and timber fragments behind. At the furthest point of the shelf stood a tower four or five stories high, the ruin of a chute for stonebreaking. Approaching it, the girl stood for a moment, clutching her bundle under her arm, her back against the overhanging upper cliff wall. A wave crashed against the lower cliff, washing to the toes of her boots. She looked round in Barnaby's direction, and he dodged back behind the ragged stone corner, hoping that he had been quick enough to have avoided her catching sight of him. Looking round again, he saw her running, as the sea-water poured back over the edge of the shelf, to climb the steps to the tower door and to disappear inside it.

He waited for several minutes, but she did not reappear. After some five minutes, he began to wonder whether there was a way out concealed from his view, leading perhaps to one of the many caves which penetrated the undercliff, through which she might return unobserved into the valley behind him. But the thought which finally drove him to break his cover and to make his way along the broken, sea-washed undercliff, was of Princess Sophie at the mercy of Abigail Rodgers.

There was no possibility of reaching the tower concealed from the view of somebody looking out from it. He could only pray that the maid was too occupied inside to keep watch over the approach to it. Like her, he waited for the breakers to ebb back across the floor of the shelf before running as far as he could, then hugged the wall of the cliff as another wave broke, drenching him to the skin, then ran on again. He reached the broken steps leading up to the tower door as a great wave broke. He dived behind them, but the crest of the wave struck his face across the step, leaving him gasping for breath and stung by the coldness of the salt water. He ran up the steps as fast as his water-filled boots would let him, and in through the broken doorway. The base of the tower was filled with mounds of stones and gravel – the relics of the final days of work at the quarry. A series of flights of wooden stairs from wooden platform to wooden platform led up to a closed door in the wall at the top of the tower, under the wooden roof. From a great beam supporting the roof-timbers was suspended the remains of the winch by which the crushed stone was raised to be sent down the chute at the top.

Barnaby mounted the stairs cautiously. He recalled Mycroft's warning that whomsoever he followed would be bound to know they were being followed, and would attempt to lead him to his own destruction. On the other hand, since he had not seen Abigail Rodgers leave, there was the strong possibility that she, and even the Princess, were behind the door at the top. The stairs seemed sturdy enough despite a few years of neglect; there was only a certain looseness of the treads causing them to wobble slightly underfoot. He reached the top. He was a tall man, and the wooden ceiling was low so that he had to stoop. He felt the icy salt breath of the sea sharp about his face where it was blowing in round the door in the wall. It was enough to warn him. He lifted the latch and pushed it open without stepping forward. What he found did not surprise him. The small platform-room which should have been at the head of the chute was gone with the chute itself. Far below him on the sea-swept rock shelf of the undercliff lay the rubble of the broken floor and walls. Abigail Rodgers and her master had intended he should fall on to it, to lie there until the

261

seabirds and the high tide had finished with what remained of him.

He clutched at the broken architrave of the door as the bitter wind buffetted him, and chilled his damp clothing. Looking back along the undercliff, over the broken roofs the quarry buildings, he saw her, still clutching the bundle under the cape which the wind was billowing about her, dodging the waves, and making her way back to the shelter of the valley path up to the village as fast as wind and sea would permit. Leaving the wind to batter the door against the outside wall of the tower, he ran down the stairs in pursuit, anxious not to lose sight of her. About halfway down, at a turn of the stairs, he saw the gaping abyss where three or four of the loosened treads had been removed since he had climbed to the top. There was no stopping his career. He tried to clutch at the rail, but his hand slipped, and he plunged between the remaining treads to fall twenty or thirty feet on to the sharp points of crushed stone below.

As he lay there only half-conscious of the blood soaking his forehead and dribbling down the side of his nose, and of the driving pain in his chest and side, the worst thing he experienced was the sense of his own miserable ineptitude and failure in trying to rescue his beloved Princess.

Chapter Twenty-Three

Mycroft decided that there was no pleasanter way of dying – unless, of course, it was to be assumed into a Better Place directly from the smoking-room of the Diogenes Club one Sunday afternoon after a good lunch. He was lying on his bed wrapped in his silk dressing-gown, propped up on the pillows, with one of Colonel Sir Rinaldo's *Romeo y Juliettas* in his left hand, leaving his right hand free to reach for his glass of brandy and seltzer.

I saw Eternitie the other nyght. . . .

Perhaps to lie on a comfortable four-poster, in one's dressing-gown, in the smoking-room of the Diogenes, would be the Ultimate Consummation. And having achieved the Empyrean, one wouldn't have to concern oneself with one's natural functions.

Mycroft had an ingrained fastidiousness, or perhaps it was a form of North-Country puritanism, which made the thought of performing into a chamber-pot during daylight hours indicative of the collapse of civilization. For that reason, he was compelled to leave his host's cigar to extinguish itself in the bedside ashtray, to desert his half-filled, swollen glass goblet on the table, and cautiously to let himself out on to the passage. Cyril was sitting there, kicking his heels bad-temperedly; *en route*, Mycroft sent him to find out from the Colonel whether there was any news from Major Barnaby or Marine Whitlock.

Mycroft returned a few minutes later to find the bed-room door he had left ajar, now shut. He wondered whether to await Cyril's return, but curiosity overcame his apprehensions. He opened it cautiously and stepped half-inside. To his surprise and somewhat to his relief, he found that Arabella and Henrietta-Louise had installed themselves in the window seat opposite the foot of the bed. They were wearing their outdoor, knitted tam o' shanters and, unbuttoned, their long, full promenade coats. Arabella was holding in her lap a paper poke containing sweet biscuits. Henrietta had a stone jar of damson jam. They were dipping the biscuits in the jam before eating them. There was a certain amount of jam around their mouths.

'Has Fräulein von Holz-zu-Birkensee never instructed you that young ladies do not enter gentlemen's bedrooms?' he asked.

Henrietta-Louise glanced at Arabella. Arabella crammed a jam-covered biscuit into her mouth, thus depriving herself of the power of speech. She shrugged dismissively instead. Henrietta-Louise gave a tolerable imitation of somebody struggling to remember something.

'She told us we should never accept an *invitation* into a gentleman's bedroom,' she said finally. 'But you didn't invite us.'

'It is quite as bad to come in uninvited,' Mycroft told them. 'It can lead to the gravest misunderstandings.'

They both stared at him. They did not, of course, understand what he meant.

'Why did you come here?' he asked.

Arabella swallowed the remains of her biscuit.

'So as we wouldn't be found out,' she said.

'So that Fräulein wouldn't be able to catch us,' said Henrietta-Louise.

'She'd never come into a gentleman's bedroom,' explained Arabella.

'Fräulein says that forty years ago you could be hanged for stealing biscuits!' said Henrietta-Louise, without displaying much concern.

'*And* jam!' suggested Arabella.

She stabbed half a biscuit into the jam jar, then ate it.

'And if I were to call for her to come and remove you?' Mycroft asked.

'You won't!' said Arabella. 'Because you don't want her to know you're only pretending to be ill, do you?'

'*We* know you're pretending because *we* do it all the time, and Fräulein has to believe us,' said Henrietta-Louise. 'Monthly sickness, you know.'

'No, he doesn't know!' said Arabella. 'Gentlemen don't know anything about it, so shut up!'

'Besides,' said Henrietta-Louise, ignoring her. 'If you tell . . .' She adopted a hoity-toity tone of voice. '. . . Fräulein von Holz-zu-Birkensee. . . .' She returned her voice to normal. '. . . about us, *we* sha'n't tell you where your Chinky-Chink princess is – so there!'

With a considerable exercise in self-control, Mycroft evinced no surprise. Quite coolly, he asked, 'Would you care to tell me how you have come to find out she is a princess?'

'Because she told us so, of course!' Arabella replied.

'When?' Mycroft asked gently.

'When we found her, of course!' said Henrietta-Louise.

'I don't think she's very comfortable where she is,' said Arabella, oozing concern into her voice.

'I don't think so, either,' echoed Henrietta-Louise.

'Is there a reward for finding her?' asked Arabella.

Mycroft went to the bed and sat down on it. He reached for his cigar and, taking more time than he needed, relit it. He drew on it several times, showing every sign of enjoying it. The twins watched. They began to shift uncomfortably and to cast surreptitious little glances at one another.

'I do feel,' he said, almost apologetically,' that I should point out to you, my dear young ladies, that, while we no longer hang young women for stealing biscuits and jam, we continue to regard extortion as a very serious crime.'

'What's that?' asked Arabella.

' "Extortion"?' asked Mycroft. 'It is the attempt to

compel somebody to give you money by threatening to harm them – or somebody who matters to them.'

'We haven't threatened to do anything,' said Henrietta-Louise.

But she sounded worried.

'Both of you agreed that the Princess is uncomfortable where she is,' Mycroft pointed out. 'By saying that, you intended – I say *intended* to cause me anxiety. You then asked me if there was a reward. It is enough to constitute a felony.'

He pointed his cigar at them, and looked gravely at them.

'Now,' he went on. They sat watching him wide-eyed, and listened. 'I may pay a reward. But it will be for taking your father and me to where the Princess is.'

'Papa?' whispered Arabella.

'Where is she?' Mycroft asked, deliberately suggesting the possibility of going to her without informing their father.

'There is a deep, deep hole,' said Henrietta-Louise. 'Up on the cliffs between Winspit and Seacombe Cliff. . . .'

She pointed out of the window to where one of the ridges ended in a cliff overhanging the sea.

'It's all hidden in fern and bracken,' she added. 'We discovered it on one of our walks with Fräulein, ooh! – long ago. Before last Christmas. And Fräulein said it looked very dangerous, and we weren't to go there ever again!'

'It's very big – like a sort of little valley with cliffs of its own. . . .' said Arabella. 'Only you don't see it until you're almost falling into it.'

'And there's no way in or out,' continued Henrietta-Louise.

'And the sides are so steep, nobody could climb out,' said Arabella.

'You have been back there sometimes, in spite of what Fräulein von Holz-zu-Birkensee told you, eh?' Mycroft asked severely.

They both nodded.

'She won't go there,' said Henrietta-Louise. 'She says that it frightens her.'

'I see. So it is rather like coming in here, I suppose,' Mycroft observed. 'It is a place you may be sure she won't find you.'

The twins nodded.

'When did you find the Princess there? Is she hurt?' Arabella shook her head.

'She's just cold and uncomfortable,' she said.

'We found her this afternoon,' said Henrietta-Louise. 'Fräulein said she was going to pay a call on that horrible German clergyman at the parsonage. We asked if we could go too, because we get most awfully bored in the afternoons with nothing to do except our needlework. And she said no.'

'So we followed her,' Arabella took up the story. 'Only, then we saw the new skivvy from the parsonage – the one with the hair. . . .'

She giggled, pretending to hide her mouth behind the palm of her hand. When she saw she was getting no reaction from Mycroft, she lowered her hand.

'She came round from the back way out of the church, and went down to the path which goes to the old quarries at Winspit,' she continued.

'And then! . . . And then,' Henrietta-Louise butted in, 'we saw Major Barnaby following her. So we followed both of them. Arabella said she's seen how spoony Major Barnaby was over Claudine – I mean, the Princess. . .'

'I have!' Arabella interrupted.

'So we wanted to see if he was going to be spoony with the new skivvy from the parsonage,' said Henrietta-Louise.

'She said she wanted to see what people actually *do* when they're spooning,' said Arabella.

'I did not!' Henrietta-Louise protested. 'That was *you*!'

'I would be most grateful, young ladies, if you would keep to the point,' Mycroft told them severely. 'I am sure you can have not the foggiest idea of the importance of what you are telling me. . . . What happened as you followed this maid – and Major Barnaby?'

'Well,' said Arabella. 'The maid went into the quarries, and Major Barnaby followed her. He followed her to a sort of tower. It's all deserted, so I suppose they thought it would be a good place to go and spoon. We didn't go any further, because it's most awfully wet and windy on the undercliff there, and the sea comes up over the ledge so our feet would get terribly wet.'

'And anyway,' said Henrietta-Louise, 'you have to come out of the quarry the way you go in so we'd probably have been caught. We scrambled up the other side of Winspit on to the path over Seacombe Cliff. . . .'

'We had just climbed to the top, when we saw the skivvy,' said Arabella. 'She was coming up the same way as we had, but I don't think she could have seen us. Anyway, we hid in the bracken. . . .'

'Did you see Major Barnaby again?' Mycroft asked.

The twins shook their heads.

'We think he must have stayed in the quarry,' said Arabella. 'We didn't see him going up the path from Winspit to Worth.'

'Deuce take it!' Mycroft exclaimed. Then he said, 'The fool! Oh the damn' fool!'

'What's the matter?' whispered Henrietta-Louise.

'Never mind!' Mycroft told her. 'Pray go on with your story.'

'We stayed hidden until the maid came up on to the top,' said Arabella. 'She was carrying a bundle under her arm. I think it was a blanket and some clothes. . . .'

'Go on!' exclaimed Mycroft.

He was so gripped with excitement he could scarcely catch his breath. He was certain that it was physically and psychologically damaging to allow oneself to become so over-stimulated, and yet he was seized – even he, Mycroft Holmes – by the atavistic thrill of the chase.

'We followed her,' Arabella continued, 'to the hole.

268

We saw her throw the bundle down into it. And she shouted, didn't she, Hetty? Down into the hole. . . .'

'She shouted something about putting them on because they were dry and warm,' said Henrietta-Louise. 'And also that somebody called Mr Huttson – or was it Godman? – was going to come as soon as it started to grow dark, and pull her out.'

'Guttmann,' said Mycroft.

'I *think* so,' said Henrietta-Louise.

'So we waited until the skivvy had gone – and she didn't stay long,' said Arabella. 'And then we went and looked for ourselves. And there was Claudine, all the way at the bottom. We asked if she had fallen and hurt herself. . . .'

'Which was pretty silly really,' said Henrietta-Louise. 'Because if she *had* fallen into that great hole, she'd have been killed. I mean, it is a *very* long way down. And she said she was quite well, only it was very uncomfortable. Then she asked – it was the first thing she said, really, apart from saying she wasn't hurt – if you had arrived at Seacombe, Mr Holmes. And we said, yes you had, only, you were taken ill. Then Arabella said she thought you were pretending. . . . Yes you did, Arabella! And Claudine said she thought that it was very likely, and we were to come and tell you you were to get better immediately so that you could go and rescue her before Mr Gumpson? Gullman? . . .'

'Guttmann,' said Mycroft.

'. . . came to pull her out,' Henrietta-Louise concluded.

'Does the Princess know you *really* well, Mr Holmes?' asked Arabella.

Mycroft went and opened the door.

'Cyril!' he shouted. 'Come here, man! The Princess is found!'

To the twins he said, 'Go and find your papa immediately! Tell him I sent you. . . . Where is the Colonel?' he asked Cyril.

'In the drawin'-room wiv Lady 'Ornby,' Cyril replied.

'You go straight to him, do you hear me?' he repeated to the twins. 'Tell him the Princess is found, and that I say there is not a moment to lose. Tell him to call out the men, and to have a rope fetched long enough to pull her up. Tell him to send somebody up on to Renscombe Hill to bring in the Marine orderly, what's the fellow's name? – Whitlock! Tell him I will be with him on the instant! . . . Fetch my clothes, man!' he called to Cyril. 'And tell your father,' he called after the twins, 'that I have cause to believe the missing documents are already planted on the Princess!'

Chapter Twenty-Four

'How can you be sure the villain don't intend leavin' the lady where she is?' asked Sir Rinaldo. 'If you're so certain he's "primed the bomb", as you put it.'

Mycroft had followed his host through the house to the gun-room. Sir Rinaldo unlocked a cupboard containing a rack of shotguns and rifles. He reached for a single-barrelled gun which looked to Mycroft like a portable piece of artillery.

'Guttmann needs to be absolutely sure the Princess will be discovered quickly, with the sealed orders on her person,' Mycroft replied. 'If the account given me by the Misses Hornby is accurate, years could pass without her being found. There is no reason why he should not set her loose: he has only to leave word with the Wareham police that there is a suspicious person on the cliff tops by Seacombe Bay – somebody he has overheard speaking Russian – and your honest but none-too-bright constabulary will rush to the conclusion that there is one of the Tsar's spies in the vicinity; as for Princess Trubetskoy, it is my belief she will not yet have realized she has the Admiralty's sealed orders about her person.'

'Gad, sir!' Sir Rinaldo exclaimed. 'You should come with us to Besika Bay. With you advising us on strategic intelligence, my command alone would make beef-steak tartare of the Russkies!'

'The reason I am here, sir,' said Mycroft severely, 'is to ensure there will be no need of that. I beg you to put away that weapon you are holding. Your service revolver will prove entirely effective as a weapon of defence.'

'Of defence, sir?' Sir Rinaldo demanded. 'Shall we not effect an arrest?'

271

Mycroft shook his head. He pointed in the direction of the bay.

'I have the fullest confidence in Sir James Swarthmoor. By now there will be a watch off-shore to take our man and such of his associates who will accompany him, at sea, without risking the life and limb of any of your people. Besides, we are none of us policemen. On what grounds will you challenge him with a citizen's arrest? Not in the furtherance of a crime; since I don't suppose for a moment he lowered her there in person, the worst he will be doing will be rescuing the Princess from the pit into which she will appear to have fallen – performing an act of charity, do you see? . . . No, sir. I have a device of my own – and I believe you have been good enough to suggest you have confidence in me.'

Sir Rinaldo gave him an honest smile.

'I have, sir,' he said. 'And I don't mind admitting it. Shake my hand, sir.'

'Gladly,' Mycroft replied, doing so.

Sir Rinaldo returned the heavy gun to the rack in the cupboard. He went to the drawer in the bottom of the cupboard and picked out a heavy Colt revolver. He loaded it from a small cardboard box, then slipped it into the capacious pocket of his coat.

'Will you go armed, Holmes?' he asked.

Mycroft shook his head. He had not the least practical knowledge of the handling and use of firearms, unless it was the common or garden twelve-bore shotgun, and he had no intention of trailing about on the cliff-tops with a shotgun.

'What about your man?' asked Sir Rinaldo. 'He seems a loyal and serviceable chap for all he's a blackie – and impudent with it!'

'Certainly not!' said Mycroft with unintended vehemence.

The thought of entrusting Cyril with a loaded revolver when there was the temptation to avenge an injury done

272

to Princess Sophie was something he scarcely dared to contemplate.

'Daresay you're right,' said Sir Rinaldo. He took two more revolvers from the drawer, and loaded them.

'Lewis can have one,' he said. 'Been a trustworthy old fellow as long as I've known him – which is as long as I've been married to the Memsahib, don't you know? And Whitlock, when he joins us. That should do the trick.'

He led Mycroft back through the house.

'You will show us the way, girls!' he shouted at the twins.

Fräulein von Holz-zu-Birkensee, still in her out-door clothes from her visit up to the parsonage, was with them.

'Why, Mr Holmes! You are up and on your feet!' she exclaimed.

'Indeed, Fräulein,' he replied. 'It was no more than a passing fainting spell brought on by the musty smell of old hassocks, I daresay. . . . Very foolish of me. I feel as right as rain now, you will be glad to hear.'

Fräulein von Holz-zu-Birkensee made a brave effort at pretence.

'Look, girls!' she cried. 'Mr Holmes is not as ill as we thought. We should be very happy, should we not?'

The twins did not evince any great manifestations of joy. On the other hand, they did not announce that they knew he had been pretending.

'You shall give them a taste of the rod when we return, Fräulein!' Sir Rinaldo attempted to bark in his best military manner. 'They may have found Lady Hornby's maid, thank God! But your charges, Fräulein, have not yet learnt discipline!'

Mycroft could see that Sir Rinaldo's revulsion at the governess's betrayal of her position of trust made it almost impossible for him to keep up the pretence of treating her as his daughters' superintendent. Still, he was clearly doing his best.

'Do you mean they are to accompany you on to the

cliffs, Sir Rinaldo?' asked Fräulein von Holz-zu-Birkensee.

'And yourself, Fräulein,' Mycroft hastily intervened.

'Oh no, sir,' Fräulein von Holz-zu-Birkensee simpered. 'We have promised to take tea with old Mrs Withershanks at Lodge End Cottage. She will be *so* disappointed, no?'

'We need the young Misses Hornby to come with us, Fräulein,' Mycroft told her. 'And since we shall be busy, we shall need you to keep an eye on them.'

Lady Hornby appeared at the drawing-room door. Fräulein von Holz-zu-Birkensee turned to her for aid.

'Lady Hornby, please!' she appealed. 'I did promise Mrs Withershanks we would be there! The dear thing will have gone to so much trouble. If the gentlemen need Miss Hetty and Miss Arabella, perhaps I may go alone to Lodge End Cottage, yes?'

'Of course, my dear!' said Lady Hornby. 'You must not disappoint poor old Mrs Withershanks. *I* will go with the gels in your place.'

'Madam!' Mycroft exclaimed. 'You shall not!'

He went to her, took her arm, and led her back into the drawing-room.

'Forgive me, madam,' he told her. 'It is of the greatest importance the Fräulein goes with us. . . . Trust me, madam. You must remain here. We want to give no hostage to fortune – or to our enemies. Lock yourself in. Receive no one, least of all Pastor August, or whatever he chooses to call himself. He is a very dangerous man indeed!'

'But the gels, Mithter Holmes? What of the gels? They are so wilful!'

'They will be safer with us than if they remained here, precisely for that reason.'

She looked at him in bewilderment.

'Madam, your husband has placed his confidence in me. I pray you to do the same,' he told her.

She nodded without much conviction. Mycroft left

her. He called to Fräulein von Holz-zu-Birkensee,

'Fräulein? I suggest you write a note to old Mrs whatever-her-name-is, this instant, and send it by one of the maids.'

He saw the look of relief on her face.

'Thank you, Mr Holmes! Such a good idea . . . is it not, girls?'

She turned smiling to the twins, then tripped away to the library. Sir Rinaldo had also seen the look of relief.

'Will you read her note, Holmes?' he asked.

'Certainly not,' Mycroft replied, lowering his voice. 'That is never the office of a gentleman! Nor shall I set a watch to see if her messenger goes to the parsonage rather than the cottage. I shall content myself with praying that we are about to flush out the fox!'

By the time Fräulein von Holz-zu-Birkensee had written the note – it took her no more than a couple of minutes – and had gone below stairs to appoint a bearer, the men from the stables and home farm had assembled, one of them with a length of rope over his shoulder, like a mountaineer. Whitlock returned from his watch to join them.

'Major Barnaby has not returned from following the maid down to Winspit, eh?' asked Sir Rinaldo as the procession moved off, past the stables and out on to the ridge.

A thin, salt-tasting drizzle was beating off the white-crested sea. Pray God, thought Mycroft, the daylight would hold long enough for them to complete their task. He did not care for the idea of blundering about the sea-cliff tops in darkness.

'No, sir,' Marine Whitlock replied. 'The foreign parson's maid set out, sir. And she come back to the parsonage an hour or two back. But no sign of the Major.'

'Nor of the foreign parson?' asked Mycroft.

Sir Rinaldo handed Whitlock one of the pistols he was carrying under his arm. Whitlock slid it under his belt.

'No, sir,' he told Mycroft. 'He ain't moved out of the parsonage. I'll take my oath on that.'

'Watts! Hawkins!' Sir Rinaldo called up two of the men. 'Take yourselves down to Winspit. See if you can find the Major.

Mycroft turned to Cyril.

'Go with them,' he said. 'If they find him, come back to me immediately and tell me what has happened to him.'

'What about the Princess?' Cyril demanded.

'I daresay you will be back in time to see her rescued,' Mycroft told him.

The wind snatched his words away.

'I want to 'elp the Princess!' said Cyril, shouting his indignation into Mycroft's ear.

'If you bring her news of Major Barnaby,' Mycroft told him, 'She will certainly regard it as the greatest of help.'

A slow-dawning smile came over Cyril's face.

'Yerse!' he said into the wind. 'S'pose she might, an' all!'

As they clambered up to the summit of the ridge, and the full blast of the bitter wind, Mycroft could see from horizon to horizon under a low, ragged sky, the cliff-promontories thrusting into the white-crested sea. For a moment or two, he had to stand panting for breath. A little way to his right, stepping through the wind-swept bracken and avoiding the thorn-patches of gorse, Fräulein von Holz-zu-Birkensee was following the twins. He was sure that it was not the wind that had caused her to tighten her lips to a thread.

Sir Rinaldo and the men with him had stopped, waiting for the twins to show them the way. They went in single file along the cliff top for more than a mile. Several times, Fräulein von Holz-zu-Birkensee looked behind her and about her to see, Mycroft had no doubt, whether there was a chance for her to break away and escape. Each time her eyes met his, and she went on. Then the twins began to run on ahead, shouting, 'Here we are! Here we are!' Sir Rinaldo shouted to them to come back, but already they were standing up on a tussock of blown grass pointing downwards.

Mycroft hurried forward as fast as his loss of breath permitted. He noticed that Fräulein von Holz-zu-Birkensee had stopped and was allowing the men to run past her. She turned with just a hint of panic, to look back in the direction of Worth Matravers, and the parsonage. Was she hoping, he wondered, to be rescued from the rescuers? He went to her and took her arm. She tried to shake him off.

'The girls,' she said. 'I must see they do not go near the edge! It is very dangerous!'

'Do you also know this spot?' he asked gently.

She stared at him wildly and shook her head. The wind caught the fur trimmed hood of her mantle and pushed it back off her head. Mycroft did not wait for an answer. The wind carried Sir Rinaldo's words across to him: 'Hodgson! The rope, man! Here!'

'I would not trust you near them,' Mycroft said into her ear. 'Not now. Not at this juncture.'

'I do not know what you mean!'

She attempted to sound outraged.

'Whitlock!' Mycroft shouted to Sir Rinaldo's soldier-servant.

He came loping through the bracken at the double.

'Sah?'

'Have a care of this woman, Whitlock. Don't let her move from this spot. Use your pistol if necessary.'

Whitlock looked puzzled. He glanced in Sir Rinaldo's direction. Sir Rinaldo nodded.

'Mr Holmes?' said Fräulein von Holz-zu-Birkensee. 'You shall be sorry for this outrage, I promise. I am the daughter of *junkers* and the widow of a *junker*!'

'Fräulein,' Mycroft replied, 'you are the creature of Carl Philipp Emmanuel Guttmann, nothing more nor less. And like all his poor, entrapped, deluded implements, you are worthy only of our pity.'

The venom in the look she gave him was as extraordinary as it was horrifying on the face of a member of what English gentlemen were brought up to regard as the Gentler Sex. It was as if, thought Mycroft, she was blood kin to her master, she displayed such a terrible family resemblance.

Leaving her in Whitlock's charge, he went to the edge where Sir Rinaldo and his stableman, Hodgson, were standing. It was an astonishing phenomenon: as if he were staring into the mouth of a volcano so long extinct that the walls down to the bottom had become cliff-face and scree, and the floor at the bottom had become a heathland in miniature, with brambles, grass, and small ash-trees.

'Jesse, here, will go down, Colonel, sir,' the man, Hodgson, said, indicating a grinning, sturdy-looking lad beside him. 'He's used to the cliffs is Jesse. Been risking his neck after gannets' eggs since he were knee high.'

'That I have, Squire,' Jesse agreed.

'Sound fellow!' said Sir Rinaldo, clapping him on the shoulder.

As the lad was roped up, Sir Rinaldo turned to Mycroft.

'There's no sign of your Princess, Holmes. I'm sorry to have to say it, but I'd not put it past my daughters to be lying. It wouldn't be the first time they've turned out the whole estate with one of their stories.'

'But not this time, Sir Rinaldo,' Mycroft assured him. 'She doesn't know who we are. She is hiding from us.'

Fighting back the sense of vertigo, he leaned over, and cupped his hands.

'*Zdrastvuytye, Knyazhna!*' he called, '*zdyes' Ya*, Holmes – Mycroft Holmes!'

'*Zdrastvuye, Meestr* Holmes,' a musical, soprano cry echoed round the cliff walls.

A small black-cloaked figure emerged from two outcrops of rock. Mycroft saw the pale little face tilted upwards, searching the lip of the chasm.

'*Kak dyela, Knyazhna?*' he called.

She saw him and waved delightedly, just like a child paddling on the shore who spots its nursemaid among the crowd further up the beach, and waves.

'*Ochyen' kharasho!*' she called up eagerly.

278

Mycroft felt a stab of joy as unexpected as it was sweet. Then she called, '*Golodny kak volk!*'

'Is she harmed in any way?' Sir Rinaldo asked. Then he saw that Mycroft was smiling. 'What does she say?'

'She says she is perfectly well, and that she could eat a horse – or the Russian equivalent. . . . I spoke to her in her own language to identify myself. There are not many Englishmen – or Prussians, I think – who have mastered her native tongue. But also to reassure her generally. Send your boy down to her.'

He leaned out once more.

'We are sending somebody down to you to help you with the rope to pull you up!' he called. 'Princess?'

'*Eta Ya!*' she called back.

'The bundle Abigail Rodgers dropped to you, earlier this afternoon! See that it is all brought up here, if you would be so good!'

As the boy Jesse was lowered over the edge, and eight sturdy fellows took the strain of the rope, Mycroft called to Whitlock, 'Bring the Fräulein here!'

He turned to Sir Rinaldo and drew him away from the cliff-edge and the men on the rope. He spoke to him as quietly as the bluster of the wind permitted. When he had finished, Sir Rinaldo stared at him with a mixture of awe and admiration.

'Devil take it, sir! I have to give it you! You are the most devious fellow I've ever met! he said. 'As devious as that old Italian fellow – what the deuce was his name?'

'Machiavelli?' Mycroft suggested.

He was not entirely sure he should feel flattered given the number of times he himself had compared Guttmann to Cesare Borgia's favourite diplomat.

'Look, Holmes! D'ye see out there?'

Sir Rinaldo pointed out over the cliff-top to the sea. There was no need for a spyglass; they could see quite clearly, just beyond St Aldhelm's Point, on the horizon, a trim, sleek grey vessel under full sail and beating down-Channel.

'Coastguard cutter out of Poole,' said Sir Rinaldo. 'Your people are on station, eh?'

'And not a moment too soon,' Mycroft replied.

They turned back again to watch as the lad was lowered down the face of the pit. Apprehension was taking its grip on Fräulein von Holz-zu-Birkensee as she stood with Marine Whitlock, only a few yards from them. The men on the rope were shouting advice down to the lad who had reached the bottom, their voice echoing from rock wall to rock wall. Fräulein von Holz-zu-Birkensee's struggle to retain some measure of self-composure finally broke.

'What do you mean to do with me?' she cried out to Mycroft.

'*Do* with you, madam?' Mycroft asked.

The twins on their hillock were enjoying a rare moment of truce between themselves. They had their arms about one another, and were watching with fascination what was happening.

'What do you suppose I should do with you?' Mycroft asked.

'I do not know, Mr Holmes!' She glanced about her, wildly, seeking perhaps for help to come at the last minute.

'Lower her into the hole!' shouted Henrietta-Louise.

'Instead of Claudine!' shouted Arabella.

They jumped up and down in their excitement at the idea.

'Gels!' barked Sir Rinaldo. 'Hold your tongues or it will be the worse for you!'

Then he caught the grin which Mycroft had not wholly been able to suppress.

'It is difficult enough to crush their insubordination,' he said in Mycroft's ear. 'Without your offering them encouragement, sir!'

The Princess was roped, and the men drawing her up, as Cyril came stumbling through gorse and bracken up from Winspit. Mycroft went to meet him.

'How is he?' he asked.

Cyril stopped to catch his breath. The climb up the cliff-path had been steep and slippery. He held out his hands: the pale, inside palms were smeared with drying mud; the heels of his thumbs were grazed, and the knees of his trousers under the skirt of his coat were caked in mud.

'h-Ain't natural!' he said. 'This sort of place. Not for 'umans, leastways!'

'The Major!' Mycroft sternly reminded him.

' 'E's alive,' said Cyril unsympathetically. 'Usin' langwidge like a gent didn't oughter. Reckon as 'e's broke 'is collarbone an' a leg – an' a couple of ribs. . . . They're carryin' 'im back to the 'ouse on an old door.'

He broke off to breathe deeply.

'She tricked 'im – that Abby Rodgers, did,' he went on. 'Tricked 'im into goin' up some broken old stairs. . . .'

'By God, I warned him against just such a ruse!' Mycroft exclaimed.

He shook his head.

'The trouble about having an exceptionally good brain, my dear good man,' he went on, 'is that one invariably underestimates the lack of intelligence in others. . . . But I did warn him of just that!'

Cyril nodded his agreement – between one highly intelligent fellow and another.

' 'E's broke 's 'ead open, too, l' he said sagely. 'But there h-ain't no signs of no brains spillin' out – prob'ly cos 'e h-ain't got none.'

'Enough of that!' said Mycroft.

The sounds of excitement and the sudden expression of delight on Cyril's face made him turn round. The Princess was standing at the edge of the pit; one of the men was untying the rope from under her arms. She was wearing a servant's woollen bonnet over her black curls, and a man's heavy black greatcoat over her servant's clothes, which was smeared with grey dirt from the rock-face. Her small, pretty Slavic-Mongolian features were patched with mud which she had attempted vainly to wipe off. And she was smiling broadly at Mycroft with relief and enormous affection. Even before the rope was finally removed from around her, she was reaching out to him.

'*Meestr* Holmes!' she cried out. '*Droog moy! Moy pryekrasniy chelovek!*'

She wrapped her arms, already limited in their reach by the bulky coat she was wearing, halfway about his girth.

'What kept you so long, dear friend?' she asked in her faultless, scarcely accented English.

'What fit of lunacy brought you here, down to Dorset, without consulting me first?' he demanded.

'Because you were not in London!' she said. 'You had gone to the wrong coast, hadn't you?'

Before he had a chance to explain that away, she added to his confusion by reaching up on her toes and kissing him on the cheek three times. Sensing his embarrassment, she released him quickly. She glanced over her shoulder at those watching.

'*Ty ochyen' Anglychaniy, moy lyubimiy!*' she laughed.

'Your coat?' he asked her in Russian. 'Is it one of the garments thrown down to you by Abigail Rodgers this afternoon?'

'Abigail Rodgers!' she exclaimed. 'So you were right, that afternoon in Dorking,' she went on, also in Russian. 'Abby Rodgers did return to serve Herr Guttmann!'

'I am not often proved wrong in my prophecies, Princess. But the coat?'

'Why?' she laughed. 'I was glad of it. I was frozen down there, after a night without food or shelter. Is it a shirt of Nessus? Does it burn up the wearer?'

'Yes, Princess. I believe so,' Mycroft told her. 'I beg you to remove it.'

She unbuttoned it and took it off. She was wearing a lighter coat under it, to cover her maid's stuff blue gown and lace-trimmed white apron. It was even dirtier than the top coat. Mycroft had no doubt that when she had first been lowered into the crater she had made every effort to climb out; she would not have been the Princess Sophie he knew if she had not done so. As he threw the coat over his arm, she turned to Cyril.

'Dear friend!' she exclaimed.

To his near-ecstatic delight, she embraced and kissed him as well.

Mycroft took her arm, and turned her about to face the others.

'Colonel?' he asked. 'I have the honour to introduce you to my very dear and trusted friend, Princess Sofya Sergeyevna Trubetskoy . . . without whose information and advice, I would not have been able to foil our enemy's wicked scheming against our Queen and Country.'

'*Have* been able, Mr Holmes?' asked the Princess.

'All but the final punctuation mark or so, I believe. Eh, Sir Rinaldo?' Mycroft replied.

He saw that the men had thrown down the ropes once more, and were hauling up the lad, Jesse. He waited until the boy was brought up over the edge. In the meantime, Sir Rinaldo was gravely apologizing to the Princess for the entertainment she had received in his home, and she was assuring him that only disaster would have ensued if his household had not treated her as a servant.

'You have one more task to perform before you return to your normal duties,' Mycroft pronounced to the men on the rope. 'You will lower down Fräulein von Holz-zu-Birkensee in place of the Princess.'

'No!' Fräulein von Holz-zu-Birkensee cried out. 'Sir Rinaldo! You cannot allow it! You cannot – as an English gentleman and a soldier!'

For a moment, Mycroft thought that this appeal would weaken Sir Rinaldo's resolve. He noticed he was biting his lip.

'Sir Rinaldo! I am a soldier's daughter – a soldier's widow!' screamed Fräulein von Holz-zu-Birkensee.

'Madam!' Sir Rinaldo replied stiffly. 'It is the greater

shame on you that you should have answered to the
ignoble vocation of spying!'

'You have no proof!' she shouted at him. 'You have
only the word of that man!'

She began screaming hysterically. Marine Whitlock
restrained her, holding her arms as she writhed and
howled with the desperation of an animal. The bystanders
looked sickened and appalled by the sudden descent from
all womanly dignity.

'Mr Holmes!' the Princess appealed. 'She is a woman!
A lady! You cannot!'

'I am sorry, Princess,' Mycroft replied. 'You should
have better cause than anyone to know that anybody
who takes service under that evil genius forfeits the right
to be treated with the respect due to rank and sex.'

Princess Sophie looked up at him. Quietly, in Russian,
she said, 'You are not so very English, after all!'

She turned her face away. Suddenly angry, Mycroft
went to Fräulein von Holz-zu-Birkensee. He grasped at
one of her flailing hands. He peeled off the glove and
ripped the lace, indoor mitten from off her palm.

'Do you see?' he demanded.

Sir Rinaldo and the Princess looked at the hand which
he was holding rigid.

'We have here an intelligent woman,' he said. 'A
woman of education and accomplishment, but one who
has the calloused hands of a slavey or a field-worker.
What do you make of that, Princess?'

Fräulein von Holz-zu-Birkensee had stopped struggling and screaming. She drew in breath, then spat on
Mycroft's face as violently as she could. Mycroft ignored
the thick slime creeping down his cheek.

'Well, my dear?' he asked her. 'Was it Moabit, or was
it some provincial gaol Herr Guttmann rescued you
from? And the crime you had committed? Even under
the harshness of your Prussian criminal code, it must
have been a heinous one for a woman like you to have
been sentenced to hard labour!'

She tried to spit at him again.

'*Scheiss*!' she screamed at him. Her throat was growing hoarse.

'*Scheiss*!' she screamed again.

'Secure her,' Mycroft told the men. 'And throw the rope down with her. But first. . . .'

He turned to face Fräulein von Holz-zu-Birkensee. He addressed her in German; 'He will come for you soon enough, the footman who released you from your prison cell to be his creature. You will not be down there as long as was the Princess – no more than an hour or two. And, since I am not as cruel as your master, and it is a cold day, I suggest you put on this coat, already worn by a lady nobler than you could ever dream of.'

He held up the coat. Fräulein von Holz-zu-Birkensee had quietened – except for the venomous glare on her face, had resigned herself to her fate. She allowed Mycroft to assist her put it on and to button it up. When he had finished, he looked to Sir Rinaldo. Sir Rinaldo nodded his agreement.

'Lower her down, men!' he called.

Mycroft and he turned away. The twins were still on their hillock. They were silent, awestruck that their suggestion of putting their governess down into the pit should be so astonishingly complied with. It was as if, all of a sudden, the whole world was at their beck and call and they had been struck dumb by the fearful responsibility imposed on them.

Mycroft looked at the Princess.

'The sealed orders from the Admiralty,' he said, 'were stolen from Edwin Barnaby while he was with you, in the house. They were stolen by the Fräulein and handed over to Guttmann, who is in the parsonage in the village. He had them stitched into the lining of the coat you have been wearing; the plan was that you were to be discovered with the orders concealed on your person, and arrested as a spy for His Imperial Majesty, Tsar Alexander II.'

'I?' asked Princess Sophie, pointing at herself in astonishment. 'A spy?'

'That was Guttmann's plan.'

'What happens to spies in this country?' she asked in a voice which was almost inaudible in the bluster of the wind.

Cyril took off his own coat, muddy as it was, and put it over her shoulders. She grasped at it and drew it about her.

'They are taken to the Tower of London; they are led out into the moat and shot,' said Sir Rinaldo.

'What have you done with the orders?' she asked.

'They remain . . .,' Mycroft replied, '. . . where I felt them to be, just now.'

The Princess glanced at the men lowering the rope down into the pit. It slackened in their hands. They threw the end down.

'Do you mean that . . . ?' Princess Sophie asked.

'It is clear the woman – Fräulein whatever her real name may be,' said Sir Rinaldo, 'is unaware, as you were unaware, that the papers had been stitched into the lining of the coat.'

'So she will be . . . ?' the Princess began.

'That is our profound hope – she and her employer, both,' Mycroft told her. 'We must hope that, in the failing light, he does not notice that she is wearing the coat he intended for you.'

He glanced out over the cliff-top to the sea. The vessel he had seen rounding St Aldhelm's Point had been joined by another sleek-looking cutter. Sir Rinaldo ordered everybody to return to Seacombe except for his orderly, Mycroft and Cyril.

Predictably, at least from Mycroft and Cyril's previous knowledge of her, the Princess refused to leave. She explained how, the previous afternoon, she had left the house as she had done before, to walk on the hillside to watch the riding-horses being exercised. There, she had been seized by two rough, gypsy-looking men, who had

286

held her in an old barn until it was dark, and had then taken her and roped her, and had lowered her into the chasm. At first, she said, she had wondered whether she had been taken for the men's own gratification; it had not been until she had been dropped down into the crater unharmed, that she realized that there was some other purpose, and had guessed whose it was. Her desperate attempt in the dark to scale the side of the chasm had been inspired by the need she felt to warn Major Barnaby in particular, as soon as possible, that Guttmann was about to strike. Now, after twenty-four hours of cold, discomfort and hunger, she was determined to see the end of the business.

As the men from the stables and the estate, with the twins in tow, straggled back along the steep ridge towards the house, the five of them who remained retreated from the edge of the chasm, and took cover in the gorse and brambles some distance away. Mycroft was sure that Guttmann would have spotted the straggle of figures returning down the ridge, and would make his move before it became dark. Sure enough, about half an hour later, there was the sound of somebody approaching up the cliff-path. Lying uncomfortably on their stomachs, on the damp ground, they tried to peer through the black, winter branches of the gorse. A shrill, falsetto male voice was calling, the words borne on the wind, 'Sir Rinaldo! Are you there, Sir Rinaldo?'

A strange, lean pantaloon-like figure appeared on the path, coming up behind them, with hanks of long grey hair fluttering from under the wide-brimmed clerical hat he was clutching to his head.

'Mr Sabine!' exclaimed Sir Rinaldo. 'Back from Salisbury already! What does he want with me here?'

It was all too clear, thought Mycroft. He wanted to express his indignation.

'Over here, man!' called Sir Rinaldo. 'Over here. Quickly!'

The Reverend Mr Sabine stared about him with a dis-

tracted gaze. He resembled a strolling player's version of
King Lear in clerical garb and a somewhat foreshortened
descent into madness. He caught sight of Sir Rinaldo.

'Ah!' he cried. 'Colonel! You will never believe this!'

He came striding through the bracken, not a whit surprised at the sight of four grown men, one of them a negro,
and a lady, lying sprawling in the damp undergrowth.

'Do you know, sir?' he exclaimed. 'I received a telegram
summoning me to appear – appear, mark you! – before
His Lordship the Bishop to answer a complaint . . .
a complaint against me, sir! And when I arrived at the
palace, His Lordship's secretary was good enough to
inform me that no such telegram had ever been sent!
There was no such summons! Not only that, sir, but he
refused to reimburse me my travelling expenses!'

Sir Rinaldo tried to signal him to be quiet and to get
down. Mr Sabine took it to mean that he should trample
nearer and talk louder.

'It must have been somebody who bears a grudge
against me and Mrs Sabine, sir!' he shrilled. 'Somebody
who regards the money for a telegram well spent for the
pleasure of causing me great inconvenience, sir – and
Mrs Sabine some inconvenience as well – though her
feelings were not involved as mine were!'

'Was Pastor von Holz still at the parsonage on your
return, just now?' asked Mycroft.

'Why no, sir,' Mr Sabine replied. 'It appears he and his
chambermaid have left – though what that has to do
with the purpose, I cannot imagine!'

'Get down, man, for God's sake!' exclaimed Sir
Rinaldo.

'Down?' asked Mr Sabine. 'Whatever for? The ground
is deuced damp at this time of the year. And I've had a
fatiguing enough day traipsing round the country without risking my health further by lying on the damp
ground. . . . Sir Rinaldo, as the proprietor of the living,
here, it is your duty, in my opinion to discover. . . .'

Both Mycroft and Sir Rinaldo reached up and dragged

him by main force down beside them. They planted their elbows on top of him. He screwed his head round to stare first at one, then at the other. A look of comprehension came over his face.

'Poachers!' he exclaimed. 'You're lying in wait for poachers, eh? Well, I'll not disturb you any further. Mrs Sabine will have my tea ready, I daresay. . . .'

He struggled to get up, but they pressed him down.

'Be silent, man!' Sir Rinaldo whispered.

'And you, Princess!' Mycroft whispered. 'Keep out of sight! Don't let him see that you have given the coat to his creature, down there!'

C.P.E. Guttmann was on the sky-line, on the far side of the chasm, a heavy, black-cloaked figure against the late afternoon light which lingered in the western sky.

'Pastor von Holz!' exclaimed Mr Sabine in his shrill voice. 'He's not a poacher!'

The figure turned in their direction. Mycroft, at least in his own good opinion, was not given to fevered imaginings: he was sure he could see with dreadful clarity the pallid, spiritual emptiness of Guttmann's eyes searching his brain. Mr Sabine too had recognized what he saw. He no longer struggled to rise from the damp earth.

'I welcomed him as a guest in my house!' he whispered. 'I let him minister to my flock!'

He began to sob softly. Mycroft said to him, 'Wiser men than you, sir, have been duped by Carl Philipp Emmanuel Guttmann.'

'Colonel Hornby?'

The rich voice penetrated the wind.

'You should not let your daughters stray! Young maidens need watching, sir!'

'Oh my God!' gasped Sir Rinaldo, his military indifference swept from him by what he beheld.

Mycroft heard the single, distressed cry of 'Papa!', then saw the two girls. They were standing on the very edge of the chasm, so close that the toes of their small boots were

289

pointing into the empty air. Behind each stood a man holding them by their arms gripped behind their backs – ruffianly-looking fellows whose leathered faces, greasy locks, and filthy, ragged clothing proclaimed them vagrants, and whose low, pithecanthous foreheads declared their malevolent but helpless stupidity.

'They were alone on the hillside, Colonel Hornby!' Guttmann called. 'I thought, perhaps, you would wish them returned to their governess!'

'The Devil!' Sir Rinaldo exclaimed. 'Devil incarnate!'

'We were coming back to you, Papa!' wailed Arabella. 'Oh please . . . !'

Her voice was snatched away by the wind.

Mycroft saw Sir Rinaldo's hand reach into his coat to draw out his revolver.

'No, Colonel,' he whispered. 'That is not the way! He will not kill them if he can help it. He is using them as hostages.'

'You should listen to Mr Holmes's advice, Colonel,' came the mocking voice. 'He is a very clever man. . . . Did you evade my walking contagion, Mr Holmes? Or is this a demonstration of the will postponing the final bout with pestilence?'

Mycroft felt the desire to reply like a temptation he could hardly resist. He fought back his own voice, uttering something like a moan.

The slight figure of Abigail Rodgers appeared on the slope below Guttmann, her straw-coloured hair blown across her face. She reached up her hand and drew it aside. Mycroft saw that she was smiling up at Guttmann and that the smile, as well as being one of affection, was filled with gratitude. In the blustered confusion which seemed to be taking over his thought processes, one point of clear understanding became fixed: that Guttmann was about to leave, taking her with him, and thus indicating that the game had been played out.

'Mr Holmes!' the voice boomed across the wind. 'Advise the Colonel that I and my associates wish him no

290

harm for the present – nor his charming daughters. We wish only to be allowed to leave your shore peacefully.'

Mycroft stood up.

'We shall allow you to leave, Herr Guttmann,' he called, 'when your men free the Colonel's daughters, and they are safely with us.'

Guttmann laughed.

'No, sir!' he called. 'A walk down to the bay will not hurt them. They are admirably healthy young women. I will release them there – you have my word on it!'

Mycroft resisted making some sarcastic comment about Guttmann's word.

'Very well!' he called back.

'Mr Holmes!' Sir Rinaldo protested, scrambling to his feet.

His revolver was still in his hand.

'Mr 'Olmes knows what 'e's up to!' Cyril exclaimed. 'Honest, 'e does, Colonel!'

Mycroft turned his back on Guttmann. To Sir Rinaldo, he said, 'He's the Devil, Colonel, but he does nothing without a purpose. There is no purpose for him in harming your daughters. So put your mind at ease.'

Sir Rinaldo gazed steadily into Mycroft's face.

'I have no choice, have I?'

'None, sir,' Mycroft agreed. 'But there is one card still to play in this game, and it is ours.'

He nodded in the direction of the sea. Sir Rinaldo returned his nod. Mycroft faced Guttmann.

'Go, Herr Guttmann!' he called.

'Goodbye, Mr Holmes!' Guttmann called. 'For the last time, perhaps? And you too, Princess, wherever you may be!'

Mycroft with Sir Rinaldo, Marine Whitlock and Cyril, stood together, the damp earth drying on their clothing in the bitter salt wind. The Reverend Mr Sabine still sat on the ground staring up at them, a look of utter bewilderment on his face.

'He should be arrested!' he shrilled. 'Impersonating a

clergyman! It is a crime! . . . And the return fare to Salisbury!'

Guttmann called to the two ruffians. He and Abigail Rodgers followed them as they pushed the twins on to the path which led to Seacombe Bay.

'Don't be afraid, gels!' Sir Rinaldo called with paternal concern. 'They aren't going to harm you, I promise you!'

There was no trace of notions of 'good hidings' or any such matter in his voice.

Abigail Rodgers turned her head as she passed, and smiled. She had grown into a quite devastatingly pretty young woman, Mycroft noticed.

'Goodbye, Mr Holmes!' she called in a sweetly musical voice.

Guttmann paused to look down into the chasm. A woman's cry – a call of surprise and desperation – echoed across the rock walls. Guttmann looked at Mycroft.

'You may dispose of the rubbish as you wish, Mr Holmes,' he said.

Mycroft and the others watched the tiny procession wind away down the slope of the cliff towards the bay. They went closer to the cliff edge to look out across the sea. The trim cutters were still on station, a mile or two out in the Channel.

Princess Sophie emerged from behind the clump of broom where she had lain concealed. She held on to Mycroft's and Cyril's sleeves to prevent the wind catching her skirts and blowing her off the cliff.

'What will you do with the poor woman?' she called to Mycroft.

Mycroft glanced across to Sir Rinaldo. He was obviously preoccupied with his concern for the twins.

'Guttmann will have informed the Wareham police already,' he told Princess Sophie, 'that one of Sir Rinaldo's servants has stolen some very important papers – documents of national importance – and that she was last seen hurrying along the path on Seacombe

Cliff. He may also have suggested that she could have fallen into a particularly dangerous cleft near the path. . . .'

Princess Sophie stared up at his face.

'And you will let her be arrested for the crime I was supposed to be committing?'

' "Why, man, she did make love to this employment," ' Mycroft quoted. "She is not near my conscience". . . . "*Hamlet*",' he explained, because the Princess was a foreigner. 'Act Five, scene two,' he added helpfully.

'But Sir Rinaldo!' the Princess exclaimed. 'He will have to swear—'

'He will have to swear to nothing,' Mycroft assured her. 'The woman will be discovered with red hands. She will be tried by court martial – an altogether more rough and ready mode of Justice than that administered at the Old Bailey, I assure you. And Sir Rinaldo will be serving his country, halfway across the world.'

'And you, Mr Holmes? What of you when you are called on to testify?'

'I shall have no qualms, my dear Princess, as I have said. In the words of Epicurus, "Justice, like the tyrant, may wear the Crown only so long as she protects the innocent from the evil intentions of the vicious" – and that woman is vicious. . . . Think, Princess: if it were Carl Philipp Emmanuel Guttmann down there, and the issue between you were not the preservation of this realm of England, but the life of your beloved sister, the Princess Orlov. . . .'

Sophie Trubetskoy turned her eyes away from him.

'That was cruel, Mr Holmes,' she said.

After a long wait which seemed even longer than it was, they heard the shouts of the twins as they came running back up the path. Sir Rinaldo said, 'Thank God! Oh, thank God!' At almost the same moment, they saw far below the cliff, riding the choppy waves, a sturdily built dinghy under sail, two lanterns suspended from its masthead, heading out towards the open sea. They were able to make out C.P.E. Guttmann and one of his ruffians sitting in the stern, their hands on the rudder. The second ruffian was seated on the windward bulwark clutching at the boom-rope. Abigail Rodgers, her hood blown off her head, her long hair billowing about her, was lying in the prow staring forward like a figurehead.

'They must see them!' said Mycroft.

He stared out at the fast-dimming horizon, waiting for one of the cutters to turn about to intercept the dinghy. Sir Rinaldo reached out to embrace his daughters. He held them in his arms.

'Look!'

Princess Sophie pointed out to sea, beyond the dinghy. The waters were boiling and seething through the turmoil of the waves as if they would open into the vortex of a whirlpool. Even Sir Rinaldo and the twins turned to watch. Through the wide-spreading disturbance of white water, a huge black cylinder, at first like a whale's back with sheets of water pouring from it, and then like some titanic black cigar, gradually rose on to the surface of the waves. The dinghy turned towards it. On the extra-ordinary apparition, halfway along its steel-plated spine, something like a riveted iron pill-box was placed. After some minutes, when the water was finally spilled off the vessel's back, the lid of the pill-box opened, and two men in seamen's oilskins clambered out. Guttmann had moved forward in the dinghy, to join Abigail Rodgers in the prow. He threw a rope to the men standing on the sea-sprayed back of the black steel leviathan, and they drew the dinghy alongside. One by one, the crew of the dinghy clambered aboard the new, strange vessel, assisted by its oilskinned seamen.

'Of course!' Mycroft exclaimed, more to himself than to anybody else. 'The steel tunnel reeking of oil! Sherlock's words! . . . That is how Guttmann has been coming and going! . . . The Nordenfeldt submersible!'

The dinghy had been cast off. Now empty, if drifted further and further from the submersible, pitching violently on the waves. The seamen helped Abigail Rodgers into the turret hatch, and down into the bowels of the craft, below the surface. She was followed by Guttmann. The two seamen followed. They closed the iron lid after them, leaving Guttmann's two ruffians out on the surface of the vessel. At first, it was clear to those on the cliff-top, even at that distance, the two ruffians did not understand what had happened. They walked up and down until the water began to lap about their feet. Then they went to the turret and began to thump and batter at the lid. They looked towards the dinghy pitching and tossing on the waves far beyond their reach. Mycroft could not be entirely sure, but the thought he could hear their voices carrying pitifully across the waves as the huge cylinder began to sink into the seething flood. He and his companions watched, held by the callous horror of the spectacle as slowly the waters embraced the spine of the monster, and the two poor human creatures were left to become two black dots in the white turmoil.

Sir Rinaldo had led Arabella and Henrietta-Louise away from the cliff edge. They were clinging to him, ashen-faced and fearful. Princess Sophie stood with Mycroft and remained watching until the black dots disappeared, pulled down into the undertow of the submerging vessel. She reached down and touched the ground with the tips of her fingers before making the sign of the cross three times.

But Mycroft had something else on his mind.

'The Nordenfeldt submersible sailed on its first trial exercises in the mouth of the St James River, Virginia, only six months ago,' he said. 'And already more than one must have been placed at Carl Philipp Emmanuel Guttmann's disposal. It is impossible to calculate the threat they would represent to an island nation should ever they become an effective weapon of offense! . . . Imagine a fleet of such objects, already capable of landing spies undetected, but modified to land whole armies, to sink our ships – and at the disposal of the Chancellor of Imperial Germany. . . .'

'We have watched two men die, Mr Holmes!' said Princess Sophie.

'Let us pray, Princess, they are not the first of many, many thousands,' Mycroft told her.

'Let us go back home to Seacombe, now,' said Sir Rinaldo, holding his daughters by the hand.

'Indeed! Indeed!' cried the Reverend Mr Sabine. ' "Sufficient unto the day is the evil thereof!" '

Everybody murmured their agreement even though none of them knew to what he was referring, since he had remained sitting among the gorse bushes unaware of the extraordinary scene they had witnessed.

Chapter Twenty-Five

Sir James Swarthmoor got down from the four-wheeler. Cyril got down after him. They both turned to assist Mycroft down on to the cobbled street. From their arrival on Tower Hill they had driven round the northern and eastern ditch of the Tower of London to the Develin Bridge, an entrance used only by the Tower garrison and staff. It had still been dark – the cold, greying, fresh-smelling dark of first dawn – when they had left 73a Pall Mall. Now, it was light over the great curve of the Thames: the trees on the embankment, the battlements before them, the high uprearing warehouses of St Katherine's Dock, and the massive brick and iron bastions of the new Tower Bridge, were all rimed with clean, white morning frost.

They were met at the gate by a senior Yeoman-Warder.

'Lord Lieutenant's compliments, gentlemen. If you would kindly step this way, gentlemen.'

He looked at Cyril with suspicion.

'Begging your pardons, gentlemen!'

'My servant,' said Mycroft. 'He remains with me.'

He did not explain that he had brought Cyril with him to assist him should he faint.

'Very good, sir,' the Yeoman-Warder replied, in the tone of voice of one who had every intention of consulting his superior at the first opportunity.

They followed their guide through the Well Tower, under the Salt Tower and along the path under the shadow of the Inner Wall. To their right the pinnacles and battlements of the White Tower reared up over the Queen's Lodgings, gleaming and sparkling in the winter sunlight. In the shadow, the cold slapped Mycroft's cheeks and he shuddered.

'This way, gentlemen,' the Warder said.

He led them into the dank gloom of the Constable Tower, across a bare wooden chamber, and up a narrow spiral staircase. They squeezed out of a narrow doorway out on to the rampart of the Inner Wall and walked northwards along it to the Martin Tower. Below them, on the grass sward of the inner bailey, the Tower ravens, symbols of the permanence of 'this Royal throne of kings, this sceptred Isle', pecked at the carrion strewn for them on the brick-hard ground.

They passed through the panelled garderobe of the Martin Tower, and out into the brittle sunlight on the stone platform of the Brass Gun Mount. It commanded the north-east corner of the Tower, a sweeping, semicircular walk connecting the inner and outer walls. The inside edge of the platform, looking down the length of the deep inner ditch between the walls to the forests of masts of the shipping moored on the Thames which loomed over the farther rampart, was unprotected by either battlement or rail, and was a sheer drop to the steep, white frosted banks of the ditch, and the gravel floor at the bottom. On the floor, a heavy wooden baulk had been planted as a post. Thirty paces from it, with their backs to the platform where Sir James, Cyril, Mycroft and a handful of others were standing looking gingerly down, was a file of a dozen guardsmen in red-plumed bearskins and grey overcoats with white cross-belts. They were standing easy, leaning on their rifles, not speaking or even looking at each other. A non-commissioned officer with black-braided sergeant's chevrons on his sleeve was watching them hawk-like, one hand resting on his pacing stick. A little way behind them, hugging the grass slope leading up to the foot of the platform, and almost under where Mycroft and the others was standing, a bewhiskered surgeon-major wearing undress blues under his grey greatcoat, and a short-tasselled pill-box hat, was standing chatting to a young subaltern in full uniform with sword, whose face under his bearskin looked as fresh as a sixteen year old's. Their breath hung like steam in the still, frosty air.

There was the clatter of a heavy door latch being raised. An orderly in bright scarlet tunic and blue trousers came out, carrying an upright wooden chair whose black paintwork looked chipped and flaky. He placed it against the post. A guardsman at the end of the rank swayed, and was caught by his neighbour by the arm before he fell. The sergeant shouted a name which sounded like, 'Ferris!' – the noise reverberating from wall to wall. The guardsman straightened up and shouted, 'Sarn't!' The sergeant bawled at him, 'Officer on parade, Private Ferris!'

The guardsman came to attention and shouted, 'Sah!'

Because of the voices echoing hollowly round the walls, Mycroft did not immediately take notice of the voice near him saying, 'Well, Holmes! I have to give it to you!'

Then he recognized the Yankee twang.

'So it did turn out to be a Prussian conspiracy, after all! Very good thinking, eh?'

'Who is this gentleman?' Sir James asked Mycroft in a voice a great deal chillier than the cold air of the battlements.

'Januarius Aloysius McGahan, sir,' the man himself replied. 'I'm accredited to your London *Daily News*, but I'm here on behalf of the *New York Tribune*.'

'You're the rascal who caused us all that trouble with your damned irresponsible reports out of Bulgaria about Turkish atrocities!' Sir James told him.

'I am, sir,' McGahan agreed. He pointed at Mycroft. 'And this, I suppose, is the "rascal" who discovered your people were being murdered not by Russians but by Prussian agents!' He smiled at Sir James. 'I don't know who you are, sir. But you look to me like somebody who ought know better than to kill the messenger!'

299

There was a stir in the ditch below them. The guardsmen were now 'at ease'. The young subaltern had left the side of the surgeon-major and had joined the sergeant abreast and facing the single rank of his men. There was a scraping hiss as he drew his sword from its scabbard to rest it at the 'at ease' position on his shoulder.

'It couldn't be a more satisfactory situation, after all,' McGahan continued, though he was now staring down at the scene in the ditch, 'for somebody like yourself, who would regard a Continental war as an unmitigated disaster – to find that the guilty party is a Power with whom, at present at least, you have no *casus belli*! . . . Ah!'

The side door set in the wall beneath them, clattered open again. A senior officer in scarlet and blue, with an ostrich-feather plumed, cocked hat, and two men in overcoats and top hats, were followed by two Tower warders half-dragging, half-supporting a limp female form. Immediately after them came a clergyman in purple cassock and surplice. As he walked along the track on the gravel caused by the toes of the female prisoner's boots trailing behind her, the clergyman intoned audibly from the *Book of Common Prayer*, '. . . We give Thee hearty thanks, for it hath pleased Thee to deliver this our sister out of the miseries of this sinful world; beseeching Thee, that it may please Thee of thy gracious goodness, shortly to accomplish the number of Thine elect. . . .'

The warder placed their burden, who was barely conscious, on the chair, tying her arms behind the back. The clergymen continued with his mindless droning of unsuitable words. The warders untied the prisoner's bonnet and removed it. For one moment, Mycroft caught sight of Fräulein von Holz-zu-Birkensee's tightly braided hair about her ears. Her eyes were open: she had come to, and had suddenly recognized where she was. She stared wildly about her, and for a second, her eyes met his. She looked as if she wanted to rise and call out to him, then the warders crammed the canvas hood down over her eyes. They walked down the ditch to take up a position

300

behind the firing-party. From the side, his back against the bank, the clergyman continued to intone the words of the Burial Service. Fräulein von Holz-zu-Birkensee began to bounce the chair on the gravel as if she was attempting to hop away on it. The young subaltern brought his sword-blade stiffly off his shoulder and shouted a command. The guardsmen smacked to attention. As the subaltern shouted the orders, and the guardsmen brought their rifles to the port, and then to the aim, Fräulein von Holz-zu-Birkensee continued to hop her chair about with quick, jerky, futile movements. The command, 'Fire!' was followed instantly by only a slightly ragged volley, and a thin drift of gunsmoke. The impact of the bullets threw the jerking figure backwards. The chair tilted but thumped against the timber baulk behind it, and was pitched forward, so that Fräulein von Holz-zu-Birkensee was left crouching on the gravel with the chair strapped to her back, like some stranded turtle. The subaltern walked out to her, scraping his sword back into its scabbard as he did so. He drew a revolver from its white leather holster, and fired it, shooting through the canvas hood. Blood soaked and welled through the canvas as the shot echoed from battlement to battlement. Mycroft turned away.

Noticing the condition he was in, McGahan took him by the arm.

'Why did you come here, old chap?' he asked.

He took a flask from his pocket, removed the cup from the base and poured into it a healthy measure. The rich smell of a single malt permeated the cold air. As Mycroft gratefully took the cup, Cyril explained from just behind him, ' 'Cause Mr 'Olmes 'as to see fings to the finish – don't yer, Mr 'Olmes!'

'Thank you, Cyril,' Mycroft replied.

They returned across the Develin Bridge to the growler waiting on the cobbles under the Outer Wall.

'Where will you go, Mr McGahan?' asked Sir James.

'Do you mean immediately? Or next week?' McGahan asked. 'Immediately, I shall take breakfast and write my piece in the first coffee-shop I find that's open – there's bound to be one on St Katherine's Wharf. Next week . . . ?'

He paused. A party of dustmen in leather caps, with sack-cloth about their waists and leather capes over their shoulders, were shovelling ashes and refuse into a cart from a ditch by the archway entrance into the dock. McGahan walked across the street to them. He picked up a placard he had noticed sticking up above the edge of the ditch, and held it for Mycroft to see. *All Englishmen who love Liberty cry Death to the Russian Tyrant!* Mycroft read. McGahan laughed and threw it into the dustmen's cart.

'Next week, I travel to St Petersburg, and from there to the Wallachian Provinces and the Tsar's army,' he called. 'I may still have my war, do you see?'

'And you, Holmes?' asked Sir James. 'Back to Whitehall and the Treasury?'

'Of course, Sir James,' Mycroft replied. 'There is the matter of the revised Naval Estimates to be considered.'

'And are you retaining this fellow's services?' Sir James asked, indicating Cyril.

'I have returned him to his true employer, the Princess,' Mycroft replied, 'who permits me to make use of him when need arises.'

The three of them climbed into the growler. As they drove round to the top of Tower Hill, Sir James said, 'Lord Derby called Baron von Schwering to the Foreign Office, you know, and gave him a piece of his mind about spying, and all that nonsense. Replying in his official capacity, von Schwering swore that the Kaiser and the Imperial German Chancellor were entirely unaware of Guttmann's activities. *Ex officio*, however, he said that Prince von Bismarck suffers from a chronically dyspeptic anxiety about finding his new Prussian Empire being assailed on two or three fronts simultaneously, and would get up to almost any trick, unofficially of course, to prevent it.'

'Which is why he employs Carl Philipp Emmanuel Guttmann!' Mycroft pointed out.

'Quite! Quite so!' said Sir James impatiently, as if he preferred to forget the existence of Guttmann. 'The last thing he wants, however, is another major war, and his intentions toward Great Britain are entirely peaceful.'

'Did Lord Derby draw the German Ambassador's attention to the threat posed to us by his country's possession of the Nordenfeldt submersible?' asked Mycroft.

'It was not even mentioned,' Sir James replied. 'You know, Holmes? I am assured by our chaps in the Admiralty that we really needn't worry about it. Such a vessel could never carry enough men to pose any threat to our shores. And its structure and function is such that it couldn't carry a gun capable of inflicting serious damage on a modern ship. They say it can be compared to the balloon; its very nature makes modification for serious offensive purposes an impossibility. You may rest assured that it is simply another of your friend Guttmann's toys.'

'It is just as well for the well-being of this country,' said Mycroft, 'that I have a great deal of respect for any of my friend Guttmann's toys, as you call them.'

'Well, well!' said Sir James. 'Maybe!'

Mycroft sat back against the cushions and looked out of the cab window at the passing street – the City of London going about its daily affairs. They were driving along Cannon Street toward St Paul's: prosperous figures in morning-coats and top hats were stepping out of hansoms, young lady typewriters were trotting along the pavements, hands thrust into muffs to keep their fingers warm for their work, chattering to one another like sparrows, clerks in paper collars and cuff-protectors and messenger-boys in brass buttons, all were hurrying to start the day's work. Everything suggested prosperity and stability – the steady, unexcited, unexcitable, honest

303

industry which made Great Britain the pattern and model of the world.

'I know it is most irregular, Sir James,' he said. 'But I wonder if you would permit me to indulge in tobacco?'

Sir James Swarthmoor visibly relaxed.

'I think we shall suffer you to do so – shan't we, Cyril,' he replied, smiling at Cyril who was sitting opposite.

'Yer!' said Cyril. 'Wouldn't say no to a smoke myself,' he added.

From his waistcoat pocket, he drew a fat Havana. Mycroft recognized the band instantly – it was a *Romeo y Julietta*. For one moment, he was about to say something, then he decided not to. Instead, he took out his case and offered it to Sir James.

'A humble *Veguera*, I'm afraid,' he said.

'I don't believe I've ever taken tobacco at this time of day,' said Sir James, drawing one out and rolling it under his nose.

All three were smoking as they drove under the façade of St Paul's Cathedral. An hour or two at the Treasury, thought Mycroft; lunch across Whitehall, at the Cock Tavern; early evening spent in the utter tranquillity of the smoking-room of the Diogenes Club; and finally, one of Mrs Turner's excellent suppers, taken in hearthside ease at 73a Pall Mall. Life had become sweet once more.